THE NIGHTMARE PLACE

Also by Steve Mosby

THE NIGHTMARE PLACE

Steve Mosby

PEGASUS CRIME
NEW YORK LONDON

THE NIGHTMARE PLACE

Pegasus Books LLC
80 Broad Street, 5th Floor
New York, NY 10004

First Pegasus Books hardcover edition 2015

ISBN: 978-1-60598-788-0

10 9 8 7 8 6 5 4 3 2 1

Printed in the United States of America
Distributed by W. W. Norton & Company, Inc.

For Lynn and Zack

Acknowledgements

Huge thanks to my agent, Carolyn Whitaker, and to all the wonderful people at Orion, especially Genevieve Pegg, Laura Gerrard, Angela McMahon and Jane Selley, who helped to make this novel what it is. As always, extra special thanks go to Lynn and Zack for putting up with me while I was writing *The Nightmare Place*, and to whom it is dedicated with much love.

Prologue

For me, it's the waste ground.

It's a real place, and although I haven't been there in years, I dream about it often. The nightmares first started in my mid-twenties, and continue, on and off, to the present day, always arriving during periods of stress. When I wake up afterwards, I feel grim and empty and *bad*, tangled in bed sheets damp with sweat. I can shower that away, of course, but the residue stays on my skin for hours, like a stain.

As in real life, it's an expanse of open tarmac, perhaps a hundred metres square, the surface scattered with dust and rubble, nails, bolts, broken glass. There used to be a factory here, a long time ago, and remnants of it remain. There are ridged steps of brick in places, while in others the land has been gouged out. It's as though the factory was not demolished so much as blown sideways by an enormous blast of pressure, and that its foundations gripped the land so hard that some were left behind, while others ripped out scoops of ground to drag away with them.

Old wire-mesh fences run down either side, the metal thin and rusted. On the far side, across from me, there is a small embankment. A footpath leads over it, worn into the hump of grass by the trudge of countless feet. Without walking across, I know what's at the other end of that path, beyond the thickets of trees: the school I used to go to. And without turning around,

I know that the Thornton estate is behind me, a malevolent presence pressing at my back.

It's a real place, and even though I haven't been there in years, I know it well. As a child, I walked across it so many times that the sight is as worn into my memory as the path on the embankment.

But I've never seen it like this.

In my recurring nightmare, the sky is an impossible aquamarine colour, a strange mixture of blue and green that reminds me of being underwater. The colour permeates the air all the way to ground level, as though the whole scene is a construction at the bottom of an illuminated fish tank. Above me, the clouds are vibrant and bright, moving far too quickly across the sky, and there is a rush to the air, as though a wind is blowing. But I can't feel it. Nothing moves but the clouds.

And that includes the figure.

It is standing in the centre of the waste ground, and is always the same: grey and colourless and wraithlike. I can't tell if it's a man or a woman, because it's ragged at the edges, as though it has been frozen in the act of moving very quickly towards me. For now, it seems to just hang in the air.

The sensation is of being out of time. This is what the world looks and feels like when it has been paused.

I have no idea what the dream means, only that it means something. My subconscious is showing me a photograph: holding it in front of my face, demanding that I recognise it, like a cop in a TV show sliding across the photo of a murder victim to unsettle a suspect.

See this.

Look at this.

Something terrible happened to me on that waste ground, but I have no idea what.

Memory can sometimes be a very strange thing indeed. If our minds are like houses, then most of what happens to us ends up distributed in the usual rooms; while we might not recall something immediately, there is always the feeling that we could pass through a doorway and there it would be. Even if we have to shift the furniture around a little – search for what we want – it's there somewhere.

And yet it doesn't always happens like that. Sometimes the things that happen to us are so awful that they get stored piecemeal, scattered about, or else are hidden carefully away. Occasionally our minds lift a trapdoor, throw an experience down the set of dark steps below, and bolt the cover back in place. Only a trace of it remains in the air. Perhaps we catch the scent of it from time to time, nervously aware that something is wrong, but we have no way of discovering what.

Those experiences still come out, of course, but they're outside of our control. They sneak up on us at odd moments. They emerge when we're asleep. For me, it's the waste ground. That's my nightmare place.

I have no idea how long the dream lasts. The clouds move, and the rush in the air increases, and the figure remains in place, and I begin squirming inside, because I realise I'm waiting for something to happen. That's what the rushing sound is. What I'm feeling is the sensation of *velocity* – of moving not only swiftly, but in a direction, towards a moment when something awful will happen. When everything will start up again, and that figure will streak towards me, and I'll finally see its face.

And just as it is about to, I wake up.

I lie there afterwards for a time, my heart pounding, or else I sit on the edge of the bed. Regardless, the same words are in my head each time, the same phrase repeating itself.

Something is coming.
Something awful is going to happen.

Part One

One

He is a very lucky man.

It's a good thought. When he allows himself to believe it, it's as though the clenched fist of his heart relaxes, splaying its warm, tingling fingers slowly through his chest. And of course, it's true: there are many ways in which he is lucky. He's young and in good health, for one thing, especially given his size. For another, he has a good job. Not only does he have a roof over his head, in fact, but in these difficult times he owns his home outright. No mortgage. No hassles or worries.

And most importantly of all, he has Julie.

He listens to her gentle snoring now, and feels that warmth inside him spreading further, just from the *presence* of her, lying so close to him. Julie Kennedy is a marvel, and whenever the thoughts of suicide rise up, he reminds himself how deeply in love they are. There is no way any man couldn't fall in love with her. She is twenty-three years old – considerably younger than him – and exceptionally attractive, in the sort of way that even people who dismiss or deride conventional beauty would be forced to acknowledge, however grudgingly. Her hair is long and thick, the colour of butter or sunshine, and her skin is smooth and gently tanned. A slim figure allows her to look good in anything, but she is – endearingly – unaware of this. In another existence she could easily have been a model or a film star, although in this one she does low-key admin in an office. She deserves better, of course, and it's surely not what she dreamed of growing up. But she never complains. And anyway, she's still so young; there's more than enough time for her to figure out what she wants to do with her life.

He met her through work. What struck him in the first instance was not her physical beauty, which is almost too intrinsic, too *obvious*, to be something you'd notice, but the kindness that accompanied it. Her manner surprised him; she was gentle and shy, and not remotely arrogant or dismissive in the way he's found some comparably attractive women can be. From the way she presented herself and talked to him, it was clear she didn't see herself as a prize, even though it was equally clear to him that she was one. And now, however many months later, here they are.

It's hard to believe how lucky he is.

But then they do say that fortune favours the brave. He remembers his mother saying that, knitting needles clittering together: *shy boys get no toys*. His father was the same. At school, despite his size, he would find himself paralysed with fear on the rain-swept rugby pitch, terrified by the thought of the hateful contacts and collisions. He despises violence, and slightly fears other men; he always has. *You have to go in hard*, his father told him bluntly, with little patience for his snivelling son; *that way it hurts less*. A punch always feels harder if you're flinching when it lands, whereas if you're angry and throwing one back, you hardly notice. It's easier said than done, but he's found there is some truth in that. Hesitate, and you're lost. Drive forward, and you make the world hesitate instead, as though it's suddenly unsure what to make of you.

It's not totally within your control, of course, but to a large extent it's true. He's a lucky man – but then you really do make your own luck.

It hasn't always been like this. In fact, the contrast between his relationship with Julie now and one he had only last year is marked. Back then, he wasn't half so brave. It pains him, actually, to remember how timid he used to be, and how that whole awful affair ended.

Her name was Sharon. She was the same as age as Julie is now, and also very beautiful. Sometimes he finds himself attracted to unconventional-looking women, but he is always aware that it's a defence mechanism: a hangover from his schooldays, when the pretty girls would never look at him, and it was far better to concentrate his mental energies on someone he might stand a chance with. When he first set eyes on Sharon, it was like seeing one of those schoolgirls grown up.

She worked in a beauty store, surrounded by fingerprints of soft dust in the air and the swirling aroma of fragrance. She wore tight dresses that showed off her figure, and kept her long black hair tied up in firm, glossy coils. He told himself that she was out of his league, and a part of him wanted to hate her for that. Perhaps a part of him even did. And yet, despite his best intentions, and the knowledge that she was unattainable, he found himself engaged in a careful pursuit. Over the course of a month, he gently courted her. It would happen almost by accident. He would find himself in town, for some reason, across the road from the shop as she emerged from work. Excuses would be found to drive past her house. After Sharon came into his life, his day-to-day actions became like trains, running on tracks and timetables that were increasingly outside of his control.

Deep down, he knew this was dangerous behaviour, and that he needed to change it. Lying in his cramped bedroom at night, he felt ashamed and worthless. But he couldn't stop, and actually, it seemed like something in the world didn't want him to. He discovered she was single. While he had been elated at that, he had also placed his head in his hands and felt the addict's low wail: *why won't it stop being there for me to take?* Even in those early days, it felt like there was a kind of inevitability to their coming together.

And so he continued to circle her, moving closer by increments. He knew he didn't have a relationship with Sharon *as such*, but he did have something. A genuine connection existed between them, and just because she was unaware of it, that didn't make it any less real. He would wake from the bad dreams, and thoughts of her would make him smile. *You are lucky.* He came to anticipate the brief contact they would have. In his head, tentatively, and without her knowing, she made love to him.

Like her life, he knew her house very well from the outside. It was a neat semi-detached property in a warren of curling, leafy streets. Out front, there was a sprawling field, with pairs of old skewed goalposts dotted about at angles, and a thatch of thick woodland beyond. To the rear of the house, a rectangular garden stretched down to a low picket fence and another road. A triangle of washing lines hung loosely from three metal posts. But the field was the easiest place to watch her from.

When reality encroached, he would thrash back and forth across the bed at night, disgusted with himself. In those moments, he blamed her and hated her, and he vowed to stop, to improve, to put this behind him and become better, normal. Yet whatever he promised himself, he was still faced by that addict's curse, and days later, he would find himself close to her work again, or her home, or the leisure centre where she swam three nights a week. Just wanting to see her again. No harm in that, surely? Except there was, because the longer it went on, the more unsatisfying it became. Because addiction always escalates.

One day, he had an idea for something else he could do.

It was dangerous, but thrilling, and he stayed up late that night almost by accident. All evening the excitement kept rising in his chest, even as he refused to acknowledge it. By not preventing what was going to happen, he allowed it to. And at two o'clock in the morning, his heart thrumming in his chest, he walked outside into the cool night air and drove to her house, still telling himself he wasn't going to do anything.

He parked on the road behind, in the shadowy space between two street lights. Sharon's garden gleamed with night-time frost, but her house, along with all the others, was black and still. When he turned the engine off, the world was suddenly heavy with silence, and every nerve ending in his body was singing with anxious life.

In the garden, washing hung on the lines: a triangle of tattered grey flags in the darkness. And once again, there was that feeling of inevitability. If he wasn't meant to do this, why did the world keep making it possible? It had only been a fantasy, after all. An idea, until now. But if the universe kept leaving its doors ajar, who could really blame him for pushing them open and stepping inside?

Outside the car, his nerves made the night air shockingly cold. He left the door slightly open behind him. Her back fence was only three feet high – the most cursory of nods to marking a boundary – and he simply stepped over it.

Move quickly.

He did so, alarmed now by the danger he was placing himself in. Everything else he'd done could be justified, but being in her garden was a clear intrusion. In a sense, it was ludicrous. If he were caught, he would be the one judged a threat, when in truth, she held all the power. Even though he was the one exposed and vulnerable, running hunched up her garden, taking this risk for them both.

He reached the lines and hesitated, trying to make out the details of the washing that hung from them. Dresses. Jeans. Blouses. Tea towels. He'd told himself he'd settle for anything – just something that was *hers* – but now that he was here, he knew he wanted something more intimate. He crept slowly along the line, checking items between finger and thumb, moving closer to the house. That was when the security light came on.

It was so bright it might as well have been a torch shone directly into his eyes. His shadow stretched back across the grass, elongated to monstrous proportions. The sudden light was like a stranger clicking fingers in front of his face, and he literally froze where he stood. It was even a heartbeat or two before the panic set in.

The light was just above the back door. In all his visits here, how had he not noticed that before? The answer would come to him later. It was because he hadn't allowed himself to acknowledge that she might want to protect herself from him, or someone like him. But for now, his thoughts were startled silent, and he simply stood where he was as the figure of a man appeared in her kitchen window, leaning on either side of the sink and staring out at him.

Staring right into his face.

And then – finally – he turned and ran.

All in the past now, of course, but remembering it still sends a spread of panic through him: cold fingers lacing over the warm. Even lying close to Julie, and with everything between them going so well, he wants to reach back and shake that earlier version of himself for being so timid. It wasn't just the security light. It was the fact that he'd wasted time, and failed to realise that he'd missed his opportunity with Sharon. A girl as lovely as her was hardly going to stay single for ever.

The important thing is that he is no longer half as timid now, and he won't let an opportunity like that slip through his fingers ever again. Now, he is a very lucky man indeed. So he lies there thinking about Julie, and listening to the soft, gentle sound of her snoring. And after a few peaceful moments, he reaches up and lovingly touches the underside of her bed.

Two

Someone is downstairs.

The thought woke me instantly. One moment I was immersed in that familiar, troubling dream of the waste ground: staring at an expanse of old tarmac, with a ghost standing there beneath an aquamarine sky filled with fast-moving clouds. The next, I was lying on my back in my bed. It was the middle of the night; the room was pitch black. But I was suddenly completely awake. Because...

Someone is downstairs.

For a moment I wasn't sure if it was true, or whether the nightmare had woken me. So I lay very still, allowing my eyes to become accustomed to the darkness of the bedroom, and listening intently. There was no sound at all, but my subconscious was insisting that something was wrong. That my space had been invaded and I was in danger. And over the years, I've learned to trust gut instincts.

I was alone at home tonight, but wherever I sleep, I always take the side of the bed furthest from the door. It's not that I'm actively *expecting* someone to break in and attack me, but it's always possible, and I figure it's better to have those extra seconds and never need them than the reverse. For similar reasons, I prefer to sit with my back to a wall, so I've got the whole room in view. As quietly as I could now, I slipped out of bed and crouched down on the bare floorboards by the wall.

The clock on the bedside table told me it was twenty-six

minutes past three in the morning. On the far side of the room, the door was open a cat's width, the way I'd left it, and the landing beyond was dark; I could just make out the banister at the top of the stairs. I listened again. For a few seconds, my ears were full of heavy, ringing silence.

And then it was broken.

A creak from the floorboards downstairs, immediately followed by a muffled thud of some kind. The kind of noises someone makes when they're trying to be quiet but not trying very hard. Someone who doesn't really care.

Inevitably, because of the main investigation at work, I wondered if it might be the man responsible – but then I dismissed the idea. Everything we knew about him suggested he was far quieter and more careful than whoever was downstairs was being – and anyway, he would have been upstairs by now. If it had been him, I probably wouldn't have had a chance to wake up at all.

Burglars, then.

I crouched right down, peering under the bed, and was met by four green circles shining back at me, like marbles illuminated by some internal light. Hazel and Willow, my two cats. They usually sleep downstairs, but would have fled up here at the first sign of intruders – not idiots, either of them. They're sisters, and I got them from a rescue centre. I guess they must have learned early on how awful human beings can be, because even now they remain timid with strangers; a knock at the door can send them scrabbling and scurrying to hide. Right now, I was glad about that, because you never know what people will do; one burglary I investigated years back, the bastards kicked the family's golden retriever in the head – for no obvious reason – and the animal had to be put down.

Not wanting to scare the cats, I reached slowly under the bed to pick up the hammer I keep there. It has a reassuring weight and heft: a good solid weapon with a polished wooden handle and a heavy iron head.

It's another habit of mine – you never really escape the

environment you grow up in. Those early years smooth or coarsen all your edges, and unless you work at it, you're stuck with those angles for life. So I have a mental blueprint of the weapons I keep around the house: the knife in the kitchen drawer closest to the front door; the screwdrivers downstairs on the bookcase and front window ledge; the strong ammonia solution in a spray bottle in the bathroom. The hammer here. There are others. If it came to it, I could defend myself all the way from the front door to this spot, always knowing where the next weapon was.

Taking the hammer with me, I walked around the bed, then opened the door as quietly as I could and moved out into the hallway, to the top of the stairs.

There's a small area at the bottom. The back door is windowed with rectangles of blurred glass, and the street light out back was casting a sickly yellow light on to the grey carpet. Beside it, the door to the front room was shut tight. I always leave it open, for the cats. More to the point, a thin bright line was visible around it. I certainly don't leave the downstairs lights on overnight.

More movement from the room below me. The noise was muffled but definitive, and it set the soles of my feet tingling. A moment later, I heard what sounded like quick, whispered conversation, and then a stifled laugh.

So there was more than one of them.

That hushed laugh again. They probably weren't laughing at me, of course. But it felt like they were.

And that really annoyed me.

'*Police officer!*' I shouted.

My voice sounded strong, which was good. The adrenalin had been keeping the fear at bay, and with the choice now made, any final trace of nerves evaporated. Confrontation. No point being timid about it now.

'I'm armed, and I'm coming downstairs. You've got about five seconds to get the fuck out of my house.'

The noise in the front room immediately ceased, but as I

trotted loudly and heavily down the stairs, it started up again – much less cautious now. Below me, something shattered loudly. They were scrambling. I supposed I should have been glad they were running, but now that I'd committed to this, a part of me resented it, and as I reached the bottom of the stairs, I realised that I actually wanted one of them to try it on. Give me an excuse to wrap the hammer round his miserable little head.

Keeping my body to one side, I kicked open the door to the front room. It banged backwards against the radiator, and the curtains over the back window wafted out. The sudden light in here was harsh, and I allowed myself a couple of blinks before stepping into the room, holding the hammer close to the head, so that it could be used for short, sharp punches if someone was standing close by.

Nobody was, which was a good thing, because I was momentarily shocked by how *wrong* the room looked. Whoever was here had already taken a fair amount of stuff, most noticeably the TV – there was too much wall showing directly opposite me. Beside it, my bookcase of DVDs had been hurriedly ransacked, and a splay of plastic cases lay in front of it. The rest of the room was in a similar state of chaos, my myriad possessions pulled from drawers and scattered about, and there were streaks of liquid over everything – *wrong, wrong, wrong* – that didn't make any immediate sense.

And then the burglars themselves.

A couple of them were a cluster of fluttering shadows out of sight in the kitchen, but the last one had only just got to the doorway. He was dressed in dirty blue jeans and a grey hoodie, white trainers, black gloves. No mask, though, the idiot.

'Hey, what about the hedge?' I called to him.

And he hesitated. It was a trick I'd learned as a teenager, when I'd been smaller than most of the children who thought they could bully me. When you say something totally incongruous, it short-circuits someone's brain for a second, just long enough to distract them as you land that crucial first punch. The burglar was too far away for that, of course, but it was enough to stall him – to make him turn to look at me for a moment, so that I got a clear view of his face.

Click.

And then he was gone, pelting outside after his friends.

I went after them, but more half-heartedly now. However pissed off I was, I knew that, legal issues aside, I'd have trouble dealing with more than one of them in an open space. Besides, they were quick: the car engine was already revving as I reached the front door and stepped out into the cold night air. A door slammed, tyres screeched, and I saw lights flashing away down the street. By the time I'd got to the end of the path – more a token gesture now than anything else – the car was out of sight.

I stood in the middle of the road, patting the solid head of the hammer against the tendons of my palm. The silence was almost eerie now: just moths pattering against the nearby street light. It didn't matter that they'd got away. I'd managed a good enough look at the last one out, and I'd recognised him. It was just a flicker of memory for the moment, but I knew him from somewhere.

Borrowed time, you little shit.

I stared down the empty street for a few moments, trying to remember – and then realised how much I was shivering. Despite the almost insufferable heat of the past weeks, it was cold out at night, and adrenalin could only add so much cover to a T-shirt and pyjama bottoms.

I headed back inside. Time to inspect the damage.

And phone the police, of course.

'Christ.'

Half past nine in the morning, and Detective Inspector Chris Sands – my partner – was standing beside me amidst the wreckage of my front room. He looked like he couldn't quite believe his eyes. Chris is always like that, though. I like him, but he seems to approach every crime scene as some kind of psychic assault on his worldview, whereas for me, it's more like confirmation: this is the way the world works. If Chris isn't careful, by the time he's forty he's going to have a face like a perpetually disappointed puppy.

Around the corner, in the kitchen, the drilling started up again. The locksmith had arrived just after Chris and was getting straight to work, no messing about: replacing the locks and installing a set of sash jams. He had special instructions to keep the barrel of the old lock, in case SOCO could collect any fingerprints. There wouldn't be any, of course, but still. Procedure.

Chris shook his head as he looked around. 'A *messy* burglary.'

'Yeah,' I said. 'It is that.'

The shattering noise I'd heard last night had been the television, dropped in a panic at the far end of the room as the intruders had scrambled out. I'd also lost handfuls of DVDs, scooped from the shelves like they'd been on some kind of fucking supermarket sweep, and my PlayStation and laptop were also missing.

But the financial damage was only part of it, and Chris was right: this hadn't been a straightforward case of breaking and taking. The burglars had found a tube of sun cream on the table and proceeded to squirt the contents around the room with gleeful abandon. The stains and crusts from it were all over the settee and walls. As if that wasn't enough, they'd also taken a bottle of olive oil from the kitchen and sloshed that everywhere. Finally, in a particularly disgusting touch, one of them had helped himself to a banana from my fruit bowl, chewed it up and spat it on the floor. The contempt they'd felt for me – a total stranger – was more than evident, and I'd spent a good portion of the night wanting to go back in time and chase the bastards a little harder.

'Scumbags.' Chris gestured around as though the damage was inexplicable, or caused by a tornado or something. 'You can sort of understand it – the burglary, I mean. There's a point to that. They're junkies or whatever. They need the money. But why not just take the stuff and get out, you know? It never makes sense to me. Why do this?'

'It makes sense to me. It's all there in the word *scumbag*.'

'I guess.'

He sounded doubtful, but I was right. These people wouldn't have known who was upstairs – whether it was a single woman like me, or an entire family – and they wouldn't have cared. It didn't matter. In their deluded heads, they probably weren't just helping themselves to other people's things, but teaching them a lesson as well. Dare to own a home and have possessions? Stupid enough to work hard and build a life? Well, look what we think of you. Imagine us laughing as we take the fruits of your efforts, trash what we don't want, and spit on what's left.

I couldn't stop thinking about the muffled laughter I'd heard. I wasn't sure I'd ever been as angry as this in my whole life.

'Prompt response?' Chris said.

'The uniforms? Oh, yes. Ten minutes, maybe. They stayed around for about half an hour, as well. One of them even went into the back garden with a torch. Which was useless, obviously, but nice of him.'

'At least they're taking it seriously.'

'That's true.'

Being police probably helped in that regard, but it wasn't just down to that. There's a common public misconception that burglaries aren't high on our list of concerns. It's simply not true; they're taken very seriously indeed, especially when the homeowner is present. It's just difficult to get a result from them. There are usually no prints, and anything stolen tends to get sold on quickly. The result is that a significant proportion of burglaries are solved by being ticked off the list when an offender gets caught for one and owns up to a handful of others, so that his cooperation can be taken into account during sentencing. Everyone's basically a winner.

But that's most burglaries – the ones where the offender just gets in and gets out again. This behaviour, though – the trashing – was closer to an engagement. There was a sense of escalation to it. A few incidents down the line, you could imagine that the individuals involved might take things further:

venture upstairs; maybe even hurt people. So they needed catching before we ended up with something far more serious than theft on our hands.

Especially in the current climate.

'You came downstairs, didn't you?' Chris said.

'Yes. Of course I did.'

'Right.'

And there he was again with the kicked-puppy face. We'd worked together for years, he knew full well how capable I was, and yet he still found it impossible not to engage his protective side. Often when it surfaced I did my best to hide how patronising I found it, but I didn't have the patience for that today.

'What did you expect me to do? I was very angry, Chris. There were people trashing my house and taking my fucking things.'

'Yeah, but you should be careful.'

'Fortunately, a floorboard keeps coming loose in the bedroom, so I have a hammer nearby.'

'Even so.' He shrugged awkwardly. 'You never know, do you? It could have been our creeper knocking around down here.'

Our creeper. As a title, it hardly went far enough. But even though it was the force's major case right now, a few officers had taken to calling him that, as though minimising him by name might make the details of the attacks somehow easier to deal with.

'Chance would be a fine thing,' I said. 'We'd have him now.'

'Or he'd have you.' But he caught the look on my face, and finally, my mood filtered through the veneer of masculinity. 'No, you're right.'

'And *our creeper*'s not in the habit of drilling out door locks.' I nodded in the direction of the kitchen, where the locksmith was still working. 'Or stomping around people's front rooms like an amateur. Maybe if he was, the women would have had more of a chance.'

'You're okay. That's the important thing.'

'Yeah, I'm fine.'

'And I bet the uniforms were pleased.'

'What? That I'd solved the crime for them? Yeah, they were thrilled.'

The name of the man whose face I'd seen had come to me while I was waiting for them to arrive. It would have come more quickly, but I didn't know him that well, and it had been a long time since I'd seen him. The kind of people I used to run with, back when I was a teenager growing up on the Thornton estate, were very different from the people I worked with now. I'd done my best to distance myself from all that, and I'd hardly thought about them since dragging myself up and out of the place. But here it was now – a small part of my past breaking into my present.

Drew MacKenzie was the little brother of one of the girls in the same gang as me. I remembered meeting him a few times at his sister's place. He'd been a cute kid – must have only been about ten at the time, and I remembered that he'd seemed clever. He had the attitude already, of course: the one children get when they grow up in that type of world, as inevitable a wrapping as the cheap second-hand clothes. Presumably the attitude had won out over the smarts, and he'd followed his sister into the family business.

Chris said, 'You're going to leave him to the rat-catchers, though, right?'

I didn't say anything.

'Zoe?'

'*Yes*. All right? Do you want me to write it in blood? I'm going to leave him to the rat-catchers.'

Chris was about to say something else, but he was interrupted by the locksmith, looming in the doorway holding a box of keys and a handful of paperwork.

'Excuse me. All done. I've left the old barrel on the counter. Just need a couple of signatures and then I'll get out of your hair.'

'Thanks. Be right there.'

'When are SOCO due?' Chris said.

'Any time now. I'll be in afterwards.'

'You don't have to. Maybe you should—'

'*Be in afterwards.*'

I gave him a look. If anything, the puppy-dog expression seemed to intensify in the face of it, but we both knew why I had to be. It was now two days since Julie Kennedy had been attacked and raped in her own home. The latest victim of *our creeper*. She'd been in hospital ever since, and it looked like the doctors might finally allow us in this afternoon to interview her.

I looked around my front room again. It was just mess and missing things, and that could all be cleaned and replaced. More than that, it could wait. In the face of what had been done to Julie, the damage here was utterly insignificant.

'I'll be in afterwards,' I said again quietly. 'That's what I should do.'

Three

You can't do this.

Jane sat down in the partially enclosed booth and waited for the button on the telephone to light up, indicating that she had a call. Thinking:

You can't do this.

Her father's voice, of course. Since his death, she'd spent a great deal of time trying to push that voice out of earshot, or drown it out with more positive thoughts. *You* can *do this. You're perfectly capable.* Sometimes she even managed to believe those things. And yet he was always there in the background, and at stressful moments he came through loud and clear.

You can't...

The light on the phone flashed red.

Jane picked up the receiver immediately. One thing she *really* couldn't do was allow herself to hesitate, because when she did, her body had a habit of freezing up. School, and even university, had been a catalogue of awkward pauses that lengthened into embarrassing silences: moments when she knew everyone was watching and waiting, and all she could do was sit there, growing red under the spotlight of their attention. Act immediately, her therapist had told her since. Fear stems mostly from anticipation, so don't give yourself time to think. If she'd let the phone ring any longer, it would have rung out.

'Hello.' Her voice was surprisingly strong. 'This is Mayday. How can I help you today?'

There was no reply at first, but the line wasn't empty. She could hear the man breathing – a slow, heavy sound that made her wonder if this was going to be a sex call. They'd been told about them during training, but nobody in her group had received one yet. She'd get one eventually, but *God*, she thought, *please not now*. That would be a baptism of fire.

Finally, the man spoke. 'My name's Gary.'

'Hello, Gary.' She didn't have to give her real name, but she decided to. 'My name's Jane. What would you like to talk about?'

'I don't know really.' He sniffed. 'I'm not sure why I even bothered calling. I just took the number with me.'

'You took our number with you?'

'Uh-huh.' The sound changed slightly, and it took her a moment to realise that he'd started crying. Or an approximation of it, at least. 'I didn't really bring anything else. I'm not going to need it. I'm in a hotel.'

I'm not going to need it. That was the moment when Jane recognised the nature of the call she was receiving. Her stomach dipped, and she looked around the small booth dividing her off from the rest of the room, fighting down the panic that was beginning to rise. Right now, she'd have given anything for a sex call. Instead, she was about to be faced with what the Mayday trainers called a 'SIP'. A suicide in progress.

Keep calm, she told herself.

You can do this.

'Please take your time, Gary. We can talk about anything you want. There's no hurry.'

'I want to talk about Amanda.' He sniffed. 'Sorry – that's no use, is it? You don't know Amanda. Or maybe you do, for all I know. No idea who you are, have I?'

'Just take your time, Gary.'

'I know her, though. Better than anyone. She just doesn't realise it.'

24

'That's fine. We can talk about Amanda.'

'I've known her for years. We worked together, and then we – you know. Hooked up. Christ, this time last year we were *living with each other*.'

That brought a fresh round of tears, and Jane felt a ghost of the man's emotion mirrored inside her. It was just enough to bring on the familiar sliding sensation of empathy, that movement towards understanding another person. Jane had always been good at that – too good, perhaps – and she took hold of the connection now. *This time last year*. She had plenty of her own examples to draw on. Her father's death. Peter.

You can do this.

'It can feel strange, can't it, looking back?' she said. 'You remember how different things were only a short time ago. It's sometimes hard to believe.'

'Yes. Exactly that.'

'You just take your time, Gary.'

As the story came out, in stops and starts, whatever Gary had taken – alcohol or drugs, or some combination of the two – began to cause him to slur his words. After a few minutes, Jane's palm grew sweaty, and she had to swap the receiver between hands. Throughout, she did her best to stay calm: to put herself in his place and imagine what he was going through; to help him, as much as she could.

For most of the call, that seemed to involve remaining silent. The longer Gary spoke for, the more obviously superfluous her presence was. He just wanted to know that there was someone on the other end of the line, listening to him.

Amanda and Gary had been in a relationship for several months, and for a time, it had been wonderful – or so he claimed. But then things had cooled. Amanda had started going out by herself more, and Gary hadn't trusted her. He'd check her text messages and emails, and find things: nothing directly incriminating at first, but enough to pass the baton from one suspicion to the next and send it running on towards another.

'She was texting her ex. They'd always been in contact. I

fucking hated it. Sorry. But she said I had to accept it, and I wanted to trust her. I tried to.'

Jane imagined this wasn't the whole truth, but did her best to suppress the thought. It was important to resist the urge to judge, or even to interpret the story he was telling her. Instead, as Gary recounted the details of the break-up, and the way Amanda wouldn't return his calls and texts, she concentrated on empathising with him: pulling similar feelings from her own experiences, emotional playing cards that she could match with Gary's own. It wasn't difficult. Breaking up with Peter had been an unhappy time. Even if she had known that it was right for both of them, the feeling of loss had seemed insurmountable at times. There had been genuine grief for the relationship, as though it had been a living thing, and the final few weeks a prolonged period of watching it suffer and die. Jane knew how much it hurt. As she listened to Gary now, she felt it again.

'She's on holiday.' The first words came out like *sheezon*. 'Here with him. Last year we were living together and now she's here with him, and so I'm here too.'

'You're there too?'

'Yes. Same hotel. It's on the coast. So when they find me, she's going to know how much I cared about her. She won't be able to ignore me then, will she?'

Jane licked her lips, thinking quickly. She understood now what Gary was planning to do. Not just take his own life, but do it close to his ex-girlfriend. After all the unanswered calls and texts, he was going to force Amanda to listen to him.

It sent a frisson of horror through her – but then, she wasn't here to judge. She wasn't here to stop him, either. It was against the rules of the helpline to intervene; she could only do so if he explicitly asked her for help. Even if she'd wanted to, there was no obvious way of doing so.

She thought carefully.

'Do you want to tell me which hotel, Gary?'

'I saw them earlier.' His words were increasingly slurred: hard to make out now. 'This morning – from out of the window.

26

There's a settee in the room here, and you can just sit. They were walking down the promenade. Hand in hand. I don't know when they'll be back. I don't care any more.'

'Gary,' Jane said. 'I have to ask. Would you like me to call someone for you?'

'Don't.'

'I won't,' she said quickly. 'Not without your permission. But if you change your mind about what you're doing, I can get someone out to you very quickly.'

'It's too late. It feels good.'

Jane's heart was beating too fast, and she forced herself to breathe slowly. Sensing that there was nothing more for her to say, she allowed the silence on the line to stretch, imagining Gary filling that space with whatever he needed to.

'It feels good,' he said eventually. 'It feels far away.'

And a moment later, the line went dead.

Jane felt light-headed as she walked out of the open booth and rejoined her training group. She'd been too lost in the call to notice, but reality had set in now, and her whole body felt feathery and strange. She sat down carefully.

The volunteers were divided up at random at the start of each session. This evening she was with Simon, Brenda and Rachel. Rachel – a small, punky PhD student in her mid-twenties – was the only one she'd really talked to before, and she gave Jane a smile now, along with a small thumbs-up from the hand resting on her thigh.

Jane smiled back weakly.

A moment later, Richard emerged from a second partitioned-off space, beside the one she'd been seated in. He was holding the sheaf of papers he'd been reading from.

'Well. That was pretty intense, wasn't it. Are you okay, Jane?'

She nodded. 'I think so. But … yes.'

'Intense. You did really well, though. That was a difficult one, and I thought you handled it brilliantly.' He sat down with the volunteers. 'Okay – questions from the group. Do any of you have any thoughts? Anything Jane might have done differently?'

Jane looked around the group, nervous. While talking to 'Gary', she'd been able to suppress the nerves and self-doubt and disappear into the conversation. It had been like she didn't exist, but now she was very much present again, and the other three were looking at her. She could already feel herself blushing, and her eyes began to water slightly.

Don't look at me.

Rachel said, 'I thought she was perfect, actually.'

Jane dared a look at her, and the girl gave her another smile, then looked away. It was a nice gesture, Jane thought, offering encouragement but not wanting to put any pressure on her. It was like when a friend called to check you were okay but knew enough not to stay on the line too long.

Simon and Brenda both tried to offer more substantive criticism, but it was clear they were struggling. Richard listened and nodded anyway, because that was what they did here at Mayday, but Jane was surprised to find that the dissection of her performance was considerably shorter than the others' had been, and at the end, Richard gave her a big smile of his own.

'Well done,' he said. 'That was really good.'

No it wasn't, she thought.

But at least she didn't say it out loud. Even just a few months ago, she had still been doing that: throwing people's compliments back in their faces. *So that's progress*, she thought. She was getting better.

After the training session was over, the volunteers either mingled with the other groups, drinking coffee and chatting, or else headed off. Jane was usually one of the first out of the door, but tonight, she dawdled a little. The conversation with 'Gary' had stayed with her. Of course, she'd known all along that it wasn't a *live* call, but still, it had felt like one at the time. And just because it hadn't been happening then and there, it didn't mean it wasn't *real*. The names had been changed, she knew, but all the test scenarios were roughly based on real calls the trainers had received.

Before she left, she spotted Richard wiping down one of the tables, moving plastic cups to one side. She hooked her bag over one shoulder and plucked up the courage to approach him.

'Richard?'

'Jane. Yes, hello. Oh – are you off?'

'Yes.' She felt awkward. Richard was in his fifties, and tall, with a halo of short grey hair. Although he was friendly enough, there was an intensity to the way he looked at you that she found disconcerting. It was as though maintaining eye contact was a matter of life and death for him. 'I just wanted to ask about that call.'

'Yes, you handled it really well.'

'Thank you.' *That's real progress.* 'I suppose I was just wondering … was there really nothing else I could have done? At the end, I mean.'

'Ah. Right. I see what you mean.' He stopped cleaning the table and turned to face her properly. 'There wasn't, no. And the thing is, I know you *want* to help them, believe me. But you just can't. What you have to remember is, it's a confidential service. And if it wasn't, you'd never be in a position to help them anyway.'

'No, I know.'

It was true. If someone like Gary had suspected that she would – or even *could* – find and stop him, he'd probably never have made the call in the first place. There was almost a paradox there, in a way. Richard looked at her kindly, and she could tell that he wanted to put a hand on her shoulder and reassure her. A fatherly gesture. He didn't, of course.

'It won't ever stop being distressing,' he said. 'What you have to remember is that the caller is an autonomous adult. They're responsible for their decisions and actions. Not you.'

She nodded. It had all been covered in the earlier training sessions; she had made notes on each one. Even so, her conscience was ticking.

Richard sighed, sensing her conflict.

'Do you know one thing I do,' he said, 'which I find really helps me cope with the more difficult calls? I tell myself they're not real.'

'Not real?'

'Exactly.' He spread his hands. One of them was still holding a tea-stained tissue. 'You won't ever really know if these people are telling the truth when they call. We have callers who tell the same story each time they phone, just changing a few details. You know they're making it up. But even the ones where it isn't obvious, you never know.'

'Right.'

'The real Gary,' he said. 'I have no idea what happened to him, and I never will. But the thing is, it really doesn't matter in terms of what I'm here for. So I can tell myself anything. I can imagine he was making it all up, or that he just drifted off to sleep and was totally fine.'

Richard nodded to himself.

'And frankly,' he said, 'when I get that sort of call, that's exactly what I do.'

Four

'All right,' I told Julie Kennedy.

But she had just finished giving us her account of what had happened, and even as the words left my lips, I flinched at them. It was too easy a thing for me to say – blasé, almost – and I should have been more careful. Because it wasn't all right. And however well she recovered from her ordeal physically, nothing was really going be all right for her ever again.

If Julie noticed my indiscretion, she didn't show it, and perhaps I was simply compounding my mistake by making it all about me: by imagining that, after everything she'd been through, she would even notice my choice of language, never mind be offended by it.

Right now, she was sitting upright in her hospital bed, looking away from me and Chris, towards the drawn slats on the blind. The covers were pooled at her waist, and her hands – one of them encased in plaster, hiding the broken fingers and wrist – rested on her lap. The small room was illuminated only by a soft lamp on the drawers by the bed, but the visible injuries were still apparent. The far side of her face was wrapped with bandages, while the other side was swollen, the skin bright and discoloured, and criss-crossed with lines of bristling stitches.

After a few moments of heavy silence, her chest inflated slowly, and she gave a steady sigh that seemed to last an age.

'I wish I'd fought back,' she said.

She'd already told us that, while relating the details of the attack. I repeated now what I'd told her then.

'You shouldn't wish that. There's every chance he could have killed you. You can't blame yourself for things you didn't do, especially when they're things you shouldn't have *had* to do. Look at me, Julie.'

After a moment, she turned her head slowly, and I stared her in the one eye I could see.

'The only person to blame here is him,' I said.

'I was just too scared.'

'I know.'

'And he was so big. So strong.'

'I know.'

It had been two and a half days since Julie Kennedy had been attacked in her home. The details were written down on the pad in front of me, but I didn't need to refer to them; it felt like her quiet voice, every word of it from the last half-hour, was still somehow echoing in my head. Julie was our fifth victim. Four other women had come before her, and she had just told us much the same story as they had. Mercifully for her, her memory was fractured and incomplete, much of the attack stored away in the nightmare place, but she remembered enough.

The attack had taken place in the early hours of the morning, when she had woken to find a man standing beside the bed. He was dressed entirely in black, and wearing both a mask and gloves. Julie said it seemed like he entirely obscured the curtains, which was impossible, and was presumably either a trick of perspective or else an exaggeration born from fear. But then, other victims had reported something similar. The man was little more than an enormous silhouette – a monster – his presence instilling terror even before the assault began. During the attacks, he never spoke. One woman had called him a concentration of hatred; another said that he smelled of violence. They were bizarre, ephemeral descriptions on the face of it, but they made a degree of sense to me. In each case,

I'd watched the woman trying to talk about the man in ways beyond words, because in her head, that was what he'd become.

Like the previous victims, Julie had been raped and savagely beaten. For hours after the man had left she had drifted in and out of consciousness, and at five a.m. she had managed to phone the police before collapsing. The subsequent two days she'd spent here in the Baines Wing of the hospital in a critical condition. For us, that period had been spent collecting evidence from her house, interviewing neighbours, pursuing leads.

'Julie,' I said. 'I know this is difficult, and you've done very well. But I want to talk about what happened before the attack.'

'Before? I was asleep.'

'No, before that. When you went to bed.'

She tried to frown, but the stitches in her face wouldn't let her.

'It was … just the same as always.'

'Did you check the door was locked?'

'Yes. I always do. Locked, chained, sash jams.'

She was emphatic about that, and I believed her.

'All right,' I said.

I didn't bother to kick myself this time, as I was concentrating on how to frame the next question. You have to be careful in this sort of investigation. You need to know, which means you have to ask, but this line of inquiry is always in danger of toppling over into blaming the victim. After everything Julie had been through, I had no wish to do that. But we needed to know how our man was getting into his victims' houses.

'All right,' I said again, rubbing my hands together slowly. 'What about the windows?'

'She claims the window was closed,' Chris said.

We were walking back through the warren of hospital corridors. I was brimming with a residual mix of anger and frustration, and while none of it was directed at him, that was how it came out.

'No. Get it right. What she said was that she didn't know.

33

She said she *thought* so, but she couldn't remember the last time she'd opened it. And she was hesitant about that.'

'You don't think she'd remember leaving the window open?'

'I don't want to *assume* anything. You know what the weather's been like. It's sweltering. Everyone opens their windows. Maybe not everyone closes them properly again.'

'It's a twelve-point lock,' Chris said. 'You need a key to open it from the inside. As soon as the handle's turned back down, it locks automatically. Clicks in place. It's like the ones I've got at home.'

'I'm aware of how windows work, Chris. Even if I hadn't been before, it's not like it hasn't come up.'

'Exactly. And it keeps coming down to this. When you've had the window open, and you pull it closed in the evening, or whatever, you *automatically* turn the handle down.'

'I do. You do. He, she or it does.' I was walking too quickly, and he was struggling to keep up. 'But what do we know about what Julie Kennedy did? Even *she* doesn't remember. Maybe the phone rang as she was closing the window. Maybe there was a wasp buzzing around outside, and she just pulled it to for a bit and then forgot about it.'

We reached the main foyer and headed out of the doors. The midday air was solid and hot, and after the artificial light of the hospital, the brightness ahead of us was momentarily blinding.

'You're grasping at straws,' Chris said.

I didn't say anything, because I knew he was right, and I don't like to admit such a thing at the best of times.

But, yes, grasping at straws. Julie's recollections matched those of the previous victims. In each case, the house had been secure when they went to bed: all the doors were locked, with any sash jams, chains or bolts in place. When the police arrived, they found a single downstairs window open. That *had* to be the exit point for the attacker, as it would have been impossible for him to leave via a door and then apply bolts and sash jams from outside. But we had no idea how he was *entering* the properties in the first place.

34

The open windows were undamaged. With those kinds of locks – and I know how windows work – you can't lever them open from the outside because the frames snap off. It's a security feature. There's no access to the locks from the outside either. But none of the victims' windows had been drilled.

One possibility was that there was some way of opening the windows that our team hadn't come across yet. If so, the numerous security experts we'd consulted hadn't come across it either. Another was that the victims were wrong: they were misremembering, and had actually left the windows ajar without realising.

The third possibility was that he was gaining access in some other way. But there were difficulties with that too. None of the five victims was missing house keys, and two of them had never even shared the property with anyone else. If the man had got in through a door, it would have to have been during the day, while they were out, because the sash jams and chains were on at night. That implied a whole different level of crazy, which was then compounded by the open window. Because if he could unlock a door somehow, why leave the house that way?

As we reached the car, I pulled out my keys and pressed the security button. The vehicle flashed and clicked once.

'You're right,' I said. 'Although it's not that I'm grasping at straws. I'm playing devil's advocate.'

'Of course.'

'Whatever. I'm driving, by the way.'

We set off. I was still thinking about it, of course.

'It can't be the windows,' I said eventually.

'What do you mean?'

'Because that would imply our man was playing a numbers game. A small number of people forget to close their windows, and he's just opportunistic and lucky. But nobody's that lucky.'

Chris nodded. 'Someone would have clocked him by now.'

'Yeah, there's that. And he's not opportunistic, is he? These women are specific targets. He's not fishing around at random.'

He didn't say anything, and I felt the frustration rising again. Because the terrible truth of the matter was that we simply didn't know.

Back at the department, I prepared myself for the incident room. Everything was quiet as we walked along the corridor, but as we got closer to the main suite, I began to hear it: the thrum of activity on the other side of the wall. It's an old building, and the walls are thin. It was easy to imagine that if I put my hand on the one to the left, I'd feel the vibration and the heat. Directly outside the door, the noise within was audible.

No pressure, I thought as I opened it.

It was like walking into a concert that had already started. Over the last two and a half months, our case had graduated from a small-scale initial investigation to become the department's primary concern; five victims in, we had every single available officer seconded to us, and the largest incident room in the building. Even so, with at least forty police working in here at any one time, it always felt crowded. There were even more here right now, crammed in along the walls and standing in the central aisle, all ready to receive the daily briefing and their updated action schedules.

I sensed a number of eyes on us as we entered, then more and more as we eased our way through the throng. The noise abated slightly as people gradually realised that the main act had arrived. Pressing through, I noticed the heat most of all; the air had the particular warmth that comes from too many people being too close together, and every time I glanced around, I saw damp hair, beads of sweat on people's foreheads. The desk fans were all on, but they weren't accomplishing much.

DCI Drake was leaning against the wall, close to the front of the room. Arms folded, face stern – no sweat on him, of course. For Drake, the production of sweat was something for other people to endure and worry about, and if they weren't currently doing so, he could certainly help them with that.

No pressure ...

36

The area at the far end of the room remained clear. It was a mini stage of sorts, raised only by a couple of inches, and there were numerous tales of unlucky detectives inadvertently face-planting on their way to a nervy presentation. No such disasters for Chris or me today. He moved to the microphone that had been set up, while I walked over to the whiteboards along the back wall. They covered it floor to ceiling, all the way across. I turned my back on the expectant gazes for a few moments, and stared at the boards instead.

Photographs of the five victims were taped across them, with information scribbled in by various hands around each one. It was all on the computers, but I found it helpful to have a visual cue as well – to be able to see as much of it all at once as I could. So here were almost countless names, dates and addresses, people of interest. We'd assumed the attacker would be someone known to the first victim, Katie Rayland, so every possible male acquaintance, every angry ex-boyfriend, had been tracked down and ruled out of the inquiry. That theory had been more or less discarded as the number of assaults rose, and a connection between the victims proved apparently non-existent. The names were still there, just in case, but it was the victims I was interested in right now.

I stared at the photographs, oblivious to the room behind me. Superficially, the women all looked very different. They ranged in height, ethnic origin, hair colour, eye colour. But still, what I'd said to Chris in the car was true: I was sure they had been targeted. Because it was clear that our man had a type. He liked women in their mid to late twenties. He liked women who lived alone. And – the most obvious similarity between them – he liked women who would be considered conventionally very attractive. All five were, in their separate ways, exceptionally beautiful.

Of course, *liked* wasn't the right word, except in the most tangential sense. In reality, he *hated* his victims. Along with his size and strength, each of them had emphasised the hate that they'd felt coming off him in waves. It seemed increasingly obvious to me that he hated them for *what* they were, rather than who. Young, attractive and successful, they were the kind of women you'd imagine finding on the arm of an alpha male, being shown off like a trophy or a badge.

If his hatred was obvious, something else was too. These photographs had all been taken after the assaults, to detail the injuries the women had received. And when you moved your gaze along the line of images, a strange thing happened. Despite the disparity in their appearances, you could trace along from the first picture to the last, from Katie Rayland to Julie Kennedy, and see damage accumulating. The victims merged into one, so that the effect was almost of viewing the cumulative destruction of the *idea* of a beautiful woman. While the rapes remained a constant feature, the assaults were becoming more vicious, more extended, more *central* to the crime. Our man was escalating. Julie had nearly been killed. It was only a matter of time before somebody actually was...

Beside me, Chris coughed.

The room had fallen totally silent. I stepped away from the boards and joined him at the table, not apologising or even acknowledging the delay. Not caring, in fact, what anyone thought, including Drake, leaning there with his knotty little forearms and his expression of impatience.

No pressure.

It wasn't true.

Five

That evening, after work, I went to visit John.

It was a pleasure as well as a duty. John wasn't my father, but he might as well have been, and a part of me actually thought of him that way – not that I'd ever admit it to him, of course. Increasingly, though, I'd started dreading these weekly visits. Dreading *seeing* him.

My mother died young, so I didn't have the chance to watch her age properly, and I never knew my real father at all. The estate housing I grew up in was single-storey and ramshackle, frequently dirty and untidy, and from an early age I was often left alone. There would be times I'd wake up in the morning and find my mother passed out on the settee, empty cans of beer littering the carpet and the smell of weed still hanging in the air. Other times I'd wake up and she wouldn't be there at all. And when she was elsewhere, I never had the remotest impression that she might be thinking about me, or worrying.

Despite all that, I loved her fiercely. My memories of her are nothing but fond. When she was around, she was the most attentive and caring person on the planet. I remember her as a young woman made old before her time: always unkempt, wearing tatty jeans and cardigans, and often – incongruously – a cheap crimson beret. Thinking about her as an adult, I notice an air of regret about her: the knowledge that her life had not gone the way she wanted, and that even on those reduced terms, she was failing to live it the way she ought to. I see the sadness of an inebriated woman dancing happily, clicking her fingers, in an almost empty pub on a sunny afternoon.

There are other memories, of course. I remember the men in drab grey suits who would turn up at our house. As a child, I couldn't understand why my mother allowed them in; she clearly didn't want them there. I'd always know when they were coming, because she'd suddenly be far more present, and would enlist me in frantic cleaning exercises, usually pretending it was a game. When they arrived, I'd sit patiently beside her on the settee, and look at the men seated across from us, sad expressions on their faces. I'd notice the difference between them and my mother – that she would always try to look happy, even when really she was feeling sad and serious, while the men were the opposite.

I didn't know why they were there, only that it had something to do with me and my mother, and whether we loved each other enough. Sometimes I'd cling to her arm while she talked to them, her voice more careful and controlled than I was used to. There was no raucous laugh; it was as though a dial had been turned down inside her. She'd place a reassuring hand on my own. *Everything's going to be okay.* And that was the kind of life we had, looking back. Never really okay, but always going to be.

I think it's to her credit that I didn't notice those things until I was an adult. Whatever flaws she stumbled so frequently over, she tried to do her best, and she loved me, and I loved her. In my head, I try to keep her frozen at that age, barely older than I am now. There are later images, of course, as the carefree young woman who liked to drink and should probably have cut down transitioned into the woman who needed to, and then the woman for whom it was too late. The woman lying in her final bed, in the hospice, as small and thin as a child. But I try not to think about that. The point is, I never got to see her age.

Not so with John.

*

He still lived in the same house he always had: a slim terrace only a short distance from the estate I'd grown up on. The road sloped steeply upwards, and John's house was close to the top, so that, standing in the overgrown front garden, you could see the spread of cheap houses stretching out in the distance.

Tonight, his house key in my hand, I stood there for a moment, looking down at it. From this far away, the haphazard sprawl of tiny buildings and warren of pathways looked peaceful and still. The sky above was pale lilac, with threads of cloud that appeared dull green in the slowly dying light. I tried to pick out the waste ground, and eventually found it. There were tiny figures crossing it: children, I imagined. At this distance, they seemed to be dissolving and rolling rather than walking.

As always, the sight of it made me think about the nightmare.

Although I had a key to John's house, I knocked hard before unlocking the front door, then called out his name as I let myself in.

'It's only me.'

The hallway smelled musty, and my shoes scuffed up an itch of dust from the threadbare fuzz of the carpet. There was another odour, as well, which I found hard to place at first. It smelled like cats, I decided finally, but John didn't have any pets.

He came slowly out of the front room to meet me. These days, he walked with a shuffling gait, as though he was a puppet on strings that were growing increasingly slack and could no longer lift his knees properly. Sometimes he looked as though he was trying to run on the spot. A proud man, he continued to insist he was fine – and perhaps he could still manage for now. But we both knew full well that the day was approaching when he would not be able to.

'Zoe.'

I steeled myself as he emerged into the hallway, and it almost wasn't enough. It had only been a week since my last visit, yet he looked months older than he had then. He was dressed in a dark suit a few sizes too big for him. Every time I saw him, the suit seemed a little looser, and yet he never bought a smaller size, as though he couldn't quite believe – or refused to admit to himself – that his body was diminishing. But it was. Former detective John Carlton looked every one of his seventy-three years, and more besides.

It didn't feel so long ago that I'd first met John – when I was fifteen, under arrest, and sitting on the wrong side of a desk from the tired but concerned man tasked with facing down my clever, cocksure teenage attitude. It *wasn't* that long ago. But the difference between that smart, neat sergeant, still youthful despite the widow's peak and worry lines, and the man before me now was stark.

I swallowed the emotions and walked to meet him, embracing him carefully. His body felt like a fragile cage of bones.

'Hello, John. It's good to see you.'

'And you.' He placed his hands on my arms; they were shaking slightly. 'What a lovely surprise to see you.'

Surprise. It worried me, that, because it wasn't like I didn't call in every week. Over the past months, I'd begun to notice that his mind was deteriorating. Increasingly he seemed to remember less, and sometimes I could see him grasping for thoughts and words, not always finding what he was searching for. He'd just shake his head: *no, it's gone.* It was as though memories were being packaged away as he prepared to move out of his life altogether.

I didn't want to accept that.

'Just thought I'd stop by to bother you,' I said. 'You know – the way you used to pester me, all those years ago.'

That brought a smile.

'Well, that's nice of you. Come through.'

I followed him patiently into the front room. The carpet here was beige and faded, and the fabric on the armchairs was worn away. Sitting on them was as comfortable as sitting on hard, bare wood. The coffee table was strewn with magazines and piles of unopened post, while bundles of old newspapers rested against one wall, below the closed front curtains.

It was always sad to see, because he'd been so fastidious and precise in the past – fussy, even. Old age had enforced untidiness upon him. It had actually seemed like the house of an old man from the beginning, as though he'd had it fixed and fitted in expectation of these later years, when he'd finally catch up with it. All that had really changed was that the three-bedroom property had become too large for him. But that was easily solved, I supposed, by closing a few doors and simply not opening them again. His living space shrinking alongside him.

'Have a seat.' John eased himself down into a chair. The movement caused him to wince; I knew he was increasingly having trouble with his legs. 'I'll make us coffee in a minute.'

'I'll do that,' I said quickly. 'Don't worry.'

'All right. But tell me how you've been first.'

'Not great. I talked to victim five today.'

I updated him on the creeper case first of all. One thing I liked about talking to John was that there was never any need to spare him the details. However fragile and doddery he looked, he was not as vulnerable as he appeared; as police, he had seen it all. Unlike my friends, the partners who had passed through my life, John was a confidant who needed no protection from the harshness of what I did.

I finished with the chewing-out that Chris and I had received from Drake after the briefing.

'Results, results, results.' I made a yapping motion with my hand. 'You can imagine. From the way he talked to us, you'd think we hadn't been working flat out on this for weeks.'

John chuckled. 'I remember Drake. Always a pipsqueak.'

'He'd have thrown us off this ages ago if he thought it would make a difference. Deep down he knows nobody else is going to cover it any better. It's crap.' I shook my head. 'It's a load of crap.'

'It's politics, Zoe. It's role-playing.'

'Yeah, maybe. I've never been too good at that. Oh – and I got burgled, too.'

John leaned forward, suddenly serious. 'I'm so sorry.'

'Oh, don't be. I just wish I'd got downstairs in time. Saw them, though. Drew MacKenzie. Do you remember him?'

He frowned, his forehead ridging with creases, attempting to attach the name to a face and a thread of memories. After a moment, he shook his head.

'Sylvie's little brother,' I said. 'You must remember Sylvie.'

I couldn't help the hint of desperation in my voice. The *must* wasn't so much a statement of fact as of hope. I was relieved when, after another few seconds of frowning, a light seemed to go on behind his eyes, and he nodded.

'Oh yes, of course. Sylvie MacKenzie. I remember her. Friend of yours, wasn't she?'

I grimaced. Not one I particularly wanted to think about. 'Once.'

John sighed. 'You try your best, but sometimes it isn't enough.'

'You can't help everyone.'

He nodded, but it pained him, I knew, when one of his kids turned out bad. One of the hardest things about old age had been giving up the outreach activity he'd continued in his retirement. For a while, he'd served on various community groups and volunteered at drop-in centres, and still gone out on cold, dark evenings to speak to the children on the street corners. Freed from his uniform, he had probably been even more effective, but throughout his career he'd always concentrated on helping people in the community around him.

I knew I wasn't the only child he'd rescued. As dramatic as that might sound, it was the truth. Without him, my life would have been very different. I doubt I would ever have escaped the gravitational pull of the place I was born into, the trajectory that was set for me.

But of course, that was another thing I'd never admit to him. It's not just old men who are proud.

'Yeah,' I said. 'Well, we'll pick him up.'

'It's a shame, but it's necessary. If not your home, it would be someone else's, wouldn't it?'

'Yeah. How about that coffee?'

He hesitated. 'That would be nice. But...'

'Don't worry.' I stood up. 'You wait here; I'll only be a second. It's not like I don't know where everything is.'

Out in the hallway, I noticed the smell again. I liked it even less now, but rather than investigating, I went through to the kitchen. The sink was full – days old, by the look of the water – and the worktops were a mess: crumbs, greasy smears of butter, crusted sauces and a flat archipelago of old coffee stains. A teaspoon was stuck to the counter near the kettle. Looking around, I realised I'd be doing some cleaning before I left, regardless of John's protestations. This must have been the source of his reluctance to let me make the coffee. Embarrassment.

It made me feel a sudden burst of love for him. Not a duty of care, as such, but a kind of privilege. *Hand over hand*, he'd always told me, about his ventures into the community. *The government won't do it. So we help each other. We keep pulling each other up.* So he had, and – for him at least – so would I.

For now, though, I found two clean cups and a teaspoon, put fresh water in the kettle, and clicked it on to boil. Then, when the sound was loud enough to obscure any other noises I was going to make, I went back out into the hallway.

There was a pantry off to the right, behind a glass door. It was filled with old bric-a-brac and not-quite-rubbish, things for which there wasn't a proper place: shelves of muddy boots and rusty cooking equipment, dusty vases, and bottles that would never be recycled.

I opened the door quietly, and sniffed – then wrinkled my nose at the intensity of the smell. A moment later, I realised what it was.

Oh, John.

My heart went out to him. I closed the door and moved back through to the kitchen. We were going to have to have a difficult conversation, John and I. It had been coming for a long time. Perhaps we should have had it before now.

There was no way I could mention the pantry, not directly. I finished making the coffee and put the teaspoon in the sink, then took the cups through. I put his down on the small table to one side of his chair, and sat down opposite.

'John,' I said gently. The expression on his face was almost unbearable. He knew that I knew. 'I want you to be honest with me, okay? Are you having trouble getting up the stairs?'

Six

Margaret is scared when she first sees them.

It was nearly an hour ago when she emptied the kitchen bin, but the next-door neighbours were loitering in the street, and she has been reluctant to go outside. She's been finding other things to do, while occasionally peering round the curtains, waiting for them to get in their cars and go. *To leave her be.*

Which is ridiculous, of course – they have every right to be there. It would have upset her once, to see how timid and subservient she has become. She and Harold always felt like the outsiders in the cul-de-sac, but at least when he was alive they could brave it out together. Laugh about it, even. Now that she's alone, it feels as if the street really does belong more to them than to her. They always look at her with disdain and annoyance: an elderly lady who doesn't matter. By hiding from them, Margaret knows she is accepting that, but the truth is, she *does* feel like an irrelevance in comparison. Harold used to tell her that nobody could make you feel inferior without your consent. Perhaps this means she has given hers.

I miss you so much, Harold.

I know you do, dear.

They spend so *long* out there, just standing around their cars, as though staking out territory. The children – a boy and a girl – are both about ten years old, but there is an air of superiority about them, as though they know they could be rude to her if they wanted and nothing would happen. The father has

47

close-cropped hair, a stocky frame and a black leather jacket. He reminds her of the stern action heroes on the covers of the spy thrillers Harold used to read. Margaret can picture him wearing a hard hat, and imagines him as the kind of inspector who walks on to building sites with a clipboard. The type who can reprimand rough men and have them listen to him.

The mother seems to pay little attention to anyone. She always looks immaculate. She has heels and make-up and long blonde hair, and she wears a pair of designer sunglasses, even in winter. Margaret has never once seen her smile.

When the street is finally deserted, Margaret ventures outside with the bag of rubbish in her hand. Before putting it in the bin, she glances around, and then up, and that is when she sees them.

Wasps.

Oh please, no.

I can't deal with this on top of everything else.

There are only a few of them right now, darting around the corner of her bedroom window, but they are close to the hole in the eaves.

There has been a break in the wood there for as long as she can remember. Over the years, birds have sometimes made their nests there, and Margaret has cautiously learned to enjoy those occasional visits. Waking on a sunny morning, it can be nice to hear them: the gentle tick of their feet; the muffled *thrum* that sounds like collective sighing. It's like having guests. They always warm the house somehow.

But wasps are different. Little buzzing curls of spite and malice, just looking for an excuse to sting. She stares up at them now, the sinking feeling becoming worse. It is the corner of the house closest to the footpath between her own house and the neighbours, and when they see the wasps, they will expect her to dispose of the nest. The woman alone is temperamental and precious enough to demand it. Margaret can imagine her wafting at them, disgusted, like royalty accosted by the poor.

But they will bother Margaret as well. In this heat, she can hardly leave the bedroom window closed the whole time.

Another challenge. Another hurdle.

Just thinking about it robs the energy from her heart.

You can do it, love.

I don't know if I can.

Margaret turns away, awkwardly hefts the full bag of rubbish into the wheelie bin, then gently closes the lid. The bushes behind it are very overgrown: yet another thing to worry about. The buds are out, at least, tiny but colourful, as though the whole ugly mess is making a fumbling attempt to be pretty.

A bee is clambering around the nearest bud. Margaret leans closer and stares. It is very small, and its black and orange fuzz looks grubby. *Homeless* is the word that springs to mind. A bumblebee, but one much leaner than the heavy, circular creatures she remembers from long-ago childhood gardens, as though the species has fallen on hard times. She watches as it moves around the bud, its legs bright with pollen ... and then suddenly it's gone, darting to another bud.

Margaret's gaze tracks it, but finds another on the way. Then more. Now that she is looking, in fact, the foliage comes alive with industry. As one bee leaves the bushes, she turns her head to follow its flight, up past her face and towards the top corner of the house. It circles around the burgeoning nest for a moment, then curls in. Another shoots straight out, as though spat, before zigzagging boozily down.

Not wasps at all.

She watches them for a few moments, almost hypnotised by the pattern of them against the sparkly brightness above, but then the sound of an approaching vehicle snaps her back into the real world. It might not even be the neighbours, but Margaret takes no chances.

She retreats quickly inside.

'Maggie? Are you here?'

'Yes,' she calls. 'I'm in the study.'

Kieran has let himself in, as he usually does. Margaret can hear him moving around downstairs: the heavy sounds of him kicking off his boots and shrugging off that thick coat he always wears, regardless of the heat.

She turns her attention back to the computer.

It sits in the centre of the antique desk in Harold's study, alongside an inkwell and a feathery quill. The latter were affectations: he never used them for writing, and the black ink has long congealed in the glass bulb. But he used the laptop, and after his death last year, Kieran tried to show her how it worked.

It was old, he told her, sighing impatiently, as though the machine had already presented him with a problem. She had no idea why it mattered that it was old. It was certainly bulky – black and thick – which Kieran seemed to dislike as well. To Margaret, that just made it seem durable. It was something that would last, like a well-made leather briefcase.

It was actually easier than she'd expected. Kieran set up a home screen for Google on the internet, and explained that she needed to type what she was interested in into the box in the middle. He showed her how to use the different tabs. It wasn't so hard.

'What you up to?'

She hears his weight thudding up the stairs, and turns to see him entering the study. As always, she is struck by the size of him. He is too large; he dresses to hide it, but not well. His jeans don't fit, and the T-shirt – a grotesque yellow smiling face covered in worms, with crossed bones behind it – only draws attention to the bloated barrel of his chest. Just from coming up the stairs now, his cheeks are red, and his forehead is speckled with sweat, with a strand of long black hair plastered across it.

'I'm online,' she tells him. 'You would be proud of me.'

Kieran crosses over and peers down at the screen. This close, she can smell him. She loves him a great deal, but she does worry about him.

'All right.' He is breathing heavily. 'Wikipedia. Bees.'

'*Bumble*bees.'

'Right. Why the interest?'

Margaret tells him about the nest. Kieran listens politely enough, but doesn't seem all that interested. That's all right, of course. It's how a lot of their conversations go. She's grateful he keeps coming round at all.

'Right.' He's got his breath back now. 'Well, I'm going to stick the kettle on. Have a quick fag while I'm down there. Is that okay?'

'Of course. I'm nearly finished.'

She listens to the creaks as he heads back downstairs, then turns her attention to the screen again.

She is pleased with herself for researching this, and also relieved by what she has discovered. Bumblebee nests are reasonably small, she has learned – often fewer than a hundred creatures – and usually only last for a few months. There is no danger of them swarming, because swarming is a way of gathering a colony together before moving to new territory, and a bumblebee nest simply dies. The only survivors are a few young queens, which head off to find new homes and begin fresh nests of their own.

She remembers her mother telling her that bees and bumblebees rarely sting because it kills them to do so, but it turns out that isn't true. Bumblebees can sting more than once, but are unlikely to do so. In general, they are peaceful creatures, and won't attack unless the nest is threatened.

So she doesn't need to get rid of them, and, in fact, she shouldn't: bumblebees are good for a garden, and also in decline. But there is something else, and it is this she focuses on now. According to the information in front of her, they usually make their nests at ground level. Two floors up, in an attic, is not unheard of, but is far from ideal. Which means the nest they are building is precarious. To Margaret, it feels as though they have arrived here as a place of last resort, a refuge. And they are welcome. She has no idea if the nest is going to thrive or fail, but whichever, it will not be down to her.

She turns the computer off and goes downstairs.

In the kitchen, she finds Kieran pacing angrily back and forth, a furious expression on his face. He peers out of the window, shakes his head, then walks back towards the front door.

'Kieran?'

'That ... *man* next door.'

He turns and paces angrily towards her. Margaret almost takes a step back.

'Can you believe it? I can't believe the ... *cheek* of him.'

The pauses are him moderating his language. Kieran has a great deal of resentment inside him, and he swears a lot, often without thinking, but he knows Margaret disapproves of it. As he reaches her, she puts her hand on his arm, and he's trembling.

'Kieran, what happened?'

'They all pulled up when I went out for a cigarette. There'd obviously been some sort of argument between them. I don't know. The three of them are trailing in. The kids. That painted-up ... *woman*. He's following them up the path. And he just turns to me and shouts at me to get the lawn cut.'

'The lawn?'

'Yeah. He's glaring over the fence at me, and he shouts it. *Get your ... lawn cut*. Like that. Like it's a threat or something.'

He starts shaking his head. Margaret is alarmed.

'What did you say?'

'I was too surprised to say anything much. It was just so aggressive, the way he said it. I was like, *what? What are you even talking about?* He just glared at me some more, like I was disgusting. With absolute *contempt*. And then he went inside and slammed the door.'

Like I was disgusting. Margaret knows how much that will have upset him. How out of place he always felt at school; how badly he was bullied, despite or perhaps because of his size. In truth, she feels it on his behalf. She knows how they make her feel. The contempt is even there in the *form* of the family, isn't it? Two successful adults, with a girl and a boy. They're a perfect vein of gleaming silver in the messy rock of society. A stark contrast to the old lady living across from them, with her misfit great-nephew, the pair of them making their ungainly, piecemeal way through life.

Margaret rubs Kieran's arm gently.

'It won't have been about you,' she says gently. 'It will have been the argument they were having. He'll just have been taking it out on whoever was nearest.'

'You didn't see him.' Kieran shakes his head again. 'I can't believe it.'

The garden has actually been on her mind. The grass hasn't been cut since early last year, before Harold died, and is now so thick that it has coiled up and collapsed on to itself.

'Well, it *is* very overgrown.'

'It's none of his business,' Kieran says. 'It doesn't affect him *at all*. Doesn't make any difference. It's up to you how you keep your garden.'

She gives his arm one last rub. When she removes her hand, he heads back towards the door. This time, he starts to open it, alarming her again.

'Where are you going?'

'For a cigarette. I was so ... *annoyed*, I just put that last one out and came in.'

Margaret glances out of the window. The properties are separated by a footpath and a fence, the front doors facing each other. The door opposite is open now. She can see the woman moving around in her kitchen.

'Maybe you should wait.'

'No, to hell with that. This is your house, Maggie. I'm not scared of having it out with him if he wants to.'

She doesn't attempt to stop him. But she stays in the kitchen, watching his huge silhouette on the doorstep through the glass door. *I don't need this. I don't want it.* She just hopes the man doesn't come out again and say something else. *Please, no more complications.* Not that Kieran would do anything if it came to it, of course. She knows that. It's just grandstanding. It's how men can be with each other.

He's a good boy really.

Seven

We were on our way back from the hospital – a third, reluctant interview with Julie Kennedy – when the call came through. Dispatch had figured we might be in the area, and they were right. A little before or after, and it would have been someone else who attended the scene, and that was something that would keep coming back to me later.

As we approached the property that had been reported over the radio, I saw an elderly man waiting by the side of the road, looking anxious.

'That'll be him,' I said. 'What was his name again?'

'Connelly.'

Chris indicated and pulled in beside him. I leaned out of the window.

'Mr Connelly?'

'Yes. Thank you so much for coming.'

'That's okay.' I got out of the car. 'What's the problem?'

The old man filled in the details, some of which we'd already had from Dispatch. He was concerned about his neighbour, a woman named Sally Vickers. Her daytime routine was like clockwork, he informed us several times, but she hadn't left the house for work this morning. Apparently they *always* had a chat, which I imagined was more at his instigation than hers. Her car was still in the drive. He'd tried knocking, and then rung her house number, but there was no reply. Having been following the news, he'd called the police.

It was the kind of report that under different circumstances would likely have been brushed off by Dispatch. But in the current climate, we were encouraging everyone to be careful and check on their neighbours, and we had to take calls like this seriously. Especially because Sally Vickers was in her mid-twenties and lived alone.

'I'm sure she's fine, Mr Connelly. But we'll check it out.'

It was a double driveway, shared with the other, unattached neighbour. Sally Vickers' side of that deal was noticeably better maintained than next door's, smothered in a layer of fresh black tarmac rather than the pitted concrete beside it. I walked around her car, then moved to the rear of the house. Behind me, I heard Chris banging on the front door.

The garden back here was as well kept as the drive: buzz-cut grass, with elegant flower beds edging the fence, the velvety reds, purples and yellows bright in the swathe of morning sun that caught them. *She's normally so reliable. Such a good neighbour.* I told myself there was probably nothing to worry about – that even the most predictable and responsible of people forget to put their bin out sometimes, or oversleep, or neglect to tell their slightly annoying neighbour that they're going away.

The drive had sloped down as it went, so I found the kitchen door at the top of a set of stone steps, level with a raised wooden deck that stretched along the back of the property, all the way to the dividing fence with Connelly's garden. I banged on the glass door first, not expecting a reply. Vickers would have responded to Chris by now if she was inside and able to. Then I slipped on a pair of gloves as a precaution, and tried the handle. As expected, it didn't turn.

I stepped on to the decking. The wood felt soft and giving beneath my feet, as though the planks there had absorbed long-ago rain and never fully dried out. The house had two large windows at ground level. Glancing up, I saw four smaller ones on the floor above.

I moved to the nearest one, cupping my hands over my eyes and pressing my face close to the glass. There was no blind, and it was obvious that this was the kitchen. Metal taps looped up over the sink, close to the window, and I could see a counter and cabinets a short distance across the room. The kitchen was small – skinny, like a galley in a narrowboat – and even in the relative gloom, I could see how clean everything was. I didn't know her, but I was already imagining Sally Vickers washing up and wiping down meticulously after every meal; scrupulous about it.

The window opened along the top, and was far too thin for anyone to fit through. Even so, I reached up on tiptoes and tried it. Shut tight.

The second window was close to the far corner of the house. A tree was overflowing the fence from Connelly's side, and it brushed against my shoulder as I peered through the glass. Sally Vickers' living room ran the entire depth of the house, so that I could see the closed cream curtains on the front window at the far end. Again, the room looked polished and spare. No obvious clutter ...

But the fact that I could see it at all meant that the curtains back here had been left open.

Despite the heaviness of the mid-morning heat, a chill ran through me as I realised that. It had taken a second to register; it's always easier to notice what is there as opposed to what isn't. Why open only one set of curtains in the morning? Or why close only one set at night? Especially if you're going away.

This window was side-hinged, and currently flush with the frame. But it was large enough, just about, to fit through. I stared at it for a moment, my ears ringing slightly, then gathered myself together and reached out to test it. I got my fingers into the join and pulled.

It won't open.

But it did.

A flare of panic went up in my chest. *Easy, Zoe.* While it was still possible that there was an innocent explanation, I knew in my heart that we had another scene here. That we'd stumbled on it fresh.

Keep calm and think.

I turned to one side and shouted – 'Chris! Round here, now!' – then back to the window. I eased it as wide on the hinges as it would go, and leaned inside carefully, looking around. There was a round glass table close by, clear apart from some paperwork piled neatly at one side. Further in, a long brown leather settee was backed up against one wall, opposite a large flat-screen television mounted over the fireplace, with a coffee table in between. At the far end, by the opposite window, a closed door. Presumably that led to the hall and the stairs.

I leaned further in and checked to my immediate right. The door that led into the kitchen was closed too. Now that my head and shoulders were inside, I realised that the air in here was strange: warmer and less fresh than outside. There was an odd kind of *silk* to it, like a glass of stale, misty water. The house itself was thuddingly silent, but felt like it shouldn't be.

'Sally?' I shouted. 'It's the police? Are you here?'

The words didn't seem to go anywhere.

A fresh scene. There was additional weight to that, of course, and the thought burrowed down uncomfortably. All the victims so far – even Julie Kennedy – had at least managed to self-report. But if Sally Vickers was in here, she was not responding.

I leaned back out, just as Chris stepped on to the far end of the deck.

'What have we—'

He froze when he saw me by the open window. Because it was obvious enough what we had. If not from the window, then from the look on my face.

'Shit,' he said. 'Seriously?'

Under different circumstances, he'd have got a sarcastic response to that. But I just nodded, feeling grim. I pressed my fingers together, warming up the muscles in my forearms.

'I'm going in.'

'Wait. Hang on.'

He started towards me, but I had no intention of waiting. Partly because I knew he was on the verge of hiccuping up some bullshit chivalry, but mostly because we needed to move quickly here. I didn't know for sure that Sally Vickers was inside, but if she was, she was badly hurt, or worse.

I eyed the window, then reached in and took a fingertip grip on the top of the frame inside. Steadied myself.

'Zoe—'

'Fuck off, Chris. If he was here, he's long gone now.'

'But how are you even going to— Oh.'

I hoisted myself up, hanging from my fingertips with my knees against the wall, feeling the tension in my forearms, shoulders and back. I used my feet to climb up the outside wall, bringing my knees up to my chest and slipping my feet through the open window, then sat down on the ledge.

'Like that,' I said. 'Make yourself useful, Chris. Call backup and an ambulance.'

'We don't know what we're dealing with yet.'

'Yes we do.'

I ducked under the top of the window, put my feet down, and stood up in Sally Vickers' front room.

Now that I was properly inside, that brief spurt of bravado disappeared entirely. There was definitely something wrong here. The air had a bruised quality, one I sometimes recognised at a crime scene. It was bullshit, but it often felt that way – as though the space in which something awful had taken place was stunned somehow by what had happened.

I checked the kitchen first, moving through to a small utility room by the back door. The boiler was on the wall above an expensive-looking washing machine; the enormous fridge-freezer had a juice dispenser in the top door. Everything was humming slightly. Through the blurred glass of the back door I could make out Chris's silhouette on the steps.

His voice came through muffled.

'Any way of opening it from in there?'

'No.'

Sally Vickers had two sash jams on the back door, both in the locked position. I could undo them, of course, but there was no sign of any keys nearby, so there was no point. Better to leave the scene as untouched as possible.

Chris started to say something else, but I was already heading back through the kitchen and then the front room. Opening the door at the far end, I found myself in a small entrance area. There was the front door, a staircase going up to the right, a box room straight ahead.

The front door – sash jams again, and a chain here as well. Vickers was security-conscious; everything had been locked up tight. Which made it unlikely that she'd left her back window open by mistake.

'Sally?' I shouted up the stairs. 'Sally Vickers? It's the police. Are you here, please?'

Nothing.

The box room was empty, so I went straight up to the next floor, taking the stairs quickly but quietly. There were two spare rooms to the left, their doors ajar, and the bathroom and main bedroom to the right. All the attacks so far had taken place in the early hours, the woman woken while sleeping. I headed to the right.

The bedroom door was pulled to, but not shut entirely. Through the crack I could make out a soft red glow – presumably the daylight smearing in through closed curtains.

I reached out to push the door fully open, then hesitated, suddenly nervous. It's not like me to be on edge, but the air on the other side of the door felt packed with presence and sadness.

I pushed the door open and stepped inside.

A minute or so later, I was downstairs again, my body moving by itself back to the open window. It was a strange sensation: I felt as though I was outside of myself, acting almost on autopilot. Perhaps I was in the beginnings of shock – although I hated the thought and did my best to push it aside. Right now, I needed to be in control.

Chris wasn't out back, but actually, that was fine. I leaned on the frame for a few moments, breathing in the fresh air from outside. In spite of the heat, it might as well have been ice compared to the stifling atmosphere in the house. It was thirst-quenching.

After a few deep breaths, I turned my head and inspected the window. There was no obvious damage to the frame, and nothing appeared to have been drilled. The handle was up on the inside, and I considered turning it – seeing if it worked, or whether it might have been interfered with in some way – but it was better to leave that to Forensics. This was certainly where he'd got out. Maybe it was where he'd got in as well, if we could only work out how. I didn't want to remove any evidence that might throw light on that. Not now.

I heard footsteps scraping on the driveway, and a moment later, Chris appeared around the corner. He hurried over.

'What have we got? Is she here?'

I looked at him and nodded.

'He's killed her, Chris. This time, he's killed her.'

His face didn't really change, but somehow it did. Something in his eyes fell away.

'She's upstairs.' My voice was small, quiet; it didn't really sound like me at all. 'He's jammed her between the far side of the bed and the wall.'

When I'd first stepped into the room, her body hadn't been visible, but it was immediately clear that something had happened. The sheets were in disarray, and there were stains spattered on the duvet, and far more extensively on one of the pillows. The red light from the curtains made it difficult to make out, but it had still been obvious that it was blood.

Sally Vickers had appeared to me slowly as I moved gingerly around the base of the bed, a stretch of pale skin at a time, her body bathed in crimson light. The gap between the side of the bed and the wall was about half a metre wide. It was possible that she'd rolled off and died there, but it looked more like he'd stuffed her down – jammed her into the space, like used clothes pushed awkwardly into a suitcase. She was naked, and

61

her limbs were tangled, with one forearm pointing up. As the sight of her had slowly resolved, I'd searched for her face; it had taken me a few seconds to realise that she was looking directly at me, and that I just hadn't been able to tell.

I shook my head. 'We need everyone here *now*.'

He was already getting his phone.

'On it.'

While he made the call, I continued to breathe in the fresh air, but the image of Sally Vickers wouldn't leave my head. I'd seen countless dead bodies before, of course, but there was something about the way he'd disposed of her that seemed to have wiped me out inside.

Part of it was that it had already been my investigation *before* she'd died. My responsibility. No matter how hard we'd worked, we hadn't caught him before he'd done this. But it was more than guilt: it was the sheer callousness of it all. The scale was different, but it reminded me of what Chris had said about my messy burglary: why not just take what you want and leave? *You didn't have to do that as well.* The violence here was just so blatant, so pointless. There didn't seem to be any reason for it, just blind hate.

Chris asked me something.

'What?'

'I said, can you find any keys? It would make it easier for you to get out.'

I shook my head. 'Better not. Let's leave everything as it is for Forensics. We want to keep it tight. We don't want to miss a single thing this time.'

'We didn't any other time either.'

'I know. But still.'

'I'll help you out, then.'

I glanced behind me, feeling the emptiness of the house again. Now that I knew for sure she was upstairs, the air felt less ominous than before. Just sadness now.

'No,' I said. 'I think I'll wait in here, with her.'

Eight

That evening, I got out of work both late and frustrated. The afternoon had been spent beginning the investigation into Sally Vickers' life – her friends and family; her movements over previous days – and canvassing the neighbours for anything untoward they might have spotted. If she'd been targeted, and perhaps even followed over time, then surely *someone* must have seen *something*? But so far, just as with the other victims, the answer seemed to be that nobody had.

It was Monday, so I did what I always do: I went to the gym. It wasn't like I was going to get much sleep anyway. Even if I could get Sally Vickers out of my head for long enough, the dream of the waste ground would undoubtedly be there waiting for me. So, close to ten o'clock that night, I pulled up in the car park of the Workhouse.

It's open twenty-four seven, but is largely unattended after hours, so I had to use my keycard to unlock the door. Normally, when I step inside, the warm, sweaty air and the *thud* of bags is familiar enough to be a genuine relief from the horrors of the day behind me. It was quieter at this hour, but the smell of the place was still vaguely comforting.

The Workhouse is a no-frills, spit-and-sawdust kind of establishment. There are nicer places closer to the centre – the air-conditioned chain gyms, where everything's colour-coordinated and the sounds are of whirring and swooshing – and I could afford them easily enough. But I prefer the Workhouse for various reasons. The main thing is that it feels like I belong here, in the way that I don't in *any* fancy establishment – whether it's pubs, restaurants, or whatever. I always suspect the owners are looking me up and down and thinking I shouldn't be there. Which is ridiculous, of course. I have money, I'm well presented and behaved, and I have about as socially responsible a job as it's possible to have. But even so, a part of me is always going to feel like the scruffy gang kid: the one the store detective follows around and keeps his eye on.

After I'd got changed, I slung a towel over my shoulder and carried my water bottle across the open-plan gym, towards the free weights area. Black rubber mats were interlocked on the floor – tacky in places, like tyres that had driven over oil – and one wall was covered with smudged mirrors, framed by an old stack-and-pulley set-up. Benches were dotted around, along with slightly rusty bars and plates, the labels long worn off the latter, the numbers on them little more than raised ridges in the iron. There was also a rack of newer dumb-bells, with rubber handles and black hexagonal ends, and I walked over to those, selecting the ones I was going to use.

There was only one man using the equipment tonight: a guy in his mid-twenties with dark shaved hair, dressed in tracksuit bottoms and a workout top that revealed the trapezius muscles on his neck and shoulders. I'd seen him a few times before. Right now, he was sitting facing the mirror, curling twenty-kilo dumb-bells – hammer raises. His arms were absurdly pumped, the veins standing out on his forearms as though the skin had been shrink-wrapped over them. As he finished his set, he placed the weights carefully on either side of his bench. Not a dropper, then. I liked that.

I dragged a bench into place a short distance to one side, dimly aware out of the corner of my eye of him tapping at his phone. Recording his set details: there'd be an app for that, for people who cared. I never bothered to count.

I lined the dumb-bells up, then shook my arms and twisted round at the waist to stretch my back. The weights I'd selected

64

today were small. Sometimes I go for heavier ones – to test myself; to mix it up and keep things interesting – but I prefer to lift light, as there's something about eight-rep sets that feels truncated to me. The sets I prefer have fifty repetitions or more, and I'm in pain for well over half of them. And that's good, because it allows me to lose myself for longer.

It's one of the main reasons I lift – to distract myself from dwelling on the day behind me: thoughts coming to life, whirling and dancing, like the mops and buckets in that Disney cartoon. Tonight, predictably, my head was all too full. A small part of it involved John; the day after tomorrow, he would be moving into the care home I'd found for him. The saddest aspect of the whole thing was that he hadn't protested anything like as much as I'd anticipated – or perhaps even hoped – he would. He'd accepted the situation quickly, so it had felt as though he was already giving up the fight. On the surface, I was worried about how he was going to settle in; deep down, I was trying to ignore the fact that he was not going to be there for as long as I wanted. That given how fast he was deteriorating, he might not need to settle in at all.

But as big as those thoughts were, they were small in comparison to those of the case. The memory of finding Sally Vickers this morning kept returning to me. The image of her. The way he'd stuffed her down there like rags when he'd finally finished hurting her.

Six rapes and one murder, and we were no closer to catching him. I tried to imagine what might be going through his head. He had been escalating before, and had been lucky not to kill Julie Kennedy. Even so, murder was still a leap. I wondered if it had shocked him – frightened him, even – taking that step. My bet was that even if he was scared by what he'd done, there'd be excitement there too, and we'd have another victim to deal with before too long: another face to tack on our boards. And at that point, it would be seven rapes and two murders. Because, having killed once, there was no reason for him not to do so again. People like our man almost never slow down. If anything, he was likely to accelerate harder, and the real question was how many people were going to suffer before he finally crashed.

The faces of the victims swirled through my head, each with its own string of dates and details trailing behind. I knew them off by heart now, and my mind kept latching on to them and exploring, moving hand over hand from one to another, searching for connections. Something that mattered. Something that we'd missed. A hundred details. A thousand. If I didn't make sense of them, another woman was going to die. Another woman could be dying *right now*.

And so you have to make sense of them.

That's another reason why I like light weights: the metaphor of them. It's one small movement, one repetition at a time. You achieve the entire set in tiny increments, edging painfully towards the end. You can always manage one more. And if you can do it in the gym, with a weight, then you can do it outside the gym, with whatever else is required of you – events, people, information. All it takes is to keep going.

The guy beside me was done for the night. He wandered away behind me, and I allowed myself to watch him in the mirror for a moment, evaluating him. There are other ways of distracting yourself, of course – of making your thoughts go quiet. But not tonight. I caught my own eye in the mirror. Made sure I knew that I was serious: that we were about to do this, and that we would keep on doing it until it was time to stop.

Then I picked up the weights and began.

I got home just before midnight, resisting the urge to turn the television on and watch the news reports on the twenty-four-hour channel.

They would be covering the case, of course, and I knew *how* they would be covering it. An investigation like this always has the same narrative in the press, and we were well into the stage of recrimination against the police for not doing enough. I didn't need to see that, or watch Drake's inevitable talking-head performance, expertly fielding the implications of the passive-aggressive questions downwards. I prefer to feel guilty on my own terms, thank you.

Instead, I warmed up some leftover bolognese sauce from the previous evening, and ate it without pasta. Then I went to bed, not giving it time to go down properly. I was going to have bad dreams anyway.

Before going upstairs, I did what I imagined everybody in the city was doing this evening: I checked that my house was safe. Every window shut and locked. Every door secured. It was foolish, perhaps, but I even searched the obvious places, just to make sure I was alone.

Upstairs, I crouched down and looked under the bed. Both the cats were there, staring back at me. It had been the same most nights since the burglary.

'You can come out, you know,' I said.

Hazel licked her lips in response, but neither of them made a move to emerge.

In the middle of the night, I bolted upright, my heart hammering in my chest, my body drenched in sweat.

For a while, I sat on the edge of the bed, my face in my hands, trying to calm myself down. I could still see the waste ground, as vivid and unreal as when I'd been asleep: the ghost-like figure; the clouds moving faster and faster. The sense that the scene was rapidly approaching a breaking point, the sudden moment when something awful would rush straight at me, screaming into my face. And the velocity of the nightmare had followed me into real life. Eventually I lowered my hands and stared at the wall.

Something is coming, I thought.

Something awful is coming.

Nine

After Jane qualified as a volunteer, the sessions at Mayday fell into a familiar pattern almost immediately. While the calls varied in length and content, and there were often unpredictable stretches of boredom in between, when she could sit with a coffee and read, she quickly came to recognise the different types of caller.

A surprising proportion were men in prison. She had no idea where they got the phones from, especially when the calls came late at night, but the conversations were often lengthy. In some ways, that was good – it made the shifts fly – but there was also the sensation that she wasn't accomplishing much. She rarely got the impression that the prisoners were in despair, so much as bored: just lonely and killing time. But then there were few rules as to who could phone the helpline, or for what reason. If someone just wanted to chat, then that was fine.

At least those calls were generally polite and comprehensible, whereas a small number came from people who were so disturbed that it was difficult to communicate with them at all. They usually just talked down the line at her, often in non sequiturs. These conversations all ended in one of two ways. Either the caller took offence at something perfectly innocent that Jane said, or else they hung up in the middle of an abandoned sentence, their voice trailing away, as though they could no longer remember why they had a phone in their hand in the first place.

The rest of the legitimate callers were ... *lonely*, Jane supposed. Some were literally alone, while others did have people around them but still felt like they were on their own. Many of them had something they couldn't talk about hidden away inside, and keeping that thing secret hurt them. Infidelity, memories of abuse, financial pressures. Whatever it was, there came a moment when they needed to share it, so they called Mayday to talk to the only person it felt like they could: a stranger, unconnected to their lives.

And then, of course, there were the sex calls.

They surprised Jane in two ways. Firstly, there were *so many* of them. And secondly, she wasn't as bothered or embarrassed by them as she'd imagined she would be. In fact, she became good at delivering a curt but polite goodbye, and hanging up as soon as she recognised the caller's intentions. *I'm sorry, but I don't have to listen to you while you're doing that.* She usually managed to inflect a little breezy jolliness into it, even when the call turned nasty.

You dirty little fucking bitch ...

'I'm sorry, but I don't have to listen to you while you're doing that.'

Click.

I'm going to find you and come all—

'I'm sorry, but I don't have to listen to you while you're doing that.'

Click.

If anything, she actually got a small kick out of that. A few months ago, she would have had trouble engaging in a conversation at all, never mind taking control of one and ending it. She was getting better. At the same time as her natural empathy helped her fade into the background with the genuine calls, she was also becoming more assertive with the time-wasters. It made her feel strong.

Whenever she was on shift with Rachel, she usually ended up giving her a lift home afterwards. The girl didn't live too far away – she had her own small house on the far side of campus

– but Jane always offered, and Rachel always accepted. It had taken her a few lifts, with the girl chattering confidently away beside her, to realise that Rachel accepted the rides not because she needed them, but because she seemed to enjoy Jane's company. *For some reason*, she thought – then told herself not to.

One night, she talked to Rachel about the sex calls.

'*Why* do they do that?'

Rachel shrugged. 'There are a lot of freaks in the world.'

'Not *that* many, surely.' Jane didn't like to feel that the world was rammed to the gills with that sort of man. 'I mean, there were three tonight, and that was just on my line.'

Rachel considered it. 'Yeah, but think about it like this. Imagine you're a man who wants to do that kind of thing. You're going to call people like us, aren't you? People who can't answer back. You're not going to cold-call the police and do it.'

Jane laughed. 'I wish some of them would try.'

'Yeah, me too. But it's a skewed sample, is what I'm saying. It's like asking why there are so many injured people in hospital.'

'I suppose so.'

'Not that I think it's particularly rare.'

'You think there are lots of them?'

It was Rachel's turn to laugh, but it was a hollow one.

'I think there are a lot of *men*.'

'That's harsh.'

'Maybe. But I think you'd be surprised. It's the anonymity, you know? When there are no consequences, people start acting the way they really want to, deep inside. And a lot of men want to do that.'

That was an unhappy thought.

'Why?'

'A million different reasons.' Rachel shrugged again, as though the details weren't important. 'A lot of them, I guess you could probably pick it apart from the story they give you while they're jerking off down the line. The things they say. But it all basically comes down to the same thing.'

'Which is?'

'That they hate us.'

Us meant *women*, Jane knew. She didn't want to believe that, but the next time she received a sex call – one of the ones that ended with violent language and threats, the words practically spat down the line at her – she thought that, actually, there was something to what Rachel had said. *The man on the other end of this line hates me*, she thought. She was someone he'd never met. He knew nothing about her, beyond the fact that she was a woman, and yet a part of him really hated her.

'I'm sorry,' she told him, a little glumly, 'but I don't have to listen to you while you're doing that.'

It was strange, as time went on, how at ease she began to feel in Rachel's company. Rachel was young, slim and pretty, and she seemed enormously self-assured, from her dyed red hair to her confident manner. She gave the impression that nothing fazed her – that she could walk into any social situation and would feel immediately at home. Why she wanted to spend time with Jane still felt like a bit of a mystery, but after a while Jane convinced herself just to accept it, and began to relax around her.

One night, she found herself telling Rachel about Peter.

'We'd been together for a couple of years,' she said. 'I'd never really questioned it before. I just sort of fell into it.'

'Was he fit?'

'I don't know.' Jane laughed. 'He was okay, I suppose.'

'Scant praise there. Come on, though. What was it that attracted you to him in the first place?'

'He asked me out, I guess.'

It came across as a joke, and Jane laughed again, but there was a degree of truth to it. In hindsight, she saw how dull Peter had been, and there wasn't much more she could say. *It's not funny, though*, she thought, *because it's true*. Ultimately, she'd gone out with Peter because she was grateful that he'd asked, and she'd stayed with him because she was grateful that he wanted her to. Even in the end, when he was drinking more heavily and they were hardly talking, it had been his decision to leave, and she'd been the one left upset.

'What happened?' Rachel asked.

'He was always telling me how much of a pushover I was. That I was too timid.'

'Nice.'

'He was probably right.'

The split had been her therapist's fault, which meant, ironically enough, that it was Peter's. Peter had always resented her father's influence on her life, weathering his frequent visits with often visibly gritted teeth. When Jane's father was present, Peter was always aware that he was now only the second most important man in the room. While he hadn't been glad when the old man died, he had certainly seen it as a chance for Jane to escape that influence.

In the most bitter argument they'd had, he'd claimed not to want a mouse for a partner. *It's always me that makes the decisions*, he told her. *You never seem to have an opinion. You're always… putting yourself out for me.*

She'd been hurt and upset, but thinking about it, he was right. And so finally, more to please him than anything else, she had nervously agreed to book an appointment with a therapist.

One evening, a short while afterwards, Peter had suggested they go to the cinema to see the latest Jason Statham film. Jane had no interest in doing that, and said so. It had been almost comical, the double-take Peter did. He really wanted to go, he said.

I hear what you're saying, Jane told him, *but no.*

She had felt very proud as the words left her mouth. Now, she recognised the same tone of voice in the way she ended the sex calls. That evening, she repeated the phrase three times to Peter. They didn't go to see the new Jason Statham film, and he sulked. *I think you're probably drinking too much*, she told him a few days afterwards. *I'm only saying it because I worry about you.* A couple of months later, it was all over and he'd moved out. Apparently he had wanted to be in a relationship with a mouse after all.

Jane laughed as she said that, and this time the humour was more genuine. Rachel gave a wry smile in return, but then shrugged again.

'You see?' she said. 'Men.'

When Jane wasn't at the helpline, it came as a surprise to her that she was often physically alone without ever actually feeling lonely. The flat she'd had since leaving university had always been too small and cramped for her to live in with Peter. Maybe it had been okay to begin with, when they'd been happy pressed up tightly, side by side, but in the later stages of their relationship that feeling had reversed and the place had become claustrophobic. Without him, it was just right again, as though it had been holding its breath for months, and could now finally get the air it needed.

Perhaps that was true of her, as well. After all this time, it was a revelation for Jane to discover that she really didn't mind her own company. She wasn't that bad.

For the first time in her life, she had begun to feel free.

Actually, it was for the first time *before* her life. That was at the root of the problem. She had been a dangerously premature baby, and it had been two months before the doctors finally allowed her parents to take their first – and only – child home from the hospital. She had then been a sickly infant, underweight and weak. Her parents were religious; they decided that their tiny daughter's life was a gift from God, and responded accordingly by wrapping that life in blankets to keep it safe. They had treated her as though any little misstep might break a bone. She was not the kind of little girl who climbed trees.

Later, on evenings when her peers and her handful of vague friends were out socialising, Jane would be in her room, studying. As a teenager, she was bookish and shy. Even at university, studying French, her year abroad had seen her father phoning every night to make sure she was okay. And until his death last year, all her bank statements had still been sent to her home address; he would open them to make sure she was spending sensibly.

Her room-mate at university told Jane – affably, but entirely sincerely – that she really needed to tell the man to fuck off. Jane had nodded wearily: she had some sympathy with that position. But she also understood that her father was acting out of love: a crushing kind of love, admittedly – one that pressed in on her from all sides and kept her life small – but love all the same. Anyway, she found it hard to stand up to people at the best of times.

Now, all that had changed.

Or *was* changing, at least. She was self-reliant, alone but happy, and, it turned out, far more capable than she'd ever given herself credit for. It was as though she'd been standing at one end of a high wire over a canyon, afraid to step out and walk carefully across to join everyone else on the far side. Now, not only had she taken the first step, she was more than halfway across – and it wasn't at all frightening. Even when she stopped and looked down, it didn't remotely feel like she was going to lose her balance.

Volunteering at Mayday had been the biggest step, of course, but it had also provided the largest reward. At worst, the shifts were challenges, and Jane had begun to realise that when you forced yourself, not only could challenges be met and conquered, but it felt good when you did it.

And so, despite the prevalence of the bad calls, she found herself looking forward to her shifts. She was looking forward to one that night.

Of course, right then, she really had no idea.

Ten

I slept fitfully after the nightmare, so got up early, and found myself arriving at the department a little after seven o'clock. The sun was just appearing above the horizon: a pale thumbprint pressed on to the sky, the edge burning where it touched the land. A new day. A fresh sheet of hours to fill. I tried to tell myself it would bring a breakthrough of some kind, but there had been too many days now, and none of them had, and I felt despondent.

Despite the early hour, the incident room was half full. The night-shift workers were stretching, ready to get home, and several I recognised from the day team were already at their stations. None of them paid me any attention as I poured a coffee, then sat down at my desk. There was a pile of actions and reports in my tray, but I doubted any of it would be important. If there had been a key development, someone would have called.

Obviously, I worked through it anyway. There was a note from pathology that the post-mortem was being rushed through and would take place this morning. I checked my watch. It would actually be in progress now, so fingers crossed we would have the results by midday. Forensics would take longer, of course, but the previous scenes had given us little in that regard, and I wasn't about to get my hopes up there.

Next, I found a compendium of witness statements, although to call them that was to mischaracterise them. It was just more of the same from yesterday afternoon: interviews with Sally Vickers' friends, family and neighbours, none of whom had reported any concerns in the time leading up to her murder. Assuming Sally had been stalked in advance of the attack, she either hadn't been aware of it, or hadn't reported it to anybody. Turning a page, I was betting on the former. Our man was too careful for that...

Or was he?

I read the final sheet in the tray for a second time. This one wasn't a witness statement. Some enterprising officer had dug back through reports on Sally's neighbourhood and found something potentially much more interesting. There was a nursery at the bottom of her street, and a week ago, staff there had alerted the police that someone had been spotted loitering nearby. He was described as a physically large man, possibly in his thirties, with a beard and wild hair. A sweep was done over the following few days, and an officer had identified the individual and confronted him. The man denied he'd been in the area before, and claimed to have just stopped to check his phone while out walking. In the event, there wasn't much the officer could do, but he made it clear that it would be wise for the man to absent himself from the area in future. But not before he'd identified him. The man had given his name as Jonathan Pearson, which had been verified from the driver's licence he was carrying.

Don't get your hopes up, Zoe.

But it was impossible not to. I turned to my computer and pulled up a search for Pearson, establishing quickly that he had no criminal record of any kind, certainly not for child-related offences. *So why were you there, Jonathan?* From another database, I accessed an online copy of his driver's licence, and studied the photograph there. He was exactly as described: a full beard, and long black hair, which for this picture had been tied tightly back into a ponytail.

I scrolled down until I found his address – and read it with a slight start. Paydale Lane. Right in the heart of the Thornton estate, where I'd grown up. Just a coincidence, of course, but not a pleasant one. I didn't exactly relish the prospect of going back there.

I scrolled up again to view Pearson's face, then took a moment to stare into his eyes. I didn't want to get my hopes up, but I felt a tingle inside.

This is something.

I checked my watch: just after half seven. Chris would be in shortly, and I knew I should wait for him before heading out. Apart from anything else, the thought of going into Thornton alone didn't fill me with joy. Regardless, though, I should wait.

Should.

You might miss him, though.

That was true – Pearson could be heading out to work soon. And that was really all the excuse I needed. I searched around the desk for a pen, and quickly scribbled a note for Chris.

Time to go back home.

As I approached it, my impression of the Thornton estate now was that it looked more like a campsite than a proper part of the city. I saw the generators first, stored in long corrugated-iron crates, behind chain-link fences topped with curls of razor wire; then came the initial spread of houses. They were uniformly ugly – flat-topped, single-storey concrete blocks, with pale faces and grey pebble-dashed sides – and weren't so much terraced as oddly conjoined: stuck together in random clusters of twos, threes and fours. The breaks in between formed a web of thin roads and footpaths, all but indecipherable to non-residents.

I kept to the main road for a while, driving past the face of the estate. The verges were dirty and unkempt, with circles and squares of grass missing, where the council-provided bins and poles had been uprooted. It was less than a mile, but seemed to go on for ever. Just before I reached the end, I indicated left, and took the last turning that would take me into the estate proper.

On the journey over, I'd been trying to kid myself that it was no big deal, but of course, now that I was here, that wasn't remotely true. The place hummed with familiarity; so little had changed that it felt as though no real time had passed. I remembered the grey fronts of the houses, cracked with disrepair and dotted with fans in meshed cages that looked scorched and burned. Broken pipes spattered water directly on to the flagstones, while sickly brown stains stretched down the walls from the rotting wooden canopies above. Many of the windows I drove past lacked curtains, and some were plastered with overlapping sheets of old newspaper. With the car window wound down, I could hear the muffled sound of televisions and radios, the louder noise of raised voices. I might as well have grown up here yesterday.

The road finished in a misshapen nub of tarmac, where I found space to park up. Wooden fences ran along one side, with a single break for a footpath. Beyond, I could see more houses. They looked like they had a second storey, but I knew it was an illusion: the estate was constructed on a slope, and the buildings ahead were just built on higher ground.

I locked the car and headed up the footpath, then took one of the many jagged stone staircases that criss-crossed the estate. It's deceptive, from the outside, just how extensive Thornton really is. The sensation came back to me now – how easy it can be to lose yourself here. The further in you go, the more it feels like you could wander through an area that is only a mile or so square without ever reaching an edge. Living here, it sometimes seemed that the area kept shifting around, reconfiguring itself to prevent you from leaving.

Occasionally washing lines spanned the paths, with towels and clothes draped over them like curtains, and the smell of wet fabric and cheap washing powder was another reminder of childhood. There were memories everywhere here, and they emerged in my head fleetingly, like half-heard snatches of laughter. The slight breeze seemed full of ghosts.

It's just a place, Zoe. No better or worse than any other.

And remember, you pulled yourself out of here.

Jonathan Pearson lived close to the centre of the estate, whereas I'd grown up in a house on the edge. I'd deliberately parked at the opposite end; I had no desire to walk past my old home. It would either look the same, or be very different, and either way, it was nothing I needed to see. Because the voice in my head was right: I'd worked hard and pulled myself out of this place, this life. There wasn't anything left for me here.

Except one thing, of course. And about five minutes after I'd left the car, close to Pearson's street, I took a ginnel that led me away from it. A couple of turns later, the land opened up ahead of me, and there it was.

Like everything else here, the waste ground was almost exactly the same as I remembered it. In fact, my nightmare had preserved it so accurately that I felt a shiver despite the heat, and had to suppress the urge to pinch myself. But no, this wasn't a dream. The sky was a normal colour, and there weren't any clouds. And it was empty: no figures of any kind standing there. *Don't*, I thought suddenly. It was irrational, and I didn't know why, but the thought came anyway

Don't.

I stood there for a few moments longer, willing a memory to come. Just some indication of what had happened here that I couldn't remember, and that only ever came out in my sleep. But it wouldn't.

Quarter past eight now.

Just do what you came here to do.

I turned and headed back into the body of the estate. It only took another minute to locate Pearson's house, and as I approached it, I could hear the sound of the television from the open window out front. Someone was home, then.

I took out my phone and dialled Chris's number. He answered immediately, and sounded annoyed with me. Understandably, I supposed.

'You've got to do everything yourself, haven't you?'

'No,' I said, although of course he was right. 'You weren't in, and I decided it was too important to wait.'

'Bullshit. Zoe—'

'Give it a rest, Chris. It might not even be anything.'

'Then why was it too important to wait?'

'Because it was. And I don't need a chaperone. Anyway, look: I've called you now that I'm here. So you can escort me by telephone, can't you?'

'Zoe—'

I moved the phone away from my ear and knocked on Pearson's door. My intention was to play it as a follow-up from the nursery incident at first: nothing serious that might alarm him. But in truth, I was glad to have Chris on the line. Just in case.

I heard bolts being withdrawn, and then a moment later the front door opened. I recognised the man immediately from the photograph online. The beard was gone now, but the wild hair remained. Of course, the picture had only shown his face.

'Jonathan Pearson?' I said.

He nodded, and my heart sank a little. At about five foot six, Pearson was shorter than me, and he was dressed in pyjama bottoms and a white T-shirt that revealed how skinny he was. Not only would I have been able to overpower him with one hand, there was no way on earth he could be the guy the nursery workers had seen, and that the officer had stopped and interviewed. You would have had to be blind to describe this guy as physically large.

I lifted the phone to my ear again.

'Stand down, soldier.'

'Why? What's going on?'

'It's not our guy. I'll be back in soon.'

I ended the call, realising that what I'd said wasn't quite right. *Pearson* might not be our guy, but I was certain that the man who had been spotted in Sally's street was. The question was, how had the bastard got hold of Pearson's driving licence?

'What's this about?' asked Pearson.

'Detective Inspector Zoe Dolan.' I did my best to smile at him, although the sinking feeling had started to be replaced by frustration and anger. 'I think we need to have a little chat, Jonathan.'

Eleven

It always happens like this, after the monster has come. He tries to forget, but after a while, it simply gets too much.

Because he is a man who loves very deeply indeed, and he never truly leaves anyone behind. In this way, he is not so unlike other people: normal people. Doesn't everybody mourn lost relationships to some extent? Whether it's with hatred, fondness, confusion, guilt or forgiveness, surely everyone looks back. However hard we try, it's impossible to unremember for ever.

In other ways, of course, he is very different indeed.

During the time he spends with someone, he is often happy. He thinks of them in the morning when he wakes up, and smiles to himself, content with the knowledge that he has them in his life, however obliquely. He anticipates the first sight of them that day, and makes plans for what they might do: dancing together at a distance. For a certain amount of time, he is able to pretend. When reality does intrude, it does so completely and utterly. The realisation of who and what he is can crush him: reduce him to nothing but a fat, heaving curl beneath the covers in a pitch-black bedroom. There is no light in the world at those moments, and yet somehow he sees himself all too clearly.

When the relationship is over, it feels much the same, only bleaker. He can walk the streets and go to work, and for lengthy periods of time he is able to forget what he has done. The woman is no longer in his life, of course, but that absence is only the vaguest of pressures at the back of his mind. Perhaps there is an odd quality to the sunlight and the air, as though the world has subtly shifted on some emotional level, but he functions.

Until he remembers.

Who he is. What he is.

Then every minute aches, and it seems impossible to imagine that he can bear an hour. He does, of course, and days somehow pass. What he experiences is not simply depression and self-hatred, but despair. True despair, he knows, is not so much an emotion as a vacuum. It is the feeling of God turning His back on you. Running through it is the knowledge that the things you have done can never be undone or made right. If a glass rolls across a table, you can catch it and roll it back along its path to where it started, but if it tips over the edge and smashes, that can't ever be reversed. The glass will forever be broken, and you will always be the man who broke it.

Even worse than the knowledge are the memories. He can still see everything that happened very clearly, and in his mind, the images play over and over, the most awful parts vivid and present. How could he have done that to them? The hate he felt for them makes no sense any more. It's the memory of an emotion, and the memory doesn't fit.

He lies in his bed, sometimes for days at a time, trying to stop himself from feeling anything at all. He calls in sick to work. And he *is* sick. Sometimes he wonders if people can sense it from the street – if the house stinks from the disease of him. He wakes up and imagines the women standing there in the corner of the bedroom. What's left of them.

It always happens like this. After a while, it simply gets too much.

Of course, this time it's different.

This time, he's killed her.

He saw the flyer while he was working at the university.

The contract was only for a week. He brought sandwiches in with him, and took to spending his lunch hours in the Union bar. The building was old; you walked in through the run-down entrance, and then down a set of stairs, and the bar was built into a large wooden booth at the centre. He would buy a couple of pints and sit, drinking slowly, losing himself in the chatter around him and trying not to think.

He could feel the students' eyes on him, because he was conspicuous in his overalls and obviously didn't belong here. He was too big not to notice, and with his bedraggled hair and unshaven face, he looked as if he had walked out of a wilderness. Whereas they were all so young and small, with their supple bodies and smooth faces. The pupal stage of an entirely different species: none of them would grow up to be like him. He tried not to look back at them. When he did, the person staring tended to turn away very quickly indeed.

The notice boards outside the bar were peppered with flyers and posters. Many were professionally done, advertising club nights. His gaze tracked across the images of young men and women in various states of undress, disco balls glinting, clusters of multicoloured bottles arranged like skittles. An alien world to him. There were also printed and hand-scrawled advertisements: rooms to rent; rooms wanted; lifts offered; musical instruments for sale. Notices for sports clubs. It was a cacophony of the small details of other people's lives. Like the students themselves, there was an air of naïve, puppyish hope to it all. Nobody would want most of these things, but they'd put them up anyway.

And then the flyer for the helpline caught his eye.

It was on the third and final board, tacked to the edge: a simple glossy black sheet with the image of a bright red telephone – an old-fashioned one, with a circular dial – and big white text.

MAYDAY.

A problem shared ...

We are here just to listen.

He stood there for a few moments, staring at the flyer, considering its message. *We are here just to listen.* Could that be true? His thoughts circled the idea, pondering the words and their meaning. He knew, of course, that such helplines existed. And they were confidential, weren't they? At least, they were when it came to the standard calls – the abuse, the depression, the loneliness. But would that be the case with him? For the special things he would talk to them about?

He ran his hand over his rough stubble. He didn't know. He wasn't sure.

Once the idea had settled in his head, though, it wouldn't leave. How good it would be to talk to someone. *What if*, he thought, *what if I could?* That would be something, wouldn't it. *A problem shared.* Because that was the point. It had always been bad in the past, but this time it was intolerable: the burden of the woman's murder was too heavy to carry. Perhaps if he *could* share that with another human being, it would bring him some degree of peace.

He didn't know.

After standing there for perhaps a minute longer, he looked carefully both ways, saw that nobody was watching, and plucked the flyer from the board. It felt like he was stealing it as he folded it away in his pocket and left. It tingled there, the possibility of some kind of release. He found himself almost huddling over it.

If he was going to do it, he realised later, he would need to be very careful.

He would have to make plans.

And so now he sits outside on a bench and prepares.

It is early afternoon, and this end of the park is mostly deserted. Across the spread of sunlit grass he can see clusters of people sitting, and a few others wandering along the dappled stone paths by the overhanging trees. There is a bandstand in the centre, and a couple of young men in shorts are on either side, arcing a frisbee to each other between the old green poles. A man is walking his dog; every now and then he throws a ball that's as bright and red as an apple, and the animal tears off across the grass. He watches them all: normal people doing normal things. They have nothing heavy to carry.

From the bench, he has a good enough view of the park to see that there's nobody nearby. Nobody close enough to overhear the conversation he is about to have. It is far from ideal, of course, but his options were limited and he needs to be safe. When he's not using the phone, he intends to take out the battery and SIM card. In case he's wrong about the call being confidential, he won't risk using the phone at home, or anywhere there might be CCTV that could catch him. He drove for a while before finding this park. It will do. If he phones again, then next time he'll choose somewhere else.

He looks down at the phone in his hands.

The plastic feels polished and awkward, as though it might slip from his grasp like a smooth pebble. He purchased it, along with a pay-as-you-go SIM card, from a dirty newsagent's just outside the city centre. It came pre-loaded with a thousand minutes. No need to enter credit card details or talk to a salesperson or set anything up. He doesn't even need to know his own phone number. He paid for everything with cash.

And now, his heart leaping, he turns the phone on and forces himself to calm down. One last check around, but there is nobody nearby. All anyone in the distance will see is a man talking on a mobile phone, having an emotional conversation. If they see anything at all.

He takes out the flyer, unfolds it, and dials the number, then presses the phone to his ear as it rings.

'Hello,' a woman's voice says. 'This is Mayday. My name's Jane. How can I help you today?'

Twelve

'He's doing this on purpose,' Chris said.

'No, he isn't.'

Late morning, and we were waiting in the reception area at the city's morgue and pathology department. We'd arrived on time for the appointment, but the pathologist, Sam Dale, had yet to appear. Under different circumstances, I might have agreed with Chris's interpretation of the delay: I quite like Dale, but he can be a prickly little bastard. Today, however, I doubted it. The pathologist had fast-tracked the post-mortem on Sally Vickers, working on it through the early hours of the morning. If nothing else, he'd be eager to get home.

While we waited, I walked over to the windows. The unit is situated on the eighth floor of the hospital, and one wall is comprised entirely of glass. Beyond the hazy width of the river, and the white eyelash curls of its folding currents, I could see the estates, the distant foundries and factories, even the beginnings of the countryside. The sun was invisible: just a brilliant white stain hanging over the city. The river below was still draped with the morning's mist, but the light made it look more like steam.

Jonathan Pearson.

He was back at the department being interviewed right now, but really, that was a formality. I'd already established everything I needed to know at his house. Pearson had denied being questioned by the police near the nursery, and I believed him, because it hadn't been him. It seemed fairly clear what had happened: our real man had given the officer a fake name. For his part, Pearson had no idea how the man could have got hold of his driver's licence. He'd misplaced it a long time ago – last year sometime, he said – and ordered a new one. But he had no idea where or even when he'd lost the old one.

The only positive thing to come out of the development was that we now had a reasonable description of our man's *face*. Presumably he had picked Jonathan Pearson because there was a superficial resemblance between the two of them that would pass if he was confronted. But that was far from positive in reality, because beards could easily be shaved off. Long hair could be trimmed short.

'Ah! Good evening, lady and gentleman.'

I turned to see Dale poking his head out of a door to the side of reception. At first I thought he was implying that we were the ones who were late, but then I saw how tired he looked. In terms of hours spent upright, it was probably approaching midnight to him.

'Join me.'

Chris rolled his eyes at me, and we followed Dale along the corridors that led to the autopsy suite. I remembered the way, of course. We'd been here a few times, although it's rare for either of us to attend a post-mortem, or – as now – turn up after one. In reality, there's little point. You've seen the victim at the scene, and you're not a medical expert, so it's generally a more productive use of your time to wait for a report to land in your actions tray, while you get on with things you're good at. Today, though, I had wanted to come.

We stepped inside the suite. The lights were very bright, and the room had a sealed quality that made our footfalls *clop* and echo on the white floor tiles. On my first ever visit, it had actually reminded me of a large high-tech kitchen. Most of the surfaces are polished steel, all kept spotlessly clean, and there are sinks and cabinets along the walls, and islands lined up down the centre. One wall is all metal, covered with a grid of what look like oven doors. Except they're not ovens, and, of course, the islands are dissection tables, with bodies lying under white sheets. The nasal sting of chemical detergent in the air doesn't quite mask the smell of death. It's a memorable combination of turned meat and old flowers.

Dale beckoned us impatiently over to the island at the far end of the room. He's a short man. Most of his head is bald – today reflecting the overhead lights – but there are neat dabs of brown hair at his temples. He also has ears that stick out almost perpendicular to his face. Chris once described him as looking like a monkey that had been shaved, and the image is appropriate enough. Dale has a wiry strength about him; you could easily imagine him hanging from things.

'Here she is,' he said, removing the sheet.

And yes. There she was.

I did my best to ignore the angry stitch marks left by the autopsy itself, and allowed my gaze to move over Sally Vickers' remains: forcing myself to see her as an object now, a person-who-once-was. It felt like a kind of betrayal to do so, because that was precisely what the man who had killed her had done, but sometimes it's necessary.

Her skin was hideously pale. Leaning closer, I could see thin tendrils of blue and red spidering below the skin: an intricate mottling and marbling. She was naked. The blood had been sluiced away now, but, if anything, its presence at the house had helped occlude the injuries she'd suffered, damage that was plainly visible now. Stark and *there*. It was most obvious on her face, where both eyes were swollen shut, the openings just tiny slits barely a centimetre across. A jagged swathe of skin was entirely missing between her top lip and her nose, exposing the teeth and ridged pink gums. Her jaw was lopsided, disconnected from its hinge below her right ear. The ear itself looked to have been half torn off at the top.

My gaze travelled down her body. The bruises and contusions were obvious, even though her heart stopping beating had halted their full bloom. They were still vivid: blue and green blossoms, a similar colour to the aquamarine clouds from my dream.

Looking down at her, even Sam Dale seemed more subdued than usual.

'Cause of death.' He gestured with a gloved hand to the damaged ear: a delicate movement. 'You can see the more obvious injuries for yourselves, but there's a bad fracture around the hairline area here.'

'A blow to the temple?' Chris said.

'Yes. Her skull has been badly fractured. It's likely she lost consciousness immediately at that point. She would have died shortly afterwards.'

'Would her killer have been aware of it?' I said.

'That she was dead? Oh yes. I would think so. It wasn't necessarily deliberate, if that's what you mean. He didn't necessarily *intend* to kill her. We see these types of injuries quite often, as I'm sure you know.'

I nodded. We did, albeit in different circumstances: drunk men locking antlers and getting into fights, not understanding that they don't happen the way they do in the movies. In the real world, you hit someone, they fall over, catch their head badly on the pavement, and die. You didn't mean to kill them, but you did.

'Of course, there's no doubt he meant to strike her,' Dale said. 'And repeatedly. But I don't know if you could say he was intending to *kill* her. He used his fists, for one thing. But obviously it's not for me to say. Anyway. Let's do the tour.'

Dale talked us through his interpretation of what had happened, referencing the injuries, the likely causes of them, what had been *done* to Sally Vickers. The results of an autopsy are always reminiscent of a story being told. As police, you arrive at The End, and you don't know for sure what transpired before that. The post-mortem helps to fill in those blanks with some degree of certainty. It gives you snatches of information – words here; whole sentences there – and if you're lucky, there's enough there for you to construct some kind of narrative, one that's at least close to what actually occurred.

So as Dale spoke, images and impressions formed in my head, whether I wanted them to or not. I pictured the attacker striking at Sally Vickers' head and face and chest with blind ferocity. Hating her. Taking pleasure in hurting her. That was what all the living victims had reported: the strength, the aggression, the violence. Something that was more like a monster than an ordinary man. I saw him as a vast shape, punching her as hard as he could, putting his body weight into it; striking her the way a man would hit another man. Then crouching over her: watching her. Listening, perhaps, for breaths that gradually stopped coming.

And what had he done next? Stuffed her down the side of the bed. Had it been a gesture of contempt, or had the act of pushing her body into the gap been a reaction to what he'd done? Not *panic*, as such, but because he realised he'd murdered her, and this was a subconscious attempt to hide her, even though he must have known how pointless that was.

It was possible, but the image that kept flitting into my head was from Poe's story about the murders in the Rue Morgue. The orang-utan, monstrously strong, stuffing its victim up the chimney.

'The rape was pre-mortem?' Chris said.

Dale nodded. 'As far as we can tell. And it was with the other victims, wasn't it? They didn't die, of course. But the rape preceded the assault.'

'Yes,' I said.

In fact, while the ferocity had increased, the attacks had all followed a predictable pattern. The women were invariably slight, and the size and manner of the offender were exceedingly intimidating. He hadn't required anything in the way of overt physical violence to subdue them before raping them. They had been so terrified at finding this man in their bedroom in the middle of the night, and so frightened by the sheer *aggression* of him, that they had done exactly what they were told.

The violence had happened afterwards. He didn't need to hurt the women in order to rape them, but he did.

As Dale and Chris continued to talk, I tuned them out and stared down at Sally Vickers' remains. Looking her over. *Seeing* her. I wanted to store the image of her away. Even though her body looked so alien now, and whatever she had been in life was long gone, I also wanted to believe it was possible she might know that someone cared. That this escalation would be where it stopped. That we were going to get him.

Amongst the thousand blank pages that would never be filled was what was going through her head as she was attacked and as she died. In one sense, that wasn't important to the investigation. In another, more nebulous one, it was the whole point of it. And so I chose to fill it in now, just for myself. I chose to imagine that, while she was still able, Sally Vickers had heard an inexplicable voice sending an impossible message to her. My voice, right now; the message not spoken out loud but *thought* at her with all the intensity I could gather.

We are going to get him for what he's done to you.

Thirteen

When the call was over, Jane sat very still for a few moments, unsure what to think or feel. She was blank. Stunned into silence. Every call involved leaving herself behind slightly, but she always came back again straight afterwards. This was different. It felt like she'd astral-projected out of her body, and someone had cut the cord so she couldn't find her way back.

After a while, she glanced at the clock on the desk. The man had been on the line for nearly half an hour. She had listened to everything he'd told her, interjecting when necessary, but the whole time that blankness had been creeping into her, alongside the horror of what he was saying.

She realised she was shivering, and that brought her back to her senses. Was it possible to suffer shock as a result of hearing something? Perhaps it was.

She turned her head slowly, and looked across the room towards the other desk. Rachel was listening to someone on her own phone. She caught Jane gazing over and mimed a yawn, then made a *yadda-yadda* gesture with her hand. Jane continued simply to stare. Rachel frowned, then mouthed: *are you all right?*

Jane shook her head, more to clear her mind than in reply, then looked away, back to her desk.

You need to talk to Richard.

Her first coherent thought since the call had ended.

Yes. That was exactly what she needed to do.

But there was something else first, and once the thought tumbled into her head, it became pressing, then urgent. She searched the desk for a piece of paper and a pen. There weren't any, of course – why would there be? But then she remembered she'd brought some translation work with her, in case calls were sparse, so she reached down to her bag, unzipping it and rifling through.

Come on, come on…

The calls weren't recorded. Unless she could note down everything the man had told her, the conversation might as well never have happened at all. And she needed to do it quickly, before she forgot anything: before something important got lost.

She pulled her translation pad out, but it was harder to find the pen – an agonising few seconds. Just as she got the pad open to a fresh page, the phone in front of her started ringing. She stared at the flashing red light on the set, almost not recognising what it meant.

Ignore it.

She began to write as fast as she could. The whole time, out of the corner of her eye, she could feel Rachel looking over at her, struggling to keep track of her own conversation.

Remember.

She had to get down every detail she could, but it was difficult: languages aside, her memory had always been a little fuzzy. She did her best, not starting from the beginning of the conversation, but writing down the things that had had the most impact on her, then using them as poles to build outwards from: what had led to them; what had come after. It took a couple of minutes to scrawl out the general content of what the man had told her. By the end, looking down at the sheet, she thought she'd captured most of it.

The *words*, anyway.

But then nothing was going to capture the crawling sensation on her skin as she'd listened to the man – the sense of horror

94

not just from *what* he was telling her, but from the tone of his voice as he did so. It would have been easier if he'd been gloating; she might then have mistaken it for a particularly grim sex call, and ended it with her usual breezy send-off. But the man had sounded so *disgusted* with himself as he told her what he'd done. Right until the end of the call, at least. At that point, he'd sounded almost peaceful. Just before hanging up, he'd actually thanked her. It was as though the awfulness of what he was describing somehow *had* been in the words, and by speaking them down the phone line to her he'd let it go. Passed it on to her instead.

Reading through the sheet again now only raised ghosts of those feelings, but the details themselves still seemed dangerous. On the surface, they were like something from the crime novels she occasionally translated, but there was an authenticity that was lacking from the pieces she worked on. Because she had believed the man. And she still did. These weren't inventions. These things had really happened.

The crimes on the news.

'Jane?'

Rachel had finished her call. She pulled off her headset and stood up, obviously concerned and about to come over.

Jane closed the pad before she could see it.

Afterwards, she would wonder about that: whether she had been shielding Rachel from what had been written there, or if she was protecting the details themselves. Strangely, it felt more like the latter: as though the man's story was something important that had been passed to her, like a treasure map, and it belonged to her now and had to be kept safe.

She pulled off her own headset and stood up.

'I'm okay.'

'You're not.'

'No, I'm not. I need to speak to Richard.'

She was cradling the pad to her chest, she realised. As she left the room, she was almost huddled over it.

*

When she knocked and walked into his office, Richard was playing Tetris on the computer. He made a token effort to turn the screen away, but it was old and stiff, so he gave up and shrugged apologetically.

'Gets boring in here sometimes.'

Jane didn't reply – just closed the door behind her and took a seat across from him without waiting for an invitation. She put the pad down on the desk in front of her and patted it repeatedly.

Richard frowned. 'What's wrong, Jane?'

'I had a call. A bad one.'

'Oh.' He leaned forward slowly, resting his forearms on the desk. 'A SIP?'

She shook her head. 'Worse.'

Much worse.

She opened the pad and read out the details the man had given over the phone. As he listened, Richard began to look increasingly uneasy. At a couple of points he pulled a face and muttered *Christ* under his breath. Jane nodded in agreement as she carried on. It felt wrong – surreal – to hear such ugly words and sentiments coming out of her own mouth. Oddly, it also made it all seem more distant. The man had told her the story, and she had written it down, and now she was telling it again. Just words. But behind them there were real women who had been attacked and badly hurt.

She did her best to speak slowly and carefully, but by the end of the report, she was rushing it. She finished almost out of breath, her heart thudding.

Richard was silent for a moment. Still. Like she had been.

Then he came to life again.

'Jesus. That's horrible. I'm so sorry you've had to deal with that, Jane. That's really very bad indeed.' He shook his head. 'How are you feeling?'

'I'm pretty shaken.'

'That's understandable. Do you want to take the rest of your shift off? I can cover if needs be.'

The words struck a slight alarm bell in her head. But she didn't yet understand why.

'Well, no. I mean, I suppose it depends…' She trailed off.

Richard shook his head again.

'Depends on what?'

'On what happens next.' She looked down at the pad. 'I mean, this is… confessing to a crime, isn't it?'

'Is it?'

'Of course. This is the man from the news. Surely.'

But when she looked back up at him, Richard was regarding her with a curious expression on his face.

'That's one explanation,' he said after a moment. 'But it's also possible that it isn't. That your caller just saw the details on the television, the same as you, and decided to… you know. *Pretend.*'

He spread his hands as he said it. It was the exact same gesture she remembered him making during training, when he'd said much the same thing about 'Gary'. Outside the confines of the call itself, you'd never know the truth, so why not choose to believe the thing that made bearing what you'd heard easier?

Jane felt a sinking sensation in her chest. That was what he was going to tell her to do. But he hadn't heard the man's voice. He hadn't heard the *way* he'd said these things.

'I know,' she said. Urgency overtook her; she had to make him understand. 'But I listened to this man, and he was sincere. He absolutely was. You could tell. He wasn't just doing it for… sexual thrills, or anything like that. If he had been, I'd have hung up on him.'

'Right.'

'I'm good at that, honestly.'

'What *did* you do?' Richard leaned back. 'How did you respond?'

Jane ran a hand through her hair. It went against her nature, but she was slightly exasperated. There were surely more important things to do right now than dissect her performance? It hadn't exactly been an ordinary call.

'He didn't need me to say much. It wasn't that kind of call. It was more like a confession than a conversation.'

'Okay.' He nodded at the notepad. 'And did you write all that down while the call was in progress?'

'No, I did it afterwards, from memory. But I'm sure of the details. And it's the way he spoke as much as what he said.'

'What I actually meant is, I'm not overly happy with you doing that.'

'Writing it down?'

'Yes. It makes me uncomfortable.' He shuffled in his seat, as though the sensation was a physical one. 'This is a confidential service, Jane. That's a *hugely* important part of what we do. If the people who contact us thought for one moment that we were recording the calls *in any way ...*'

'I think this is a bit different. Surely we have to report it?' She waited. 'Don't we?'

'To the police?' He was visibly disappointed with her. 'Absolutely not. It's out of the question.'

'But don't we have a duty? Doesn't it make us ... I don't know. What's the word? Complicit?'

'It's an anonymous service, Jane. We have legal protection. And anyway, we have no ability to trace the calls.'

'I'm sure the police could.'

'We'd fight tooth and nail against that. The privacy of the people we serve is paramount.' He shook his head sadly. 'Jane, you *know* all this.'

Despite herself, she nodded. Because yes, she did understand. But then again, there were various kinds of complicity, weren't there, and what they might be obliged to do legally didn't seem to cover all of them. When it came to suicide, she could appreciate it. The people calling were responsible for their own actions, making their own decisions. But this was different. The man was describing something horrific he'd done to *somebody else*. Something he'd done to others. Something that, for all she knew, he was going to do again.

'But what if it could help stop him?'

'Jane, you're not thinking straight. *Stop* him?' He shook his head. 'Stop *who*? For all we know, it's just someone who wants the attention. Someone very unpleasant and disturbed: yes, I grant you that. But not the man who's out there doing these things. They've been all over the papers, the television. I mean, there's nothing you've written down there that someone couldn't have come up with from reading the newspaper. Is there?'

'I don't know.'

'All we'd likely achieve is scaring off other people from calling.' He leaned forward, resting his forearms on the desk. 'People who genuinely *need* our support, but then won't seek it because they know they can't trust us to do something as basic as respect their privacy.'

Jane felt the urge to reply *yes, but* – then realised there was nothing that she hadn't said already. He was right, as far as it went. And perhaps in his position she'd even have felt the same. Some of the confrontation went out of her; a little of the old Jane returned. The old Jane reminded herself that Richard had been doing this a lot longer than she had.

'Has this happened before?' she said.

'Not to me,' he said. 'No. I've never heard anything quite like this before. But other things, yes, of course. I've had to grit my teeth listening to people tell me they've abused their children, and they're going to do it again. I do my best to tell myself it's all made up. Just a prank. But of course that doesn't always work. And so I have to remind myself of what's important here.'

'Which is?'

'That the conversation is privileged information. Without total confidentiality, it would never have happened in the first place. That's the flip side to what we do here. We comfort and help people, and it *has* to be anonymous for us to be able to do that. The by-product is that we occasionally have to listen to things we'd rather not. We have to keep them secret. That's why it's such a difficult thing to do, Jane.'

He paused, leaning back in his chair.

'It's why not everyone is cut out for it.'

That last sentence, he could have said it as a threat, but some kindness had returned to his voice. A part of Jane heard it as a threat anyway, and she felt a lurch inside herself. Mayday was important to her, and she didn't want to lose it.

'But I think you are,' Richard said softly. 'I think you're very good indeed.'

The compliment made her blush, but she clung to it anyway. She forced herself to acknowledge it.

'Thank you.'

'You've just had a rough call. That's all.' He corrected himself. 'Well, worse than that. Even I find it hard to imagine what it must have been like to listen to that, and I've been doing this for ten years now. But the principle stands.'

He leaned forward again now, wanting to emphasise the last point but also making it clear that, in his mind, the conversation was over.

'You are *not responsible* for what happens outside of the call itself.'

Jane nodded.

She tried to believe that.

Part Two

Part Two

Fourteen

I parked up on the main road by the Thornton estate, and left the car engine idling as I stared at the buildings.

It was nearly eight o'clock in the evening, but the sunshine was still just about hanging on. An angle of it rested across the tops of the houses, while tufts of grass shivered at the bases. My thoughts went beyond the buildings, though, all the way to the waste ground. *Something awful is coming.* That familiar night-time sensation, brought forward into the day. It felt as though, when that *something* finally arrived, I wouldn't be able to get out of its path in time. That I'd simply be blown away sideways, like the factory that had once stood there.

But I wasn't going back in there tonight. Instead, I turned off the engine, got out of the car and faced the opposite side of the road, my back – quite literally – to my past.

It had been weeks since the break-in at my house, and Drew MacKenzie had failed to materialise. However messy the burglary, crimes only stay on the radar for a certain amount of time before newer, fresher ones push them off to the sidelines. MacKenzie would get picked up eventually, I was sure, but not because anyone was actively looking for him. For whatever reason, that wasn't good enough for me.

Perhaps it was simply pent-up frustration from our investigation, but Chris had been right in what he'd said over the phone: I did want to do everything myself. I'd wanted to go after MacKenzie from the beginning. And this evening, as I left work, I'd decided I wasn't prepared to put up with waiting any longer. The rat-catchers had had their chance, and missed it. It was my turn.

According to the reports on file, the last known address we had for him – across town – had been a washout. Which didn't surprise me. I knew the area, and it was sublet city: residents came and went, and nobody kept a register or a headcount. MacKenzie probably hadn't lived there for years. Like me, though, he was a Thornton kid. You can escape from that sometimes, but you can't ever really change where you come from. Pull the plug out of our lives, and for people like me and Drew, this will always be the place we'll swirl back down to.

On the far side of the road there was a small row of shops and businesses. The bookie's was shuttered up for the night. The off-licence was open, a homeless man half lying close to the door, little more than a pile of brown clothes and bristling grey hair. Beside that, an alleyway. And then the Packhorse.

Even if I hadn't grown up here, as police I would have known the Packhorse by reputation. It's not the Wheatfield, and you're not going to read about shootings and stabbings here, but it's rough enough to be raided from time to time. The drugs are fairly blatant. Right now, I could see a cluster of people smoking by the door, and I was sure at least some of it would turn out to be cannabis. They just stand there and don't give a fuck. It would almost be a dare, except there was nobody here to take them up on it. The world around was more or less oblivious.

In the evenings, the younger contingent from the estate tend to colonise the place, and it gets louder and more lively. Once upon a time, that would have been me. I remembered it well. There'd be at least one fight a night, but none of them would be reported unless they had to be. It was mostly just the same people facing off, warming over old arguments and slights. Nobody ever got barred for very long, simply because there was nowhere else for them to go, and nobody else to replace them. If Drew was back in Thornton, there was a good chance he'd be here.

I considered my options.

The alleyway to the side led to a beer garden at the rear of the pub. It was totally enclosed, surrounded by high brick walls on all sides, with a few benches scattered around, standing lopsided on cobbled ground so covered with old cigarette butts and roach ends that it was impossible to ever sweep clean. The underage drinkers used to perch on the metal steps of the nearby fire escapes, while dealers used the alleyway. I imagined none of that would have changed much. A side door from there led into the pub proper.

Along with the front door, there were two exits, then. If MacKenzie was inside and saw me coming, I couldn't cover both. I weighed it up, and decided it was better to go through the front.

I crossed the street and approached the door. Aside from the group by the door, there was an alcove with two more smokers: a shaven-headed man with a field of acne scars across his cheeks, and an old woman in a soft blue tracksuit, her own face a mess of wiry red veins. As I'd suspected, the air reeked of dope, and the man barely moved to let me through. From his body language, it was as though he hadn't seen me. But I felt his gaze following me inside.

It was a shock at first: not so much the familiarity of the place, but how busy it was. The pub was heaving, and the raucous mingled noise of all the people was overwhelming. The bar was in the centre. An obese young woman was serving. She waddled awkwardly along, her mottled forearms the same enormous width from elbow to wrist.

I edged through the crowds of people, wafting away a fly and trying not to breathe in too deeply. Searching for familiar faces. Finding none. There were old men lined up along the bar itself; clusters of younger drinkers forming circles with their backs out; lonely strays. Workmen in bright yellow coats and clumpy muddy boots. Close to the open door to the beer garden, an elderly woman was stamping and clapping along to music I could barely even hear.

I didn't recognise anybody, and I felt woefully out of place here now. That was a good thing in some ways, of course, but less so in others: the atmosphere wasn't threatening, as such, but I'd definitely been clocked as not local, and I caught a few less friendly looks pointed my way. Perhaps, I admitted to myself reluctantly, this had been a mistake. I decided to finish looking around, check outside, then get the fuck out as quickly as I could.

Past the side door, at the far end of the pub, there was a lower section, slightly grander-looking than the rest: red carpets, and walls panelled with dark mahogany, like a private room in an old-fashioned gentlemen's club. Most of the space was taken up by a pool table covered with stained green felt, and the rest was full of men, the majority in their late twenties and early thirties. Some were playing pool, while the others were watching football on an overhead screen. I stood at the top of the stairs, my gaze moving from one face to the next.

One of the men by the table was leaning over it, his fingers gripping the underside, his face obscured by the low-hanging lamps. As I watched, he lifted that side of the table off the floor, then banged the legs down hard, the balls on the table shifting back and forth with the movement. From inside the table I heard a rolling and a clattering, and then the white ball emerged into its bay with a rattle.

When the man leaned away again, I recognised him.

Hello, you little shit.

The sight of him took me right back to the night of the burglary, and despite the environment in here, my first instinct was to walk straight down there, elbow through the crowd, and arrest him. But that wouldn't be the wisest course of action. I turned and examined the throng behind me. A few people back there were still eyeing me suspiciously, and they weren't the types to look away when I caught them. Chances were, nobody was going to actively assault me, especially if I identified as police, but I could hardly count on good-hearted bystanders either. Nobody would need to interfere directly; they could make it hard enough for me without really trying. Just an accidental sidestep; a blocking. I turned back, more concerned about the men at the bottom of the stairs. They were MacKenzie's crew, after all – career criminals, in their own small way – and he probably wasn't the only person down there who'd been in my house that night. Even if he was, he had a good twenty friends with him.

The sensible thing was to go back outside and call in for assistance. Not escalate the situation more than I needed to.

My gaze moved from MacKenzie over the other men.

Back to him.

I remembered the laughter as they'd trashed my house.

Decisions, decisions.

You've got to do everything yourself, haven't you?

I went to the bar and ordered a vodka and Coke. It arrived in a small glass with lipstick stains on the rim. I gave it a rub, then took it over to the stairs, standing to one side at the top. The drink was warm, but it would do. I sipped it, kept a vague eye on the television screen by way of pretence, and waited. Sooner or later, he'd need the bar or the toilet.

It only took ten minutes, but it felt like an age. Behind me, back towards the front of the pub, the karaoke had started up: awful, tuneless renditions of 'My Way' and 'Mack the Knife'. I began to wish I'd made the vodka a double.

But then, finally, there was MacKenzie, standing at the bottom of the stairs, facing away from me. He was holding up an empty pint glass, waggling it. There was a chorus of approval. I looked at the stairs. They were big and solid: thick oak struts at either side.

Don't think. Just do it.

I put my glass on the side and met him halfway down, blocking his path. He almost bumped into me, then steadied himself with a hand on the banister and glared at me.

'What the—?'

I smacked one half of the cuffs over his wrist, then leaned down swiftly and attached the other to one of the struts of the staircase.

Click. Done.

'Shit! What's going on?'

'You're under arrest, Drew.'

I made my way quickly back up the stairs, my heart going off more than I wanted to admit, and threaded through the bar. The shouts from behind me were drowned out by the karaoke, but I knew they'd be coming.

'Excuse me. Excuse me.'

I edged my way between people as quickly and efficiently as I could. Whatever they thought about me, none had seen exactly what I'd done, and nobody tried to stop me. MacKenzie's crew were another matter. I glanced over my shoulder; a few of them were making their way after me.

'Oi! Stop her!'

I ploughed on, trying to reach the door before anyone understood and decided to make things difficult for me. But just as I got there, my way was blocked by two people coming in from the outside: an elderly woman, and a younger one. The younger was perhaps in her early fifties, but it was difficult to tell. Her hair was ragged and unkempt, and she had an enormous scar running down her forehead and across her cheek all the way to her ear. It was a horrific injury, as though the top quarter of her head had been sawn away and then reattached. The eye sectioned off within it was pink and blind.

I know you.

But that was all I had time to think before my momentum carried me past the pair of them, almost pushing them to one side, and I half fell out of the door into the evening air.

Car across the street – I ran for it and got in, locking the doors after me. Five or six of MacKenzie's friends fanned out on to the pavement opposite, and two started to cross the street. I slapped my ID face out against the car window, which stopped them, although didn't make them retreat any.

Regardless, it was done. I'd got him. With my free hand, I pulled out my phone.

Now I would call for assistance.

But as I waited for backup to arrive, MacKenzie's crew loitering grudgingly on the far pavement, my thoughts kept returning to the woman at the entrance of the pub.

I know you.

Except I had no idea who she was.

Fifteen

It is important to keep active.

Two mornings a week, Margaret leaves the house early and catches a bus into the city centre, then walks slowly through the busy streets, heading for the library. The first thing she does is return the three books she took out on her last visit, always feeling a pang of nostalgia for the weathered old cards replaced by the computerised system. Then she spends half an hour browsing, moving slowly through the aisles.

The vast majority of books hold no interest, but she finds it comforting to recognise the same titles and patterns on the spines, visit after visit. She finishes at the romance aisle, where the shelves are full of narrow paperbacks, the mostly pastel covers tattered and worn. The titles here are all but indistinguishable, but Margaret can usually tell from scanning the first page whether she has read one before.

It takes time, of course, but that is the point. So much of her life now is spent finding ways to fill her day. Killing time. A question always hovers underneath such moments. What is she killing time *for*? With Harold gone, there is nothing much to anticipate or look forward to, and so the answer is depressing: she is killing time simply to get to more time. Her days pass for the sake of it. But it always feels a little different here in the library. Meandering and browsing take her out of herself. The pleasures on offer here, however small, are one of the few things she lives for.

When she has selected three books she'd like to spend more time with, Margaret checks them out at the counter, then begins the slow walk back through town to her bus stop. Sometimes she window-shops. Today, the heat is so strong that she decides to rest along the way.

She reaches a tea room with an ornate front. It looks old-fashioned and homely, not one of those indistinguishable chains. The bell above the door tinkles gently as she opens it. Inside, the shop is pretty and elegant, but small: there are only six tables, and five of them are taken. The room is also dimly lit, and it's because of this that Margaret first notices her. *How strange to be wearing sunglasses in here*, she thinks – and then realises that the solitary woman at one of the tables is her next-door neighbour.

Even in here, Margaret thinks.

Even here, she can't get away from them.

At the same time, she can hardly retreat now, and the woman isn't paying her any attention. There is a large-brimmed cup of tea to one side on the table, untouched for the moment as she scribbles into a small black book. The metal clasp taps against the table as she writes. A *Filofax*, Margaret thinks, pulling the word from somewhere. Something busy people need.

Margaret approaches the counter and orders tea from the young woman serving there, then moves to the free table. To reach it, though, she has to pass her neighbour, and as she draws closer to her, she finds herself hesitating. The Filofax has gone away now, and the woman looks *miserable*. She has moved the tea across and is stirring it, lost to the world. What happens next is a whim.

'Excuse me,' Margaret says. 'May I?'

The woman looks up quickly, and Margaret smiles and gestures to the empty seat at the table. In truth, she isn't sure which of them is more surprised. Her heart feels like a bird in her chest, unexpectedly startled.

'May I sit here?'

'I suppose so.' Then the woman gathers her manners together. 'Sorry. I mean, yes. Of course.'

She moves her cup back, although there is no real need, and Margaret sits down.

'I don't want to interrupt. I just saw you here and thought it might be good if we had a chat. We never really have, have we?' But the woman only looks confused at that, so Margaret has to explain. 'I live next door to you. It used to be my husband and I, but he died last year.'

'Oh. Yes. Of course.'

'I'm Margaret.' She holds out her hand. After a moment, the other woman shakes it carefully. Nervously, almost.

'Karen.'

'It's nice to meet you properly.' Margaret takes in the woman's clothes. She's wearing a white uniform, a little like a nurse's. It occurs to her again that she really has no idea what her neighbours do for a living. 'Are you on your lunch break?'

Karen nods, and is about to say something else when Margaret's pot of tea arrives. They sit in silence for a few seconds while she pours. The sugar cubes are rough and hard. She *plinks* two into her cup, and then it's her turn to stir incessantly.

'If you don't mind me saying so, you look like you've got the weight of the world on your shoulders.'

'Do I?' Karen gives a hollow laugh, then takes off her sunglasses and rubs her eyes. She is a lot older without them, especially close to. 'Oh, I'm just tired. It's hard work bringing up two children. Three, sometimes, if you count Derek.'

Margaret smiles; despite the undercurrents, it's clearly at least an attempt at a joke. But she also thinks, *Derek*. So these are her neighbours. Karen and Derek. They aren't so frightening after all.

'Why are you in town?' Karen says.

Margaret holds up the books in a carrier bag.

'Shopping. If you can call it that at the library.'

Karen looks at her; it's clear that she feels she should be able to come up with some casual reply but isn't good with small talk. It makes Margaret like her a little more. They aren't so different, really. In an odd way, she feels more in control here than she expected to.

'So you like to read?' Karen says eventually.

'It keeps me occupied. Don't you?'

'I used to. It's hard to find the time.'

'It must be difficult.' Although in truth, Margaret has no idea. She and Harold tried to have children, but neither of them were too bothered when it refused to happen. Anyway, that was a very long time ago now, and they were always happy enough, the pair of them ...

Even though it has been well over a year, she suddenly feels the same burst of loss that went through her on the day Harold died. It has never left her. How can an absence leave you? Although the time between its keenest moments has increased, the intensity of the loss has remained.

How could you leave me, Harold? How unfair of you.

I know, love. I'm sorry.

She does her best to keep it inside. Nobody wants to see an old lady cry. They never know what to do.

'It is difficult,' Karen says. She means her family. But when Margaret doesn't reply for a moment, she thinks about it, then adds: 'And I'm sorry about your husband. I do remember him.'

'Thank you.'

'What happened to him?'

'He had a heart attack.' Strangely, she finds this territory easy. 'It was very quick, they told me, and he wouldn't have suffered. He was driving when it hit. According to the people behind, he indicated suddenly and pulled in. He ended up across the pavement with his hazard lights on.'

The doctors explained this to her, but initially she had no idea what it meant. She knew very little about cars, and for a time, when she told the story, it felt like she was speaking in a foreign language. *Hazard lights.* It almost came as a surprise when people understood the words. Now they are more nat- ural, and amidst the grief she feels the familiar dab of pride for Harold: a man who never went out without a waistcoat, and with his hair combed just so; a man who even in his final moments had the presence of mind to do the correct thing. The indicator. The *hazard lights*.

When it happened, Margaret was at home, reading one of her battered paperbacks. It still seems ridiculous to her that there was a period of time when Harold was dead and she was happy. A period when the world was already this awful and ruined and she did not know the truth about it. That was the most unfair thing of all. She should have been with him.

'I'm sorry,' Karen says again. But then she checks her watch, and Margaret thinks she has been waiting to do that, because the surprise that follows seems a little staged. 'Oh. I have to get back to work.'

'Of course. It's been nice talking to you.'

'And you.'

On impulse, she says, 'I'm sorry about the garden, by the way.'

Karen is on her feet and is gathering up her handbag, but she pauses now, clearly confused.

'The garden?'

'That it's so overgrown. I keep meaning to have it cut, but it's hard for me, with Harold gone. I will get it sorted.'

Karen still doesn't understand.

'But it's *your* garden.'

'Well, yes. But I know it's a bit of an eyesore. And your husband – Derek – he said something about it. He was quite angry.'

'That sounds like Derek. I wouldn't take it seriously. He's not bothered about your garden, honestly.' She gives a hollow laugh. 'We'd probably just had an argument about something, and he was throwing his toys out of the pram.'

Margaret smiles again. Karen does her bag up with a snap and loops it over her shoulder. She is clearly about to leave, but then she pauses, considering something, and turns back to Margaret.

'I'm sorry if he was rude to you, though. Derek can … well, lose his temper sometimes. Come across quite aggressive. He lashes out without thinking.'

There is something troubling about the way she says that, and Margaret remembers how miserable Karen looked when she first approached the table. *He lashes out without thinking.* But in the circumstances, it somehow seems impolite to press.

'That's all right,' she says gently. 'It wasn't me he spoke to. It was my great-nephew. And he can be exactly the same, I promise.'

Karen grimaces at that. 'Your great-nephew?'

'Yes. Kieran.'

'I don't like him very much.'

'Oh?'

'I don't like the way he looks at me sometimes.'

Margaret hesitates, because that seems a very forward comment to make to a stranger about a member of her family. The urge to defend Kieran is there – but it often is, and that's what bothers her most: that Karen's complaint feels so plausible. Kieran has always been a little antisocial and awkward. *Gauche* was Harold's word, but to Margaret that never went quite far enough. She could imagine, if you didn't know him, that her great-nephew's behaviour might come across as odd.

'He can be a bit strange sometimes,' she admits cautiously. 'But it's like you said about Derek losing his temper. Kieran's a sweet boy really. He means well.'

Karen considers that, then nods.

'Perhaps it's just me, then.'

The way she says it, it's as though she's used to men looking at her, and just finds it distasteful in this instance because it's Kieran. But Margaret is still thinking about it as she watches her leave. Because she does worry about Kieran. She knows in her heart that he would never hurt a fly, but her thoughts keep returning to the argument he had with the man next door. With Derek, another man who can lose his temper and lash out. She sips her tea, remembering the way Kieran paced back and forth in her kitchen, and the look on his face, which scared her for a moment, but most of all the way he talked about Karen.

That painted-up ...

That pause as he fought down the language he really wanted to use.

That painted-up ... woman.

Sixteen

I surprised myself that night by not having the nightmare, but then I hardly slept. My thoughts were occupied by the woman I'd seen on my way out of the Packhorse. After backup had arrived, I'd gone back inside with them, ostensibly to assist with Drew MacKenzie's arrest but also to look around for her. The place had emptied somewhat by then, as the regulars had known the police were on their way and many had decided to clear out. Whoever the woman was, she had disappeared with them.

I know you.

Except I didn't – or at least I didn't know how, or where from. She had been considerably older than me, I was sure, but I couldn't think of anyone I might have known growing up who even remotely fitted her description. Casting my mind back over previous cases, she didn't obviously figure in any of them. The scar had been hideous, but presumably she hadn't had it when I'd known her, or else I'd remember her more easily. On balance, she was a stranger to me. At the same time, she was utterly familiar, and something about that made me feel incredibly uneasy.

I was still thinking about her as I arrived at the department the next day, wondering not entirely half-heartedly if there was a simple way to trace her. Distracted, I almost walked straight into Vicky, a young sergeant based on our team.

'Zoe,' she said. 'I've got a live one in suite four.'

'A what in what?'

'This young woman.' Vicky nodded to the closed door beside us. 'She came in about an hour ago, says she's got vital information about the case.'

I rolled my eyes.

'Oh, superb. That means we can all go home.'

'Ha ha, yes. I know what you mean. But she's pretty insistent. Seems quite scared too, to be honest.'

'Of what?'

'Our boy.' Vicky nodded at the door again. 'Jane Webster, her name is. She says he's been calling her.'

'Right.'

I closed the door to the interview room behind me, perhaps a little too aggressively. The woman sitting there looked at me hesitantly. From her body language, you'd have imagined that she'd been caught shoplifting and dragged in here for questioning, rather than coming in of her own accord.

I sat down across the table from her. She was probably in her mid-twenties, but still resembled a little girl more than a proper grown-up: small and slight, with astonishingly pale skin. Looking at her, I imagined a child who had been forbidden from playing outside, where she might pick up even the mildest of tans or bruises.

'It's Jane, isn't it? What can I do for you, Jane?'

'It's about the case that's been in the news,' she said. 'The women who have been attacked.'

'Yes, I know. That's why you've been directed to me.' *That's why I've been dragged in here.* 'I'm actually the lead officer on the investigation.'

The tone of my voice caused her to flinch slightly, and she rubbed her hands together anxiously. For a moment, she didn't reply, and I looked at her carefully. Her white cotton blouse was undone just enough to reveal a small silver cross hanging on a chain, and her blonde hair was pulled back into an approximation of a ponytail, with lock-pick ridges of split ends poking up. The glasses she wore were very large and very circular. All in all, she reminded me of the unkempt girl in one of those high-school brat-pack movies: the one who gets a makeover two-thirds in and ends up looking pretty.

'Sorry,' she said finally. 'Of course you are. It's just difficult to explain. I don't know where to start.'

'Me neither. Let's try, though.'

'I'm not sure if I should be here really.'

I feel the same way.

Under other circumstances, I would probably have said it out loud, but despite my impatience, there was a fragility to Jane Webster that kept the reply private. She seemed so timid, with her knees pressed together and her shoulders slightly hunched, as though she had real trouble looking at the world. And although she didn't remotely resemble our creeper's usual choice of target, I didn't want to scare her off, not if she knew something important. We needed something important. We needed it months ago.

'Can you try to explain, please?' I said. 'It's something about a phone call, isn't it? That's what I was told.'

She nodded. 'I had a call. I think it might have been him. The man who's been doing all those things.'

'Right. That seems pretty unlikely to me.' None of the other victims had reported any contact prior to the attacks. He stalked his targets, certainly, but they'd never been made aware of it before. 'You mean a threat of some kind?'

'Oh, no. I'm not explaining this very well. I work on a helpline – I volunteer. Mayday?'

She said it as though she expected me to have heard of it.

'I have no idea what that is.'

'It's a local organisation. A confidential service. We offer support, that sort of thing – just listening, basically. People can call us up and talk to us, when they're feeling lonely or depressed.'

'Okay.'

With every faltering word, my impatience was growing. Now,

I imagined a tiny room full of meek do-gooders like Jane. Probably eating lentils out of plastic pots.

Hear her out, at least.

'We get all sorts of calls,' Jane said.

'Depressed, miserable people ...'

'Sometimes. That's what it's there for, anyway. But a couple of nights ago, I had a phone call from ... well, I think it's this man. No, I'm sure it is.'

'He called your helpline?'

'Yes.'

'And threatened you there?'

'No, no. He wanted to talk.'

The penny finally dropped. I felt myself groaning inside.

'Listen,' I said. 'When any case becomes as high profile as this, you always get idiots crawling out of the woodwork. It's *highly* unlikely that the man who called you was the offender. Far more likely that it was just some crackpot. We get them all the time here.'

And Jesus, didn't we just. False confessions from outright lunatics; twisted phone calls from oddballs craving attention; useless tip-offs from busybodies who'd added two and two and somehow come up with rapist. Of course, we rely on information from the public, but find me a single detective who doesn't face dredging through it with all the enthusiasm of a plumber approaching a drain, and I'll show you a detective with a news camera trained on them.

'I know,' Jane said. 'I can imagine you do. We do as well. Most of the calls we get are sex calls. But this was different. I didn't want to believe it either. Not the first time, anyway.'

'There's been more than one call?'

'Yes. Two, so far. The second was last night. The first one *felt* genuine, but Richard – my boss there – he said pretty much the same as you. That it was probably just some weirdo. A lot of sick men use us as an outlet.'

I leaned back, considering her. From her manner alone, I could tell she wasn't lying to me. That she *had* received these two calls, and that the man on the other end of the line had really managed to convince her he was responsible for the attacks. Of course that didn't mean it actually *was* him. Still, I felt some sympathy for her. It must have been unpleasant enough regardless.

'What was it that convinced you?'

'The second call.' She said this immediately, more definite now. 'After the first one, I told myself it hadn't been real. It was shocking while it was happening – while he was talking – and it was shocking afterwards too. But then I spoke to Richard and started to doubt myself. It began to feel a bit unreal. So I told myself that it couldn't have been him, however genuine it felt at the time ...'

She trailed off and shrugged helplessly. She actually looked apologetic, as though she'd been sitting on a crucial piece of evidence all this time.

I prompted her.

'But then the second call ...?'

'It gave me the exact same feeling. And this time, I was sure he was telling me the truth. There was an atmosphere on the line.'

An atmosphere, I thought. God help us.

'What did he say?'

'He was relieved to get through to me. I think he must have tried a few times before he did. And then it was just like the first call. He wanted to talk about the crimes. About what he'd done. Reliving it, I suppose.'

'Like one of those sex calls?'

'No, no. Because he wasn't enjoying it. You can usually tell. But he was crying. It was like he was *unburdening* himself of it. As though he was upset about what he'd done, and talking to me was a way of making himself feel better.'

'Like a confession to a priest or something?'

'Yes.' Jane nodded emphatically. 'Yes, *exactly that*. Because the calls are anonymous, you see. We guarantee confidentiality. So he knew he could talk to me without getting into trouble.'

'And yet.' I picked up a pen and twiddled it. 'Here you are.'

Her pale skin gained a flush of colour at that, and she looked down at her lap, embarrassed. I decided not to press it. Presumably she and her colleagues took their vow of silence seriously. Putting myself in her position, I realised that it must have been a tough decision to come here today and report this – a breach of confidence that she might very well get in trouble for. Well, she didn't need to worry about that, at least. I could pretty much guarantee the confidentiality of this conversation.

Follow it through anyway.

'I'm guessing you don't have this individual's phone number to hand?'

'No. We don't see the numbers.'

'Someone does?'

'I don't know for sure. But you're the police. You can trace it, can't you? You could force them to reveal it. If you had to, I mean.'

'I imagine that would take a court order. But I don't think it's going to come to that, Jane. And I really don't want to get you in trouble for no reason. Like I said, we receive a lot of calls like that too ...'

I trailed off, because she seemed to be sinking into herself as I was talking: slumping down further in her chair. She thought she was doing the right thing, coming in here, at real personal expense, and I was just dismissing her.

'All right.' I sighed. 'What about the *content* of the calls? Let's see if there's anything there. What did he talk about?'

'He talked about what he did. Described it.'

'Tell me.'

Jane took a deep breath and began. The more she spoke, the more certain I felt. The information she was giving – that had been given to her – was nothing exceptional or revealing. There were no details that hadn't been in the papers or on television, no special inside knowledge that couldn't have been picked up from the news and that would indicate he knew more than he should.

He was a crank.

Of course he was. Serious offenders don't suddenly get an attack of conscience and confess everything to strangers – and certainly not *this* offender. The violence accompanying the attacks had escalated steadily, and he had become much better at what he was doing. Even if he'd panicked after Sally Vickers, that wouldn't have lasted. He wouldn't be feeling the slightest hint of regret for his actions, or crying down the phone. He *hated* these women.

'He said he killed the last one,' Jane finished. The memory of the conversation was clearly distressing her. 'He said he raped her and beat her, just like the others, but this time he decided not to stop. He was crying when he was telling me.'

'Sick bastard,' I said. 'Look, I know it's upsetting. I've had people confess the most awful things to me, and it's never pleasant to hear, and sometimes you're shaken afterwards.' That wasn't true; most of the time I was just pissed off at them. But I wanted to make her feel a bit better about herself. 'In this case, I want you to know, I highly doubt that this is the individual responsible for these crimes.'

'Really?'

'Really.' I leaned forward. 'And listen. You did the right thing coming in and reporting it. I can imagine it was a tough decision, but you're not going to get in trouble for it. You've done everything you can. But there's nothing in what you've told me that he couldn't have got off the news. There's nothing that hasn't been reported. I'll keep a note of it, but we're so stretched at the moment.'

Jane nodded slowly. She still looked miserable, but I thought I detected a hint of relief there now as well. She seemed lighter somehow. *Unburdened.* As though what the man had said was a physical weight he'd passed to her, something heavy that had become increasingly uncomfortable to carry. By coming to see me, she'd effectively passed it on. *Here: you deal with it.* And I had.

'Is that it, then?' she said. 'Are we finished?'

'We are.'

She stood up.

'It's rubbish, isn't it?'

'What is?'

'That somebody would do that. Phone up *pretending*.'

I pictured Sally Vickers' body, seeing it vividly in my head. The man who had done that was a monster, but there was something similarly despicable about the kind of man who would phone up *pretending* he had. The same pool of misogyny, just more towards the shallow end.

'Yes,' I said. 'If it was up to me, he'd be hung up by the balls too.'

That made her smile: a small, secret little thing that was quite nice to see, but one that she put away quickly. I have no patience with mice, but I felt for her anyway. How dangerous she seemed to find it, interacting with another human being. Imagine going through your life like that.

'That's exactly how Rachel feels,' she said. 'Rachel's a friend of mine who volunteers there too. She doesn't have a lot of time for the sex callers.'

'She sounds spot on to me.'

'Why would someone do something like that?' Jane moved over to the door of the interview room. Standing up, she looked even smaller than when she'd been seated. 'It's the way he talked about it. I keep seeing it in my head.'

'Try not to.'

'I can't, though.' She turned the door handle. 'I keep imagining it. Him stuffing her down the side of the bed like that. Like a piece of rubbish. That was how he put it.'

The image came back to me again. A detail that hadn't been made public.

'Wait,' I said.

Seventeen

Why did it feel like she'd made a terrible mistake?

As she sat in the passenger seat beside DI Zoe Dolan, Jane tried her best not to think about it. Instead, she watched out of the window as they left the main roads behind and headed into the smaller streets of Woodhouse. The policewoman seemed to know her way; Jane had asked if she needed directions, and Zoe had just shaken her head as though it was a stupid question. Actually, that was exactly the problem. She'd felt stupid walking into the police station in the first place, and then this woman had made her feel worse. Even now, finally being taken seriously, she felt like a child who didn't understand and kept saying and doing the wrong things.

A mistake.

She'd just been trying to do the right thing. And maybe, as it turned out, she actually had. But Jane couldn't escape the feeling that she'd messed up badly, and that all of this was going to blow up in her face in some unexpected way.

It was a poor area round here: mostly student houses and families crammed into red-brick back-to-backs. A few of the smaller university faculties were scattered amongst them, nestled inside houses with cramped staircases and tiny offices that had once been bedrooms.

Mayday wasn't officially part of the university, although it was vaguely connected on some kind of funding level. It occupied a building halfway down a steep hill. There were only two parking spaces in front. One was empty right now, and Zoe swung the car into it.

'You're not meant to park here,' Jane said.

'What?'

'They're reserved for the volunteers.'

Zoe gave her that *stupid* look again, this time shot through with disbelief. Jane felt herself blushing, embarrassed. With everything that was going on, she was concerned with a bit of pointless bureaucracy.

Zoe was still staring at her.

'You're a volunteer, right?'

Jane nodded.

'Well then.'

When they got out, the policewoman set off ahead. Jane hesitated slightly, looking at the building. Taking it in. The large front door, and the bay windows that bulged out on both storeys. The fact that, from the courtyard, it always looked unoccupied. After barely a month of shifts, it already felt so familiar to her, and even if she *was* doing the right thing, it wasn't just stupid she felt, but guilty as well. The Mayday team weren't exactly family, but she was a part of whatever they were. Or rather, she had been.

Zoe was walking up to the front door.

'It's round the back,' Jane called.

'Is it?' It sounded like even that irritated her. 'Well, come on then.'

There was an open gate between the building and the hedge that separated it from its neighbour, and a path led round behind. Zoe was already heading down it.

Come on then.

Taking one last look at the front of the building, Jane raced to catch up, feeling sick over what was about to happen inside.

'Jane, what is going on?'

She didn't know whether it made the situation better or worse that Rachel had been on duty when the pair of them arrived. Better in some ways: Jane couldn't deny it was nice to see a friendly face. At the same time, the girl's presence brought home the inherent betrayal of what she had done, and not only to Mayday itself. The friendship the two of them had built up, while important to Jane, still felt tentative and uneven, and this might just end it altogether. It was also embarrassing to think how weak and powerless she must appear to Rachel right now. She couldn't even look her friend in the eye.

What is going on?

That was what Jane wanted to know too. She stared at the door to Richard's office. Zoe had been in there for nearly ten minutes, and had closed the door behind her after entering. However hard she strained to hear, Jane couldn't make out anything of the conversation that was going on inside. She wondered what on earth the two of them were making of each other.

'Jane? Please talk to me. You're scaring me.'

Finally, she turned to face Rachel.

'I think I've done something stupid. So stupid. Maybe, any-way.' She put her hand over her face. 'Oh God, I don't even know.'

'What do you mean?' She felt Rachel's hand on her shoulder. 'Come on. Calm down. Who was that woman you came in with?'

'A policewoman.'

'What?'

'A *policewoman*.' Jane took her hand away from her face. 'Oh God. I just feel sick, Rachel. Honestly. I don't know what I've done.'

'Whoa, whoa. Back up a little. Why are you here with a policewoman?'

Jane hadn't been exaggerating: she really did feel sick. Her stomach was tight, and she had to keep swallowing.

Don't cry.

'I had a call. Well, I had a couple of them. Have you been following the news? About those poor women being attacked?'

'Of course. But—'

'They were from the man who did it.'

'Okay. You're going to have to explain a bit more than that.'

So Jane told her, as best she could. After the first call, when she'd finished in Richard's office, Rachel had asked her what had bothered her so much, and she'd fudged the answer: just said it was horrible and she didn't want to talk about it. Now she told her the truth, and then about the second call.

'And I just thought I had to do *something*. I couldn't live with myself if he did it again. Not if there was a way I could have helped stop him somehow. Even if...'

She trailed off, not wanting to say it. Rachel looked over at the door to Richard's office, understanding.

'Oh shit, Jane.'

'I know.'

'You did the right thing.'

'I'm not sure. I just don't—'

'No. *Look* at me.' Jane did as she was told. Rachel was looking at her with complete sincerity. 'You did. I have no idea how Richard is going to react, but that's really the least important thing right now.' She gestured around the room. 'All of this – all that confidentiality business – forget about it. The fucker killed the last woman he attacked. If you've told the police something that might help catch him, then that matters more than anything else.'

'He told me a detail about what he'd done to the last woman that hadn't been made public. The policewoman in there wasn't taking me seriously before I mentioned that. But after that, she really, *really* was.'

She didn't mention that she'd almost been relieved at being dismissed at first, because that meant she'd done what she could, and none of it was going to come back and make her life difficult. A nice line drawn: the end. Obviously, that had all gone to pot now.

'So what are the police going to do?' Rachel said.

'I don't know. Trace the calls, I guess.'

But she remembered what Richard had told her when she first reported her concerns: that Mayday would fight against it. Would it really come to that? DI Zoe Dolan didn't seem like the kind of person who was going to take that very well. Jane could imagine her behind the closed door right now, increasingly irritated by Richard's passive-aggressive *I'm-really-sorry-but* stalling. She suspected that Zoe was nothing like as scared of confrontation as she herself was.

She got the answer a moment later, as the door to Richard's office opened – a little too violently – and Zoe emerged, throwing it closed behind her with equal force. She barely broke stride, and it was obvious from the storm on the woman's face that the meeting had not gone well.

Zoe came across to the pair of them, then stood at a slight angle, looking off to one side, narrowing her eyes at the wall as though she wanted to murder someone. Maybe she did. She was barely taller than Jane herself, but there was real energy to her beneath the suit. She looked toned and strong, as though she could move very quickly if she wanted to. Right now, with the anger pulsing off her, Jane felt slightly threatened just being in close proximity.

'That didn't go well,' Zoe said finally.

'No.' Jane didn't know what to say. 'This is Rachel, by the way.'

'Yeah, that's great.'

Zoe took a deep breath, then gathered herself together.

'Right.' She checked her watch. 'I'm going to ask you to come with me for a bit, Jane. When we get back to the department, I'll have to make a large number of phone calls, and they'll be a lot easier to make once I've got your statement down in writing. I'll need a lot of detail. Okay?'

It wasn't really a question.

'Of course.'

'Good. Let's get going.' Zoe already had the car keys in her hand.

'Did you leave him alive in there?' Rachel said.

'For now.' Zoe took the other girl in properly for the first time, then gave her a brief smile. 'Hang them up by the balls, right? Nice to meet you, Rachel.'

Eighteen

Looking back on the night that changed my life, I realise that the plan for the robbery was almost painfully simple. To be fair to us, though, we were only fifteen years old.

Rather than planning it weeks in advance, we more or less decided it on the night in question. The target was an Indian restaurant called the Paladin, which was about half a mile away from the Thornton estate. The front of it faced out on to a main road, but there was a car park behind, and the entrance to that was on a quieter residential street. The back of the restaurant consisted of nothing but a steel door and illuminated storeroom windows, half blocked off by metal bins and stacked crates, but it was well known that the Paladin kept alcohol in the storerooms, and that the back door was frequently left ajar. A number of kids at school had boasted of sneaking in and lifting some, which should probably have given us pause: indicated that the staff might be watching out. Instead, it simply affirmed that it was an easy enough thing to do. In fact, I wasn't even thinking of it as a crime as such, more just something that was there to do.

Four of us set out from the park that night. It was winter, and the air was sharp and sparkling with the cold. The tarmac glittered. Above us, the sky was black and clear, the stars just a shivery prickle dotted across, as though they barely had enough temperature in them to shine.

Sylvie led the way, of course. She always did. The MacKenzie family was notorious on the estate. Sylvie was lean and angry, quick to fight, and already following in the footsteps of her father and cousins. You messed with her, you messed with them, and nobody wanted that. Sylvie was a gateway kid. There are always people when you're young who offer access to boys, drugs, parties, all the mysterious stuff going on below the skin of the world that seems so important at that age. That was Sylvie. Natalie kept up with her, staying close enough to make the link between them clear. Sylvie's little beta. Nat was all right when you got her on her own, but the slightest hint of a pecking order and there she was, right up in second place. She was the kind of kid who stands behind the bully, smirking. Of course, none of us thought of Sylvie as a bully, not when she wasn't bullying us.

I trailed slightly behind the pair of them, walking with Jemima. It was never entirely clear what my place in the gang was. I was smart without being sly, and I could fight, but I was scrappy rather than tough. I was at least as confident as Sylvie, but in a different sort of way. Maybe that was why she kept me around: not because I fitted in, but because she couldn't work me out, and in the meantime I seemed happy enough not to challenge her.

Jem's position was much clearer. She was sweet-natured and pretty, and a natural athlete, but shy and timid. In another school she'd probably have coasted through quietly and anonymously enough, but her family had downsized to Thornton the year before, and she'd made few friends since arriving. I guessed we were better than nothing, but it couldn't have been by much: Sylvie didn't quite keep Jem around as a comedy mascot, but it sometimes seemed to fly close. Already that evening she'd been bawled out twice. Once for her ridiculously bright green coat, and then for questioning our little expedition. There'd be boys joining us later, and Sylvie wanted alcohol, but Jem had wondered why they couldn't bring it themselves. Sylvie had rolled her eyes like she couldn't believe the stupid shit she was hearing. Jem was still in the doghouse, and I walked with her more out of solidarity than anything else.

We reached the car park about eight, which meant we could steal some alcohol then hook up with the boys in the park, with plenty of time to get drunk and fool around into the early hours. Play the night by ear. At the open gate, bathed in the orange light from the street light above, we clustered together.

'Four's too many,' Sylvie said. 'And that fucking coat's visible from space. Me and Nat'll go in. You two wait here, keep watch. Okay?'

I nodded, because now that we were here, that suited me fine. Jem, who I'd imagined would feel the same, apparently didn't.

'Keep watch? What are we supposed to do?'

It earned her a flash of outright disgust.

'What the fuck do you think? Duh. Keep an eye out. If it looks like anyone's coming, then shout. It's not hard.'

Jem nodded, looking stung. For what it was worth, I wasn't entirely sure what we were supposed to look out for or shout either, but it didn't make any sense to piss Sylvie off. But she was still staring lasers at Jem, and I felt the need to take some of the heat off her.

'Synchronise watches?' I suggested.

It was cheek, and Sylvie's glare flicked to me, but I'd gauged it right and a second later she grinned.

'Won't be long. Stay tuned.'

And with that, she and Nat ducked into the car park, then moved around the corner out of sight.

I sniffed and moved closer to Jem, who still looked as though she'd been slapped.

'Don't worry about it,' I said. 'Just concentrate on keeping watch. Very serious business.'

That got me a smile, albeit a miserable one.

'I suppose at least we don't have to do anything.'

'There is that,' I said. 'Hang on to it.'

About twenty seconds passed, and then I was aware of two figures bolting out past me, only resolving into my friends once they were across the street and disappearing off into the distance.

'Shit,' I said.

Jem – the natural athlete – started running after them, leaving me standing alone beneath the street light. That was lucky. I was about to take off myself when a number of men came pelting out of the car park entrance. Four of them, dressed in black trousers and white shirts, chasing my friends down the street. And very clearly not just chasing them *off*; they were scissoring their arms and pounding down the middle of the street like sprinters racing for the line. They meant to catch them.

I stood there for a second, fighting my body's stupid instinct to run in the same direction, then turned my back on the chase and walked slowly up the hill towards the main road. Lucky, lucky, lucky. They'd been so intent on chasing the others, they hadn't noticed me standing there.

Once I was on the main road, I began walking steadily along it, sticking my hands in my pockets and pulling my coat tighter, trying to do my best impression of a girl out for a walk. When I reached the ornate front of the Paladin itself, I stood for a moment perusing the menu on the wall outside, and breathing in the heady aroma from the open door, before moving off again. A little further down, after passing a shuttered-up bank, I came to a stop and considered what to do.

The chase had been intense enough that it was likely over now, one way or the other. Either the waiters would have burned out and given up, or they would have got someone. Even though she'd set off last, it wouldn't be Jem. Sylvie was quick. I wasn't too sure about Nat. Fingers crossed everybody would be okay. Even if someone had been caught, none of us was going to give up the others, not to the police. In Thornton, that was practically religion.

Despite the adrenalin still blaring in my chest, I was golden.

I looked up at the sky. Even though I couldn't see any clouds, I remember that it had begun to snow slightly – just a speckling, drifting in the air around me, almost an afterthought. The safest thing to do, I decided, was just keep walking; find a convenient side street to disappear into, then work my way back around to the estate. See who turned up at the park.

And I was about to do that when the van screeched up beside me, the side door already open, and the bastards pulled me inside.

'I know my rights,' I said, two hours later.

'Do you.'

The policeman sitting opposite me didn't even bother to phrase it as a question. It was more a weary rhetorical statement. *Obviously you do; you all do.* He was old, with a ruddy complexion and a stippling of shaved silver hair that didn't quite cover the top of his head. His neck was wrinkled and thin. Coupled with the starched straightness of his uniform, it gave him the air of a tortoise, its aged head poking out of a smooth shell that was slowly becoming too large for the creature inside.

He looked very tired indeed. I smelled blood, and leaned forward, tapping the table with my finger.

'Yes. What they did to me was totally unacceptable. And we both know it. Kidnap. False imprisonment.'

'Yes.'

'Anything could have happened to me. I'm in shock. I'm actually in shock. I'm ... I want medical attention.'

He looked at me, figuring it for sarcasm, but it wasn't entirely. I'd been dragged into the van by three men from the Paladin before I'd even had a chance to react. I'd managed to strike out at a couple of them, but it hadn't achieved much, and they'd held me pressed to the metal floor as they drove the short distance back round the corner. From there, I'd been strong-armed – spitting and shouting by this point – in through the back of the restaurant and straight upstairs, where I'd been thrown down on to an old armchair.

What followed could, realistically, have been worse, although that had only started occurring to me afterwards. In the meantime, I'd been faced with several men pointing and shouting, demanding information from me about my friends and talking amongst themselves in a foreign language. I assumed they'd called the police, and that we were waiting for them, but it was well over an hour before an officer arrived at the restaurant.

Anything could have happened to me. The realisation of how vulnerable I'd been, coupled with guilt at being caught, was making me volatile now, and I wanted to lash out at the detective in front of me. Like most teenagers, and many adults, I was very adept at reflecting my own failings on to others.

'What they did was against the law,' I told him angrily. 'Assault. Abduction. False imprisonment.'

'You've said.'

'It should be them in here, not me.'

'They performed a citizen's arrest, Zoe.'

'No they *didn't*.' I managed to inject a pleasing amount of contempt into my voice. 'They never said anything to me. And anyway, if they wanted to perform a citizen's arrest and physically detain me, I would have had to be in the course of committing a crime or fleeing the scene.'

He looked even more tired, but raised an eyebrow.

'Is that so?'

'You know it is. What are you doing? Impersonating a police officer?'

'I'm thinking that most girls your age aren't reading up on the law unless they're intending to break it.'

'I read a lot of things. And I have done nothing wrong. Whereas *they* have. And *you* know it. So what are you intending to do about it?'

The policeman considered that.

'Yes,' he said eventually. 'They did entirely the wrong thing, I admit. So I suppose I'm *intending* to have a word with them about it.'

'That's not good enough. I want to press charges.' I could

feel him backing down, and was determined to push him harder until he did. 'They shouldn't get away with what they did.'

'Maybe not. But this isn't the first time they've had an attempted robbery. Put yourself in their position. They're angry about people helping themselves to their stock, and I can understand that.'

'Yeah, me too. So what?'

'Well, that *is* what you were intending to do.'

'No it's not.'

'You were just out for a walk, were you?'

'That's right. Free country, last time I checked.'

'What if I said we had you on CCTV hanging around the entrance to that car park, waiting for your friends to come back out?'

I pictured the scene in my head. Although I'd been talking to Jem, I'd had enough chance to look around – *keeping watch* – and take in the sights.

'I'd say that's a lie. There aren't any CCTV cameras there.'

He didn't reply, but gave me a pointed look, and it took me a second to realise what I'd done.

Shit.

'I imagine, anyway,' I added.

But it was too late, and we both knew it. He stared at me for a few more seconds, not quite smiling, but almost. Then he leaned forward, looking weary again.

'Zoe, let's just cut all this out, okay? We both know you were there. I can probably guess a few of the others who were there too, not that you'd tell me, would you?'

'No.'

'And look – you just admitted it again, didn't you? You're not half as street-smart as you like to think. Maybe you should stick to reading.'

I didn't reply. After a moment of silence, he sighed.

'I don't want to see you in here again, okay? What I'm suggesting – intending, in fact – is that we should all leave it at that. On both sides. What do you say?'

'But those men—'

'Were in the wrong, yes. And I'll be having a word with them about that. A strong word, actually. But I also know they're good people who are having their business disrupted, and who are understandably very angry about it. They have a hard enough time as it is. So. What do you say?'

At first I didn't say anything.

Looking back on that night now, I realise that Detective Sergeant John Carlton was employing wisdom, rather than the letter of the law; that he was being compassionate and trying to make the best of the situation for everyone. Trying to do the right thing, not the legal thing. These days, I'm not sure I'd do the same. My instinct would probably be to caution me and have the waiters at the Paladin prosecuted within an inch of their lives. But back then, as a kid, I recognised an escape route when I saw one. And I wasn't so cocky as to look a gift horse in the mouth.

'All right,' I said finally.

And that was supposed to be the end of it. John did his best to extract a promise that I'd behave myself in future, and warned me that people would drag you down if you let them. I half listened with a kid's ear, my mind on the fact that it was still early enough to get back to the park and make something of the night. But I do remember thinking *I'm already down*, and that the real problem was a lack of people dragging me up. I didn't realise that, in his own small way, that was what John was trying to do.

Regardless, that was supposed to be the end of it. I never expected to see him again.

I had no idea what a problem he'd become for me.

Nineteen

He seems so diminished.

That was my first thought when I saw John now.

The hospice was built on two storeys, centred around a reception area below and a communal sitting and eating area directly above. From each, a web of corridors led off to the residents' rooms. After I signed in, a nurse led me to John's, which was up on the first floor.

'Mr Carlton had an unsettled night.'

She walked slightly ahead of me, her brown ponytail swinging.

'He's having problems with his liver and kidneys, and he required attention for his breathing on a couple of occasions. We're doing our best to make him comfortable. But he's settling in well overall.'

'That's ... good. I guess.'

Good on the one hand, and yet it still brought a pang of sadness. The corridors were clean, but partially obstructed by wheelchairs, half folded up, as though hunching their shoulders to let us pass, and laundry trucks with faded yellow hazard stickers plastered to their sides. It brought it home to me that this was the last place John was ever going to live. That he was no longer in the end stages of his life, but the very last. I didn't want to think of him *settling in* to that.

'He's been a joy,' the nurse said. 'He's a lovely man.'

'Yes.' There was no need to be uncertain about that, at least. 'Yes, he is.'

'Are you a relative? I'm sorry, I can't remember.'

'A friend.'

'You're very lucky.'

Given the circumstances, that could easily have sounded glib or out of place, but her tone of voice assuaged that somehow. It's amazing how different something can sound when it's obvious the person saying it actually cares.

Dinner was being served in the open-plan space upstairs, and the smell of food cooking in a distant room permeated the area: an artificial but comforting aroma that reminded me of school dinners; the smell of being looked after, of having things prepared for you. Barely half the seats were taken. The nurse had explained to me that many patients had their meals in private, and that included John. Most of those who were there now were dressed in papery white gowns, and they ate slowly and in silence, accompanied only by the gentle clink of cutlery.

I glanced into some of the open doorways we passed. The bedrooms were utilitarian, but well decorated, and not as uncomfortable-looking or prison-like as I'd been expecting. It wasn't even quite like a hospital. Each room had an adjustable single bed along one wall, an armchair, a desk, a television. There was a narrow wardrobe, and the kind of partitioned-off bathroom unit you find in cheap hotels – identikit blocks of plastic that are simply slotted into place and drilled in.

'Here's our boy.'

The nurse rapped once on the door, although it was slightly ajar, and pushed it carefully open. A doctor was sitting on the bed, making some notes on a clipboard resting on his knees. It took a moment for me to recognise that the man sitting beside him was John.

He seems so diminished.

He was dressed in a white gown with a V neck that partially exposed a wiry tangle of grey hair at the top of his emaciated chest. Through the fabric, his ribs looked oddly misshapen

– tangled, almost, like the roots of a tree. His legs were bare below the knee, and the mottled, hairless skin there gleamed as though it had been shaved and polished. His forearms were painfully thin, and his hands fretted in his lap, knotty fingers rolling nervously over each other.

But it was in his face that the deterioration was the worst. Viewed side on, his head seemed too large for his neck to support, and the shape of his skull was clearly visible. When he turned to look at me, his eyes were small and set back in their sockets, almost lost in the dark skin surrounding them. It was only when he smiled – and the lines at the sides of those eyes crinkled slightly – that he finally resembled the man I'd known for so long.

'Hello, John.' I said it too quietly, scared that my voice might somehow bruise him.

'We're nearly done,' the doctor said.

The nurse headed off back down the corridor. I lingered by the doorway as the doctor felt John's chest, his lower abdomen, unsure at first whether it was all right to watch, or even be here. He prodded his fingers gently beneath John's ribs, quickly removing them when John cried out: a sound that cut through me. But I felt a responsibility to be here for him, the way he had been for me in the past. For his part, he didn't seem remotely self-conscious about my presence.

A minute later, the doctor had made his notes and left. John remained on the bed, and I sat down in the armchair opposite him, leaning forward so as to be closer to him.

'It's good to see you,' I said.

'Is it?' He seemed bemused by the idea. 'I know how dreadful I look. I can't imagine it is.'

'You don't look too bad to me.'

'Considering.'

There was some relief: he sounded more lucid than I'd become accustomed to over the last few months. Perhaps fighting the physical decline had been taking up too much of his energy, and now that he had stopped, that energy could be concentrated elsewhere. All his remaining heat, burning in a single room.

'I thought I was gone last night,' he said.

'Don't be silly. You're not going anywhere for a while yet.'

'No, I mean it. I kept waking up because I couldn't breathe properly. But then when I was awake, it was hard to do anything about it.'

'You should have called the nurses.'

'I did. In the end, they had to put me more upright.'

'Is it easier to breathe like that?'

He chuckled. 'Don't you remember anything I taught you? It's easier to do everything when you stand up straight.' But the chuckle died away. 'I still had to concentrate, though. It's like when your sinuses are very blocked and you try to breathe through your nose, and so, so little will go in. Like that, but everywhere somehow.'

'John—'

'Everything was very grey and distant. Just the tiniest little thread of breath keeping me here. And I thought maybe I wouldn't really care if it snapped.'

'You might not, but I would.'

'Yes.'

'And you did too, or else you wouldn't have called the nurses.' I gathered myself together. 'So enough of this crap, John.'

'I just panicked.' Another chuckle. 'I surprised myself, actually. Because I thought I'd made my peace; that I'd accepted what was going to happen. But it turned out I hadn't. When it felt like it was coming to it, I realised I wanted to live. So much.'

'Fight to the last. Something else you taught me, remember?'

'You never needed me to tell you that.' He smiled at me, his eyes watering slightly. 'You always had more than enough fight in you. I just turned you slightly, pointed you right. Maybe not even that. You'd have got there on your own.'

'Yeah.'

But it gave me pause, because I knew deep down that it

wasn't true. After that night at the police station, I began to see John more and more – just around the estate or thereabouts. I didn't realise at first that he was keeping track of me, but when I did, I think I was more flattered than annoyed. From my mother to my 'friends', nobody had ever seemed to care that much about my future, or encouraged me to make something of myself, and here was this stranger who was doing both, simply because it was in his nature to help people. To do the right thing.

Over the weeks and months that followed, a strange thing happened. I found myself moving away from Sylvie and Nat and the rest of them. Even Jem. I spent more time on my own, I worked harder at school, I applied myself. It was a gradual thing, but it happened. And looking back, I really wasn't sure I would have had enough fight in me to do it on my own.

So a part of me wanted to reassure John now. To disagree. To let him know how much he'd quietly done to make my life better – me and so many others. But it was hard to admit that I'd never been as self-sufficient as I liked to pretend. Chris's words came back to me again. *You always have to do everything yourself, don't you?*

And he was right, of course.

In the end, John broke the silence first.

'It's okay.'

'What is?'

'Not knowing what to say. It must be hard. It is for me.' He frowned. 'I am very frightened, you know. I'm not ashamed to admit it. For the first time in my life, I think. I've never been this scared.'

I leaned further forwards.

'Do you remember what you told me once, when we talked about death?'

'Not as well as you do, I imagine.'

'You said death was nothing to be frightened of. That you weren't scared about growing old and dying.'

143

'That sounds like something I would have said. People do say things like that, don't they?'

'You said it was because death would either be wonderful, or else it would be like nothing at all.'

'Maybe tonight I'll stay asleep and find out.'

'You won't. But the point is, nobody knows. And if it turned out to be nothing, then being scared of it would be like being frightened of the time before you were born, when you didn't exist. And nobody's frightened of that, are they?'

'Yes.' He nodded. 'I do remember that. I have to say, I stole that from somewhere. It was an observation from someone else. I can't remember who.'

I leaned back. 'Still true.'

'In a way. But I'm not scared of being dead. Maybe I'm not even frightened by dying. Perhaps it's … sadness. Because I know there'll be a time without me. There'll be so much happening that I'll miss, and it doesn't feel fair. You, for example. I'd love to see you grow up properly.'

He gave me a pointed look, and I shifted in my seat.

'Yes, well. Can we talk about something else?'

'Of course. Tell me about work.'

'I can do that.'

So I did. I told him about finding Drew MacKenzie, and how I'd handcuffed him to the staircase, which got me another chuckle – I loved that sound. Then I told him about the creeper investigation, and how I thought – or hoped – that we might have had a breakthrough of a kind. I even lost my temper a little when I was explaining about the obfuscation at Mayday, but it got me another chuckle, so it was worth it.

'I'm surprised you didn't handcuff him to the desk and rifle through his filing cabinet.'

'Huh. If it was as easy as that, I would have done. Should have dragged him in for obstruction, at least. Court order's being fast-tracked, though. We should have the number tomorrow morning.'

'And then this man.'

'Fingers crossed.'

There was another night to get out of the way first, though. Another night when he could be hurting a woman the same way he'd hurt the others. That image of Sally Vickers came to me again. *We are going to get him for what he's done to you.* If we didn't do it in time, the temptation to revisit Richard Oakley at Mayday was going to be strong.

When I was done recounting it all, we both fell quiet for a time. John still looked mildly amused, and I was reluctant to break the mood. Then I realised there was something I wanted to ask him.

'When I arrested Drew MacKenzie, I saw someone else. A woman.'

'A woman?'

'She was in the pub. I only got a quick glimpse of her, but I'm sure I recognised her from somewhere. She had long brown hair, and these scars on her face.' I made a motion across my own. 'Maybe just one scar. I wondered if you knew who she might be?'

He frowned. 'How old was she?'

'Late forties, early fifties.'

'It does ring a bell...'

And it obviously did, because he was frowning, an expression more reminiscent of the John I'd become used to over the past few months. A man struggling to recall something that should be where he'd left it, but that had been inexplicably moved.

Please, John.

I wasn't sure why it was suddenly so important, but it was. *Please remember.*

After a moment of thinking, he blinked and shook his head. 'I'm sorry,' he said. 'It's gone.'

Twenty

You don't need to come in tonight.

Jane sat in her small flat. As usual, she was alone, but for the first time in a while she also felt lonely.

The worst thing about the phone call from Richard was that he hadn't even sounded annoyed. The phrase 'more in sorrow than in anger' had kept coming to mind during the brief conversation, and Jane had found herself wondering if Richard ever got angry about anything. Perhaps he was just treading carefully for legal reasons. Regardless, she could hardly imagine a more polite sacking.

The closest he'd come to addressing the issue was to remind her that confidentiality was key to Mayday, and that whatever the merits of the action she'd decided to take, it wouldn't be appropriate for her to come in for her shift. *You don't need to come in tonight.* He hadn't added *or ever again*, but it had been implicit enough for both of them to hear it there anyway.

So that was it. She was no longer a volunteer.

With the evening now free, she ate a quick dinner on her knee in front of the television. The news continued to cover the attacks, but there was nothing she hadn't seen before. Not yet, anyway. Assuming the police managed to gain access to the phone records at Mayday, there might be a development soon, and as upsetting as the reports were at present, there was some comfort in knowing that when this man was caught, she would have played a part in making it happen. However miserable she felt right now, it was a worthwhile sacrifice in the grand scheme of things ...

You see? You couldn't do it after all.

Her father's voice, stronger than it had been in weeks. Jane put her plate to one side on the settee and looked across at the telephone. Her therapist's number was on a small business card beside it, and she considered calling her now. Eileen had told her it would always be fine to do so, and anyway, it wasn't as though the circumstances were normal.

You couldn't do it ...

She stared at the phone for a few seconds longer, then looked away. No, she wasn't going to call. She was going to deal with this herself.

I couldn't do it, no. But there were other things I could do.

She closed her eyes and, as she'd been taught, worked methodically through her feelings about the day. As she thought back on everything that had happened, the foremost sensation was a cringe of embarrassment, left over from how she'd felt at the police station, and then in the car. It was the same feeling that always prompted her to apologise – not for doing something wrong, but for doing anything at all. It had been there again during Richard's call, as though she had been caught talking in class and was being told off by the teacher.

But that wasn't fair.

Here are some of the things I could do.

For one, she had felt scared of going to the police. There had been the fear of making herself the centre of attention, and of not being taken seriously, but there had also been the risk of losing something that had become very important to her.

And I did it anyway.

It had turned out that she wasn't being ridiculous – that the information she'd provided to the police might be crucial to their investigation. She had been correct that the man on the phone was the man they were looking for, and they now had a much better chance of catching him before he hurt someone else.

That's because of me.

And no, she hadn't been able to abide by the rules that Mayday set down, but she'd been good at the work while it lasted. The old Jane wouldn't have dared to volunteer there in the first place, *but I did it* – and yes, Mayday was closed off to her now, but there would be other challenges. She'd always been petrified of running into life's knots, but she was beginning to learn that she could often untie them when it came to it. Challenges were never half as frightening as they seemed.

And when I find a new one, I'll face that too.

But most of all, this:

I did the right thing.

After washing up, Jane went through to her bedroom.

She didn't turn on the main light, but flicked on the lamp on the desk and sat down there in the soft glow. If she wasn't volunteering, she might as well get some extra translation work in. She opened up the laptop in front of her make-up mirror and loaded up a linked pair of documents: the French file she was translating, and the one she was gradually assembling in English. They sat side by side on the screen, different versions of the same story.

Fiction was her particular speciality, and the original file was a short crime novel. It was time-consuming work, but it paid reasonably well, and she enjoyed the process. Jane had always been a reader, and still harboured vague dreams of writing a book herself – dreams which, she told herself often, were on hold rather than dashed. While she suspected she had little flair for writing, she knew that was pretty much how she thought about *everything*. In the meantime, the translation work gave her a degree of creative outlet. The original text was set, of course, but she still had to use her imagination to pick the right words for the English version. She aimed not just to recreate the author's sentence in her own language, but to convey the exact meaning as well. To get it precisely identical below the surface.

Eileen, her therapist, had seemed interested in the whole

process, and especially by her choosing this profession in the first place. By then, Jane had been clued up enough to realise what the woman was getting at. In some ways, the work did reflect her personality, because it made her a conduit – a catalyst, even. She changed one thing into another, but she was invisible throughout, and she vanished at the end. While essential to the finished translation, she was never obviously present in it.

She worked for a couple of hours now, losing herself pleasantly, and then decided to have an early night. She saved the documents and closed down the laptop.

As she did so, she glanced sideways at the photograph she kept on the edge of the desk. Her and Peter: an image captured in different, better times. The two of them were embracing, and Peter was holding out the camera to take a self-portrait, with a lush green garden and fountains behind them. It had been good enough – even Jane agreed – to print and frame.

But right now ... the position of it was slightly off.

She was used to seeing it from this perspective, and she was certain. Only a little, perhaps, but it had definitely been moved. It was as though somebody had picked it up and looked at it, then put it back down at a slightly different angle.

A shiver ran up her back.

Without moving her body, she turned her gaze to the mirror at the back of the desk. It gave a view of the bedroom behind her.

Of the bed.

And of the wedge of black space underneath it.

She stared at the bed, the silence growing louder in her ears until it filled the room with a high-pitched ringing sound. In the mirror, it seemed like the dark space was moving closer to her.

But there couldn't be someone under there.

Could there? The door had been locked when she got home. It was locked again now. She felt the pressure of the keys in her jeans pocket. But then ... was that what the other women had thought too?

The dark space stared back at her. For a moment, Jane imagined she could hear soft breathing, but then she swallowed and the sound disappeared. Maybe it had just been her.

With her eyes still on the space below the bed, everything else seemed to be whiting out of view. She forced herself to blink. How quickly could she reach the door and get out? But that was the wrong question. If she was going to get out, she needed to move *slowly*. If someone really was there, he'd know she was panicking and come straight out after her. If she gave the impression that she didn't know, she'd have more of a chance.

She sat there for a few more seconds, wondering what to do and how to make her body do it. She listened very carefully.

Just that ringing silence.

You can do this.

As calmly as she could, Jane pushed the chair back and stood up. No longer able to see the reflection of the room, she could feel her back tingling, but she made herself stand at the desk for a moment, faking a yawn and stretching. Feigning that she didn't have a care in the world.

Then she walked steadily to the bedroom door.

Everything behind her remained silent.

At the doorway, she hesitated, then turned slowly around. The bed seemed somehow alive now. Humming with presence, like an animal down on all fours that might pounce at any second.

She slipped the keys out of her pocket, finding the one for the front door between her finger and thumb. Ready to walk quietly downstairs and let herself out...

Yeah, and then what?

It would be even more ridiculous than before to go to the police over this. After the second interview, Zoe Dolan hadn't seemed to think there was any reason for Jane to be concerned – or she certainly hadn't mentioned it if there was. And confidentiality went two ways, didn't it? There was no way the man could find out who she was. It was probably just the events of the day. The crime novel she'd been working on. She couldn't just *leave*.

No…

Instead, she moved across the hallway and into the kitchen, taking out the largest knife from the drawer. She had absolutely no intention of stabbing anyone – doubted she even could – but an intruder wouldn't know that. Then she moved back to the bedroom doorway and got down on her knees. She leaned forward slowly, pressed the side of her face against the carpet. Looking under the bed.

There was nobody there.

Jane's heart thudded suddenly, as though starting up again, and relief ran through her like water. She stood up quickly, feeling a little foolish. Nobody there. Of course. It was just her imagination playing tricks. Except for the photograph, obviously, but when she looked at it again now, she began to doubt herself.

Just her imagination.

Even so. She kept hold of the knife, and spent the next twenty minutes checking every nook and cranny of the small flat. The air still felt tingly, but she was totally alone. The downstairs door was locked, and the chain was on. Every single window was shut and bolted. There was nobody in here with her, and no way anybody could get in without making a hell of a lot of noise.

You're safe.

Lying in bed later, Jane made sure that her phone and keys were within easy reach on the bedside table. It took her a long time to fall asleep.

Tomorrow, she told herself. She'd look into something. It was unnecessarily paranoid, perhaps, but regardless, she'd do it: find some way to make the house even more secure.

Because however safe you are, you're never safe enough.

Twenty-One

Margaret takes a torch up into the loft.

The hatch is on the landing, and she can reach it if she stands on tiptoes. A sliding ladder pokes out over the dark lip above. It's metal, but light as a feather, and even under her meagre weight the flimsy rungs creak and bend as she climbs. Her body trembles a little too.

She goes high enough for her head and shoulders to pass through, then reaches up and shines the torch around. The attic is a high, cavernous space, with webs plastered to the beams like thatches of old hair. It is surprisingly cold up here too, and she can hear a rush of air, as though she is somehow both inside and out at the same time.

She shines the torch into the corner, at the beams and the taut blue sheets stretched between them like sails.

The bumblebee nest is in there somewhere, she knows. But she can hear nothing for now but that rush of air.

Over the past days, she has found herself going out into the garden more and more. It is always when the neighbours aren't there, so it is a half-victory at best, but still. She sits on the doorstep with a cup of tea and a book, and it feels as though her small patch of the world is a little more friendly than before.

Following the conversation with Karen, she senses a kind of unspoken truce. Even if that is just in her head, the neighbours no longer seem quite so threatening. *Karen and Derek*. She tries not to worry about the messy tangle of weeds in the garden. Kieran remains adamant that he won't tackle it, but Margaret recognises that particular brand of masculine stubbornness – that constant, wearying *competition* – and knows there is no point to it. She will either persuade him to help or else hire someone who will. Anything for a quiet life. She will meet the neighbours in the middle.

Most of the time outside she spends watching the bumble-bees. She admires their industry, the way they work at the buds, then loop upwards, laden down with satchels of pollen. She can never keep track of them for long individually, but by not focusing, she detects an underlying pattern to their movements. A tiny piece of organisation occurs within each bee, as though they are all small, separate parts in the same hugely intricate piece of clockwork. Occasionally, one buzzes close to her face before swirling away, and she thinks *hello there*, as though the creature has come to see her. And that is how she feels about the nest as a whole. In a strange way, she is almost humbled that they have chosen to come and stay with her. That an old lady's house has purpose again.

As she watches them today, she loses herself slightly, transported back to idyllic memories of childhood: a bright, primary-coloured garden; the smell of the flowers and tousled grass; a rusty fence and the polished, evergreen gleam of holly. Just fragments, really, but they cohere in an odd way, and somehow make her feel young and hopeful without reminding her that she is not. There were always bees back then. It is as though the arrival of the creatures now is tying the beginning and end of her life in a bow.

'You've got bees.'

Her eyes are closed, and the sound of his voice shocks her. She opens them to see him standing opposite, right up against the fence. *Derek*, she remembers. He is staring over at her, his forearms resting on the wood. Karen is standing a little way along the path, her sunglasses on, looking down at her feet.

'I'm sorry?'

'Bees.' He nods at the roof. 'You've got a nest up there.'

'Oh, yes. I know.'

Margaret stands up. She can't retreat inside now – not in the middle of a conversation. And anyway, what is there to be scared of? He isn't threatening her, and with his body obscured by the fence, he doesn't seem as intimidating as he usually does. Perhaps Karen has spoken to him and he is even trying to be friendly. To look out for her. She forces herself to walk a little way down the path towards the fence.

'They've been there for a bit. They're bumblebees.'

Up close, Derek seems much younger than his wife. His face is tanned and smooth, and his receding hair is cut short and neat. Those forearms are thick, and not so much muscled as meaty, as though he is a man who doesn't need to work out, who is just naturally strong.

As Margaret reaches the fence, he still hasn't replied to her, and it throws her a little. Yes, she has bumblebees, and they've been there for a week or so. Surely it is his turn to speak now? The silence makes her feel flustered and awkward. She looks at Karen, who is still staring down, and then back to Derek.

'I quite like them,' she says. 'They're very pretty when you see them up close. Nice to watch. And they're not really bothering anyone, are they?'

His expression flickers slightly at that, but she doesn't have time to read whatever was momentarily there.

'You need to get rid of them.'

The words are so definite that everything sinks inside her, and for a moment she accepts the encounter on his terms. *Why* does she have to get rid of them? It's not fair. All she really wants is to be left alone. Derek and Karen on that side of the fence, and her on this. That doesn't seem too much to ask.

'I don't think that's necessary,' she suggests. 'They're not causing any harm.'

'They're bees. Sooner or later you're going to get stung.'

'They don't sting unless they're threatened.'

'They'll sting when they swarm.'

That makes her feel a little brighter.

'Oh, but they *don't* swarm,' she says. 'They're not like other bees. And there aren't that many in there really. The nest doesn't even last very long.'

She expects him to see sense at that, but if anything, the expression on his face has hardened. *He isn't listening*, she realises. In his mind, this isn't a conversation. He has stated what he wants done, and that is not going to change, regardless of anything she has to say.

'You need to get rid of them,' he repeats. '*You've* not been stung. But it's not just you. Do you *really* not understand that?'

Margaret blinks. 'I'm sorry?'

'It's like with the state of the garden. You think you live in a bubble.' He turns slightly, gesturing past Karen, who remains standing still, to his own well-kept lawn. 'I mean, look. They're down here too. Why should I have to put up with them? Why should my wife?'

'I...' But she doesn't know how to answer. Does he really expect such total control and dominion over the world that he thinks he should be able to shut nature out of his property? That the potential danger of his wife being stung outweighs Margaret's rights over her own home?

'Karen—' Margaret says, but Derek interrupts her.

'Are you having trouble? Finding someone, I mean. I know you're on your own. I can have someone come round if you don't know how. I know people.'

He sounds genuine, but even so, the insult lands. *If you don't know how.* It hurts to have it confirmed – that he thinks of her as a feeble, incapable old woman. Karen remains silent. Perhaps she thinks that too. In some ways, of course, they are right, but she is coping. It's not that she needs help getting rid of the bees. It's that she doesn't want to.

And she surprises herself by saying so.

'I don't want to.'

'You don't *want* to?'

Her resolve hardens.

'No. I don't. They're not bothering anyone.'

'They're bothering me. And they're bothering my family. You need to get rid of them.'

The final sentence is firm, not phrased as a command, but clearly intended as one. *I have said it, and so it shall be done.* And with that, Derek walks off down the path, brushing straight past his wife, heading for the car.

For a moment, Margaret feels despondent. She likes the bees; they have made her house feel a little like a home again, and have, in some small way, given her back a piece of the outside world. He isn't going to take that away from her.

'I'm not going to.'

He is too far away to hear her now, but the words reach Karen, at least, and she finally raises her head to look at Margaret. With the sunglasses on, it is hard to make out her expression, but she seems to be reappraising Margaret, and a moment later a slight smile appears on her face. There is something about it that seems conspiratorial. *Don't worry. I'll talk to him. It's fine.*

Margaret nods at her, and then Karen turns and walks towards her husband. She moves a little oddly, and Margaret finds herself hoping that she's all right.

She takes one last look at the bumblebees meandering around the hedge, and then goes back inside.

Twenty-Two

For the day and a half that Drew MacKenzie had been in custody, he'd belonged to Burglary. They'd spent the time gently persuading him that he was totally fucked – basically – and then teasing out the details of the long list of crimes he was prepared to take off the books for us.

It was standard procedure, and MacKenzie was not about to inject any originality into the process. He stonewalled at first, and then capitulated when it finally filtered through to him that copping to other offences wasn't going to make his predicament dramatically worse. If anything, a sentencing judge was going to see him in a better light afterwards. It was dispiriting in some ways, but at least it gave the affected households a modicum of closure. *The guy who did this to you, we got him.* He hadn't been overly forthcoming about his accomplices, or how he'd got rid of the goods he'd stolen, but again, not bucking any trends there.

A day and a half with Burglary.

And now he was ours.

Nine thirty in the morning, and Chris and I were sitting across from him in an interview suite; one of the newer ones in the department, with polished steel surfaces, hi-tech recording equipment and a wall mirror that looked like it might have an observation suite on the other side. It didn't. Anybody watching would be doing so via the video feed from the camera in the corner of the ceiling.

A number of people upstairs would be glued to their monitors. The court order for Mayday had come through twenty minutes ago, and that was being pursued right now. In the meantime, MacKenzie had gone up in the world. Overnight, he'd become a person of interest to us.

'No comment,' he said.

'You think this is a film?' I said. 'What do you think that even means, *no comment*? You want to spend this whole interview like a little kid with his fingers in his ears? It's not going away, Drew.'

'No comment.'

'That is a comment. And it's not one that's making things look particularly good for you right now.'

He stared at me, a sullen expression on his face. At the Packhorse, with his crew and in his sauce, he'd come across as strong and cocky, but a day in police custody has a way of diminishing the hardest of people. In an interview suite, everybody always looks significantly smaller. He was dressed in T-shirt and jeans, and was much skinnier than I remembered. His thin frame suggested that a great deal of his calories came from alcohol, and he had the pale, unhealthy pallor of an addict.

I was fairly sure that he hadn't recognised me. But I – at least – knew we'd both come from the same place, and it was odd to see him like this, on the opposite side of the polished steel desk. Our lives had diverged radically since childhood, and that distance was represented by the width of the metal between us.

The more I looked at him, the more I saw traces of the cheeky little boy I remembered. But it was clear that an attitude that had been endearing when he was young had curdled badly with age, becoming something altogether more unpleasant. There was a sneer to his mouth now. A total blankness in his eyes as he stared right back at me. He could have done anything with his life, and he'd done this.

'No comment.'

I stared him out for a few seconds, until it became apparent that he wasn't going to look away. It was childish to continue, so I tried to convey *yeah, well, only one of us will be going home tonight* with a slight smile, then turned my attention to the document in front of me.

'To repeat myself, what I have here is a list of burglaries you have admitted to carrying out. There are fourteen addresses on this sheet.'

The last was mine, although I wasn't going to mention that. Either he hadn't committed an offence since, or he wasn't copping to it, but that didn't matter much to me. I was more interested in one a third of the way down. I tapped it now.

'In the early hours of September the twelfth last year, you have admitted to breaking and entering an address with the motivation of theft. A semi-detached house on Wesley Street, Haydon.'

I turned the sheet round for him to see. He only glanced at it for a second before looking at me again, so I turned it back.

'That address belonged to a woman named Sally Vickers. Does that name mean anything to you, Drew?'

Saying her name out loud made me a little angrier. My mind pulled out an image of her, covered in blood, stuffed down the side of a bed. And then as a still white form in a mortuary. This time, I held his stare.

After a few moments, he shook his head.

'Subject indicates no,' I said. 'Don't you watch the news, Drew?'

He shrugged, as though wondering why on earth he would do something like that.

'Sally Vickers was murdered in her home a few days ago. Doesn't ring any bells?'

That got more of a reaction than I'd been expecting, but it took a couple of seconds for it to arrive. You could see the cogs turning, clicking into place. He still didn't know who she was, but he understood where this might be going.

'That's got nothing to do with me.'

'I didn't say it did.' I stared at him again, and this time he was the one who looked away first. 'Why so quick to deny it?'

'I know what you're like. Always bothering us. I've told you everything, and that's enough. You're not pinning that on me as well.'

I shot Chris a glance, and he rolled his eyes at me. As well as growing up sullen, it didn't seem like Drew MacKenzie had ended up all that smart. He seemed to believe it was possible we were going to try to unload a murder on to his charge sheet as well.

I leaned forward.

'Drew. Listen. Right now, I don't believe you raped and killed Sally Vickers. *But here's the thing.* We still don't know how her attacker gained access to her property. All we know is that he did, and that he was a bit cleverer about it than you. And you know what? It strikes me as a bit of an odd coincidence that you did it less than a year ago.'

Which was true, although I still wasn't sure what it meant. We had checked out priors on the properties from the very beginning, of course, but out of the six victims we had so far, Sally Vickers' was only the second to suffer a break-in. The third victim, Mary Jones, had also been burgled, but that had been over three years ago. Ultimately, we'd discounted the connection.

Now we had burglary number two. As thin as it was, I was willing to seize on anything – grab it and shake it, in fact, and not let go. Even if I couldn't see the significance yet, there was something here. I was sure of it.

But MacKenzie was shaking his head.

'I don't know what you're trying to say. I don't know what you're fucking getting at.'

I pulled a sheet from my file.

'This is a list of addresses, Drew. I'm going to read it to you, and you're going to tell me if you magically missed some of these out.'

I read out the addresses of the other victims. It was unlikely but possible that they'd suffered some kind of break-in without reporting it. But to each one MacKenzie just said no, obviously without thinking about it. As an afterthought, I asked about Jonathan Pearson, the suspect I'd visited on the estate.

'What about Paydale Lane?' I said.

That at least got his attention.

'In Thornton?'

'That's the one.'

'That's where I'm from,' he said. 'You don't shit on your own.'

From the way he looked at me, I wondered if he'd clocked me – if he'd remembered who I was. But he hadn't. It was just bravado. Just pretending he had some kind of code when he didn't. I could tell that in his own head he felt superior to me and Chris. Thought that we didn't know what it was like. That we'd had things easy.

'All right,' I said. 'What did you *take*?'

'What?'

'For God's sake, Drew. From Sally Vickers' house in Haydon. When you broke in that night, what did you take?'

'I can't remember. How the fuck am I supposed to remember that?'

'Try.'

'Stuff. The usual.'

I'd read the report before coming in here, and knew full well what had been taken; it was all there for the insurance claim. Not only had MacKenzie and his friends broken in using the same lock-drilling technique they'd employed at my house, they'd apparently taken much the same things. The TV, the Blu-ray player, a laptop. High-value items, basically, along with a scattering of movies and games. He hadn't thrown stuff around the way he had at mine. A tidy burglary.

'*Stuff*,' I said. 'But you can't remember what.'

'The TV, probably.'

'Yeah, you love TVs, just not the news. What about the kitchen? You scoop out any drawers?'

'What?'

'The kitchen drawers. Is that something you'd normally pay attention to?'

'Maybe. I don't know. Why?'

'Because that's often where people keep a spare set of keys.'

I allowed that one to settle in his head. For me, now that I'd said it out loud, the feeling that there was *something* here grew even stronger. If Sally's killer had got the keys to her property from somewhere, the prime suspect was sitting in front of me right now.

He looked down at the table.

'I don't remember. I don't.'

'No,' I said. 'Well, you're going to have to give us some names, then, aren't you? The people who were there with you. The people you passed the gear on to.'

'I can't do that.'

'You really can. And you're going to.'

He shook his head again, still looking down, his misery evident in what I could see of his face.

There was enough of the kid there, in that expression, for me to remember him more vividly. One time round at Sylvie's, before John's influence made us drift apart. Drew had been sitting on a threadbare settee, his bright yellow hair home-cropped short, weaving a battered third- or fourth-hand toy aeroplane in figures of eight in front of his face. His legs were so short that his feet didn't touch the floor. I concentrated on the image, trying to think about him like John would. Just an innocent little kid. Still too young to have an ounce of any real badness in him.

I leaned further forward, trying to catch his eye, speaking more quietly now.

'Drew. Listen to me. A woman is dead. Others have been hurt. And the man who did it, he's going to do that again. *This is more important.*'

I let it settle.

Come on, Drew.

But after a moment, he lifted his head and looked at me, and from the expression on his face I already knew what the answer was going to be.

'No comment,' he said.

Out in the corridor, I was ready to start punching the walls. Not simply because MacKenzie wouldn't give us the information we needed, but because I'd *wanted* him to on more than one level. Right now, I wished I could take that mental image of him as a child, hold it up and fucking burn it. The way he'd looked at me too, as though I couldn't possibly understand the life he'd chosen to lead. *Chosen.*

Instead of attacking the paintwork, I turned to Chris and prepared to vent, but I didn't get the chance. We were met at the lifts by a sergeant from the incident room upstairs. His face was flushed, but he was beaming.

'We've got him.'

Twenty-Three

Two hours later, Chris and I were parking up outside a battered old newsagent's on the outskirts of the city.

I was still quietly seething about Drew MacKenzie, but he mattered less to the investigation now. *Fuck him*, I thought. Because with the shadow of DCI Drake hanging over them, IT had moved quickly. Within an hour, having run a trace on the Mayday caller's number and discovered it was turned off, we'd retrospectively pinpointed the locations the man had phoned from: two parks on opposite sides of the city. Two marks on his invisible map revealed. They were of little obvious use to us right now, but the trace on the number remained active, and we'd have him the moment it connected to the network.

Given the severity of the situation, the phone company had been equally swift to comply, and a SIM card is far easier to track and trace than you'd imagine. It's surprising, in fact, how much is recorded. From the number alone, we got the batch and shipment date, along with a specific manufacturer's code. The distribution centre noted the SIM card in and out. There's no such thing as an anonymous call any more; we could literally draw a detailed map of the card's movements over time, from the moment of its production to its arrival at this shop here, on the edge of the city, two months ago. It was only what had happened to it afterwards, and precisely where it was now, that remained a mystery.

'Doesn't look great,' I said.

From the outside, it did indeed not look particularly auspicious. The sign along the shopfront was old and broken – faded lettering read NEWS – OFF-LICENCE – GROCERIES – COMMS – XXX – and the windows below were totally obscured by flyers and hand-written adverts, aside from a square of dull neon lettering that spelled out 'Phones Unlocked Here'. Through the glass door, the shop looked dismal and shadowy. If it hadn't been for the hand-scrawled note pasted to the glass, I'd have guessed it was closed, and possibly had been for some time.

'We're not here to do our shopping,' Chris said.

'Yeah, that's funny.'

It wasn't quite as bad inside as I'd been expecting, although the sign out front would have done well to put the XXX at the beginning: most of the magazine rack was taken up with pornography, and there were two dump bins full of similarly themed DVDs. The groceries consisted of a few shelves of basic jars and packets, and a single fridge containing milk and cheap, plasticky-looking sandwiches. Round the corner, I could see that the walls were taken up with an extensive selection of alcohol. Of the promised 'COMMS', there was no immediate sign.

A desk fan was whirring away behind the counter, next to a bored-looking elderly man. He was sitting on a stool and watching a small black and white television, apparently with the sound turned off. He didn't even look up as we approached him.

'Afternoon.' I showed him my badge, which at least caught his attention. 'Detective Inspector Dolan. This is DI Sands.'

'Oh God. What's he done this time?' The old man stared at me for a moment, then turned and shouted across the store: 'Simon! Get out here now.'

'Simon?' I said.

'The little bastard. It's about the booze, isn't it? I've told him to check for ID. Warned him about it. It was his fault I got in trouble last time. *Simon!*'

A gangly man in his early twenties emerged sheepishly from the door to a back room.

'What? What are you talking about?'

Before the old man could reply, I held up my hand to cut him short.

'It's okay, Simon. You can go back to … wherever you just came from.' I looked back at the man behind the counter. 'It's not about the booze. Or the videos. Although we can certainly talk about those things if you like.'

'What, then?'

'You sell phones.'

He grunted, glaring at Simon again. 'Not many, I don't.'

I smiled. 'Even better.'

'Shit,' Chris said. 'That's our guy?'

'Yes.' I stared at the screen, a knot in my stomach. 'I think it is.'

We were sitting in the store's cluttered back room area – empty of Simon now – reviewing the security footage. The truth was that we'd been enormously lucky so far. Not only did the shop have a camera installed, but the owner had remembered our guy almost instantly. He wasn't lying about the phones: he had only shifted three in the past month, and two of them had been to a woman and a teenage friend of Simon's. Right now, we were looking at the third customer. He'd picked an out-of-the-way shop, and that had been a mistake. Although we couldn't be certain this was our guy, I was convinced it was.

And then our luck had come up short.

Chris said, 'They might as well not bother with CCTV at all.'

I was already mentally framing the video footage to release on the news, but Chris was right. It was not going to be easy. The feed would have been terrible even without the enormous smudge of dirt across the lens, and all that was really obvious was that the man was physically very large, with unkempt hair

166

and dark stubble. Aside from that, he was wearing dark glasses that made his face impossible to make out. Despite the heat, his body was obscured by a long coat, so that you couldn't even tell whether he was overweight or muscled. He managed to be simultaneously both hugely distinctive and utterly unrecognisable.

A ripple ran up the footage, like a wave moving slowly over the scene. Everything rolled with it, apart from the smear of dirt.

'Someone's going to know him,' I said.

'Maybe. Are they going to recognise him from this, though?'

He sounded despondent, and I felt the same. But as I watched the man handing over the money, I told myself that we were at least getting closer. Both of us would have preferred a crystal-clear image, but at least this was *something*. Distinctive and anonymous was still distinctive. Someone must know him. Someone would recognise him.

'We need to get this feed over to the department,' Chris said. 'Get the IT guys on it and—'

But at that moment I felt a buzz in my head, and I immediately tuned him out. I watched as the man on the screen stuffed his change into his pocket, and something clicked.

A shiver of familiarity.

Chris was still talking, so I held my hand up.

'Wait.'

I closed my eyes, because I didn't need to see the figure on the screen any more. Instead, I forced myself to relax, to concentrate. Without consciously thinking about it, I allowed my mind to flick back through its mental files, waiting for a sense of recognition to kick in, for my memory to pull out what I needed.

Click.

There it was.

And I understood. Everything made sense.

I opened my eyes in time to see our man trudging out of the frame.

'I know him,' I said.
'What?'
I was already on my feet, searching for my mobile phone.
'And you do too.'

Twenty-Four

When Jane had eventually got to sleep, she'd stayed there: it was ten o'clock when she woke, and from the kind of dense sleep she knew would leave her tired and groggy for hours.

Light was streaming in through the curtains, and the air in the bedroom had already been warmed and turned by the morning sun. Another hot day. She needed to open a window: the bedclothes were tangled around her.

She showered, turning the temperature right down, then dressed and made breakfast – just a couple of slices of toast and a cup of tea – and took it through to the front room, tucking her legs underneath her on the settee and staring through the blank screen of the television as she ate.

She had no real plans for the day ahead. The weather was nice, but she'd never really been able to take the heat: she'd be an embarrassing and sweaty shade of red within minutes. She should get on to what she'd been thinking about while trying to fall asleep. Start making plans to contact someone about beefing up the security on the house. But in the sunny warmth of the day, the nerves and fears of last night seemed a long time ago. And even a little silly now. She was perfectly safe here.

Maybe spend the morning doing some more work, she thought. She was ahead of schedule on the translation, but the quicker it was done, the sooner she could take on a new project. Money mattered, after all, and her profession was especially hand-to-mouth in comparison to other types of work. There might be nothing for her next week, or the week after.

She licked butter off her fingers and brushed the crumbs on to the plate, then took it through to the sink. As she put it in the bowl and started the water running, she felt a single vibration of the mobile in her pocket.

A text.

She dried her hands, then picked her phone out and read:

Hey you. Missed the ride home last night! No, but seriously, I hope you're okay. Free today if you fancy meeting up? Pint by the Park? Rach xx

She had to read it twice, the second time with a feeling of relief. She couldn't remember giving Rachel her mobile number, but supposed she must have done at some point, and it was so good to hear from her. She hadn't had time to talk to her before leaving yesterday with Zoe, and had only realised later on that she had no way of contacting her. She'd never even seen which door she went in when she dropped her off. Of all the things she was going to miss about volunteering at Mayday, Rachel was easily the biggest.

Pint by the Park, though? Midday drinking wasn't really Jane's thing. She hardly drank at all, and more than a glass or two would probably send her funny, especially in this heat. Still... it would be nice, wouldn't it? Crazy behaviour in some ways – especially for the old Jane – but what did it matter? *Let your hair down a little for once. See how it feels.* Maybe midday drinking could be her thing if she let it. Whatever, it would be good to chat to Rachel. Really good.

She texted back suggesting meeting early afternoon, although she had to ask where. She didn't know which park or which pub: presumably it was a studenty hangout that Rachel was familiar with. Then she made another cup of tea and went through to the bedroom. There was time to get on with some work before she set out.

She was just beginning to get into it when the doorbell rang. The sound made her freeze up mid-sentence, her fingers poised over the keys. She wasn't expecting any visitors or deliveries. Could it be the police? Zoe had her address, of course. Perhaps there'd been a development in the case and they needed to talk to her about something.

The bell rang again.

Jane trotted down the staircase to the front door. It had two panels of marbled glass, and she could make out a large blurred figure through the panes. Not Zoe – she could tell that much – but it was impossible to see anything else, and the size of the figure made her feel momentarily nervous. She wished she had a spyhole to look out through. But then, she was being silly again. Her flat was above an estate agent's on a busy street, the figure was surrounded by bright sunlight, and she could hear the steady rush of cars going past. It was the middle of the day, for God's sake; there would be lots of people about. What on earth did she think was going to happen?

Even so, she left the chain on after unlocking the door, and opened it only as far as it allowed.

The man standing on the pavement outside was enormous, with wild dark hair that seemed to be heading off in all directions at once: tousled and out of control, like untended shrubland. The rest of his face was almost entirely obscured by stubble and a large pair of mirrored sunglasses, and he was wearing blue overalls with a logo on the chest pocket.

He smiled at her – and it was actually a nice smile, as though he was used to his size being intimidating and knew he had to compensate. It also made him much look younger than she'd initially thought. He was in his early thirties at most.

He held out an ID card.

'SSL Security. Detective Inspector Zoe Dolan asked us to come round and install some new locks and bolts for you.'

Jane shook her head. 'I don't know anything about it.'

'Me neither. Usually when it's a police request, they're concerned for someone's safety, but I don't know any of the details. It's gratis, though.' He sniffed. 'Or rather, the police are picking up the tab. It'll only take about ten minutes. Probably not even that.'

'Right.'

So that meant Zoe *did* think she might be in some kind of danger after all, unless this was just a standard precaution. Whichever, it wasn't like it hadn't been on her mind anyway. Problem solved.

She undid the chain.

'Come in,' she said.

'Thank you very much, Jane.'

And he stepped inside, giving her that nice smile again.

Twenty-Five

Chris and I led the procession, pulling out of the department car park with three vehicles behind us: two carloads of backup officers, and the van belonging to the door team. Assuming that Adam Johnson didn't open his front door, the latter would do it for him. I knew them. They'd be looking forward to it.

On my order, there were no sirens. I didn't want Johnson – or anyone else – to have the slightest idea we were coming for him. It was early afternoon, and traffic was relatively light, so I drove quickly. All the attacks had taken place at night, so in theory we had time; while it was possible that he was in another woman's house right now, chances were that nobody was in immediate danger. But I certainly wasn't going to give him an opportunity to bolt. Not now. I wanted the bastard in custody within half an hour.

Beside me, Chris was talking on a headset while tapping on a tablet resting in his lap: gathering data; making arrangements. We were moving, but in a sense still very much playing catch-up. Chris finished a call.

'SSL say he's not at work today. Called in sick this morning.'

'Maybe we'll get lucky then,' I said. 'Maybe he's at home.'

'Maybe. No criminal convictions.'

'Obviously. They wouldn't have hired him otherwise.'

'They're sending through a list of his jobs for me now. They said it was lengthy.'

'And they'll all be there. All of them.'

It was clear now how he had been able to open the windows without damaging them. Because it was easy to open one from the inside. He had simply needed to find a window key, and most people keep one around, often just lying there on the inside ledge for ease. The window had only ever been his exit point. From his point of view, it had probably seemed like a transparent piece of subterfuge – just something to give us pause and make us ask questions, to wonder about how he was gaining access to the houses. The truth had been there all along.

He got in during the day, when the victims were out and the chains and sash jams were, necessarily, undone. He locked the door behind him, found a place to hide, and when the women woke to find him in their bedrooms, the reality was that he'd been in their house for hours. He was there when they got home, when they locked all their doors and windows, when they turned off the lights and went upstairs to get washed, to brush their teeth, to slip beneath their bed sheets. He was there as they fell asleep, blissfully unaware that, the whole time, they were not alone.

And now we knew where he'd got the keys from.

Adam Johnson had worked for SSL Security for eight years, specialising in fitting those new, special kinds of locks, the ones that were undrillable, with the unique keys that had to be individually ordered and constructed. As hi-tech as plain metal gets. At the end of the installation, he handed the homeowner the keys to their property, along with the spares. The security man at SSL had told us that three came as standard for each barrel.

After my burglary, he'd given me one spare.

How were you supposed to know?

I swung a slightly overeager left, just beating a red light. Glancing in the rear-view, I saw that the other vehicles had followed me through regardless.

Slow down.

'Shit,' Chris said.

'Yeah, I'm doing my best.'

174

'Not that. List of his jobs has just come through. It's still downloading.'

'Eight years,' I said. 'How many jobs a day? It's going to add up.'

And that would have worked to Johnson's advantage in a couple of ways. Firstly, it introduced him to an enormous pool of potential victims to choose from. Only a small proportion would be the young, single women that met his criteria, but the numbers ensured that *some* would be. Secondly, there was little obvious to connect him to the victims, or them to each other. Yes, Sally Vickers had been burgled, but she was only the second victim who had been, and both break-ins had taken place months previously. And the other victims? What's the first thing you do when you buy and move into a new property? You call someone up to come and change the locks. It's what everybody does.

A red light ahead. The car in front of me stopped for it, so I had no choice.

Chris tilted the tablet towards me. 'You hate to say someone looks the type. But he does look the type.'

The screen showed a driving licence photo of Johnson, but I only half glanced at it. I remembered him well enough from his visit to my house: a big, bulky man, unkempt and messy, who'd only partly managed to tame that wild appearance for work. A slight sheen of sweat over his forehead, the base of his hair damp. Personable enough at the time. Chris was wrong. You can't tell.

He *did* look like Jonathan Pearson, though – facially, at least, which would have been enough for his purposes. We'd find Pearson on his list of jobs too, I was sure. Someone who looked just enough like Johnson for him to keep a key, revisit the property, and steal some photographic ID that he could have on him in the event that he was ever stopped for acting suspiciously.

I tapped my finger on the steering wheel, waiting for the lights to change.

Thinking.

Planning ahead.

The best-case scenario was that we took Adam Johnson now, quickly and easily, at his home. The next best was that we ended up with a siege situation, where at least he was contained and nobody else was at risk. The worst was that he was inside his next victim's house right now, waiting for tonight.

If that was the case, we had a real problem. The list of his previous jobs was extensive, and there would be no obvious, easy way to sieve it for potential scenes. It wasn't like the security company recorded the age and sex of the people who booked in to have their locks changed. If Johnson wasn't home, we'd have to hope there was some indication of where he actually was. If we couldn't find any, we'd have to trawl his jobs as best we could, and hope he wasn't planning an attack for tonight. And in case he returned to the house, we'd have to do all that without announcing a police presence and scaring him away.

'He'll be home,' Chris said.

'It's like you can read my mind sometimes.'

'Sometimes it's more open than others. He took the day off sick.'

'No, he took the day off on purpose.' I didn't want to say it, but it was true. 'He could be anywhere right now.'

'Or maybe he's just sick.'

The lights changed. I set off, not replying.

Because I don't believe in best-case scenarios.

Johnson lived in Horsley, a suburb about five miles north-west of the city centre. It was a mixed area, but generally upmarket. There was an estate – of course – but it wasn't notorious so much as cheap and practical; obviously distinct from the nicer cottages and clusters of clean new-builds, but hardly a trouble spot. It was closer to the countryside here, and it showed. As we drove, there were fewer and fewer side roads, and more expanses of fields and wooded groves. Approaching Horsley itself, the main road ran close to the canal, separated only by a sloping stretch of grass dotted with horses, then obscured by a row of quaint old cottages, all three-storey and crammed in tightly side by side.

A street away from Johnson's house, I found a decent length of free road. I indicated and parked up, and the cars and van followed suit, pulling in behind. Most of us got out, and Chris and I met the head of the door team by the middle car.

Sergeant Connor is a no-nonsense bull of a man, with a shaved head that looks polished to a sheen. I like him. He never seems bothered enough to look other men in the eye, and when he does, you tend to see them shrink a little. Now he rested an oversized tablet on the bonnet and began pointing out the salient details on the map he'd loaded up.

It was an overhead view of Adam Johnson's house, zoomed out enough to show the blue pulse of our GPS position on the next street. He ran his finger just above the screen.

'Obvious approach.'

'Obviously.' I leaned in and pinched the screen, zooming in to get a good view of the property.

It was a detached cottage, set alone and slightly back from the main road. There was a field on one side, with what looked like a small car park and a playground. On the other side, a thatch of woodland, separated from the house by a dusty footpath. The path led into the woods, which spread out behind the area, reaching all the way down to the canal. What appeared to be a short fence separated the property from the field, but it seemed entirely open to the footpath and woods on the left-hand side. At the rear of the building, there was what looked like a gravel parking area, and then another fence against the tree line.

'Not great,' Chris said.

He was thinking about containing the scene – possibly that Johnson could head into the woods if we didn't handle the situation correctly. But at least the field was open: we'd see

177

him if he took off in that direction. And if he didn't know we were coming, we'd have the advantage.

'Could be worse,' I said. 'Let's see the house.'

Connor swiped and tapped. A moment later, we were rewarded with a street-view image of the cottage.

'Looks the type,' Chris said again.

This time, it was harder to disagree. There was some irony in Johnson's house being close to that playground, as it looked very much like the sort of building children would tell each other ghost stories about. It was a two-storey cottage, with a wide chimney sprouting from the front, and stone walls coated in tangles of ivy. What passed for a front garden was massively overgrown.

In some ways it should have looked homely and welcoming, but everything about the structure was slightly off. The whole building was set at an odd angle to the main road, so that it faced the world with an oblique point, turning a shoulder to it. It was difficult to imagine how the interior was organised. There were several windows, but they were oddly spaced and in locations that didn't look like they would work with each other. From the road, you couldn't see where the doors were. As a whole, it looked more like an object than an actual home: something predatory that had seen a house once and was pretending to be one.

'How do you want to play this?' Connor asked.

'Like this,' I said.

A minute later, we split up. Chris got in one of the cruisers behind, and I drove alone, allowing his vehicle to overtake me, so that I was second in the queue.

In the silence, I had time for the reality of what was about to happen to sink in. Maybe it was strange, but I didn't feel much in the way of nerves. I never do, really, in situations like this. I've always found waiting to be harder. If you're getting on with it, and dealing with the problem outright, then you don't have time to be nervous. It was the same when I was a teenager, especially after I fell away from Sylvie and lost whatever nominal protection I'd enjoyed there. When I knew someone had a grudge and was coming for me, it was the anticipation that was the worst; it always felt better just to march up to them and get it over with, however it played out. This was no different. And in this case, we had a good team and we were going to get him.

That was what I told myself, anyway. That one way or another, this was all going to be over. Maybe in the next few minutes. Definitely in the next twenty-four hours.

Up ahead, Chris's vehicle signalled, then turned into Johnson's street. I did the same. And just like that, we were on. To the right, almost immediately, I saw the field, with its small playground. A car was parked up, and a family was playing in the tarmac area: a man, a woman and two children. I saw them stop and watch us as we approached.

Then everything accelerated.

Chris's car passed the playground, followed by mine, but the one behind me turned quickly, veering off into the car park. The officers inside would spill out across the field, towards the side and back of Johnson's property. The van with the door crew sped up to fill the gap.

Johnson's house came towards me on the right.

Chris took a hard turn down the wide path on the far side. He and the officers in that vehicle would park up past the far corner of the property, covering the rear and the woods.

I pulled in on the main road, blocking the entrance to the path.

The van screeched up behind me.

A second later, most of us were out, hitting the pavement at the same time. In the field to the right, I saw four officers fanning out towards the cottage. Up ahead, further down the dirt road, Chris and another three officers were heading around the back.

I ran down the path, my feet kicking up the sun-baked dust. The front garden was open to this dirt road, but didn't appear to have been cut back in years, and the brambles had grown high enough to collapse into themselves, filling the yard like dense coils of barbed wire. As far as I could see, they reached the short fence by the field, and filled the space down the side as well; no way Johnson was going to be escaping through that.

I found the front door halfway along the structure, opening almost directly on to the dirt road. Further round, the back yard looked in better condition – tarmacked over in a rectangle behind the building. Chris and the other officers were covering that. So the property was contained.

No car, though.

He's not here.

I banged on the door as hard as I could, shouting:

'Adam Johnson. Police. Open this door!'

There was no response. I took a step back as the door team caught up with me, and glanced at the windows. In real life, they seemed even more strangely placed, like eyes in a malformed face, all of them dark and blank. The nearest – a kitchen, I guessed, from the glasses and disinfectant spray on the window ledge inside – was grey and grimy, thick with triangular webs in the top corners.

I gestured at the door. 'Open it.'

Two officers moved in front of me, holding an iron battering ram between them by its massive handles. In unison, they swung back only slightly, then forward, the rounded end landing with a painful thud against the lock. The frame split and the door wobbled inwards, tottering back like a shoved drunk.

I was through it first, moving into a small entrance area. Glancing to the left, I saw the kitchen, the tiled floor greasy and the air misty and opaque, as though something had been burned in there a long time ago and the air had never cleared. A cheap blind hung down at an angle over the window, letting the sunlight through it like a batwing.

There seemed to be only one other room down here, a living room to the right. When I saw it, the feeling of wrongness intensified. The carpet was a faded swirl of pinks and browns and yellows, organised in ornate patterns, and the settee and chairs rested on elegant wooden feet. The textured wallpaper was a Braille of beige curls and crowns, interrupted only by the ancient three-column gas fire hanging from one wall by metal brackets, like a half-detached circuit board. Adam Johnson was in his early thirties, but this was the living room of a pensioner.

The staircase led up in front of me, curling around to the left, growing darker as it went. I started up, the door team fanning out below me into the kitchen and front room. Despite my certainty that the house was empty, I took the bend carefully, raising my arms in front of me, ready to deflect any attack with my elbows. None came. The upstairs landing had three rooms off it. Two doors were open, one revealing a dirty rectangle of bathroom, the floor thick with plastered-down whorls of hair, while the other led into Johnson's bedroom.

I leaned through the doorway. It was impossible to take it all in at first glance. The room was too full: a confusion of cluttered possessions. Johnson's single bed was against one wall, dividing the rest of the space into a horseshoe shape tightly packed with belongings. My gaze picked out details. An awkward construction of shelving filled with trinkets and toys, empty bottles, odd figurines. A wardrobe without doors, the top bulging down under the weight of the suitcases and half-crumpled boxes stuffed in above, pressing up against the ceiling. A mess of strewn clothes and snaking cables on the floor. An old television, grey plastic, shaped like an astronaut's helmet. An antique wooden dresser, the drawers all open to different lengths, like bad teeth. And then the posters stuck to the wall above the bed.

They were old and faded, and not really posters at all, but pages cut from magazines; one long side of each was feathered from awkward scissoring. I recognised that technique, as it was one I'd used myself as a child, cutting out pin-ups. Johnson's were typical of a teenage boy: they showed beautiful women in exaggerated poses. Bikinis. Pouts. Thin bare legs leading up to impossibly tiny waists, like half-open compasses. One was a large image of a woman's face, her black eyeliner running around her eyes, as though smeared by crying and rubbing, her perfect lips slightly parted. Sunlight had faded the bottom corner, and the paper had curled around the drawing pin he'd used to attach it to the wall, like a tiny hand around a nail.

I stepped back out on to the landing. One of the door team was perusing the final door up here.

'Padlock,' he said.

'Let me see.'

He moved, taking a couple of steps back down the staircase. When he was safely out of the way, I aimed a solid kick against the door, close to the lock, breaking it open in a crunch of splinters.

'I could have done that,' he said.

'Yeah, and so could I.'

I stepped into the room.

Christ.

The curtains were closed in here, and the room was filled with a meagre blue light. It was the same size as Johnson's bedroom, but practically bare. The only item of furniture was an armchair, positioned with its back to the nearest wall, so as to face the one opposite. The rest of the room was empty and spotlessly clean.

I stepped in, saw the wall and immediately felt sick.

Looking from the display to the armchair, it was easy to imagine Johnson sitting there, perhaps for hours on end, with no extraneous possessions to distract him from the view. I crossed the room slowly. Beneath my feet, the carpet felt lush and bouncy. There was no itch of dust in the air in here, just a tingle of electricity from the space being so off-kilter, an obvious physical manifestation of someone's bizarre inner world.

The far wall had been divided into square spaces, drawn neatly on to the plaster with a pencil. Each one was about half a metre wide and high, and had a single nail driven into the wall at the top. One had been painted entirely black, and some were empty, but twenty or so were in use. In those ones, a key hung from the nail, and a name had been scrawled on the plaster beneath it. I scanned them, recognising some as belonging to the women in our case. But there were far more keys here than victims.

Below the names, he had used drawing pins to attach pieces of paper. Some of the squares were so full that the pieces overlapped. There were printouts of women, photographed from a distance. Sheets of notepaper covered in writing: a small, tight script that was hard to read, but which I could tell contained observations and details on their behaviour. My gaze flitted across dates and times, comments, even what looked like short poems.

But it wasn't just paper tacked to the wall. There were also items of women's underwear, socks, rings, gold and silver chains. Mementos, of course. All of them. Things he'd stolen from people's houses, either after attacking them or in the weeks beforehand, when he'd been inside their houses without them knowing. When he'd let himself in and out as though he was a part of their lives ...

A possibility suddenly occurred to me, and brought with it a slice of panic – a visceral, physical sensation in my stomach. The squares that were in use were spread around the wall rather than lined up, perhaps in a pattern that meant something to him, so there was no way of telling which one was *last*. I had to scan them all quickly, crouching down, searching the squares closer to the carpet ...

And there I was.

Zoe Dolan. My own name, written carefully on the plaster.

Below it, there were no secret photographs of me. Perhaps he'd been worried I might recognise him, that I'd be paying special attention as a cop. But there *was* a photograph. It showed me as a teenage girl, standing beside my mother, one gangly arm lifted so my elbow could rest on her shoulder, a cocky expression on my face. My mother looked smug too, smirking almost, beneath the tilted beret she wore. *Think you shouldn't mess with me? Wait until you meet my daughter.*

It was from the album I kept in my bedside drawer.

Beside it, I recognised the piece of black underwear he'd tacked to the wall. But I only glanced at that for a second, my attention returning to the photograph. For some reason, that annoyed me far more.

Chris crouched down beside me.

'Oh,' he said.

I could hear the awkwardness in his voice, and feel the sudden tension of his body, as he recognised what he was seeing. Then I realised that the door team would come in here shortly and see this. That other officers would follow. For a ridiculous second, I resented them all.

'He's been in your house.'

'Obviously he fucking has.'

It's not Chris's fault, I told myself. But the protectiveness in his voice infuriated me, and I had to fight the urge to turn around and hammer my fists at him. I half wanted to tear my underwear off the wall too, but forced myself to stand up instead, direct the anger at Adam Johnson. Because I *wasn't* embarrassed, and I wasn't going to let anyone make me be.

'Zoe …?'

He's been in your house.

'My key's missing.' I turned and walked out of the room. 'He's there right now.'

Twenty-Six

Jane lay very still on the bed, her whole body immobilised by the fear. Aside from the shivers, which rolled over her in regular waves.

He's going to kill you.

She listened to the sounds of him moving about downstairs, hearing thuds and bangs. They gave no clue as to what he was doing, so her mind conjured horrors. She heard the rattle of a kitchen drawer being yanked open, and the terror she was feeling intensified.

Knives. Forks. Corkscrews.

It didn't seem possible for her to be any more afraid, and yet it kept happening. Because this was him. The man who had raped and mutilated those women, killed the last one, told her all about it over the phone...

And he's going to do exactly what he described in the calls.

She didn't even know where she was. Once properly inside her flat, the man had quickly overpowered her. It had been ludicrous, really – she'd never stood a chance against him, because of his size, but also because she'd been too startled to fight. It had all happened so fast. Holding her in place on the stairs, his knees either side of her arms, he'd immediately stuck the tape over her mouth, then rolled her over on to her chest and wrapped more of it around her wrists, and then her ankles.

The whole time, the front door was ajar behind him. Until he'd flipped her over, she'd been able to see the cars going past, and she could still hear them. There'd be people. She'd tried to cry out, but the gag had muffled the sound.

'Right.'

He had sounded out of breath. Scared – upset, even. And that was when she'd recognised his voice.

She *had* started fighting then, but by that point it was useless. He was monstrously strong, and with her hands and feet bound, there was no way of making an impact. He'd just scooped her up and carried her outside into the sunlight like a man taking his bride over the threshold.

Help me, she'd thought. Because it was absurd: the world was bobbing around her, and she'd seen several people nearby, some of them staring back with eyes as wild as hers must have been. She was being abducted in broad daylight, and nobody was doing anything, and that was ridiculous. But then, all these people's ordinary days had just been interrupted by the incongruous sight of a huge man carrying a tied-up woman out of a house. They had no idea how to react at first, and so they didn't, and those few seconds were all the man needed.

While inside her house, he'd left the door of his car open and the engine running. Once outside again, he'd laid her down on the back seat, then pushed her legs inside. The door had slammed, hitting the soles of her feet, and she smelled warm leather and an air freshener like off fruit, and saw an *A to Z* stuffed in the pocket on the back of the driver's seat. A moment later, it had bulged towards her as the man got in, still breathing heavily.

'Hey,' someone was shouting. 'What—'

But the driver's door slamming cut the sound off. A couple of seconds later, the car had rocked and then they were moving: heading off quickly, the tyres screeching. Somewhere behind them, a horn had blared.

The whole thing had only taken a minute, maybe less.

As the man drove, Jane had concentrated on not rolling into the footwell. That was easy enough, but trying not to panic was much harder. *You've been kidnapped.* For a short while, she decided that couldn't be true, because it didn't make any sense, but reality settled in quickly. She'd been kidnapped by *him*. The memory of what he'd done to those women came back to her. The way he'd described it. The words he'd used. And then she couldn't fight the panic any more.

Unable to scream, she had started to cry. She wanted her father, whatever he might say to her. She wanted to turn back time and do everything differently.

Please let me go. Please don't hurt me.

I can't do this.

I don't want to.

The man was still clattering around downstairs. Every noise he made sent a blare of terror through Jane's body.

She forced herself to roll over, towards the edge of the bed closest to the door. Even with her hands and feet bound, if she wriggled on to her stomach, she thought she'd probably be able to manoeuvre herself off – get herself into a standing position. But what was the point? Fighting was out of the question, and she couldn't walk, never mind run. Where would she go anyway? Into another room, perhaps, but certainly not downstairs. She wouldn't be able to get outside...

That was when she realised what he was doing.

Once again, the terror stepped up a level.

He's fortifying the house.

Even if nobody had directly intervened outside her flat, someone must at least have got his registration number. It would have been reported, which meant someone would be looking for her now. When they realised who she was, and her connection to the case, the police would guess who had taken her. And the man must have known that.

Which meant that this time he wasn't trying to get away. He was anticipating the police turning up here – wherever *here* was – and he was barricading the pair of them inside while collecting the things he was going to use to hurt her. That was his plan – that neither of them was going to leave this house alive.

Oh God.

And then she heard his footsteps on the stairs.

They were huge, heavy sounds. Out of instinct, she rolled back across the bed, only just stopping short of falling off the far side. *I stuffed her down there when I was finished with her*, she remembered, and those words, coupled with the sound of the bedroom door opening, sent her rolling over one more time. She tumbled off the side of the bed, landing hard on the floor.

'What?' the man said. She couldn't see him, but he sounded concerned. 'No. Wait. Don't do that.'

Jane heard him heading quickly around the bed. She'd landed on her side, facing underneath it. Two cats stared back at her, directly beneath the middle. And centimetres from her face, between her and them, there was a claw hammer.

She could have wept. With her hands tied together behind her, there was no way she could reach it. So it was like a taunt, and she started crying again. A second later, she felt herself twisted on to her back and saw the man looming over her, impossibly large, filling the world.

'Come on. I know you're scared, but it will be okay. Honestly it will.'

Jane kicked up at him. Bracing her back against the floor, she summoned a surprising amount of force, landing both feet into a gut that was softer than she'd been imagining. The man grunted, and half fell over on top of her. She was screaming through the gag, but it just came out muffled and nasal.

'Don't,' he was saying. 'Please.'

But she kept twisting and kicking with her legs. Now that he had hold of her, though, she didn't have the distance to generate any kind of strength to the blows. Just like back at her flat, he hoisted her up with ease, and put her back on the bed, propping her up in a seated position on the pillows against the headboard.

'There. Is that comfortable?'

She shook her head quickly.

'I'm sorry.' He ran one hand through his hair. 'It's the best I can do right now.'

The overhead light glinted in the beads of sweat on his forehead. While he'd been downstairs, he'd taken off the sunglasses, and she could see how wet and flushed his cheeks were. His eyes were too small for his face, and were ringed with red, as though he hadn't slept properly, or had been crying.

He started to say something, but then, in another room, a phone began ringing. His head jerked to one side, in the direction of the noise, but all he did was listen. After about twenty seconds, it went quiet. The man moved to the corner of the room by the window, and very carefully lifted the edge of the curtain to look outside. Jane saw his gaze moving here and there, and then he replaced the curtain and stared off to one side for a few moments, blinking rapidly.

'Right. Right.'

He stepped back around the bed and walked over to the set of drawers beside the door. On top of them, there was a kitchen knife. As he picked it up, the blade caught the overhead light and glinted. He turned back to the bed, the expression on his face incredibly sad.

Behind the gag, Jane felt herself beginning to hyperventilate. It was impossible to get enough air in through her nose, and her chest was heaving. Breath whistled in and out, in and out. *Don't be sick, don't be sick.* But at the same time, what did it matter? Perhaps it would be preferable to die like that, choking on her own vomit.

The man sat down on the bed, by her feet. Instinctively, she pulled her knees up, retreating as far as she could. But he didn't seem to notice. His concentration was focused on the knife in his hands. He kept turning it over and over. Jane couldn't keep her eyes off it. The reflection of the light flashed and faded, flashed and faded.

'They took you away from me,' the man said.

She shook her head, not understanding.

'From the helpline,' he said. 'I needed to talk to you last night, and you weren't there.'

How does he know that?

Perhaps he could have worked out she wasn't available by calling often enough, but that wasn't what he was saying. *They took you away from me.* That meant he knew the helpline had let her go. But *how* could he know that? And how on earth had he found out where she lived?

'You weren't there.'

Finally, he turned to look at her. She forced herself to look back. His eyes were so tiny and pink that it was impossible to work out what might be going on behind them. They didn't even seem to have any whites to them.

'That's all I want. Someone to listen. I want you to listen to me now.'

He *was* crying, Jane realised. Just a little.

'I want to tell you about the monster,' he said.

Twenty-Seven

For three days after the security light incident in Sharon's garden, he was consumed by panic.

All his illusions about their relationship had been shattered, and the reality laid bare. There had never been anything between them outside of his head. She had a boyfriend, and had even secured her house against men like him. But although the familiar feeling of self-disgust was stronger than ever, it was still drowned out by the panic. Because Sharon's boyfriend must have seen him very clearly from the kitchen window, and would surely have called the police. He spent seventy-two hours sick with worry, anticipating a knock at the door.

When the knock finally came, it was almost a relief.

Before that, though, there was what felt like infinite time for both worry and self-recrimination. Why had he carried on with what he was doing when he had *known* he was being stupid? In his head, he wound events back, like cotton on a spool, but the real world was beyond him; his actions couldn't be undone. With clenched fists pressed into his eyes, he prayed for time to reverse, but of course he remained firmly in the present. It almost felt like the universe was mocking him. It had kept leaving its doors ajar, yes, and he had walked through each of them, feeling that sense of inevitability. But when he was safely inside, it had swung one of them shut behind him, trapping him.

He still went to work, and while it was possible that he'd get away with what he'd done, he anticipated a phone call at any moment. The jobs took longer. He would find himself holding a drill, shaking, unable to keep his hands steady. At home in the evenings, he watched the local news, expecting to see an item about himself, perhaps with an artist's impression of his ragged features. He watched to the end, because he knew it wouldn't be a lead item: he wasn't that important, and he never had been. It was fitting in many ways that his life would be destroyed by something so pathetic and ineffective. Something so ultimately *pitiful*.

He bought all the local newspapers as well, tearing through the pages, searching for anything. By the third day, he was almost daring to believe he might have escaped – that either it hadn't been reported or it wasn't being investigated – but deep down he knew that was delusional thinking. It was the exact same complacency and self-deceit that had led him to Sharon's garden in the first place. In reality, he had never been that lucky.

And then, on the third evening, he found the report.

It was on the fourth page of the newspaper, and only a small sidebar, but it was there.

WESTFIELD WOMAN ATTACKED IN HOME

Police are today appealing for information about a serious assault on a Westfield woman in her Cragg Road home. The assault occurred on 4 May at approximately 2 a.m., after the woman, 25, returned home from a night out with colleagues at Eyecatchers Beauty.

'This was a heinous and wholly unprovoked attack on a defenceless young woman in her own home,' Detective Superintendent David Barlow told press. 'We are determined to catch the assailant, and we urge members of the public who may have seen anything, or have any information at all, to come forward now.'

DS Barlow said that the police were pursuing several lines of inquiry, and that there was no reason for

the public at large to be concerned, but stressed, 'We
advise any member of the public travelling late at night
to be safe and stay vigilant.'

He read it again immediately, the panic looming larger now.
From the details given, the woman referred to in the article
had to be Sharon – and yet the story was confusing. The night
was correct, and the time was about right. But he'd only been
in the garden ... hadn't he?

It was suddenly difficult to remember, and he pressed his fists
into his eyes again, moaning softly. He couldn't have done that
to her. However much he had sometimes hated her, he would
never have done anything to hurt her. Anyway, the man had
scared him off – the boyfriend – so it was impossible that he'd
gone into her house ...

And then he stopped rubbing his eyes, and slowly moved
his hands away, staring down at the article. Remembering the
man's shape in the kitchen window, staring out at him from
the darkness.

He'd assumed it was a boyfriend.

That had been his first mistake – or his second, if you
counted going to Sharon's house that night. His next came an
hour later, when there was a knock at the door, and he opened
it expecting to find the police on his doorstep.

Adam tells all this to Jane as best he can, although he knows
he's panicking, and that the words are coming out jumbled,
the story out of order.

It's not like talking to her on the phone, when he was upset
but still calm enough to think clearly. Now he can see how
frightened she is: still watching him wide-eyed, still convinced
he's going to kill her. His heart goes out to her. He puts the
knife down for now, but it doesn't seem to help. The important thing is, though, that he's unburdening himself. *A problem
shared.* How much time does he have left to do so? He keeps

checking carefully out of the side of the curtains, and every time he does, the street seems even more full of police vehicles.

'But you see, it wasn't the police knocking at the door that evening,' he tells Jane. 'It was the monster who found me.'

How to describe the monster, though?

A physical description will hardly do. The man is large and strong, but wouldn't necessarily stand out in a crowd. In many ways, he is entirely average, and when Adam thinks about him, his mind supplies the kind of photofit he expected to see on the television: sketchy details that add up to a face and a body, but which don't seem entirely real. He thinks he knows why. When someone has a distinctive feature, you tend to focus on it, and fail to absorb the rest of their appearance. What is distinctive about the monster is not his physical features, but what lies behind them.

How do you use words to conjure up the purest forms of hatred and aggression? How do you convey absolute emptiness? A photograph of a void is blank by definition. Even when the monster holds still, he has violence beating off him like heat from a fever. The first time he saw him standing there, Adam could already feel the sheer force of the monster's presence. It wasn't a man that was on his doorstep, but something elemental and unstoppable, something that despised everything in its path.

None of which is possible to explain.

'Sometimes when I see women,' he tries, 'I think they look like the beautiful girls at school, all grown up. And that's the only way I can really describe the monster. He's like one of the tough boys, the ones who used to bully me, all grown up as well. When I used to be afraid of them at school – the dread I'd feel – that's exactly what he is. That fear. Standing there like a real person.'

But not standing there for long that first evening. The monster stared at him for a few seconds, tilting his head slightly, as though perusing a lower species, then walked past him and inside. The strength emanating from him wavered like a magnet: Adam moved to one side to let him pass, then felt himself pulled along after him.

There was no point asking who he was – Adam already knew. Equally, there was no point denying he had been seen in the garden that night.

How did you find me?

The monster didn't answer. He didn't say anything, in fact – just stalked from room to room, looking around the cottage. His face remained impassive throughout, his eyes dead. *Don't get too close to me*, his body language commanded. Despite the fact that this was his home, Adam obeyed.

What do you want?

No answer. The monster walked upstairs, his body seeming to expand and fill the stairwell. Adam followed nervously, and it was only as they reached the landing that he realised he'd left the door to his key room open.

But the monster looked into his bedroom first, so he had a chance. It was another moment he'd look back on later, wishing that he could turn back time and do things differently. While the monster was in his room, Adam reached out to secure the lock on his key room. All he needed to do was press the link down. And then take control of the situation, of course – order this man, this *thing*, to leave his property. But instead, he stood there with his hand on the padlock, staring at the man's back, and he didn't *dare*. The sense of threat coming off the monster was simply too great.

Things might have been so different if he had.

He tries to tell Jane all of this, along with what happened afterwards. The monster stood in the middle of his key room, gaze darting here and there over the wall, then looked at Adam as though he was suddenly a little more interesting.

Tell me about this.

And again, Adam did as he was told.

He tries to explain it all, but he's crying, and Jane still looks so frightened, and the phone keeps ringing, and he can hear the police outside now, without even looking. There are loud-hailers and shouted instructions, the blare of sirens, bangs on the doors and windows. He doesn't have much time left. Maybe he has none at all.

In the end, though, despite the tears, he feels a degree of light-ness inside: a sensation he hasn't felt since before the monster's first visit, and even for many years before that – perhaps as long as he can remember. But there is sadness there too, of course. If only you could reach back and do everything differently. If only you could make the smashed glass whole again. If only.

Adam's hand is trembling as he picks up the knife again.

'I'm sorry,' he tells Jane. His voice is clogged, and he forces himself to swallow down as much of the loneliness and fear as possible. 'I'm so sorry for what I'm going to do to you.'

For a moment, it feels like he won't actually be able to. Cour-age is required here, and he's always been lacking in that. So he searches for his mother and father in his head, and after a few seconds, he finds them. *You have to go in hard*, his father says bluntly, *and it hurts less*. His mother is there too, of course. *Shy boys*, she tells him.

Shy boys get no toys.

Twenty-Eight

My bedroom.

Mine.

Except it didn't feel like it any more. I stood in the doorway, and for a few moments I was unable to process the state of the room in front of me.

Adam Johnson's body was half on the bed. He appeared to have collapsed – dropped like a stone, rather than slumped – and had landed awkwardly, so that his head was turned to the side, one fat cheek pressed intimately against the bottom of the bed. His knees and hands were out of sight on the floor. If it wasn't for all the blood, it would have looked as though he'd been kneeling there praying and had just fallen asleep.

From this angle, the wound to the side of his neck was clearly visible, wet and red in the light. The covers at the base of the bed were crimson, soaked through as thoroughly as tissue paper. The fabric glistened. A spray of blood had also landed on the wall, and there was a great deal on the floor, pooled over the bare boards and already clotting in the thin gaps between. On the bed, Johnson's hair and beard were bedraggled with it. I could see enough of his face to make out a single eye, which was open, and pointed sightlessly off to one side of me.

I moved as far into the bedroom as I could. There was a hush to the air here, like distant traffic heard from an open window, but it was more of a sensation than a sound. Just behind Johnson's body, a kitchen knife lay half submerged in the blood. Was it one of mine? I couldn't tell. Presumably he would have brought a weapon with him, but who knew?

I stepped back.

My head was a mess. The day had been intense – a wave of incident and adrenalin – and right now, a hundred thoughts and questions and threads of understanding were mingling together. The most immediate was a visceral reaction to how incongruous the whole scene was. It's always a shock to see a body, of course, but the effect was enhanced here because this was *my bedroom*. The feeling of unreality was hard to deal with. Despite all the police work going on, the officers in the house around me, there was still a sense that this could not really be happening. That I might shortly wake to find myself lying in the bed rather than staring down at it.

It's going to be a fucker to clean up, too.

The thought came unbidden, and the flippancy of it was almost welcome. But far from enough to settle me.

Would I even *want* to sleep in here again anyway?

It was bad enough knowing that Johnson had broken in and spent time in here – that he'd taken my things and spied on me. But he'd ended his life in here too. The whole house felt soiled by his presence in a way that would be hard, maybe impossible, to clean by conventional means. Everyone believes in ghosts a little in the middle of the night. How was it going to feel to wake up in the pitch-black and imagine him standing there at the foot of my bed? How was I going to deal with that?

I took a deep breath, then let it out slowly.

All those details would take care of themselves. Of course they would. Right now, the important thing to remember was that this was over. Adam Johnson wasn't going to hurt anybody else, not the way he had in the past. The relief the knowledge brought was palpable, and it was that thought that I needed to focus on.

I crouched down and peered under the bed, seeing Hazel and Willow in their usual place. There was a large carrier in the spare room, and they were both small enough to fit in it together. They always seemed to prefer that, in fact.

'Going to be a pain getting you out from there, isn't it?'

They just blinked at me.

'Have to do it, though.'

But as I stood up, something else occurred to me, and I paused in the doorway, turning back to reassess the scene behind me. Because actually, something about it *wasn't* incongruous, after all. It reminded me a little of what I'd found in the bedroom at Sally Vickers' house: the closed curtains; the blood on the bed; the body on the floor. It wasn't the same, but it was similar.

I remembered how it had been to see her – how in some strange way it had felt different from other crime scenes I'd visited. Standing here now, at the end of the case, it was impossible to escape the idea that an echo had escaped from this moment right now, travelled back, and reached me then. An echo that had told me: *this means something important to you.*

Rubbish, of course. But still.

The feeling of strangeness was only amplified when I stepped outside, carrying the cats in the holder. The scene was both familiar and ridiculous at the same time. My street had been transformed into a circus, filled with police cars and vans, many with their lights flashing silently. There was an ambulance to one side, while officers were busy unrolling a yellow cordon around my property. What I presumed was Johnson's car was parked outside, caught within that perimeter.

There was no media presence yet, but that was going to change very shortly. Several of my neighbours were out on their doorsteps, and I felt their eyes on me as I walked down my path towards the cordon. A part of me actually felt like waving at them.

Hi there. Yes. This is about me.

Bit too busy to be sorry about that right now.

I headed to the ambulance. Jane Webster was sitting in the open back, slightly hunched, with her hands gripping the edge of the vehicle and her feet only just reaching the tarmac. With a blanket draped over her shoulders, she looked like the world's tiniest boxer recovering from the world's hardest fight. Which I supposed was fair enough.

Actually, Jane had surprised me. She had proved much tougher than I'd have given her credit for. When she first came in, I'd pegged her as a timid little creature who would skitter under furniture if you raised your voice. And then at Mayday, she'd been borderline pathetic, practically hugging herself at all the *conflict* going on around her. After everything that had happened today, I'd have expected her to crumble into pieces. And yet she hadn't.

We were still debating the best course of action to address the siege situation we were faced with when Jane had unlocked and unbolted the front door and simply let us in. She'd looked a little dazed, certainly, but not obviously in shock. *Determined*, more than anything. 'He's upstairs,' she'd said, and walked down the path. For a second, nobody had even tried to stop her. Now she watched me approach the ambulance, and the gaze she kept on me seemed just as purposeful.

'I need to talk to you,' she said.

'I need to talk to you as well.' I walked straight past where she was sitting and opened the door of the nearest empty cruiser. 'Join me.'

I put the cats on the passenger seat for now, and when both of us were ensconced in the back seat, I leaned through and pressed the button to dim the windows for privacy. As the glass grew slightly darker, I noticed Jane watching it with something close to relief. However brave she was being on the surface, that instinct to hide clearly hadn't gone away completely.

'There,' I said. 'Now let's quickly run through exactly what happened.'

'Just like that?'

'What do you mean?'

'Well ... doesn't it have to be recorded, or something?'

'Eventually. We'll do it officially later. In the meantime, I just want to get an idea of the chain of events today. Preliminaries, really, to help us out.'

'Right.'

'So let's start with how you ended up here.'

'He turned up at my house this morning,' Jane said. 'He showed me his ID through the door – the security company he worked for. I was half thinking about calling someone anyway, but he told me you'd sent him.'

'Me?'

Jane nodded.

'He said that you were concerned about my security.'

I wished I'd had the foresight. For a second, I was quiet, wondering how on earth Johnson had found out where she lived. But then I shook my head. He had fixed the locks on my house after the burglary, and must have overheard the conversation between me and Chris. A coincidence, of course, but a fortuitous one for him. He'd taken items from my house, but I was a good ten years out of his age range, and hardly in the same league as the other women he'd gone after. No, he'd been interested in me because of my connection to the case, and just because he hadn't taken covert photos of me didn't mean he hadn't been following me from time to time. One of those occasions must have been when Jane first reported the calls. He could have trailed us to Mayday, realised who she was, then switched to following her when we left.

I said, 'What happened after he got inside?'

It was Jane's turn to shake her head. 'I'm not even sure. There was a moment when I realised it wasn't right; that he was just *off*, somehow. And he must have seen that I knew, because one second I was thinking about what to do, and the next he had hold of me.'

She'd fought, she told me, but that was always going to be futile against a man of Johnson's size. He'd tied her up and carried her out of the house in plain daylight. At that point, presumably, he had known what he was going to do and didn't care about being seen.

'He put me on the back seat,' Jane said. 'He was apologising the whole time, but it was hard to listen. I was panicking. We drove for a while. Not long. Then he picked me up out of the car again, and carried me in there.' She nodded back in the direction of my house. 'I didn't know where I was. He took me upstairs.'

Even though on first glance it didn't seem like Jane had been raped or assaulted like the other victims, I was still dreading the next question.

'And then?'

She took a deep breath. 'He apologised again. He told me how sorry he was, and he promised that he wasn't going to hurt me.'

'Okay.'

'I didn't believe him. I thought I was going to die.'

'I can imagine. Did he untie you?'

'No. He left the tape on my mouth, too. He said he was sorry about that as well. But he told me he didn't want me to scream, or even talk to him. He just wanted me to listen.'

I frowned.

'Just listen?'

'Yes. Like when he rang Mayday.'

'Why?' I said. 'Because he liked talking to you?'

'Yes. That's what he said.'

'And that's why he abducted you?'

'I think so. He didn't say it, but that was the impression I got: that confessing to me helped him a little – helped him to deal with what he'd done. When I got sacked, he didn't have that outlet any more. It was like his safety valve had been taken away.'

'Why didn't he just talk to someone else there?'

'I don't know.' There was a flash of anger from her at that. Another new experience. 'I don't know why he wanted *me*.'

'All right,' I said. 'I'm sorry.'

Actually, I could think of a couple of reasons why Johnson might have wanted her. For one thing, although I'd not been privy to the conversations, I imagined Jane would have been far less confrontational than another volunteer might have been. More to the point, it was becoming clear that Adam Johnson formed genuine relationships with the women he encountered – even if only in his head. Once he was fixated on someone, he concentrated on them, at least until it became clear that they were far from interested in him in return. Until reality intruded and drove him into a frenzy of rage and hate. It wasn't so hard to believe that he felt he'd formed a bond with Jane, and that it would have distressed him to have it broken.

'A safety valve,' I said.

Jane nodded. 'Like I told you before. During the calls, it felt like he was unloading what he'd done. Passing the burden on to me. Without that, he couldn't cope any more.'

'And what about today?'

'He killed himself in front of me.'

Suddenly Jane looked like she was going to cry. Whatever else I'd seen during my career, I'd never seen what she'd had to witness today, and I almost reached out to put my hand on her shoulder. But she had already gathered herself together. Her hands were bunched into fists on her thighs. *No. I have to get through this. It's important.*

'Jane,' I said. 'I know. It's okay.'

'It is okay. Because I'm sure that was what he was planning all along. Which means it was *his* decision. He couldn't deal with what he'd done, and needed to end it all. And before he did, he wanted to confess.'

'Everything he'd done?'

'No.' She shook her head. 'Everything he hadn't.'

'What do you mean?'

'He never touched those women. It was the monster.' Jane looked at me. Stared at me, to make sure I understood. 'The phone calls he made, the things he said ... none of it was true.'

She looked away and took a deep breath.

'The monster's still out there.'

Part Three

Twenty-Nine

Sitting on the rattly bus, her head resting at an angle to her own sunlit reflection in the window, Margaret realises she is smiling. In recent months, returning from the library has always made her slightly nervous. The outings are moments of freedom, whereas at home she has always felt slightly under siege. But that has changed, she realises.

It's changed.

With the sun beating down on her, she makes her way steadily up the cul-de-sac, the bag of books growing heavy in her hand. As she approaches the end, she sees that Derek is out in his garden, wielding a hosepipe at waist height. Because of the weather, a ban is in force, but he clearly doesn't believe it applies to him, or else he's confident that nobody will say anything or report him. He is whistling to himself as he sprinkles water over his ornate flower beds.

Margaret decides to ignore him. There has been no interaction between them since the argument over the bees, and if he is upset with her for not getting rid of them, at least he hasn't pressed the issue. Most likely it was just as Karen said in the tea room that time, that he's been taking things out on her, and that deep down he isn't really bothered.

She walks past the bottom of the neighbours' garden and then turns up the footpath between their houses. It doesn't occur to her to wonder what Derek is doing there at this time of day. She's too busy concentrating on ignoring him as she steps on to her own path, and that's when the first one crunches very softly beneath her shoe.

Immediately, Margaret stops.

And then she looks down. The path ahead is dotted with them. At first, the sight doesn't make any sense, because it is like the ground has been scattered with the tiniest clumps of earth. But then she realises how quiet and still the warm air is. Nothing is flying. She looks at the hedge. Even when she stares through it, no movement appears.

She steps back carefully, and then crouches down. The bumblebee she has trodden on is dead, but some of the others lying on the path are not. Here and there, a mandible or a leg is quivering slightly. One of the bees appears to be chewing hopelessly at the air. She looks upwards at the corner of the house, and there is no movement there at all.

She stands up slowly, refusing to accept that it has happened. It is impossible. This is *her* house. Surely he wouldn't dare.

Behind her, Derek is still whistling happily to himself. When she turns to face him over the fence, he glances across, and with his free hand he throws her a mock salute.

I can have someone come round if you don't know how.
I know people.

Then, still whistling, he goes back to watering his garden.

Margaret stares at him for a few seconds more. She is trembling, but she doesn't know whether it's from anger or shock, the invasion of what he's done, or simply the sheer *meanness* of it. Right now, it is so difficult for her to comprehend what has happened that she can't believe it actually has.

I have said it, and so it shall be done.

After a few moments, she turns her back on the man and walks the rest of the way down the path, careful not to stand on any of the dead or dying bees. For some reason, that feels important. When she gets inside, she locks the door against the outside world, and something is snuffed out inside her. A feeling leaves. She leans down awkwardly on the kitchen counter and begins to cry.

Thirty

Detective Inspector Zoe Dolan
Detective Inspector Chris Sands
Ms Jane Webster

ZD: But he never gave this woman's full name?

JW: No. He was rambling a bit. It was all jumbled the way
he told it, and I think he kept forgetting bits and then
having to go back. I would have asked him if I could have
done, but he never took the tape off my mouth. I was just
there to listen. That's what he said. That's all he wanted
me to do.

ZD: What about where she lived?

JW: Not the area, no. I've already told you about her house,
though, the way he described it. There was a field out front,
and a back garden where she hung her clothes out to dry.
And a security light, I guess, because he said he tripped it
the night he went there.

ZD: Which is when he saw the man in the kitchen window?

JW: Yes. He presumed she must have got herself a boyfriend
he hadn't known about. She was single when they met, he

thought, but I got the impression he'd been stalking her for a while. So at first he just thought he'd 'missed his chance' with her.

ZD: Can I just clarify? Those were his words?

JW: That was how he put it. I remember, because he was so upset. It was obvious that he'd barely even spoken to this woman, but the way he talked about it, it was as though he'd just waited too long to ask her out. That he just hadn't moved quickly enough, and so he'd lost her to someone else.

ZD: But then he changed his mind about that.

JW: He read about it in the newspaper a couple of days afterwards. That was the evening the man came round to his house to see him.

ZD: This is the man he alleges he saw in the window of the property? The supposed real attacker?

JW: Yes. 'The monster.' That's what he kept calling him.

ZD: How would that man have known who Johnson was, or where to find him?

JW: I don't think Johnson knew. He guessed that the security light would have given the man a good view of him, but beyond that, he wasn't sure. As far as he knew, he'd never met the man before. And he asked him, but never got an explanation.

ZD: Why did the man go and see him? It seems to me like that would be pretty risky behaviour, if what Johnson was telling you was true. He could have placed him at the scene.

JW: Yes, but I don't think the man saw it that way. The impression I got was that he thought of Johnson as some kind of kindred spirit almost. Johnson said the man just invited himself in, and that he saw some things in the house that made him think they were alike. Or at least that he could use Johnson.

ZD: Why didn't Johnson go to the police?

JW: He didn't say. I presume he was scared about his own involvement. But the way he talked about this man, I think he was also very scared of him. That he felt incredibly intimidated by him. When he was speaking about him, he always called him 'the monster'.

ZD: And 'the monster' came round more than once?

JW: Yes. He kept coming back. It sounded to me like he was trying to *groom* Johnson for a while, but then he was disappointed because Johnson wasn't really like him at all. He was a bit, obviously. I mean, he did stalk those women, and he did go into their houses when they weren't there. But I don't think he could ever let himself go through with actually hurting them. It was always the other man who did that. Johnson was really upset about it, and he had to listen to it every time the man came round, but he was too scared of the man to do anything. And so he had to keep doing what he was doing.

ZD: Which was?

JW: Listening to everything he'd done. And giving him the keys.

'Ten pages of this.'
DCI Drake slapped Jane Webster's signed interview statement down on the desk between us.

'If it wasn't so thick, do you know what I'd do? I'd make it into a paper aeroplane and throw it out of the fucking window.'

He shook his head in disgust, then stared at the window to the side of him, as though he was actively considering it.

I could sympathise with him, but only to an extent. Our commanding officer had been somewhat overeager to position himself in front of the media outside my house that day, and had managed to give the impression the case was closing – that the creeper had been identified and was now deceased. Jane's statement, if true, had the potential to embarrass not only the department, but Drake specifically.

At the same time, and being as charitable as I could manage, I knew it wasn't only image he was concerned about. All of us had breathed a quiet sigh of relief when the investigation had reached a conclusion. None of us wanted to believe the man responsible might still be out there.

'I'm sure Webster's telling the truth, sir.'

Drake turned to look at me.

'You believe *a single word* of this?'

Sitting beside me, I could feel Chris sinking down in his chair. Drake's office had that effect on him. He seemed to anticipate the fairly regular verbal beatings with a slightly pathetic sense of resignation. I made an effort to sit up straight. Neither of us had done anything wrong, and neither had Jane Webster.

'That's not what I said, sir. I said *Webster* was telling the truth. Which is to say, I believe that this is an accurate enough account of what happened in my house. This is what Johnson really told her.'

'And what do you make of that?'

'I don't know, sir.' I shrugged. 'Not a paper aeroplane.'

That got me lasers. 'Well, let's run through it, shall we? Johnson claims that a mysterious stranger – a *monster* – shouldered his way into his house and began helping himself to his collection of stalking memorabilia? Is that basically about the size of it?'

'Yes, sir. And kept coming back. Every time he did, he told Johnson the details of what he'd done.'

'Why would someone do that?'

I shrugged again. 'Maybe it's like Webster thinks, and he was trying to groom Johnson to be more like him. Or perhaps it was a kind of safety valve for him.'

'A safety valve?'

'That's why Johnson phoned the helpline. We've seen an increase in the violence during the assaults, so it's obvious the perpetrator is escalating. It often reaches a boiling point for this kind of individual. Maybe this was a way of letting off steam. Sharing the responsibility.'

'I notice the present tense there,' Drake said.

'Just keeping all options open, sir.'

He snorted. 'A *monster*. Tell me, why would Johnson be that scared of someone? He wasn't exactly small.'

'As hard as it might be to understand, sir, some men are intimidated by overly aggressive males.' Out of sight, under the desk, I kicked Chris's foot. 'But maybe this man was doing what Johnson *wanted* to, deep down. On one level, he was disgusted, but on another, it excited him. So he was living through it vicariously.'

Drake stared at me, as though wondering if, like Jane Webster's statement, I was too big to fold.

'But that's supposition,' I added.

'Yes. It is.'

He rested his knotty forearms on the desk, one on either side of the statement.

'All right. We'll come back to all that in a moment. I had the pleasure of visiting Mr Johnson's former address yesterday afternoon, and I've never seen a more disturbing house in my entire career. Please tell me everything you know about it and him.'

I turned to Chris, to let him know it was time for him to do something in here other than shrivel. He lifted himself up in his seat and began running it through for Drake, although there wasn't a great deal to tell. We'd already known that Adam Johnson had no convictions on record, and further digging had failed to turn up a single instance of him crossing our path in any way at all. The cottage, as I'd suspected, had belonged to his parents, both of whom had been deceased for several years. It appeared that the front room had been left untouched in their absence, and Johnson's existence in the house had been limited mainly to his bedroom – another time capsule, in its own arrested way – along with what had once been his parents' bedroom.

'Ah yes,' Drake said. 'His key room. Now tell me about everything that's been found in there.'

'One wall was divided into a grid,' Chris said. 'It was covered with details of all the women he'd been following, along with photographs, personal items, things like that.'

When Chris said *personal items*, Drake's eyes flicked to me, and I hated him a little more. We kept our gazes on each other as he said:

'Evidence, then, of his connection to all six victims?'

'Yes, sir.'

'And other women too,' I said. 'Including me.'

'These are all the women he'd presumably been stalking? Have you cross-checked—'

'Yes,' Chris said. 'Every woman listed on the grid had at some point been a customer of SSL, and Johnson was down as the attending locksmith.'

There had been nineteen in total. It was obvious that he'd paid more attention to some than to others, the victims especially. We'd been in contact with the rest of them, and none of them had known anything or reported concerns. It was as though this other man, assuming he existed, had taken a perverse delight in targeting the women Johnson was particularly attracted to.

'They've all been informed,' I said.

'Well, I'm sure that brightened up their day. Let's concentrate on the six actual victims for a moment. We have a link between

Johnson and all of them, don't we? He changed the locks at their houses, and had the opportunity to keep copies of the new keys. We know he went into their houses and stole their possessions. We know he followed them and obsessed over them. Yes?'

'Yes, sir.'

'We also know that he called this Webster woman on more than one occasion and *confessed to the crimes over the phone.* In fact, that's how we caught him.'

'Yes.'

'Which brings us back to this.' He tapped Jane Webster's statement. 'Assuming this is even close to verbatim, what evidence do we have, exactly, that this mysterious second man ever existed?'

'None,' I said. 'Only Johnson's word.'

'And do you know how highly I rate this man's word, especially when it's placed against all that other evidence you just described to me?' He held his index finger and thumb a millimetre apart. 'Not even that much. Not even that.'

He was right, of course. The possibility that Adam Johnson had told the truth was exceedingly slim: it was far more likely that Jane Webster had been listening to the ramblings of a madman trying desperately to minimise what he'd done in the final moments of a self-destructing life. Johnson couldn't deny parts of his involvement – the stalking; the keys; the stolen possessions – and the mystery second man was an invention that slotted conveniently in between them. Even the language he had used fitted. A monster. Not a separate individual at all, but a part of himself that frightened and upset him, its visits symbolic ones.

Not only was there no evidence that a second man existed, there was no evidence that he *needed to*. Everything we had pointed to Johnson acting alone: we simply didn't need to conjure up a mysterious partner to make sense of what had happened.

I knew all this. But even so.

'We don't want to end up with egg on our faces. Sir.'

Drake stared at me for a long time, considering that, then finally looked away.

'Oh, I'm well aware of that, Detective. And I'm not saying for one second that we should simply *discount* the possibility that this other man exists. So you tell me. Who is he?'

'We don't know, sir.'

'And what about the victim? Who is she?'

'Again, we don't know. As I said, all the women on Johnson's wall have been accounted for. They're either victims we already knew about, or else they've never been attacked.'

'But if he'd been stalking her, surely she would have been there as well.'

'Unless he erased her details. She was the first victim of this other man – let's say – so he might have been upset enough to remove her.'

'Christ.' Drake rubbed his eyes. 'We don't know when this incident took place. We don't know where. We don't even know if it was a rape.'

'Actually,' I said, 'I think we know it wasn't. We looked at other rapes, and I've looked at them again. There aren't any that match the description Johnson gave. But there was a huge pile of borderline cases we went through at the time. If the attacker didn't have the keys back then, and if he was interrupted, we wouldn't necessarily have connected the MO.'

'How many?'

'I couldn't say. Into the hundreds, probably, but I don't know how many would fit.'

Drake stopped rubbing his eyes and stared at me for what felt like an age. Then he sighed.

'All right,' he said. 'Let's go over them again.'

Thirty-One

I'm sorry.

I'm so sorry for what I'm going to do to you.

It kept coming back to Jane at odd times, what Adam Johnson had done to her. She had expected to revisit it in nightmares, but for the last couple of days her sleep had been sound. Perhaps the memories weren't deep enough down for that yet. Instead, it emerged during the day. She would be sitting on the settee, or preparing a meal, or trying to work, and she would find her body was suddenly still, and she was reliving the events in her mind.

I'm sorry.

When it was obvious that Adam Johnson had finished talking to her, she'd been terrified, convinced that he was going to kill her. He'd stood up, sobbing to himself, then moved to the head of the bed beside her, holding the knife. She'd tried to roll over, but he'd put his free hand on her – gently – and stopped her. She could still feel the pressure there.

Hold still.

His voice had been so soft that she'd done what she was told. Johnson had leaned down again, and carefully cut the tape holding her ankles together.

Roll over.

A second later, her hands were free.

As he stepped away, Jane had scrabbled back into a sitting

position by the headboard, then stared at him, wide-eyed, as he walked to the base of the bed.

Thank you.

He'd stood there for a long time, with his eyes clenched shut, before suddenly raising the knife to his throat and violently cutting it. His body had dropped instantly. As he lay there, half on the bed, half off it, Jane had listened to the hideous noise of the blood leaving his body, like tap water gurgling down the sink, and thought: *oh God, oh God, oh God.*

She heard it again now, then flinched, brought back into the present by the sound of the doorbell.

She shook the memories away and checked her watch. It was a little after twelve, and whoever was downstairs was her first *visitor* of the day. God, she'd actually started to imagine it might be over. The last forty-eight hours had been a gradually diminishing scrum of press attention that had kept her constantly on edge. The phone rang endlessly, though she'd stopped answering it on the first day; she had no idea how they'd got her number. And the last time she'd opened the front door, she'd been confronted by a man with a camera for a face, angling back across the pavement to get a shot of her. For a second, she'd been taken back to that day, when Adam Johnson had attacked her at the bottom of the stairs. She'd closed the door quickly, and ignored it ever since. A trimmed-down photo of her had appeared in the papers anyway.

The doorbell again.

Leave me alone.

And yet she got off the settee and moved to the top of the stairs.

The thought had been building: perhaps she *should* talk to the press. Because it was clear the *police* weren't taking her seriously. After everything she'd been through, and all the details she'd given, there had been no follow-up calls, and nothing in the papers about the man Johnson had told her about. The monster. The implication was clear enough. They didn't believe her – or him, at least. They were probably just glad to have the case closed.

It wasn't that easy for her, though. Just as with his calls to Mayday, Adam Johnson had passed knowledge to her, and it sat like a stone in her chest. She had tried to give it to the police, but they wouldn't take it from her. What was she supposed to do? It was a desperate feeling. As much as she might have wanted to leave it alone, she knew that she couldn't. If she did, the knowledge would only ever get more and more uncomfortable.

The front doorbell rang again.

What are you going to do?

Jane hesitated.

And then she decided.

I'm going to go downstairs. I'm going to open the door wide. And I'm going to tell the media exactly what Adam Johnson told me.

Perhaps it would spur the police into acting. The press would demand answers, and wouldn't be fobbed off as easily as she'd been. The idea of making herself the focus of attention was terrifying, and it would be the most confrontational thing she'd ever done in her life, but it needed to happen.

You can't do this.

Yes I can, she told her father's voice. *Because I have to.*

Jane began trotting down the stairs. Go quickly; don't hesitate. She was halfway to the door when the letter box clicked open, and she saw a couple of fingers protruding in between the brushes.

'Jane?' The voice was muffled. 'It's me. It's Rachel. Are you there?'

Despite her decision, relief flooded through her. The press could wait.

'Yes,' she said. 'Hang on.'

It was only early afternoon, but Rachel had brought a bottle of red wine with her.

'I thought you could maybe do with it,' she said.

Jane surprised herself by not even pausing, never mind arguing. An hour later, sitting at her kitchen table, they'd got through most of the bottle, and she had told Rachel everything.

'Shit.' Rachel sat back in her chair. 'I've been following the news. Obviously I have. But there's been nothing about this. I mean, the police haven't said anything.'

Jane shook her head. They'd drunk the same amount of wine, but whereas Rachel seemed relatively untouched by the alcohol, Jane could feel herself getting more than a little fuzzy. *Midday drinking.* Maybe it wasn't for her after all. She pushed the current glass slightly away from herself.

'The police don't believe me.'

'Really?'

'Well, they probably *believe* me. But they don't seem to be taking it too seriously. They don't believe *him*, is what I'm saying. As far as they're concerned, they've got their killer, and he's dead, and that's that.'

Rachel considered it.

'Are you sure they're not right?'

Jane started to answer, but then thought about it. It wasn't the first time she'd considered it. The whole reason she'd gone to the police in the first place was that she'd believed Adam Johnson when he was calling her, but it had turned out that everything he'd told her over the phone was a lie. Who was to say he'd been telling the truth in Zoe's bedroom? And yet she was convinced he had been.

'I'm sure,' she said. 'He was telling the truth – clearing his conscience before he ... did what he did.'

'So why the phone calls?'

'In a weird way, they *were* true. To him, anyway. This other man had told him all the details, and in his own head, he was responsible for that.'

'Because he was.'

'Yes. Kind of, anyway. But you should have heard him, Rachel. Seen him. As bad as it had been before, I think maybe the murder pushed him over the edge. He was so upset. I don't know how to explain it, but I'm sure.'

'Hey, hey. Okay. That's good enough for me.' Rachel shook her head. 'But assuming it's true, that means this other guy is still out there.'

'Yes.'

'So what happens when he goes after someone else?'

'I don't know. Maybe he won't.'

'What do you mean?'

'Maybe he'll just think he's in the clear now. Johnson's dead. So if he stops, it would mean he'd get away with it, wouldn't it?'

'Men like that don't just stop. Trust me.'

Jane thought about it, then nodded, feeling miserable.

'At least the police would *have* to take it seriously then.'

'Yeah.' Rachel gave a hollow laugh and lifted her glass. 'But then it'll be too late for someone, won't it?'

Jane picked up her own glass again.

'What about you?' Rachel said.

'Me?'

'How are you holding up?'

She hesitated. Because aside from reliving the moment of Adam Johnson's death, Jane was surprisingly okay. She remembered the terror she'd felt in the car, just after he'd taken her, and then in what had turned out to be Zoe's bedroom, but that was all growing distant now. Every day seemed to cover the memory with a thicker blanket, muffling it. She could remember wishing she'd kept herself safe, and that she would have done anything to go back in time and wrap herself back up in her father's cotton wool, but even that seemed almost like it had happened to another person.

Maybe she was made of sterner stuff than she'd thought.

'I'm all right, actually.'

'Really?'

'The main thing that bothers me is that perhaps there was something I could have done.'

'Like what?'

'I don't know.' Jane shrugged. 'Something that would have stopped him killing himself. But then that's stupid, isn't it? It's like Richard always said: we're not here to intervene. And that's what it was, really. A Mayday conversation.'

'A pretty fucking extreme one.'

Jane sipped the wine, raising her eyebrows. 'Mmmm.'

'But there was nothing you could have done.'

'Maybe not.' There was no *maybe* about it, of course. She could possibly have rushed him while he was standing there with the knife, but who could blame her for not doing that? And she'd been gagged. There was no possibility of reasoning with him. 'But there is something I can do now. Because the police aren't taking me seriously. I'm thinking about going to the press.'

'What? Why?'

'To tell them about this other guy.'

Rachel was shaking her head, so Jane pressed the point.

'It's just like you said. What if he hurts someone else? It feels like Johnson has made me responsible for doing something about that.'

'No, no, no.' Rachel was still shaking her head. 'That's the *last* thing you should do. I mean, *think* about it, Jane.'

'Think about what?'

'Your house has been on the news, you know? Your name is out there. How do you think I knew where you lived? It took about five seconds searching online.'

Jane sipped some more of her wine. She hadn't thought of that.

'What I mean,' Rachel said, 'is that this guy could easily do that too. He knows that Johnson abducted you from your home. The papers are reporting the Mayday angle – the fact that he called you and talked about the crimes. What might he be thinking? You don't want to be drawing attention to yourself.'

Jane didn't say anything.

'It's not safe here anyway,' Rachel said, putting her glass down firmly. 'You can't stay here.'

'I don't have anywhere else to go.'

Rachel stared at her for a few seconds, exasperated, then reached out and put her hand over Jane's.

'For God's sake,' she said. 'Of course you do.'

Thirty-Two

When a bad thing happens in someone's home, the place can sometimes end up tainted as a result. That makes sense to me. Space that previously felt safe and secure has been tarnished and undermined; the warmth in the hearth goes out. And sometimes, what happens in a person's house is so serious you wonder how they *can't* move. I knew that two of our surviving victims were already resident at new addresses. Their old houses had simply become inhospitable.

'I can't afford to leave,' Sharon Hendricks told us now, as though reading my mind. 'The market's fucking collapsed, and I'm just having to hang on. Believe me, there's nothing I'd like more than to get out of here. I hate this fucking place.'

Sitting across from her in her front room, I smiled politely. Under different circumstances, either Chris or I might have pulled her up on the language, but not today. In an attempt to validate what Adam Johnson had told Jane Webster, we'd searched through the files for crimes that matched the description he'd given, and what had happened to Sharon Hendricks last year was one of the few real possibles we'd come up with. That meant raking up an event in her past I was certain she would prefer was left buried. If I were her right now, I'd probably swear too.

I knew very little about her life subsequently, only that she had left her job at Eyecatchers, the beauty shop where she used to work. She still looked like the kind of woman I'd encountered in my few forays into such places: twenty-six years old, slim, with jet-black hair, and undeniably beautiful. She was thinner – more gaunt – than she appeared in the case-file photographs, but her hair was carefully styled, and she had a serious amount of make-up on, even though she hadn't been expecting us and didn't seem to be on her way out anywhere.

But traces were visible. There was a real steel to her now; I doubted it had been as strong before. While her body language was somewhat jittery and nervous – knees together, slightly hunched, smoking constantly, her cigarette hand darting here and there – there were constant flashes of *don't mess with me* in her eyes. They came across as angry, but there was a sense of pleading there below the surface.

She spoke quickly: no mess, no nonsense.

'My father helped me with the deposit. It was only a couple of years ago, just after I finished university. We looked around together, and I loved this place the moment I saw it. You would, wouldn't you? It was supposed to be perfect. And now …' She gestured around with the cigarette. 'Well, I just fucking hate it.'

Her father. That figured. Obviously she wouldn't have been able to afford this house – a decent semi in a good neighbourhood – on her own. I'd been given grotty police housing when I started out, then saved up judiciously for my first real place, and it was nowhere near as nice as this. I tried to imagine having a parent rich enough to help me buy a house. But that was old resentments surfacing, and I reminded myself that this was hardly the time for them.

'Can't he help you out now?'

'He could, yes. He offered to.' Her face went hard at that. 'But I decided I didn't want him to.'

It was an obvious full stop on that line of conversation – and again, fair enough. As much as she hated living here, I could understand her thinking that way, that maybe she didn't want to rely on a man after what had happened, even one close to her. Not wanting to feel that power being wielded, however benign her father's intentions might be.

'So,' she said. 'This is about what he did to me?'

I nodded. 'Yes. I'm sorry.'

'Don't be. It would be good to get some closure. To know that the bastard's dead. God knows I've killed him in my head enough times. Adam Johnson. Be nice to give him a name.'

'We're just pursuing a lead right now. We don't know for sure he was involved at all. It's only a possibility.'

'So what do you want to know?'

'We've read the case file,' I said. 'But it would help to hear your own recollections of what happened that night. If that wouldn't be too painful.'

She shrugged, stubbing out her latest cigarette. Then she stood up and walked to the far end of the room – to the doorway that led into the small entrance hall. Chris and I followed her over. She gestured vaguely at the bottom of the stairs by the front door.

'This is where it happened.'

We already knew most of it.

In the hours after the attack, Sharon Hendricks was understandably distraught and had difficulty making an official statement. A clearer and more detailed account had emerged the following afternoon. Having her go through it again now, over a year later, felt cruel, but it was important. I was curious to see whether anything had changed – if she'd remembered something new.

But the story she told us now was practically identical to the one given at the time. She talked quickly, and without apparent emotion. She used the word *I*, but her tone of voice was decidedly third-person throughout, as though the events had happened to someone else. They had been locked away: memories that would now emerge only from oblique angles, or in nightmares, or spoken out loud like a story that wasn't real.

She had been on a night out with friends in the city centre. It was a works do for the beauty shop: six young women breezing from bar to bar in a cloud of perfume, buying rounds from a kitty. Sharon had chatted to several men that night, but that wasn't unusual – a group like that was bound to attract attention – and it had all been good-natured. There hadn't been any altercations or trouble, and nobody stood out in her mind as having been strange or pushy. Subsequently, all the individuals who could be identified from CCTV coverage in the bars had been eliminated from the inquiry.

At the end of the evening, Sharon took the night bus home. It was about two o'clock in the morning. There had only been two of the group left by that point, her and the manager, and they lived at opposite ends of the city. Sharon lied about having enough money for a taxi for herself, not wanting to borrow from the boss, and ended up taking the bus instead. It was very busy: lively with drunks. Again, there had been no trouble. The camera footage had been reviewed, and nothing untoward was spotted: nobody had bothered Sharon, and no male had seemed to be paying her undue attention. Other passengers had got off the bus at the same time, but her stop was also covered by CCTV, and nobody had followed Sharon as she headed up the hill that led to her street.

The walk took her along a winding road at the bottom of the field opposite her house. It was dark and quiet, but there were little cottages on the left-hand side, and the area was well lit. She'd walked it countless times, she said, so it felt safe to her. And it was.

As she approached her house, Sharon didn't glance at the field, which would have been pitch-black at that time. Keys in hand, last drink a way behind her, she was distracted: already thinking about what might be in the fridge for a snack when she got in. She walked up the short path that led to her front door, unlocked and opened it, and that was when he attacked her.

'He pushed me forwards,' she said. If anything, she sounded even calmer now. 'I remember that clearly: that it wasn't like in the movies. When someone gets picked up with a hand over their mouth? I've noticed that since, and they always get pulled backwards slightly. Always kick their heels a bit and scream. But it was more like a rugby tackle. And I didn't have a chance to scream. I didn't even know what had happened. He pretty much smashed me straight through the front door.'

I glanced out of the front room window at the field opposite. There were trees there, close to the road, and a man could easily have been lurking behind one, all but invisible in the dark. Just waiting for an opportunity. Finding one. I imagined him sprinting, quick and silent, across the street, then barrelling her inside. Sharon was a tiny woman. She wouldn't have stood much of a chance against an average man, never mind one the size of Adam Johnson.

If it was him.

'I was stunned by it. But I do remember. He was very calm and controlled. He just closed the door behind him, and put the chain on.'

She paused. For the first time, she looked upset.

'And then?' I asked gently.

'And then ... by then, I'd stood up. He was big. Dressed all in black, and he had some kind of mask on.' She made a circular motion in front of her face. 'I made to move to try to get into the front room, but he punched me in the face. I'd never been hit like that before.'

The blow had spun her around, so that she'd landed face first on the stairs. The man had then continued to assault her, punching her in the arms and sides, along with blows against the back of her head. He'd repeatedly grabbed her hair and smashed her face into the rough fabric of the carpet. At some point, he landed a far more focused and deliberate blow to the side of her head, which had rendered her unconscious.

'I woke up after a bit. I don't know how long I was out for. But the man was gone. The chain was off and the door was open a bit. I couldn't believe it. I sat there for a while, just shaking. Because it wasn't real.'

She took a deep breath.

'But then, yeah. It turned out it was.'

I wanted to give her a few moments to compose herself, but Chris had already taken the photograph from the back of his notebook.

'Do you recognise this man?'

Sharon looked at it and nodded.

'It's the man from the news. Obviously.'

'What I meant is—

'No, I don't recognise him from that night. I already told you. He was wearing a mask. Do you think I haven't watched the TV and thought about it? I think about it *every single day and night.*'

'I'm sorry,' I said.

'Don't be.' She looked at me. '*I'm* sorry I can't be any more help. I wish I could.'

'You've got nothing to apologise for.'

'I try not to think about it, but sometimes I can't stop myself. He seemed to hate me so much.' She took out a cigarette and lit it, her hands shaking slightly. 'I remember thinking the same thing that night too, while he was hitting me. *What have I done to make this man hate me?*'

'What do you reckon?' Chris said.

'I reckon you should let me show people photographs in future.'

'Okay. But do you think this is the attack Johnson was talking about?'

'I don't know.' I sighed. 'I just don't know.'

We were standing on the street behind Sharon Hendricks' house, looking up the back garden towards the rear of the property. There was a low fence: easy to get over. There was a triangle of washing lines further up the garden. A security light over the back door.

'It fits with his story,' I said.

'It does.'

'But there are differences from the other crimes.'

'Similarities, too.'

I nodded. Sharon Hendricks was definitely our man's *type*, the level of violence was comparable, and nobody had been arrested for the attack, which suggested to me it had been committed by a stranger – someone the original investigating officers had been unable to connect to Hendricks. But all our official victims had been woken in the night and attacked in their beds. The doors were found locked, with just that single window open. And our victims had been raped, whereas there had been no obvious sexual element here.

At the same time, those discrepancies still fitted with Adam Johnson's story. The *monster* wouldn't have had access to Johnson's keys at that point, so would have needed to either break or force his way in. And it was possible that, having subdued Sharon, the man had gone to get a drink from the kitchen, spotted Johnson halfway up the back garden, and immediately left the scene.

I stared up the garden towards the back of the house, imagining that.

It was possible. It did fit.

Chris said, 'Of course, just because Johnson got the details right, it doesn't mean he was telling the truth, does it? Doesn't mean this other guy actually exists. It could have been Johnson that did it. The other guy – the monster – could still be a total invention.'

'True.'

He was right. Whether the assault on Sharon Hendricks was linked to our series was one question. But even if it was, we still had no evidence for the involvement of a second individual. As things stood, all we had was Johnson's testimony, and second-hand at that.

I stared at the back of the house for a while longer, thinking about the ways our surviving victims had described their attacker. The size of him. The terror. The hate coming off him in waves. And the way the crimes had been escalating. *A safety valve*, I'd suggested to Drake, when he'd asked why this possible second man would tell Johnson everything. But of course, if that were true, the man would now have lost that along with access to the keys.

The other guy – the monster – could still be a total invention.

'I hope so,' I said.

Thirty-Three

Unlike Sharon Hendricks, I had absolutely no intention of moving out of my house. Equally, though, I had no desire to stay there in its current state.

After the scene had been released, I'd organised for a professional crime-scene cleaning operation to come in and scrub all traces of Adam Johnson's presence from the bedroom. Brand-new sheets and curtains had been ordered, along with a new bed and chest of drawers. Several floorboards would also be taken up and replaced. But all that would take time, and until the work was completed, I'd moved myself, a few basic possessions and the cats into John's old house.

That was where I drove to after work that day, and even though Hendricks and the possible second man remained on my mind, I stood in the garden for a time and stared down the hill towards the estate, picking the waste ground out from between the surrounding buildings. It was totally deserted this evening, and yet even from a distance, it unnerved me. The sight of it brought the images and feelings from my nightmare out into the real world. The fast-moving clouds. The wraithlike figure. The sense that *something awful is coming*.

But I still had no idea what that something was.

And why was that the case? Because I always woke up before it happened. I wondered about that now. I'd always assumed it was the nightmare that did it – that whatever happened next was simply too terrifying for my sleeping mind to endure. But thinking about it, maybe that wasn't the case. Maybe it was me that woke myself up. Not because the truth was frightening in itself, but because I was too afraid to find out what it was. Because deep down, perhaps, I didn't want to.

The conversation I'd had with John in the hospice came back to me now. I'd told him that death would either be wonderful, or else it would be like nothing at all. And what had he said in reply?

Maybe tonight I'll stay asleep and find out.

I stared down at that empty waste ground for a little while longer, and as I went back inside, I thought to myself:

Yes.

Maybe tonight I will.

I dreamed of other things at first: regular dreams, interspersed with long stretches of blankness. My sleep kept breaking, but every time I drifted back off again, I willed the nightmare to arrive.

Let's do this. Come on.

And sometime close to dawn, it did.

It turned out that the regular waking had been fortuitous, because it blurred the edge between states, and I was still thinking clearly, convinced I was awake, when I realised the waste ground was in front of me. The familiar jolt of panic went through me, but I had the presence of mind now to dampen it down. The membranes were too thin at the moment, and if I got scared, or didn't concentrate on the scene in front of me, I knew I'd immediately find myself back in the bed. Normally, that would have been a blessing. Tonight, I wanted to see.

So keep calm.

It was easier said than done, but the additional awareness helped. I forced myself to look at the scene before me, amazed – even slightly awed – by the level of detail my sleeping mind was conjuring up. The strangeness aside, it was indistinguishable from reality. The only differences were those fast-moving clouds and the strange green-blue colour of the sky – and the figure, of course, hanging there ominously in the centre of the waste ground. As always, it was grey and ragged and sketchy, as though scribbled on to the scene in pencil. And it was very obviously being held in place for now, leashed there in this moment of frozen time.

As the rushing sensation began to build, I told myself:

There's nothing to be frightened of.

Except I didn't think that was true, and I suddenly wanted to escape. It was a strong urge – one I had to fight – and I knew I'd been right, and that it was why I always woke up.

It's just a dream.

But it wasn't. Something awful was coming, and I felt the terror of that running through me. *Get out of here*, my mind was telling me. *What are you doing? I've spent so long hiding this from you: protecting you from it; keeping it secure and out of sight. You shouldn't be here. Get out now.*

The clouds were moving faster and faster, and the rush in the air was louder than I ever remembered it being. The sense of impending velocity was reaching its pitch. On other nights, I must have—

Get out now.

I desperately wanted to, but I would never have a better chance than this. As I watched the grey figure on the waste ground, it seemed to be gaining substance. Its edges were shivering now. If I'd stared at it any longer, I might have woken up, so instead I looked up at that oddly coloured sky, that strange mixture of blue and green. The bright clouds were moving across it as quickly as I'd ever seen them, but they didn't seem to be accelerating any more. The nightmare had reached a tipping point and balanced there. I stared and stared, but everything remained in place. Nothing else was happening.

You don't want to know, my mind told me.

And that mattered, I realised. It was both the reason behind all this – the explanation for why it only emerged here in my dreams – and the key to unlocking it. I watched the clouds for a few moments longer, weighing all the competing impulses inside, and then I made my decision, for good or for bad.

I want to know.

Immediately the rushing noise ceased.

The clouds were suddenly still, but for a second or two that odd colour remained, permeating the world. Then the blueness above began to intensify steadily, as the other colour faded and the sky began returning to normal. In my ears I heard birdsong, and then I felt the warmth of a summer sun on my upturned face.

Very slowly, I lowered my gaze.

The figure remained frozen where it was, but it had become solid now, and it was no longer grey. As the green drained from the sky above, it was coalescing in the person hanging in mid-step on the waste ground, rendering her increasingly distinctive. Already I recognised her, and I also knew who the scarred woman at the Packhorse really was. She wasn't older than me at all. She just looked it because of whatever had happened to her.

When the colouring was complete, the girl in the bright green coat finally began moving again, quickly and purposefully. But not towards me. Instead she was heading away across the waste ground, towards the embankment and the path and the thicket of trees it led through.

I tried to move, but I couldn't, and then I tried to wake up, but it was as though my mind had decided that I'd made my choice and could live with the consequences.

Don't! I screamed as the girl in the bright green coat reached the embankment.

There was no way she could hear me, of course, not here and not now, but I shouted it anyway.

Jemima, don't!

Thirty-Four

The dream remained vivid after I woke the next morning: I still had that clear mental image of Jemima walking away from me across the waste ground. But however hard I thought about it, there was no real-life memory to anchor it to. I couldn't remember ever seeing her walk away from me like that, and I had no idea what had happened to her afterwards. Not yet, anyway.

But my head was full of other memories, and they played over and over as I showered and dressed. I drove to work early, in a kind of daze the whole way.

I remembered the night of our attempted burglary of the Paladin, and how Sylvie had torn into Jemima about her coat and her attitude. Jem had always been a figure of fun in our gang, and I found myself wondering now if some nasty little part of me had even been glad it was her that was Sylvie's target that evening, rather than me. I didn't like to think that might be true, but how could I be sure? It was the kind of emotion you could easily airbrush out of your past, if all you cared about was keeping it a pretty picture.

After that incident, we'd both separated ourselves away from the group. For Jem, that had happened almost immediately; she had never been cut out for Sylvie's kind of behaviour, not really. It had been a more gradual transition for me, though, so I was able to observe first-hand how Sylvie's derision for Jem only intensified. She never stopped being that figure of fun. Once she was outside the group, all that really changed was that it became more malicious – the bullying more overt and cruel. She never made any new friends that I knew of, and the rest of her school days were spent isolated and alone, hardly daring to show her face on the estate. To the extent that I remembered her at all, she was always hurried and huddled. Always trying to make herself invisible, to get from one place to another without being noticed.

It was different for me. I didn't make any new friends either, but I didn't want or need to. I'd always been happy enough with my own company anyway, but now I was keeping my head down, working as hard as I could: focused on making something of myself and escaping the traction of Thornton. In reality, I was only ever the vaguest of targets for Sylvie and her circle of friends. Leaving the group removed any protection they might have given me, but there was still something about me that kept Sylvie at a distance, shy of actual confrontation. They left me alone.

But I recognised the danger. I knew how easily that could change. So it wasn't just the desire to be alone that caused me to blank Jemima Field in the school corridors, and to shut down her attempts at conversation on the few occasions they occurred. It was mainly the fact that she had trouble written all over her – and by association, I would have too. I didn't want that kind of attention. And anyway, if I could survive on my own, why couldn't she?

Why couldn't she?

I was thinking about all of that as I pulled into the department's car park. There was a sense of dread about what was to come, and I sat in the car for a minute, preparing myself. But I was halfway there, and had to finish. While I still couldn't remember what had happened to Jem, the file would be there to read. I had no choice now but to do so.

It was still early. The incident room was completely vacant, and walking in provided a stark contrast to the twenty-four-hour flurry of activity of the last few months. It wasn't just the lack of people, but also the files, which had been collated and organised, and were now neatly stacked and tied ready for storage. The investigation technically remained live, but after Johnson's death, many of the seconded officers had returned to their original postings. Some would be in later, but there was nothing to justify or occupy a round-the-clock presence any more. For a short while, I would have the place to myself.

I dumped my bag on the desk, and felt a slight tingle in the air as I took off my jacket. The ghost of the case, perhaps. But no, it was mostly Jemima. As I turned on the computer and opened the database, I was steeling myself for what I was going to find.

The file only took a moment to load, and then there it was, right in front of me, a seventeen-year-old investigation. I began reading.

Oh God.

I *had* known this, I realised, somewhere deep inside me. Because flickers of it came back to me as I read. They were as indistinct as sudden memories of a long-forgotten dream, but they were there.

You knew this.

It had been 8.14 p.m. on a Saturday evening when Jemima was found lying in the small patch of woodland, known locally as the Edith Copse, which lay on the far side of the embankment, separating the waste ground from the school and shops beyond. That evening, a man named Joe Gardener had been taking the footpath and spotted what he thought was a girl's body between the trees. Police and ambulance crews had been on the scene within minutes.

She wasn't dead, of course, but in some ways it was a miracle. The file included photographs of her injuries, taken at the hospital, and even across a distance of years I could hardly bear to look at them. She barely resembled a human being any more. But at the same time she was somehow still recognisable as the girl who had once been my friend. The girl I'd pushed away and turned my back on. I forced myself to look at the photos anyway, and as I did, I found myself remembering her shy smile, and how kind and sweet she had been. A promising athlete.

I'm so sorry, Jem.

I read on.

Following emergency surgery, Jemima had been in a coma for two weeks, and then remained in rehabilitative care for over a year. On the evening in question, she had been severely beaten and raped. It was unclear exactly how long the ordeal had lasted, but it had culminated in an act of attempted murder, when the perpetrators dropped a paving slab on her head. It had been found at the scene, still angled between the ground and what was left of her face. There were separate photographs of the slab, of course, and it was obvious just from looking at it why the report suggested more than one attacker. One person on their own, however strong, would have struggled to lift it.

I stared at the slab, thinking of Jemima as I'd seen her in the Packhorse, looking a good two decades older than she should have, with a scar that seemed to divide off the top quarter of her face. An eye that was pink and blind. This was what had caused it: an ugly piece of concrete that had left her skull in pieces and her life in ruins. She had been walking into the pub with an elderly woman – her mother, I presumed – which meant that both of them must be resident on the Thornton estate. And that seemed the cruellest aspect of it: that after all these years, they still had to live in the place where it had happened. At school, Jem had always seemed like a girl who would manage to escape eventually. But no. In the end, the place had done what it so often did. Destroyed someone and kept them.

Of course, I knew it wasn't really Thornton that had done that. The estate was just run-down buildings and people, and none of them were all that different or worse than you'd find in many other places. It was *specific* people who had done this to Jem. I scrolled through now to find their names.

Already knowing deep down what I'd find.

Ben MacKenzie – a cousin of Sylvie's, one I'd never met – had actually been arrested *before* Jemima was found. He'd entered

Swaine's off-licence just before eight o'clock that evening, and the manager had called the police based on his appearance and behaviour. MacKenzie was dishevelled, acting erratically, and there was blood on his clothing. Five other people waiting outside were then detained at the scene. It didn't surprise me to see Sylvie's name amongst them, although I didn't recognise any of the others. Even Nat, apparently, had bailed on the group by that point.

It was later established that the six of them had spent most of the previous two days drinking and taking drugs, drifting from house to pub to house. Several other reported confrontations subsequently came to light, but nobody had phoned the police at the time. Nobody wanted the trouble. I racked my brain now, wondering if I'd seen anything, but if I had, I couldn't remember it. I read on. Late that afternoon, the group had ended up in the Edith Copse, where the binge continued, reaching its climax when Jemima (*don't*, I thought suddenly, seventeen years too late) had taken that short cut to the shops and crossed paths with them. And this time, the natural athlete hadn't had the chance to run.

Ben MacKenzie and the two other men present were sentenced to twelve years each. The three girls each received eight. Jemima was eighteen at the time. Even if her attackers had served their whole sentences, the last of them would have been free five years ago. I wondered if she ever encountered any of them in the Packhorse, or around the estate.

Christ.

I scrolled back through.

The only explanation for the nightmare was that I'd known what had happened to Jem and suppressed it. The awful thing I'd always felt coming for me had simply been the truth about that. But even now, the memories wouldn't come. I cast my mind back, but the date of the attack was meaningless to me. I would have been eighteen then too, and looking forward to heading off to university in a couple of months, but the day itself didn't stand out in my memory. I hadn't seen her that day – I was sure I would remember now if I had. Perhaps that was why I was never really present in the nightmare.

But I did know something. All I could think was that I must have learned what had happened, flashed on that image, and then immediately frozen it. *Don't think about it.* Back then, I had been so single-minded, so determined, so selfish. No distractions. No guilt. I was looking forward to university, pulling myself up and out, and wouldn't have wanted to think about anybody else.

You've got to do everything by yourself, haven't you?

Yes. And yet the truth was that I hadn't. John had given me a hand up, but even back then, I'd been too arrogant to acknowledge it. And I'd already become too dismissive and self-oriented to extend one of my own downwards. I could have been Jemima's friend and stuck up for her. I could have made things easier – or even, in some small way, helped to pull her up and out with me. But I didn't. That wasn't the type of person I was back then, and it wasn't me now either. I'd never been as good a person as John. Maybe it wouldn't have made a difference to Jemima if I had. But maybe it would.

I stared at the screen for a while longer, feeling a mixture of emotions. After a little while, it was the guilt and shame that won out.

Maybe it would.

Thirty-Five

When Jane woke up, she had no idea where she was. Her body felt cramped and awkward, the muscles in her legs were aching, and she didn't recognise the room around her. It sent an immediate jolt of panic through her: a flashback to her abduction. *Tied up on the back seat of a car.* She scrambled into a sitting position.

Then she remembered. Of course, Rachel's house. She was on the settee in the girl's cluttered front room. Rachel had offered to top and tail in her bed, but for some reason Jane had preferred to sleep down here instead. The blanket Rachel had given her was tangled away at the back of the sofa. Evidently the heat of the night just past had caused Jane to fight it off.

She sat there for a few moments in her pyjamas, rubbing her eyes and waiting for her heart rate to slow. Then she yawned, and stretched her arms to ease some of the tension from her muscles. Rachel was already up, and in the kitchen. Jane could hear her whistling through there as a kettle boiled. She presumed it had been Rachel getting up and passing through the room that had woken her.

Another flashback then. As well as the physical discomfort of the night, there had been bad dreams. The earlier ones had already vanished, but she remembered the most recent one clearly. There had been a phone ringing, and she didn't want to answer it because she knew it would be *him* on the other end. Adam Johnson. Calling to tell her in grotesque detail about something he had done, or was pretending to. There had been someone else there with her – Zoe, she thought – telling her with increasing urgency that she needed to take the call, that she had to, that it was very important. And the phone wouldn't stop ringing, so eventually she did as she was told and picked up the receiver.

It wasn't Johnson. At first, in fact, it didn't sound like there was anyone there at all, and yet the silence seemed too heavy for the line to be entirely empty. After listening for a few seconds, Jane thought she detected faint breathing, and then something that might have been a faraway voice, or the ghost of one. She couldn't make out any words, but there was somehow the idea of them.

Jane didn't say anything; she simply listened. After a few moments, she heard a second voice on the line. And then another. And then another. None of them were any more audible than the first, and they all seemed to be saying different things, but despite that, they somehow began to coalesce into a whole: a single voice, made from all the overlapping words being spoken and the gaps in between. It was still too quiet for Jane to make out what was being said, but she could tell it was a woman speaking: a single voice that was struggling to form itself from the combined static of the others.

'Coffee?' Rachel asked brightly, leaning around the door frame from the kitchen.

Jane rubbed her eyes again.

'Mmmm. Yes please.' She was a little hungover, but not half as catastrophically as she'd expected. 'Morning, by the way.'

'It is, you're right. Sorry: I didn't mean to wake you. I was going to try sneaking out in a few minutes and just leaving you with a note and a spare key.'

'I'm glad you didn't.'

Rachel came through washed and dressed for university, her cheeks still warm and red from the shower. She was carrying the cup of coffee with both hands, fingers splayed around the top and base so that Jane could take the handle.

'Thanks.'

'No worries.'

She retreated, then came back a moment later with her own cup, shoving the rolled-up blanket to one side and perching on the opposite end of the settee from Jane.

'Sleep okay?'

'Oh, probably as well as I could hope.'

They chatted for a bit, making small talk as they sipped their drinks. It was just after eight o'clock. Rachel had supervisions to handle from nine until the middle of the afternoon, and would be back around five. She told Jane that she was welcome to do whatever she wanted in the meantime: hang around and work here; let herself out; *whatever*. Then she gave her the spare key and asked whether she'd be staying over tonight too.

'Because it's totally not a problem if so.'

'I don't know,' Jane said. 'I might need to pop home to pick up a few things whatever I do.'

'Yeah, that's cool. But you're welcome, is all I'm saying. And … well, you know what I think.'

'That it would be a good idea.'

'Yeah. At least for a few days.'

'Okay.' Jane smiled. 'I'll see. Thank you.'

'It's cool. Make yourself at home.' Rachel stood up and stretched on her tiptoes, holding her empty cup out to one side. 'You'll be able to find anything you need. If not, just give me a bell.'

Make yourself at home.

It wasn't something Jane was used to, imposing on others, and it went against her instincts. But Rachel sounded like she meant it, and as though she'd actually be disappointed if Jane felt too awkward to accept. They were friends, after all, Jane reminded herself. If the situation had been reversed, she would have said the same things to Rachel, and felt the same way.

After the girl had gone, Jane showered and dressed, then made herself some more coffee. There was bread and eggs in the fridge, so she cooked up some scrambled eggs on toast.

Afterwards, she washed everything up, dried it, and put it away in the cabinets and drawers. Polished the counter, as well. It seemed the least she could do.

Then she unpacked her laptop and organised her notes for the translation she was supposed to be working on. With the events of the past few days, the project had fallen behind. She made some progress now, but the time dragged and her attention kept wandering. It was hard to concentrate here. There was too much of a sense of *displacement*, and it wasn't entirely down to the unfamiliar surroundings. It felt like there was something else she *needed* to be doing but was subconsciously avoiding. It brought back the urgency of the dream. Zoe's voice. *Answer the phone, Jane. It's so important.*

She set the laptop to one side on the settee and tried to think. It was Johnson, of course, nagging at her. The police weren't taking what he'd told her seriously, but despite the fact that he'd lied to her in the phone calls, she believed that in Zoe's bedroom he'd finally been telling the truth. And if that was the case, this other man – *the monster* – was still out there somewhere.

So what was she supposed to do?

Stay here for ever?

Her instinct had always been to leave things to other people to deal with. To not interfere. To not get in the way. But she wasn't the same person now, was she? She was stronger. While her father's *you can't do this* was still there, it had gradually slipped as far away as the voices in last night's dream. In reality, there was nothing stopping her from doing whatever she wanted.

Just look, then.

What harm can it do?

She picked up the laptop again and minimised the windows that were open for the translation work, then opened the web browser. *Make yourself at home*, Rachel had said, so she checked around the back of the television, finding a tall black box with pale blue lights running down the side. She could tilt it enough to see the label on the back, and read the password for the wireless. It wasn't like Rachel was going to mind.

She spent the next hour searching for information online. The attack Adam Johnson had talked about *must* have been mentioned in the media, because that was how he'd learned about it, but she had no real idea where to look. She started with the websites for the local papers, using the search boxes to find any story that might be relevant. All she knew was the little that Johnson had told her, and she wasn't sure how trustworthy her memory was, so she stuck to the key facts. Woman. Assaulted. Home. And it would be a story from sometime last year.

The immediate problem she had was that the keywords were too vague. Or rather, that the number of stories they applied to was absurdly high. Using just those simple terms produced pages and pages of results.

Painstakingly, she checked each article. The more she read, the more she felt herself growing numb from the accumulation of detail. Most of the reports were cases of domestic violence: petty squabbles that had escalated, with a few serious assaults scattered amongst them. But several were more disturbing: a woman and child who had been inexplicably killed by her partner; a revenge attack by a woman's jealous ex-lover, who had thrown bleach in her face; a woman beaten, then shoved from the fifth-floor balcony of a block of flats, all in the presence of her daughter.

The worst thing was that Jane couldn't remember even *hearing* about most of the cases. They had all taken place over the last eighteen months, and had clearly made the news, but she hadn't taken them in. Laid bare by the search terms now, the extent of the violence was shocking. After nearly an hour, she was almost ready to give up. There had only been a handful of articles that might have fitted the description Johnson had given, but in each case someone had already been arrested. While it was possible that the police had got the wrong man, it seemed unlikely. The attacker she was looking for would still be out there.

Just a couple more.

And then she found it. There was no way of knowing for certain that this was the one, but a tingle crossed the skin of her back as she saw the headline – WESTFIELD WOMAN ASSAULTED IN HOME – and then read the article that followed.

She stared at the screen, trying to extract more detail from the small number of lines, and failing. She opened a new window to do some follow-up searches on the same incident, but there was nothing: no mention of the assailant having been caught, and no further information on the victim, or what had happened to her since.

She returned to the original article and read it again.

The details fitted. The age of the victim. The time of night. An attacker who didn't appear to have been caught. And the vague address and the place of work would have given Johnson enough information to recognise the woman from the report.

So now what?

Go to the police? She wished she could, but this wasn't going to be enough. It wasn't like they were amateurs. Presumably, at some point in their investigation, they would have examined this case and discounted it for some reason. Perhaps it hadn't appeared similar enough: just one more assault on a woman in her home with nothing obvious to connect it. Whatever their reasoning, she was positive they would know about it already. At the same time, there wasn't much here to pursue on her own.

God.

Are you actually *thinking of doing that?*

She leaned back on the settee, closing her eyes. Searching online was one thing; it would be another entirely to follow up on this herself. The laptop jittered slightly on her thighs, the underside warm against her legs. Was she really going to do that?

After a moment, she thought: *Yes.*

Yes, I am.

She opened her eyes and read the article for the third time. Not much to go on, it was true. Cragg Road in Westfield. She'd never been there before, but she could find it easily enough. Then what? Knock on every door and ask about this woman? Not totally out of the question, but hardly appealing.

Eyecatchers Beauty, though. That was surely a better option.

Are you actually—

She cut the voice off. Enough with it. She would keep moving forward, one step at a time, just as her therapist had told her. Because one step at a time, when you knew you could stop at any moment and yet didn't, was what got you where you wanted to be. It was the way to approach every challenge.

Jane returned to Google and began typing.

Thirty-Six

It was possible to drive for a short distance along the towpath of the city's canal, but not as far as we needed to go, so with a good half-mile still between us and the scene, Chris parked up in a large turning space by Horsley lock. The tyres crackled slowly on the crumbly ground as he manoeuvred us in behind the two police vans already present.

The side of one of them was open, and an officer was sitting on the sill drinking coffee. As we got out of the car, he stood up and walked towards us.

'Morning, sir.'

Chris nodded by way of reply.

I closed the car door. The sound echoed, but didn't seem to go anywhere. Aside from the trickle of the water in the lock, it was deathly quiet here. On this side of the canal, there were two huge metal containers, like something you'd see being loaded on to a ship. A short way behind us, a black metal bridge spanned the water, and on the far side a lush field dotted with yellow dandelions sloped gently up to the first trees of the woods, where a footpath disappeared into the shade. Officers were stationed at the entrance to the woods, and also directly on the far side of the bridge. Not doing anything for the moment: just helping to secure this end of the two-mile stretch of towpath that had been sealed off this morning.

Under different circumstances, it might have been idyllic, but knowing what awaited us further on, the silence seemed too heavy, and the tranquillity of the scene an illusion. The hush felt more like one of shock than peace.

I joined Chris and the officer, who was gesturing vaguely over his shoulder, further down the canal. It was blocked off by a triangular metal gate, strapped across with more police tape. I interrupted whatever he was saying.

'We know where we're going.'

'Of course, ma'am. Morning.'

'Isn't it just.'

What had been done to Jemima remained in my thoughts, but I'd had to put it to one side for the moment, after the news of what had happened out here. It made me feel even more guilty – it was just like when I'd pushed her out of my mind in the past – but I was determined that this time would be different. When this case was closed for good, I was going to do something, even if I didn't know what yet. But in the meantime I needed to concentrate on this.

On the possibility that the monster really was still out there.

Beyond the lock, the water was flat and still, perfectly reflecting the bright blue sky, and I watched as a swan and cygnets sailed slowly along by the far bank, small ripples spreading backwards. The trees there were close to the edge, the beginning of the woods that lay directly behind Adam Johnson's cottage. His former home was less than a mile away.

I glanced behind me at the footpath. On the journey here, I'd studied a map of the area. That path snaked up the sloping land, between the trees, until it emerged on the Horsley road, directly at the side of Johnson's house.

It could be a coincidence, of course.

'Pathologist on site?' I said.

'Yes, ma'am. Sam Dale.'

'Right.'

I took a deep breath, thinking of Johnson's second man, the *monster*. But we couldn't know anything for sure right now, not until we'd attended the scene.

'Let's go and see her.'

We encountered other officers as we walked, along with SOCOs in bright white uniforms who were combing the tree line to the side of the towpath. The land fell away quickly on this side: steep embankments, thick with coils of undergrowth, leading down to factories and construction sites below. There were flatter stretches, where we passed wooden benches, and at one point we came close to the thick metal struts of a pylon, wired off from the path in a square of overgrown brambles. The only sound was the electricity buzzing ominously in the air.

'God, it's desolate here,' Chris said.

I nodded, although that impression was partly due to the circumstances. Normally the footpath would have been much busier than this, and would probably have seemed more friendly, more welcoming. The canal threaded through the suburbs and then out into the country, and it was a popular route for walkers and cyclists. Never exactly crowded, but you wouldn't have felt threatened or isolated at any point on the route. There would always be other people around. Today, though, desolate was the right word.

Because of the way the canal curled and straightened, we saw the scene a good minute before we reached it. A hundred metres ahead, a white tent had been erected over the footpath, with just enough space for people to move around it. The area was teeming with officers, and a dive team were in the canal to the side. From this distance, they looked like seals bobbing in the water. The SOCOs stood out against the trees, bent over and moving steadily, searching the nearby undergrowth.

Neither of us spoke as we approached. Jemima aside, I imagined Chris was thinking much the same as I was. The proximity of this scene to Adam Johnson's house. Too much of a coincidence.

Sam Dale edged out of the tent as we reached it.

'Gentleman,' he said. 'And lady. How are we doing this morning?'

'We've been better,' I said.

'You could be worse, believe me.' Dale glanced back behind him. 'Yes indeed, you could. Oh look, here comes the not-so-good sergeant.'

The officer in provisional charge of the scene joined us from the other side of the tent. DS Gregory Timms was old and a bit fussy, but a good officer, and I was glad he'd been out of earshot for Dale's reproach. Timms knew us well enough to be aware that we wouldn't be poaching the investigation off him if we didn't have to – and also, that we really wouldn't want to. Like the rest of us, Timms wanted it all to be over. For Adam Johnson to have been the end of it.

'Greg,' I said. 'What have you got?'

'Zoe, Chris.' He sighed. 'A headache, to be honest. And an upset stomach. Victim is a young girl – well, early twenties, at an estimate. It looks like her name is Amanda Jarman. We found ID in a handbag over there in the trees, along with some of her clothing.'

He gestured to the far side of the tent. The trees were further away from the path up there: a semicircle of grass with another of the wooden benches. A thin path wound back through the wood, out of sight. It made me think of Jemima again.

'You think that's where the attack took place?'

'Yeah, it looks pretty certain. There's a small clearing in the trees.'

'A copse.'

'Yeah, I guess. Anyway, it's covered overhead, and you wouldn't see it from the path. That's where we found some of her things. There's a lot of blood in the undergrowth too.'

'So why move her body to the path?'

'He didn't. He dragged her out and put her in the water.'

'Ah.'

'Right,' Timms said. 'Tell me about it. I have no idea why he did it. He covered the body up a fair bit with foliage, so it wasn't like he wanted it to be found, but he wasn't exactly hiding it either. Maybe he was trying to erase evidence.'

Dale glanced at the canal dubiously.

'Maybe he was trying to improve the water quality.'

'That's nice, Dale.' Timms shóok his head. 'A walker noticed her first thing. It was impossible to miss her, really.'

Between them, Timms and Dale filled us in on what appeared to have happened. From a preliminary examination, Dale estimated she'd been in the water for several hours, and he thought it likely she was dead when she went in. Coupled with the fact that it was unlikely that her killer had brought the body here, the evidence pointed to her walking along here sometime last night or early evening; her assailant had been waiting on the bench, or possibly back in the tree line, and had grabbed her as she went past.

'There's evidence of sexual assault.'

'Getting her into the water would have been tricky,' I said.

'Why? Because of passing traffic?'

'Yeah. It would have taken a bit of time. We might get lucky there.'

Timms said, 'Someone would have come forward by now.'

'Only if they saw it directly. He would have checked the path was clear first, so it's possible someone saw *that*, and wouldn't necessarily have reported it. Yet.'

Dale was frowning.

'Another possibility is that he might have sat with her for a while, back there in the trees. Maybe waited until the early hours. Much less busy then.'

'That's a dismal thought.'

But he was right, and I closed my eyes for a moment, imagining it: picturing him cross-legged at the side of a small clearing, a woman's body lying in the centre. Maybe calming himself down after what he'd done. Waiting. It was an odd scenario, though, because it implied caution, but what had he done afterwards? Made a poor attempt to hide her body in the water. The crime was a strange mixture of thought and non-thought, organisation and carelessness, as though the killer had been clear-headed one moment and lost the next.

I opened my eyes and looked at the tent.

'Can we see her?'

'Of course.'

Not that I wanted to. As we approached the closed flap of the tent, my mind pulled out a memory of Sally Vickers, lying bloodied and stuffed down the side of her bed. And then of Jemima's face in the hospital. Preparing myself for comparable horrors, I lifted the flap and stepped into the unpleasant heat of the tent, holding it open for Chris behind me.

The body of Amanda Jarman had been retrieved from the canal and laid carefully face down on a sheet on the ground. Her head was turned to one side. The single eye I could see was completely closed, and her jaw was dislocated and distended below the ear. Patches of her scalp had been ripped bare. There was little blood, of course – the water had taken care of that – but in some way that made the injuries appear even more abhorrent and alien.

The white blouse she was wearing had been reduced to clingfilm, covered with detritus from the canal – weeds and leaves – but she was naked from the waist down. One hand rested close to her face, two of the fingers clearly swollen and broken.

I tried, somehow, to view her remains dispassionately.

'What do you think?' Chris said quietly.

'I don't know. It looks like our guy, doesn't it?'

'Yes.'

'And we're close to Johnson's house.' I stared at the inside wall of the tent. 'That's an enormous coincidence.'

'Even if Johnson was telling the truth and the second man does exist, there's no reason to think he lives nearby.'

'Well, he would have to have encountered Johnson *somewhere* in order to have recognised him, so it makes sense for him to be local. The violence is comparable. The MO's different, what with it being an attack outdoors, but then he's lost his locksmith, hasn't he? Limited options for him now.'

Chris didn't say anything for a few moments. Then he puffed up his cheeks and blew out slowly.

'We'll need to get Jane back in as soon as we can,' I said.

'See if there's any additional detail she can give us. Something that might have come back to her.'

'Bring the Hendricks case in too.'

'Yes. Go over that again from scratch. Because if she was this guy's first, then there's got to be a connection there. Something that was missed at the time. There'll be a reason for him to target Amanda, too.' I looked back down at her. She was, or at least had been, our man's type. 'I don't think he did this just on spec. We need to move quickly.'

'Because he's escalating.'

I nodded. 'And deteriorating. He only half hid the body. He doesn't care as much any more.'

It was a bad sign. Killers often conform to certain patterns. It's not uncommon for attacks like these to increase in frequency and ferocity, as the man gradually loses his grip on reality, taking less and less care. Killers like that end with a supernova. If it was true here, then we were going to see more victims, and more quickly. It would be over soon, but not before other women died.

I stared down at Amanda Jarman for a few seconds more, then turned and walked back out of the tent into the sunlight.

Thirty-Seven

The quickest route to Amanda Jarman's house took us along the Horsley road, past Adam Johnson's cottage.

As we approached, I stared out at the playground on the right. It was empty today. While the media had retreated from the boarded-up cottage, the police tape remained, and I imagined local residents would feel uneasy bringing their children to a place so obviously tainted. *A monster lived nearby.* And perhaps one still did.

Even without him, Johnson's cottage remained an awkward, uncomfortable sight: a wedge of darkness amidst the green, sunlit surroundings. I made a mental note to have somebody check that the place was secure, but as we passed it, my thoughts remained with the playground behind. *A monster lives nearby.* There was something about it. I just couldn't work out what.

We turned down into the heart of Horsley.

The old stone cottages along the main road wore the early afternoon's sun well. With the window down, and my arm resting on the sill, we drove past the two pubs at the centre of the village, and then turned left on to the road where Amanda Jarman had lived with her husband, Michael.

Their house was a semi-detached, second from the end and a little run-down. The garage door was hanging down at an angle, and the front lawn was overgrown and untended. The other gardens in the street were pristine: trimmed crew-cut neat and bobbing with bright flowers. The neighbours probably hated the couple. But this was an affluent area, and the Jarmans were young. Presumably they'd flung their aspirations as high as their finances would allow. If the ID on the body turned out to be correct, it was as high as they ever would.

We parked beside a police car, then walked up the short path. There was a black wheelie bin beside the front door, with discarded cigarette ends on the ground around it. Presumably one of them came outside to smoke, but lacked the will to stub them out and lift the lid on the bin. There was still a faint trace of smoke in the air. Michael Jarman, then.

There was no bell, so I rapped hard on the glass door and waited. A moment later, it was opened by a woman in police uniform. I passed her my ID, and she showed us into the front room.

Michael Jarman was sitting on a threadbare settee, in a jittery, half-praying position. His elbows were on his knees, his hands knitted together in front of his face, and his feet were drumming repetitively against the exposed floorboards. Despite the time of day, it looked as though he'd only just got up: he was wearing a red and black tartan dressing gown over jeans, and his dark hair was dishevelled. Black stubble prickled his jawline. He stood up, slightly hesitantly, as though unsure whether he was allowed to, but there was an expression of hope on his face, and it broke my heart to see it there.

'Mr Jarman?' I showed my ID again. 'I'm Detective Inspector Zoe Dolan. This is my partner, DI Chris Sands.'

'Is it her?'

I started to close my eyes, only just managing to turn it into a blink instead.

'For the moment, we don't know. But we'll come to that. What have you been told?'

'Just something about them finding a body. They were asking whether Amanda had come home last night. I don't really understand what's going on.'

'Okay. Have a seat again, please. The most important thing

right now is that we get as much information as we can. I know this is upsetting, but please try to keep calm.'

'I am calm.'

He wasn't remotely calm, but he sat back down at least. I'd seen the same reaction numerous times before. It was the stage of denial in between being informed of a loss and fully comprehending it: a nebulous, vague space in which you can't be sure what's true. For now, Michael Jarman was maintaining an air of disbelief, his mind refusing to accept that this was actually happening. Soon, he was thinking, it would all be sorted out, and his world would be restored to how it was meant to be. The nightmare would be over.

'Do you have a picture of Amanda I could see?'

'Over there.' He nodded at the mantelpiece. 'There's a couple of them.'

'Thank you.'

They were at either end. The one on the left was a black-and-white photograph of the two of them with their faces pressed together, filling the frame. They were both smiling, and a city I couldn't identify stretched away far below them. A honeymoon shot, maybe. The other was a professional colour photograph from their wedding, with the pair of them in the centre and family to either side. Michael wore a straightforward black suit, while Amanda had chosen a dress with a red top and blue trimmings, like a princess in a Disney cartoon.

It was definitely her. We'd require a formal identification in due course, but I'd seen enough of the body by the canal to be sure.

I turned back round, feeling sick but trying to keep my expression neutral. The look of hope on his face threatened to derail that, so I took a seat on a chair opposite him and rubbed my hands together, trying to concentrate on them instead.

'It's not her, is it,' he said.

It wasn't a question, so I decided not to answer it directly. But there was no use in pretending, either.

'Michael, can you tell us the last time you saw Amanda?'

'Yesterday morning.' He said it immediately. Either he'd already been asked, or else he'd been preparing the answer in his head: going over everything that had happened. 'Just before she left for work.'

Chris, who was still standing, pulled out a notebook.

'What time would that have been?'

'She leaves about ten to seven. The bus into town is on the hour, so she always has to leave a bit before. If she misses it, she gets in late.' He leaned forward. 'Look, have you not contacted Abbie yet? I'm sure this is all some kind of mistake.'

'Abbie?'

He nodded emphatically.

'Abbie who?' I said.

'I don't know her surname. I mean, why would I? But Mandy works with her. They go out for drinks sometimes. That's what they did last night.'

Chris was scribbling this down, but it didn't make sense to me. If Amanda had gone out for the night with a colleague, why had she ended up at the canal?

'What does she normally do after work?'

'Comes home.' He looked confused. 'What do you mean?'

'How does she get home? Does she take the bus?'

'Mostly, yeah. Sometimes she gets off early and walks. She hates going to the gym, so that's what she does for exercise. Not that she needs to.'

For now, I didn't want to ask the obvious question. *Does she walk along the canal?* I thought I already knew what the answer would be.

'The drinks out with this Abbie. Was that prearranged?'

'Yeah, yeah. Although she forgot to tell me.'

'What do you mean?'

'She texted me after work – said how sorry she was, that it had slipped her mind.' He smiled, but there was no humour there, and it vanished quickly. He knew. 'She's got a terrible memory. Airhead, you know? That's what I always tell her. She just forgot, is all.'

'Have you still got the message?'

'Of course.'

'May I see it, please?'

'Sure.' He fumbled in the pocket of his dressing gown, then checked the screen, presumably for messages, and looked disappointed. He pressed some buttons on the phone and passed it over.

'Here.'

I read the message, which had come through at 17:48 yesterday evening.

Hi there. Sorry – totally forgot. Night out with Abbie. Will make it up to you. See you later. Love you xx

'There's another,' Jarman said. 'You just scroll up.'

'Thanks.'

I found it. The second message had come through much later, at 22:16.

Hi again babe. Bit sozzled, so probs going to carry on a bit then crash at Abbie's. Hope that's okay. Will see you tomorrow. Love you. Night night xx

I passed the phone back.

'I'm going to need you to keep those messages, please.'

'Of course. What's the matter?'

'We don't know yet.'

But I did. Amanda had been killed at the canal, and it was hard to imagine that she'd changed her mind and caught a bus, then taken her stretch of exercise, that late at night. Which meant those messages had been sent not by Amanda, but by her killer. Because he knew that if she'd been reported missing, the police might have searched the canal area before he'd had a chance to ditch the body in the water and leave the scene. There had never been drinks with Abbie. And the time difference between the messages suggested that her killer had waited with her body for several hours.

'Obviously we'll need to trace Abbie.' For my next sentence, I concentrated very hard on using the present tense. 'Where is it that Amanda works?'

'I don't know the name, sorry. I should, but I'm just not interested in that stuff. Amanda's obsessed, but she's beautiful without it, you know? All that make-up stuff. But it makes her happy. Has done since she was a kid.'

Which made me think about the playground again. *Has done since she was a kid.* Kids go to playgrounds, I thought. And the second man, the monster, had to have encountered Johnson somewhere. Kids go to playgrounds. Who do they go with? They go with their parents...

And then I caught what he'd just said.

'Amanda works with make-up?'

'Yeah, one of those places in town.'

I felt a tingle. Sharon Hendricks had worked in beauty. None of the other victims had. But then these were the only two victims the monster had picked out himself.

'How long has she worked there?'

'Oh, I don't know. Not long. A few months. What's the name? God, why don't I know this stuff? I should *know* this about her.'

I knew, though. I leaned forward. 'It's—'

'Eyecatchers.' He turned back to me suddenly, pleased with himself. 'That's it. Eyecatchers.'

Thirty-Eight

Eyecatchers Beauty was a small boutique built into the ground-floor corner of a larger shopping arcade. It was a plush area of the city centre, and the building itself was grand: constructed from sleek black marble flecked with grey, and separated from its neighbours by tiled pedestrian walkways dotted with fountains and seating areas for the cafés, tea rooms and bistros that lined the sides. Every unit here was either a high-end chain or a small bespoke company: hand-made cards and trinkets sitting next door to designer fashion.

Jane parked up opposite.

The pavements were busy with people: women clearly on shopping expeditions, carrying bags in awkward bunches; groups of students meandering; businessmen weaving through, phones pressed to their heads. All the sunlit tables were occupied. Jane hated busy cafés, the kinds of places where you had to queue for a spot and then spend twenty minutes pressed in between strangers, simply because it was the place to be. *Let's go in there, it looks busy.* When she'd been studying in France, her friends had all been that way, saying they shouldn't go into a particular restaurant because nobody else was eating there, whereas Jane was always willing to forgo high-quality food if it meant she could have some space. Give her a quiet pub any day. Sometimes she felt like an alien around other people.

She felt even more nervous about going into Eyecatchers. Whatever make-up she wore, she picked up almost at random from the supermarket, and just studying the outside of the salon now made her feel apprehensive. It would have been a challenge for her to go inside at the best of times. She always imagined that the women working there would look at her and sneer, as though she didn't deserve the products, and anyway, what good would they do someone like her? With the questions she was here to ask, she was going to look even more ridiculous than she would normally.

You can't do this.

The feelings it conjured up were all too familiar. But as Jane recognised the tightening in her chest, the shame in her mind, she pushed back at them. *Do you know what, Dad? The more you say that recently, the more determined I become.*

She got out of the car. The worst that could happen was that she'd look like an idiot, and a few people she'd never met before and never would again would think she was stupid. That was hardly so bad in the grand scheme of things.

She waited for the lights to change, then crossed the street. When she reached Eyecatchers, she removed any last traces of hesitation from her mind, pushed open the wooden double doors and stepped inside.

The first thing that hit her was the smell: a complicated, cloying mixture of aromas that hung in the air, thick as powder, a little like walking into a sweet shop. Everything was so very bright in here, as well: even more so than the sunlit street behind her. All the shelves, drawers and cabinets were white and clean, and there were rows and rows of rainbow-coloured products, the jars and boxes arranged in size order, like small families. Soft classical music was playing in the background.

There was nobody behind the counter, but a young woman in a clinical-looking white uniform was standing by one of the displays, slightly on tiptoes, hands clasped in front of her, giving her the air of a ballerina. At first glance, she was very beautiful, but as Jane looked at her, she wondered if that was more down to the fact that she appeared to be wearing an entire mask of make-up. Her face was tanned, with the centre of each cheek sporting a smeary sun of red. Amidst all that, her eyes were large and almost preternaturally white.

Could it be her? The victim from Westfield?

'Hello there! Can I help you with anything?'

Jane closed the heavy door behind her. Despite the friendly welcome, she felt even more nervous than before. Now that she was here, she wasn't sure what she was actually going to *say*. But as she approached the assistant, at least one immediate concern was taken away – she was in her early twenties at most, and likely still a teenager. The victim described in the papers had been twenty-five, so this couldn't be her. There was some relief in that. Jane wanted to talk to the victim, of course – that was the whole point of being here. But one step at a time.

'Hello,' she said. 'Yes, possibly. It's a bit strange, though.'

The girl laughed, but frowned at the same time. 'Okay?'

'It's about something I read in the newspapers. I was wondering... well. Have you been working here long?'

The girl shook her head. 'A couple of months. I started in... April, it will have been. Why?'

That meant she wouldn't know much, if anything, about the attack.

'Is there somebody else in? Someone who's been working here a bit longer?'

'Well, yes, there's the manager. She's been here for years, I think.' The girl rolled her eyes a bit at that. 'She's in the stock room at the moment. Do you want me to see if she's available?'

'Yes, please. If you could.'

'Okey-dokey.'

She moved around to the other side of the counter, almost bouncing on her toes, heading towards a closed door behind. But as she reached it, she paused, and then turned back to look at Jane. The frown was there again.

'You look familiar,' she said. 'Have I seen you somewhere before?'

'I don't think so.'

But the girl continued to stare at her, as though Jane was

264

a question she was determined to tease out the answer to. A moment later, her eyes went wide.

'Oh God. You're *her*, aren't you? The woman in the news.'

Jane nodded, feeling herself beginning to blush. She wanted the girl to look away, but she just kept staring.

'The one that man took? *Holy shit.* I mean, sorry for the language, but holy shit.' She pressed a hand to her chest. 'That must have been so awful. I can't imagine. It's like my worst nightmare or something.'

Jane nodded again. 'It was horrible,' she said. 'Yes.'

The girl still had hold of the door handle, but she let go of it now and came back to the counter.

'God, yeah. I can imagine. A while back, I had this feeling someone was following me? You know, when I was walking home? And that was bad enough.' She shook her head. 'But you're okay, right? He didn't hurt you?'

'I'm okay. It could have been a lot worse.'

'Well, yeah. Especially with what he did to the others. I couldn't read about it, to tell you the truth, although obviously I did. But it totally freaked me out.' The girl's eyes widened again. 'Wait a minute. Are you here because of what happened to Sharon? Don't tell me you are. Are you?'

Sharon.

'Maybe,' Jane said. And now that it came to it, there was no point in not explaining. 'I read something in the newspaper. It said there was an attack on a woman last year. That she worked here.'

'Yeah, yeah, there was. That was Sharon. I wasn't here then, but it's not like they don't all still talk about it. They told me about it on a night out: first week I worked here, I think. They all made sure I got a taxi.'

'Do you know what happened?'

The girl shook her head. 'Not really. Just that she was attacked when she got home. The creep was waiting for her.' She realised something. 'And *they never caught him*. Is that why you're here? Do the police think it might be this guy that did it?'

It was Jane's turn to frown. Did the girl really think that if that was the case, the police would have sent her to make inquiries on their behalf? That was ridiculous. At the same time, maybe it would encourage her to talk.

'I don't know. It's possible. I was just hoping to track her down, to be honest. Does she still work here?'

'No, no. She quit pretty much straight afterwards.'

Sharon.

'Do you know her surname?'

The girl shook her head. 'No. I mean, I never met her. I don't know anything about her really, apart from what the others told me.'

She looked a bit miserable at that for a second, but then perked up again.

'Karen will know, though. Hang on, I'll get her. Oh – here she is now.'

The door behind her opened just as she turned around. Jane expected to see a woman emerge, but it was a man that came out first. He was short and stocky, his leather jacket open over a black T-shirt stretched across his frame. His hair was close-cropped and the expression on his face was absolutely furious.

'Come *on*,' he called over his shoulder.

As he strode around the counter, he was swinging a set of car keys. Jane took a step back, but she could feel his presence from feet away.

A second later, a woman emerged, harried and upset, running a hand through her hair and walking a little awkwardly. She was almost beautiful, and once upon a time she might have been, but something about her seemed *off* to Jane. She was too skinny, too tanned. And it looked like she'd been crying. The eyeliner she was wearing had fragmented into stretches of Morse code.

'Abbie,' she said quietly. 'I'm leaving early.'

'Ah, okay. Well, listen, just quickly, this lady was wanting to talk to you about something.'

Karen slipped on a pair of sunglasses and turned to face Jane. Immediately, with the wrinkles around her eyes obscured, she looked about ten years younger.

'Oh?'

'Yeah,' Abbie said. 'She's the woman from the newspapers. You know? The one the creeper took? She wanted to talk to you about Sharon.'

Jane nodded. 'Only if you've got time, though.'

Karen didn't respond. Jane looked at her stern, motionless expression, and then over at the man she was leaving with. He had stopped by the door and was staring at her. He didn't look away when she looked back, and his gaze unnerved her.

'I'm not prepared to talk about that,' Karen said. 'It's nobody's business. Certainly not yours.'

'I—'

But Karen was already moving over to join the man at the door, and Jane closed her mouth on the unspoken words. She was momentarily bewildered. After the warm welcome from Abbie, that was not the response she'd been expecting. Maybe when she'd first come in, but not now.

The man pulled the door open as Karen reached him, holding it for her to go first. The whole time, he was still looking back at Jane. He no longer seemed quite as furious as before, but she couldn't read the expression on his face at all. He looked utterly blank.

'Please.' She took a step towards the pair of them. 'Can you at least tell me her surname? That way I can—'

'It's none of your business.'

With that, Karen stepped outside and was gone.

A second later, with one last glance at Jane, the man followed.

Thirty-Nine

The man and woman next door are arguing when they arrive home.

Karen and Derek – Margaret can hear their raised voices from the front room. It is none of her business, of course, and anyway, it is hardly surprising. They do seem like the type of couple that fight. Over the years, she has heard people say that everyone does, and that it's the sign of a healthy relationship, but she can't remember ever raising her voice to Harold, or him to her, and she can hardly imagine that anything would have made them.

Despite herself, she moves over to the window and peers cautiously through the gap in the curtains, keeping out of sight to one side.

Derek is halfway up their front path, just standing there, looking back down the garden in the direction of the road. Karen is hovering at the gate. She is without her sunglasses right now, and appears to be crying. Her hands are pressed to her eyes, and black streaks of make-up have run down to her jawline. Her shoulders are trembling, and she is half leaning against the gatepost, as though she is about to faint.

Her husband is red-faced and talking angrily to her. He's no longer shouting, and Margaret can't hear what he's saying, but he's speaking so deliberately quietly that it's somehow even more threatening. There is a violence to his posture. Even from across the path, from behind the safety of her locked door,

Margaret feels intimidated. She can't imagine what Karen must be feeling, standing so close to him. The rage beating off him must be almost as scorching as the afternoon sun.

You horrible man, she thinks.

You hideous little man.

Although she can't make out the words, his intentions certainly become clear a moment later, when he strides back down the path towards his wife and takes her by the arm. It doesn't look like a particularly painful grip, but she cries out anyway, and he doesn't wait for her to respond – just turns and walks towards the house with her trailing behind him. Clearly he has no expectation that she might resist, and she does not. From his manner, it is as if he's gone back to collect something he's dropped, rather than a human being. Rather than his wife.

They go inside, and he slams the door behind them.

Margaret's heart is beating faster than it should, and she feels chilly despite the afternoon heat.

She replays in her head what she has just seen, and, really, it is minor. But for some reason, it does not feel that way. Something about the encounter has shocked her.

It takes her a few moments to realise that it reminds her of a holiday she took with Harold, many years ago, in a static caravan on a sprawling campsite in the south of France. The temperature was much the same as it is today, and she remembers the hot, powdery sand pushing between her toes whenever they walked on the nearby beach.

They were sitting outside one evening when an argument broke out between a German couple two lots along. The woman was short and overweight, with hair that needed washing, while the man was tall, with long hair and a blonde goatee. It seemed to come out of nowhere. She heard sudden shouting, and looked up in time to see the man throwing the woman over one of the plastic chairs, sending her sprawling to the ground. Margaret was still trying to comprehend what was happening as the man dragged the woman into the caravan by her hair, then slammed the door shut behind them both.

For a few moments, nobody on the campsite responded. Beside her, Harold put his newspaper down, folding it once, and stared across the path. A number of other people stopped what they were doing and gazed at the closed caravan. The sudden violence had shocked everyone into stillness and silence.

Then Harold stood up and went over. He was the first person to do so, but others joined him immediately, hammering on the door to the caravan until the man opened it. Someone – not Harold, thank God – then pushed their way in to make sure the woman was all right. Afterwards, although she was proud of him, Margaret remonstrated with her husband for putting himself in danger like that. Harold nodded, then told her: *But anything could have been happening behind that closed door, Maggie. Anything.*

And that is how she feels now, looking across at the closed door opposite. Despite not seeing anything comparable to the violence she witnessed that day, there is a similar feel to it. The sensation that anything could be happening in there.

Should she go over?

Perhaps even call the police?

Margaret considers both options – but then, all she's seen is an argument. The violence, if it can even be called that, was relatively insignificant. It would be an overreaction, she thinks, based more on her dislike for the man than any genuine need for help. Despite how she feels about him, she has never seen him be explicitly violent. Aside from her bumblebees, of course.

Eventually, she moves away from the window. It is none of her business. Perhaps the two of them even deserve each other – although that thought is uncharitable and unkind, and she immediately regrets it. But regardless, it is not her concern.

She heads into the kitchen. Kieran will be finishing work soon, and calling round. She should tidy up.

The police arrive shortly after Kieran does.

Margaret is still finishing the washing-up, while Kieran is in the front room, where he has drawn the curtains and is looking intermittently out of the window. Strange behaviour, even for him, but her mind has been elsewhere, and she hasn't thought to ask him what he's watching out for. Now, with her hands deep in the tepid water, she sees the police car swing up at the end of the cul-de-sac. Her initial thought is that something serious has happened next door after all – that the argument must have escalated. But then she sees Kieran smiling to himself by the front room window, and she understands that this has something to do with him.

'Kieran?'

'They're here.'

He is beaming as he walks into the kitchen.

'Don't worry, Maggie. I'll take care of it all.'

'Take care of what?'

'The bumblebees. I called them about it. I'm sorry, but he can't get away with doing that. Uh-uh. No way.'

'Oh, Kieran …'

Finally, she understands. They had this discussion yesterday, when Kieran called round: after she'd told him what the neighbour had done, he was livid on her behalf. Raging, actually. And although she was still angry herself, his intensity frightened her. He insisted that he wanted to go next door and talk to the man; she had no idea how much of that was bluster, but she still worked hard to persuade him not to. Then he mentioned going to the police. She hadn't even considered it, and the idea made her crawl inside. Trespass, Kieran insisted. Criminal damage. Harassment, even. And maybe all that was true, but she still resisted. As hurt as she was, it was better not to cause a fuss. What could it achieve?

And yet he went against her wishes anyway. She shakes her head now, drying her hands with a dishcloth. Two policewomen are heading up the path.

'I'm sorry, Maggie,' Kieran says again. 'But he can't be allowed to bully you like that. It's totally unacceptable. I'm doing it to look after you.'

He sounds like he means it, but she wonders whether it's

really true. He does care about her, of course, but she's well aware that the argument about the garden began an unspoken conflict between him and the neighbour.

'All right,' she says wearily. 'All right.'

There is a knock at the door. As Kieran goes to answer it, Margaret heads back into the front room. Perhaps it is a good thing he's done this, irrespective of his reasons: Derek is clearly in the wrong, and really he shouldn't get away with what he's done. Even so, she doesn't want to be involved. She sits down on the settee, not listening to whatever Kieran is saying to the officers in the kitchen.

She feels very tired.

'They're going to have a word with him,' Kieran tells her a minute later, walking back into the front room.

'Are they?'

'Yes, they are.' She can tell from the tone of his voice that he's still beaming. 'Do you know what? I think I might go outside for a cigarette or two. Enjoy the view.'

'Kieran, *don't.*'

'Oh come on, Maggie. I'm not going to miss this. I want to see the look on the … on his face. He's got it coming. You have to admit.'

She wants to stop him, but he's already heading back into the kitchen, so she just sighs to herself. She hopes he enjoys it, for what it's worth, because it's her that will have to live with the effects. She's the one who has to stay here and see the neighbours every day. As she contemplates that, she puts her head in her hands. Why can't anything be easy?

Why won't people just leave me alone? she thinks.

Then:

I miss you, Harold. So much.

I wish you were here to look after me.

For a while, she's lost in those thoughts – and loses track of time. So it might be five minutes later, or as little as one, when she hears the commotion out front. Shouting. Thudding. She turns to the window just as Kieran's broad back slams into the glass, and then she is on her feet as he disappears from view, and all she can see is the neighbour, Derek, his face contorted with rage and hate, staring down at the ground.

For a moment, she simply stands there.

They're actually fighting.

She has no idea what has happened. How can it have escalated to this point? Regardless, she has to intervene – make them see sense. And where are the police? She hurries through to the kitchen, where the door is slightly ajar.

As she pulls it open, she hears the man next door. He is grunting and shouting.

'Fucker. *Die*, you fucker. *Die*, you fucker.'

She can't really see Kieran. He is lying on his back in the garden, his upper body obscured by the tangle of undergrowth, his legs on the path. The neighbour has his back to her, and is stamping repeatedly down at where Kieran's head should be.

'Stop it!' Margaret screams.

But the man ignores her. It's like she's not there. He just keeps shouting – *die, you fucker* – as he lifts his powerful leg and drives it down. Desperately, Margaret looks around. The door opposite hangs open, but there is no sign of the police. She looks back at the fight. Kieran is not moving at all.

He's killing him.

The man has become a single muscle dedicated to the task at hand. She can feel the solid strength and power of him from the doorway, and every instinct makes her want to flinch back and close the door. Instead, she looks to one side, sees the washing-up, soap suds still sliding off metal, and reaches out on instinct, picking up the heavy saucepan.

She has never hit anybody in her life; she doesn't really know how. But she hefts the pan as best she can. It spins round in her hand as she swings it, and she almost loses her grip, but the man is too distracted to realise that the blow is coming. The pan hits the top of his head with a heavy *thonk* that knocks it out of her hand. He stumbles sideways, half falling, as the pan clatters on the path.

Margaret is trembling as he looks up at her. The expression on his face is barely even human.

'I've called the police,' she says – even though it's pointless; even though the police are already here, or should be. 'Leave him alone now. I'm warning you.'

The man stares at her for a few more blank seconds, then his face contorts into a derisive sneer, although it goes nowhere near his eyes. A moment later, he stands up straight, turns and simply walks away down the path. He doesn't even look back. On the concrete, Margaret can see the bloody footprints he leaves as he goes.

Forty

'Am I under arrest?' Karen Cooper asked.

'No,' I said.

Not yet, anyway. But the situation was so fluid, and moving so quickly, that I had no idea how long that would be the case. In truth, I was struggling just to keep up with events, never mind get on top of them. Chris and I were sitting in an interview suite with the one woman who should have been able to help in that regard, and she was giving us nothing. Every now and then, there'd be a polite knock at the door, and an officer would deliver a swiftly jotted update. It wasn't exactly interrupting the flow of conversation.

'Then I want to go.'

Karen half stood, but then didn't seem to have the willpower to complete the move. I just stared at her until she settled back down again.

'If I'm not under arrest, then I don't have to stay here.'

'No. But I think it's in everyone's best interests if you talk to us. Don't you?'

'I don't know.'

'Anyway, where would you go? I'm sure you understand that your home is out of bounds for the time being. That it's currently a major crime scene.'

'I want a lawyer, then.'

She was staring down at the table, so I risked a curious glance at Chris, and he returned my expression. *Am I under arrest? I want to go. I want a lawyer.* They were all phrases that would normally have set alarm bells ringing. And yet, as far as we knew, Karen Cooper wasn't in any trouble. She was as much a victim of her husband as everyone else he'd hurt, the exact details of which we were still trying to work out.

We could be sure of at least three others. It was nearly two hours since the incident at Petrie Crescent. A young man named Kieran Yates was presently in a critical condition and unlikely to survive, while two WPCs were both in hospital. Sergeant Melanie Connor remained critical but stable, while Sergeant April Graves, who had been less seriously injured in the attack, was awake now and able to talk about what had happened.

The facts on the ground were these. A woman named Margaret Smith had placed an emergency call just after three o'clock this afternoon. She was obviously in extreme distress, and told Dispatch that a relative of hers had been badly assaulted and needed an ambulance immediately. The attacker had already fled the scene, but she'd given a basic description of his vehicle over the phone – a black Range Rover of some kind. The man lived next door, and his name was Derek, but she didn't know his surname.

Officers and an ambulance crew had been in attendance at the scene within minutes, where they found Margaret Smith in the front garden, sobbing quietly, her clothes soaked with blood, cradling what appeared at first glance to be a body in the undergrowth. The young man, subsequently identified as Kieran Yates, had been severely injured. His face was a mask of blood and his breathing was weak. As paramedics cleared his airway, he suffered a heart attack, and they'd worked hard at the scene to save his life.

Margaret Smith explained that she'd managed to fight the attacker off, causing him to flee the scene. The police were already next door, she told officers: she'd shouted for them, but they hadn't come out, and she'd been reluctant to leave Kieran alone in the garden.

When officers entered the neighbouring property, they found

the two WPCs on the kitchen floor. Graves was semi-conscious, and had managed to prop herself up against the cabinets, while Connor was unconscious. Both were bleeding heavily. Karen Cooper herself had been found huddled in the front room, in the corner between the radiator and the door. She had her hands pressed to her eyes and was rocking gently. After an initial examination by paramedics, she had been brought to the department. The assailant had been quickly identified as her husband, Derek Edward Cooper, whose whereabouts were currently unknown.

Officers down.

'I really don't think a lawyer will be necessary,' I told Karen now. 'For the moment, we're just trying to get a handle on what happened this afternoon. It's important that we do that quickly, so we can locate your husband. A lawyer is only going to complicate things and get in the way. That's not in anybody's interests, is it?'

'I don't know,' she said again.

'Trust me, then.' I leaned forward. 'Let's start with this afternoon. You left work early, is that right?'

'Yes.'

'And why was that?'

'Because I was upset. Derek came to pick me up.'

'What were you upset about?'

'I can't remember.'

Despite all the make-up, Karen Cooper didn't strike me as much of an actress, and I didn't think that was true. But I filed it away for later.

'All right. So Derek picked you up. Is that normal? Does he usually come to get you?'

'Not always. Sometimes.' She shrugged. Her manner was frustrating. At first, it had been as though she didn't understand the severity of the situation – as if what had happened this afternoon was just some minor inconvenience that really ought to have been sorted out by now. And then, as reality had settled in, she'd become more sullen.

What the hell is wrong with you, Karen?

But then, I reminded myself, it was likely she'd suffered a great deal of trauma. There was bruising beginning to appear around her left eye, and tears had spread her make-up in streaks down her face. It was obvious that she'd been assaulted by her husband this afternoon, and it was difficult to believe it had been the first occasion. In an earlier interview with Margaret Smith, the elderly woman had alluded to this. Perhaps Derek Cooper's violence was now such a natural setting for Karen that she was having trouble comprehending why the outside world would care. Perhaps she was even in shock.

I said, 'Your neighbour told us she'd spoken to you last week. In a café?'

'Yes, I remember that.'

'She told us you mentioned that Derek had a temper. That he could lash out.' I left a pause for her to reply, but she didn't. 'Is that what happened when you got home today?'

'Derek was … yes. Derek was very angry.'

'Does Derek get angry a lot?'

'Yes.'

'More and more angry recently, right?'

She looked awkward. 'There's a lot of pressure on him.'

'Why?'

'He was made redundant. He's always been a proud man. It's been hard.'

Chris took out a pen. 'When was this?'

Things had been moving so quickly that we were playing catch-up for the moment. I hadn't even known what Derek Cooper did for a living. Karen told us now that he'd been a manager in a construction firm until last year, when the company had downsized and he'd been let go. He'd been unable to find work since. Before then, the money had been good, and they still had savings, but now they were beginning to struggle.

'So he was under pressure. I don't think that excuses him getting angry, does it?' I gestured at her eye. 'Not this kind of angry, anyway. So he's *lashed out* at you before, Karen?'

'Yes.'

'And did you report it?'

'No.' She shook her head, looking small. 'Like I said, he's under a lot of pressure. And ... well, you don't cross Derek when he's like that. Nobody does.'

King in his own little domain, I thought. Well, it was one thing ruling over a downtrodden woman behind closed doors, another altogether facing down an entire police department. *Officers down*, I thought. *You don't cross Derek.* He was going to find out.

I pulled a sheet of paper from the file in front of me: a hastily printed transcript of the testimony April Graves had given from her hospital bed.

'Your husband attacked two police officers immediately after they entered the property,' I said. 'They were there to address an issue regarding your next-door neighbour, but the front door was ajar, and they heard shouting and crying coming from inside, so they moved into the kitchen.'

'I didn't see them.'

'No, but your husband confronted them. Sergeant Graves was closest to the living room, and he struck her on the side of the head with a rolling pin. There was no preamble. She wasn't anticipating it, and didn't have time to see it coming. The blow knocked her unconscious.'

It looked as though the other officer had had a chance to fumble with her Taser, but not enough time to use it. Derek Cooper had struck her several times, the last few most likely when she was already incapacitated on the floor. He'd then gone outside, walked casually down his path and up his neighbour's, and attacked Kieran Yates with his bare hands, beating the young man almost to death.

'We found the rolling pin in the kitchen bin,' I told Karen Cooper. 'He'd stuffed it there like it was a regular piece of rubbish that he was done with. Nice of him to tidy up after himself, I guess. Weird, but nice.'

She looked at me, trembling slightly, but didn't reply.

'Where is he now, Karen?'

'I don't know.'

'Let's go back, then. You left Eyecatchers at what time?'

'I've already told you all this.'

'We'll do it as many times as we need to.'

'About half one. Oh God.' She dabbed at her eyes. 'Maybe a bit after.'

'Because you were upset.'

'Yes.'

'You still haven't said why.'

'We had an argument, all right? Derek had done something I didn't like.' There was a sudden pleading tone to her voice. 'Can't we leave it at that?'

I stared at her for a few more seconds.

Derek had done something I didn't like.

'No,' I said. 'We really can't leave it at that. What was it that he'd done, Karen?'

'I don't want to talk about it.'

'I'm sorry, but we have to. Do the names Sharon Hendricks and Amanda Jarman mean anything to you? They've both worked for you.'

'Yes, but—'

'They were both assaulted and badly beaten. You know about Sharon, of course. She survived. But Amanda was attacked last night. She died as a result of her injuries.'

'Oh God.' She went pale. 'Oh God, no.'

'Was Derek out last night?'

'No.'

'Was that what you were arguing about?'

'No.'

'I don't believe you. He didn't come home last night, and that was what you were angry about.'

'He *didn't* go out.'

'You're lying, Karen. Why bother protecting him now?'

She didn't answer, but it was clear to me that that was what she was doing. It was frustrating, as I could see straight through it, but many victims experience a kind of Stockholm syndrome, and I forced myself to remember the kind of pressure she must be under here. Not that it made the situation any less urgent.

'Where is he now?'

'I don't know.'

'Friends? Other family? Somewhere else?'

'*I don't know.*'

Finally I lost patience with her.

'Listen to me, Karen.' I leaned forward. 'I get that you've been through a lot, and that this is hard for you to deal with. But if your husband hurts anyone else, and you could have stopped it, *you'll* be partly responsible for that. Do you understand me? Do you not—'

'*I know that,*' she screamed. '*Don't you think I know that?*'

And then before Chris or I could respond, Karen Cooper began clawing desperately at her own face, as though she might not know the answers to our questions, but a woman hidden deep beneath her skin might, if only she could find her again.

So, Derek Edward Cooper.

Are you our man?

Back in the operations room, I was sitting at my desk and looking at the only photograph we had of Cooper. At the end of the interview, Karen had needed to be restrained and sedated, and she wouldn't be talking to us again for the time being. But her husband – the man on my computer screen – remained at large. So far there had been no sightings of either him or his vehicle.

There would be other photographs soon, taken from his home, but for now this was all we had: the passport-sized photograph from his driving licence. It was a few years old. Cooper had lost the licence for a while, following repeated points for speeding, which seemed to fit the growing picture I was building up of him in my head. A man who felt that the rules applied to other people, not him. A man who didn't like it when things didn't go his way.

In the photograph, his hair was receding and close-cropped, and his face was strong and broad in a way that suggested his body would be too. He looked *hard*, and nowhere more so than in the eyes: the glare he was giving the camera was the kind designed to back another man down in a bar. Even in a still image, he seemed full of barely suppressed rage.

I thought about how the victims had described their attacker. The words they'd used. *A monster. A concentration of hatred.* The photograph was silent, of course, as it had to be. But it reminded me that our attacker always had been too. That he seemed to hate his victims too much for words.

Are you our man?

We could link him to Sharon Hendricks and Amanda Jarman through his wife's employment, but to an extent they remained satellite investigations to the main one. He had lost his job not long before the attack on Sharon Hendricks, and had been unemployed since, which would have given him the opportunity to access the victims' homes in the daytime. But obviously that was all circumstantial.

What else?

The Coopers had two children, both nearly in their teens, which made me think again about the playground by Adam Johnson's house. *Who goes to a playground?* Children and their parents. It was local to the Coopers, and Johnson had lived in that strange cottage there since childhood. It seemed possible that Derek Cooper had seen Johnson near the playground, and then recognised him in Sharon Hendricks' back garden on the night of the attack. And that, upon visiting him, he'd found someone he could dominate and use.

Possible.

Then there was the psychological angle. The escalation in our creeper had been evident from the increasing ferocity of the attacks. Whatever the reason behind it, it seemed clear enough that Derek Cooper was also undergoing a meltdown of some kind, and that this afternoon he'd boiled over. The officers had only been there about some dead bees, but perhaps he'd suspected otherwise and attacked them before they could arrest him for what he thought they were really there for. Sticking the rolling pin in the bin also suggested disassociation from reality.

It's you, isn't it, Derek?

It had to be. I was sure that both Sharon Hendricks and Amanda Jarman had been attacked by the same man as the others, and that led straight to Eyecatchers. It could hardly be a coincidence that a man associated with the shop had also gone ballistic today and vanished off the grid. Cooper must have known that attacking Amanda would bring us to his door. Which meant either that he was out of control, or that he no longer cared about getting caught.

You're the monster Adam Johnson talked about.

I pulled up the online file for Johnson's attacks, then scanned through to find a number for Jane. Perhaps something about Cooper would jog her memory – remind her of something else Johnson had said. But the only number we had was her home phone, and it went to voicemail. I could have kicked myself for never taking a mobile contact for her.

I left a short message.

'Jane, it's Zoe Dolan. We really need to go over what Adam Johnson told you again. It's a matter of urgency. Can you give me a ring as soon as possible, please?'

Since I didn't know for sure where I was going to be, I gave her my mobile number, then hung up.

'Result,' Chris said.

I shook my head. 'What?'

'We've found his Range Rover.'

On the far side of the incident room, there was a flurry of activity. Officers on phones were clicking fingers at each other, everybody already moving.

'Where?'

'It's in that open-air car park by the side of the bus station. No ticket or anything. Looks like he's just abandoned it.'

'Shit.'

That was bad news. The city's bus station was a long,

double-sided building, with local buses leaving from one side and coaches dispersing from the other, threading out all around the country. With a two-hour head start, Cooper could be almost anywhere by now.

Chris said, 'He ditched the vehicle because he knew we'd be looking out for it. Figured he wouldn't get far enough in it.'

'Obviously.'

'The station will have CCTV.'

'Which we'll now have to sort through to find out exactly which coach he's on. He'll have paid cash. By the time we discover where he went, he'll have been there for hours. And if the coach made multiple stops, we're even further behind.'

Unless we were incredibly lucky, Derek Cooper would have at least one more night on the loose, and a man in his situation could hurt a lot of people in that space of time. Especially when he had no reason not to.

'We're already tracing friends and family connections,' Chris said. 'All this does is broaden the net.'

'To most of the country.'

Something else was bothering me, though, and it took me a few quiet seconds to work out what it was. Even though Cooper appeared to be in meltdown, there were still flashes of cunning in his behaviour. He'd waited with Amanda Jarman all that time last night. He'd been careful with the text messages. And even something as bizarre as the rolling pin he'd used to attack the officers in his kitchen – stuffing it into the kitchen bin was pointless, but it still showed a flicker of awareness. And then there were—

'The windows,' I said suddenly.

'What?'

'At the victims' houses.' I turned in my seat to look up at Chris. 'He always climbed out of the window afterwards. He got in easily through the front door, but never left that way.'

'So what?'

'It was always just a stupid piece of misdirection. Maybe he even did it on impulse the first time. But think about what he'd done to those women. Think about how they described him – that he exploded at them. How violent he was. He must have been half out of his mind with rage at the time, and that's probably the state he's in now too. So how do we know he's not misdirecting us again?'

'Meaning?'

I turned back to the screen.

'I don't know. Meaning that maybe this is the same. Leaving his vehicle somewhere that will stretch us in the wrong direction. Maybe it's not a coach he's on at all. Perhaps there's somewhere in the *city* he wants to go. It would take longer to get the CCTV from the local buses.'

'Where, though?'

'I don't know, do I? *Christ.*'

Chris leaned against the desk and folded his arms.

'All we can do is pursue it,' he said gently. 'We'll get him eventually, Zoe.'

'Not in time.'

'We can only work with what we've got.'

I closed my eyes for a moment, rubbing my forehead. I was annoyed at his tone, but it wasn't his fault, and deep down I knew he was right. It was the worst-case scenario, this, but we could only follow the leads that were open to us. For Chris and me, as tough as it was going to be, the next few hours would be a waiting game.

I opened my eyes and turned my attention back to the screen – to the photograph of Derek Cooper – and then clicked through to set it printing. When it emerged from the machine a moment later, I took it and stood up.

'Where are you going?'

'There's no use both of us just sitting here, is there?' I grabbed my bag and car keys. 'I'm going to find out for certain whether he's our man.'

Forty-One

After the frustrating experience at Eyecatchers, Jane wasn't sure what to do next. She was emboldened by at least having gone in and *asked* – but at the same time, she still felt a little silly for having done so, and the lack of any real result only compounded that.

Sharon.

All she had was a name. She sat in her car outside the shop feeling that she'd failed, and wondering what was the best thing to do next.

The obvious thing was to give up, go back to Rachel's flat and get on with work. If she wasn't careful, she'd be in danger of missing the project's deadline: a professional first for her, and not one she was keen to add to her CV. Of course, that wasn't the only reason it would be sensible. She wasn't the police, and she wasn't a private investigator, and perhaps it was pointless to waste an afternoon pretending she was. What exactly was she expecting to achieve? If she carried on, come evening, chances were she was going to feel even more stupid than she did now.

But set against that was the same determination she'd felt in Rachel's flat earlier. She needed to do *something*. If the police weren't taking her seriously, then she had to make them. Never mind the danger to herself; she owed it to the *victims* to make them listen.

But that would require more evidence. She still needed something that couldn't be simply brushed aside and dismissed.

So.

Cragg Road, then.

Are you really—

YES, I AM!

Despite the doubts, it made her feel a little brighter. And what had happened in Eyecatchers hadn't been a total washout: she had a first name now, at least. That meant she might only have to knock on a few doors before finding someone who knew a young woman called Sharon living on the street. And if she didn't manage to turn anything up, at least she would know she'd tried. The ... bloody *universe* itself could think she was silly if it wanted. What did it matter? It felt important *to her* to follow this as far as she could, and that was reason enough to risk a little ridicule.

Jane wasn't sure where exactly Cragg Road was, but she knew how to get to Westfield, and from there she'd be able to find the exact address on her phone. She did a quick mental calculation. The route along the ring road would take her close to her flat, so it made sense to call in there first, gather some things together. She had no idea how long she was going to stay with Rachel, but she could certainly do with some more clothes, and perhaps a few books to read. It would only take a few minutes at most.

She peeled off to the left at the turning, grateful to leave the afternoon traffic behind. A few minutes later, she pulled up a little way down from her flat; someone had parked a battered old car in her usual spot, one of the perils of living on a main road. As she approached her building, though, Jane felt that sense of dislocation again. The sight of it felt off, somehow, like something familiar seen from an unusual angle.

She unlocked the front door and went in.

Inside, the flat was silent – abandoned, almost – and the stillness and quiet seemed judgemental. She glanced up the stairs; the landing above was gloomy, and the air already felt stale, as though the place had been empty for much longer than a night.

Which was ridiculous, of course. And yet, as Jane started up the stairs, the flat did feel suddenly alien to her. She walked over the spot where Adam Johnson had attacked her and tied her up, and it didn't evoke bad memories so much as the sensation that she no longer quite belonged here. As she reached the landing, she counted the time spent here backwards in her head.

Four years.

That was how long it had been. Her father had bought the place for her in her third year of university, after she'd come back from abroad. It was hers now, aside from the slimmest of mortgages. Before now, she'd never even considered selling it and moving somewhere else, but maybe it was time to think about that. It would be a break from the past, wouldn't it? However comfortable you were, there could still be something stagnant about remaining in the same place for too long. And why not? There was nothing really to keep her here.

It was something to think about, anyway. Something she *could* do, if she decided she wanted to.

First things first, though.

She went straight through to the bedroom, pulling an old gym bag from the bottom of the wardrobe and beginning to pile folded clothes into it. In theory, she wouldn't require much – just enough to get by for a few more days – and yet as she went, she found herself peering into drawers, and at the outfits hanging in the wardrobe, and selecting far more than she needed. Dresses that she hadn't worn in years, and wouldn't any time soon, but which had sentimental value; jeans that were too small for her, but which she couldn't bear to throw away. She emptied drawers, the stained wood at the base smelling like long-forgotten school desks.

Personal possessions next.

Out of instinct, she turned to the desk on the far side of the room. There were photo albums in the drawers there, letters and trinkets, probably a few other things she had forgotten but which she liked to have close to her. And the photograph, of course – the framed one of her and Peter, smiling in the sunshine. The photograph that was now lying face down on the desk, the strut sticking up in the air.

She stared at it for a moment, frozen to the spot.

Behind her, the bedroom door closed.

And Jane turned around to find a man standing there.

Forty-Two

The victims.

It all came back to them. It always does.

In truth, I didn't have much of a plan, but it wasn't like I'd be achieving anything by sitting around in the incident room waiting for news. To link Cooper to the attacks, we'd have to talk to all the victims again eventually. So with the printout of his photo in my pocket, I headed out. I was hoping that one of the surviving victims might at least recognise him. His eyes were distinctive, after all, and despite the mask, they'd all seen them. Or maybe it hadn't always been Adam Johnson doing the following and stalking, and one of them would remember spotting Cooper at some point. It was slim, but possible, and I had to start somewhere.

So start at the beginning.

In this case, that meant a second visit to Sharon Hendricks. She was the least promising, in some ways, as she'd presumably encountered Derek Cooper at work, but hadn't recognised him during the attack. But maybe his name, his image, would jog something. Start at the beginning. Then I'd move on to the others.

By coincidence, I ended up driving the exact same route that Sharon would have taken on the night she was attacked. I followed the main road out of the city centre, heading west, before splitting off into the suburbs where she lived. Driving slowly, the day dimming around me, I found it easy to imagine her walking alongside me.

I parked up outside her house. The field across the road was still visible in the gloom, separated from the pavement by the trunks of old felled trees. Directly opposite Sharon's house, there were a couple of large stone pillars, with enormous trees on either side, their sweeping branches hanging down almost to the ground, creating a shadowy doorway. In my mind's eye, I pictured Derek Cooper there. Dressed in black, and peering around the stone column. Knowing Sharon was out with his wife. Waiting for her to come home.

Outside the car, a slight but welcome breeze was making the thin branches rustle together. I walked up Sharon's front path, but even the sound of my shoes on the tarmac was oddly subdued and quiet: a peaceful whisper, hardly louder than the breeze in my ears. The world felt slightly *off* somehow.

Just past her front door, the front room curtains were open, and I could see the television on in the corner of the room: silent images flashing against the glass. That was good. She was at home, at least.

I rang the bell.

While I waited, I took the printout of Derek Cooper from my pocket and unfolded it. The creases had drawn a cross over the centre of his face: one line down the centre, the other bisecting his eyes, making his countenance even blanker than before.

After a few moments, I rang the doorbell again.

Again, nothing.

I stepped back and looked up at the house. The curtains were closed in what I presumed was the bedroom, but the light was on behind them, the bulb showing through the fabric like a hazy sun.

I pressed the bell again, then moved over to the front room window, cupping my hands around my eyes and pressing my face to the glass. The room was lit only by the flickering images from the television. On the carpet, by the base of the settee, there was a full mug of coffee, and an ashtray with an unlit cigarette angled against the rim. Close to the door, something dark stained the carpet.

I moved quickly back to the door and tried the handle. Locked. I banged hard on the wood, then crouched down and lifted the letter box flap.

'Sharon? Are you in there?'

No response. Rocking slightly on my toes, I was granted an awkward, shifting view of the stairs. The stains were there too. A streak was swiped over the white wall beneath the banister. Without the glass in the way, it was obvious that it was blood.

Shit shit shit.

I moved back to the window. The hinged section was closed, but I reached out and pulled, and it came open with a creak, the small golden hinges stretching out.

A few seconds later, I had Chris on speed-dial.

'What's up?' he said.

'I'm at Sharon Hendricks' house.' My heart was hammering. 'I need backup immediately, and an ambulance.'

'Wait, what—?'

'He's been here. Cooper.'

Chris was silent for a moment.

'What about Hendricks?'

'I don't know yet.' I looked at the open window. 'The house is locked, but there's blood in the front room and on the stairs, and the downstairs window is open.'

'Zoe—'

'I'm not going in, Chris. Just get me backup.'

He started to say something else, but I cut him off and slipped the phone back into my pocket, then stared at the open window in front of me, thinking.

What on earth was going through Cooper's head? Obviously he knew time was running out, and had decided to revisit the first woman he'd attacked. She'd got off more lightly than his other victims, after all. Perhaps he'd intended to rectify that before he was caught. The thought made me feel sick.

I stared at the open window. I'd told Chris I wasn't going

in, and at the time I'd meant it. It would be madness. Cooper was larger and stronger than me, and it was possible he was still in there.

And yet.

I had no idea what kind of condition Sharon Hendricks might be in. I flashed back to finding Sally Vickers' body stuffed down the side of the bed – but that was different. That had already happened, and so that was what I'd found. Right now, it was possible Sharon was still alive in there, and my hesitating might make the difference.

Too risky.

I brushed the edge of the curtain aside, then carefully leaned a little way in. It was definitely blood on the carpet. In patches, the coils of fabric were still glistening with it. If Cooper was here, he'd already know he had company, so there was no point being coy.

'Sharon? Are you in there? Can you answer me?'

Nothing.

I pushed the curtain a little further, trying to get a better view of the room, but this time, it didn't move. This time, the back of my forearm met a solid object.

Immediately, a hand clamped hard around my wrist, and I was yanked forward, my chest slamming into the window ledge. My head and shoulders were already through the window, inside the stale warmth of the front room. Another hand grabbed hold of my hair, and I began kicking and screaming as I was dragged in over the sill, my thighs scraping against it. A moment later, the back of my shoulders hit the floor, all the breath knocked suddenly out of me. I tried to suck in air, and it wouldn't come.

Above me, I saw Derek Cooper closing the window, then heard the click as he turned the handle and locked it. As he stared down at me, he seemed to fill the world.

Forty-Three

There were a couple of seconds when it didn't feel strange to see Peter standing in her bedroom.

After all, he'd lived here with her for over a year, and she was used to seeing him around: lolling on the settee or sprawled on the bed; sitting at the small kitchen table with an empty bottle of wine beside him, turning his glass absently between his fingers as he stared off into space. His presence was familiar, and she had countless memories of him being here against which to match the sight of him now. He was not out of place.

That was the first moments after seeing him.

But then ... he had moved out long enough ago for there to be a slight feeling of unease. *No, there's a reason why he shouldn't be here.* There had been no contact between them since he'd left. Even if there had been, he had absolutely no right to be here in her flat right now. Nothing belonging to him remained. She had not invited him in.

And so the panic set in.

Jane swallowed it down and took a step back. Peter didn't seem to notice. He just stood there with his back against the bedroom door. Swaying slightly.

Staring at her.

Only a few months had passed since they'd broken up, but his appearance had deteriorated badly in that time. His face was pale and clammy, the eyes sunken, ringed with dark circles. His cheekbones jutted. Staring back at him, she could easily make those familiar features disappear and visualise him as a skeleton.

The effect was only emphasised as she looked at his arms, which emerged from the sleeves of his dirty white T-shirt as thin as bones. He was holding a bottle of vodka, and his knuckles looked bruised. He'd been in some kind of fight, then. She wondered if he even remembered it.

'Peter,' she said carefully. 'What are you doing here?'

He swallowed heavily.

'Came to see you.'

The slur in his voice confirmed that he was drunk – very drunk, in fact. She was used to hearing him talk when he'd had a few drinks, and he'd always remained contained and controlled. If you didn't know him well, you probably wouldn't even have suspected. But this, right here, would have been obvious to anyone. The words swayed with his body.

Still staring at her, he took a step forward, away from the door. Jane took another one back, and he frowned at her.

'Don't seem pleased to see me.'

Don't make him angry.

The thought seemed to come from nowhere. Until now, she had been more surprised than frightened. Towards the end of their relationship, there had been things thrown, especially when he'd been drinking, but they'd never been thrown at *her*. And while he could be aggressive verbally, he'd never been physically violent. There was no obvious reason for her to be afraid of him now.

Except that he was here and he shouldn't be. She was locked in with him. And he was blocking the only way out of the room.

So don't make him angry.

'I'm just surprised,' she said. 'I didn't know you still had a key.'

He winked at her and patted his back pocket, but the movement unsteadied him, and he took an accidental step forward. She matched him again, the backs of her calves now touching the bed.

He certainly shouldn't have a key. He'd posted it back through the letter box when he moved out. She remembered it clearly: it had never been settled exactly when he would be done moving, and then one day she'd come back in and stood on it. He hadn't even bothered to put it in an envelope.

Obviously he'd decided to keep a copy.

'Right,' she said. 'Well, that's—'

'You don't seem pleased to see me. Pleased to see *you*.'

He gestured at her with the bottle, a vague sweeping movement that made the liquid inside slosh. It was only a third full, and there was no telling if that was all he'd had today.

'Really nice to see you again.' He slapped his chest proudly. 'I know you feel same. Deep down.'

Jane didn't know what to say, so she said nothing. A moment later, he gestured again, this time off to one side.

''Cos you kept the photo of us.'

The photo.

That slight shift in its position. At the time, she'd imagined it was Johnson – not that she'd known his name back then – and then, later, had decided it must have been her imagination. Of course, it could never have been Adam Johnson, because he didn't have a key to her house. When he'd abducted her, he'd needed to ring the bell. But it hadn't been her imagination, either.

A chill went through her as she pictured Peter in here while she was out, going through her things. She saw him pick up the photograph, perhaps as drunk as he was now, then replace it at that slightly wrong angle. In her house. Invading her space. As though he had every right in the world to be here.

All without her knowing.

'You kept it,' he repeated, looking over at it. He sounded both happy and sad at the same time.

'I just hadn't got round to moving it.'

'Don't say that.' It got her a frown, one he used his whole face to emphasise. 'Know it's not true. And it's not nice to tell fibs.'

'Peter,' she said carefully. 'We broke up.'

'Don't say that.'

He took another step towards her, and this time she had no more room to retreat.

Forty-Four

I was barely conscious as Cooper dragged me upstairs.

It was a small mercy, I supposed, because he hauled me like he was moving a heavy sack, gripping my hair and one of my arms. My head thudded against each of the steps. The next thing I was really aware of was him crouching over me on the landing, silhouetted against the small window.

The pain in my scalp registered then, although it had been there the whole time, along with the tightness where he had been clasping my upper arm. It took another moment to make sense of what was happening and where I was. I had no memory of what had taken place downstairs, or even how long I'd been in the house. I must have tried to fight. The right side of my vision was blurred, and the cheek below it throbbed badly, as though there was too much of it to feel.

I managed to roll over and rest for a moment on my knees and forearms. An inch from my eyes, the carpet was sparkling with curls of light. They formed, turned and faded.

It looks like it's been charged with electricity.

And then he kicked me – stamped on me, really: down on my lower back. I barely saw it, but it turned me over on to my side. For a second, the pain wasn't there, and then suddenly it was: the same raw, scraping agony as falling hard against a rough stone wall. I gritted my teeth and bit down as it flared. I had no idea what would encourage him, whether it would be fighting back or playing docile, but I didn't care, didn't want to give him the satisfaction.

Chris will be here, I thought.

But not in time. And when backup arrived, the house would be locked up tight.

Cooper stamped down at me again, this time driving his whole weight on to the side of my knee. It mashed my leg against the carpet, but didn't do any real damage. Then he was crouching on me, and I wrapped my hands around my head as he began raining blows down on me: pounding on my upper arms and the backs of my hands. My biceps blew up, and then went numb from the repeated impacts. Each blow was like an earthquake, setting the whole world moving, and I could hear both of us grunting. When he stopped, and I opened my eyes, the landing seemed to be shuddering from the after-effects of the violence. But I was all right.

The pressure lifted from my legs as he stood up, and then he spat on me. The spray landed on the back of my hand and upper arm, my hair.

Chris, Chris, Chris.

I was begging him to get here. Force the door down. Get in and save me. How long could it take?

Too long.

'Get up.'

It was the first time he'd spoken, and his voice was full of contempt. I remembered again how the other victims had described him. A monster. A concentration of hatred. Not speaking as he assaulted them, either as though they were animals unworthy of communication or because he was too full of rage for words.

'Get up.'

He took hold of my hair again and yanked me to my feet. I went dead, but as soon as I'd got my feet under me, I pushed down and launched myself into him, aiming low: my shoulder into his solar plexus. He was too solid, and it wasn't hard enough to wind him, but at least it nudged him slightly off balance, forced him to take a step back. It was a small space up here, and I thought maybe I could send him, or both of us, down the stairs. He wrapped his hands reflexively around me, and for a few seconds we wrestled on the landing. But then he let go and hooked a quick jab into my ribs. As my body moved with the blow, he caught me with a punch to the face and it sent my head flying into the wall.

Stars everywhere – and a second of no sound at all.

Then I was falling. He caught me and threw me backwards. I was expecting to hit the wall again, but this time I went through space, a bright light flashing ahead of me, and my upper body landed on the softness of a bed.

Stand up. Immediately.

And that was when I saw her.

Oh God, no.

Sharon Hendricks was lying at the foot of the bed, naked and curled into a foetal position. Blood had matted in her hair and spread in watery rivulets down the back of her shoulders, like hair dye that had run. More blood dotted the wall beside her, and the bottom of the duvet. But she was moving, at least, breathing softly.

I turned around, the room moving slightly faster than me. Cooper was standing in the doorway, just staring at me, his fists bunching and unclenching by his sides. It was the first time I'd seen him clearly in the flesh. He was solid and physically compact, but not as tall as I'd been expecting. There were fresh grazes down one side of his face. Not from me, I didn't think. I couldn't be sure they had come from Sharon Hendricks either, but found myself directing a thought at her anyway: *good for you.*

See what else I can add to that before we're done.

'Police are on their way,' I said.

It surprised me how strong my voice sounded, but Cooper continued to stare at me with the same dead eyes. Silent again now. He didn't care. Beneath that blankness, he barely even seemed human any more. It was like facing off with someone who had completed their transition into a literal monster. This was always going to be his final destination.

Suddenly, moving like a boxer, he came at me.

I managed to block the first punch, more out of instinct than design, but he was already throwing another. I had no chance. The room blew up, the centre of my vision flashed bright white, and my legs went from under me. *Shit.* I rolled on to my side on the bed and cupped my face, moving my hands away just enough to see blood all over my fingers, but then my eyes filled with tears and the sight blurred. Bizarrely, the impact had been so hard that there wasn't much pain yet.

He was going to kill me.

It wasn't like I hadn't known it before, but a part of me had suppressed the thought. Chris would save me, or else I'd fight him off. But neither of those things was going to happen. He was going to kill me, and Chris would look down at me and think, *you always had to do everything by yourself, didn't you?*

Cooper grabbed hold of one of my heels and yanked me back, so that only my upper body rested on the bed. I felt his hands fumbling at my belt, but it was more of a sound than a sensation: the clink of metal. I didn't have the strength to fight him. I just wanted to cry. *Ridiculous.*

And then my phone started ringing.

At first, it was just a buzz against my upper thigh. Then the chirruping sound was loud in the bedroom.

Cooper paused.

A moment later, his hands left me, and I felt him step away.

'Answer it,' he said.

Lying on my back, still cupping my face, I said, 'What?'

He tapped the outside of my leg playfully.

'Answer your phone.'

Forty-Five

They talked – or rather, Jane listened.

Peter was very drunk already, and he kept swigging from the bottle of vodka. It was difficult to understand him through the increasing blur of the alcohol, but she could follow enough. Since he'd moved out, he had found life hard. The plan had been for him to stay at a friend's house for a while, but the friend had quickly grown frustrated with Peter's failure to move on, and with the promises of help with the rent and utilities that failed to materialise. In the end, he'd thrown him out.

At first, that had been okay, but then Peter hadn't been able to afford his own rent. He didn't say, but it was obvious he'd begun drinking more and more, and as cheap as the vodka he was holding now might be, it still cost money. He was due in court in a couple of weeks for non-payment of council tax. The way he described it, necking from the bottle, you would have thought the whole thing was desperately unfair: that it was something that had happened to him rather than something he'd caused.

All these months, he said, he hadn't stopped thinking about her.

She was sitting beside him on the bed when he said that, and she didn't reply. She simply rubbed her hands together and waited for him to go on.

Inside, though, it felt strange to hear. Because she hadn't thought about him very much. While the relationship had been deteriorating, she'd talked to her therapist about it, and had been comforted by the woman's advice. *Part of breaking up with someone is that you're no longer responsible for how they feel.* That seemed right, and it had been a relief to be excused from feeling guilty about whatever Peter might be going through. And after he'd delivered the key through her letter box so casually, she'd more or less put him out of her mind, rarely thinking of him at all.

She hadn't considered that he might miss her. In fact, she'd thought so little of herself that it seemed impossible he would. His life since their break-up was a blank spot in her head, entirely unknown to her; she had filled it, if anything, with happiness for him. A period of adjustment and recovery, perhaps, but always with the idea that he must be dealing with things at least as well as she was, if not much better. He'd always seemed the stronger of the two of them.

Apparently, she had been wrong.

'I never stopped missing you. Messed up. You meant everything to me.'

When he said that, she believed him – or at least believed that *he* believed it. Because it was more likely that what he really regretted was the direction his life had taken, and that he didn't need her so much as *someone*. Regardless, she didn't need him. She was sure of that. She didn't want him either.

It seemed like on some level he knew that.

'You're with her now, aren't you?' He drained the last dregs from the bottle. 'That fucking dyke.'

It took her a moment to work out what he meant. When she did, she almost laughed. She hadn't thought about Rachel like that. She'd never even considered it.

'Don't call her that.'

'I've seen you with her. Are you happy?'

'I don't know what I am, Peter. But yes, maybe I am. I'm certainly happier than I was.'

'That's good.' But he sounded miserable when he said it. 'Can I have a hug anyway? I've missed that.'

'Yes.'

She wasn't scared. Despite the situation, having listened to him, it felt like she was now the stronger one. So she turned to face him, and put her arms around him. It was a second before he returned the gesture, as though he was afraid of how it would feel, and then his hands pressed gently against her back. She smelled the familiar scent of his neck, then turned her head away, looking over his shoulder towards the headboard of the bed, just holding him.

'I've missed this so much.'

He sounded far away. A minute or so later, he was snoring on her shoulder.

Jane eased away from him, then laid him down gently on the bed, making sure he was on his side. Let him sleep it off, she decided. When he woke up, they could talk properly. She would explain that it was over between them, and that it was unacceptable for him to come here any more. She would have the locks changed if it came to it, but she didn't think that would be necessary. She was much better at saying no than he was used to.

He was still snoring as she picked up the heavy sports bag and left the bedroom.

Through in the lounge, she checked the phone on impulse, finding two messages. She listened to them. They were both from the police, one from a man asking her to get in touch, and the second from Zoe, who indicated that the matter was urgent. She had left a mobile number.

Jane noted it down on the pad by the phone, then hung up and dialled.

Forty-Six

Afterwards, I could never remember the call.

I have no idea why – whether the trauma of what I was undergoing pushed the memory into the same nightmare place where what happened to Jemima had gone, or if I was simply too woozy from the assault to take it in.

There is no transcript, but Jane has been interviewed, and I've been told how the conversation went, at least as far as she remembers it. Upon answering the phone, the first thing I said was:

He says to tell you that I'm going to die.

I said that over and over again, apparently, without any emotion in my voice at all.

He's going to rape me, and he's going to kill me.

He wants you to know that.

He wants me to tell you.

I don't remember any of that. I'm glad there's no recording of the phone call – that the conversation is gone now – because I'd hate to hear myself say those words. I do have one vague recollection, though, albeit more of a hint at a memory than an actual one: I was struggling to hear Jane while she was talking to me. Not because I was disorientated, but because it sounded like there were other people on the line. There were women talking over each other, all at the same time. I couldn't make out their voices, as they were too far away, but sometimes they dovetailed with what Jane was saying, and sometimes they obscured it. If I didn't know better, I would have thought it hadn't just been the two of us on that line. That we hadn't been alone.

From her testimony, I know that Jane began panicking, and obviously had no idea what to say. She understood what she was listening to: that she was talking to a woman who was about to be murdered, that help was far away and wouldn't reach me in time, and that there was nothing she could do about it. All those things were clear. For a few moments, she said, her head went blank.

But then the training kicked in. If she couldn't do anything else, she told the police afterwards, she wanted to console me. So using her natural empathy, and without even thinking about it, she put herself in my position, and in that moment she regressed to her own abduction. She recalled exactly how she'd felt when Johnson had taken her, and everything that she'd seen, and suddenly she realised that there might a way she could help me after all.

So she blurted something out.

That's the only bit of it I really remember.

Zoe, there's a hammer under the bed.

She was confused, of course. A moment after she said, it, I realised she was thinking about *my* bedroom – that she must have seen the hammer when Adam Johnson abducted her and took her there, and presumed that that was where I was right now. There was no way she could know what Sharon Hendricks kept in her bedroom.

Even so, the urgency with which she said it was compelling. *I have suddenly remembered something important* was the tone, *and it's vital that I tell you.* I sensed a thin, impossible web of connections, an interlacing of voices and history, and even if Jane couldn't possibly know what she was saying, I still believed her.

Cooper had moved back over to the wall while I'd been on the phone, leaning against it with that vacant expression on his face. Now he unfolded his arms and walked back towards me.

I threw my phone at him as hard as I could. There wasn't really time to aim, or even try to, but the distance between us was so short that I was bound to hit him somewhere. Some unconscious instinct took the projectile straight into his face.

'Fuck!'

The contact was only solid enough to slow him for a moment, not to do any real damage. I scrambled backwards across the bed, turning as I went, knowing I had a second or two at most. As I did so, I caught sight of Sharon Hendricks, her back to me, and then I half fell off the far edge, my forearms landing hard on the carpet, blood pattering down from my nose, head full of stars and close to passing out. *Stay with us!* I pressed my chin to my chest and looked backwards under the bed.

It was there.

Not like mine at all. This hammer was a professional DIY tool, made of moulded black and yellow plastic.

I scrabbled for it, knocking the handle and setting it turning. My legs were still on the bed, though, and I felt Cooper's hand encircle my ankle – and then he was dragging me backwards across it. My arms lifted off the floor, but I clung to the underside of the bed with one hand, concentrating on finding the hammer with the other. I couldn't even see it now. It was just my fingers stroking at the carpet, searching, searching, and then closing around the plastic handle as my grip on the bed gave out and he hauled me back towards him.

I turned over as I went. The momentum took me to the far side of the bed, close to him, and once again I didn't have time to aim: just punch up and out with the hammer as best I could. The head landed firmly, straight in his mouth, and I knew it was a solid blow from the way he jerked backwards, half falling away from me, hands flying to his face.

I felt a burst of exhilaration as I got to my feet, still unsteady but *shrieking* at him now. I don't know if it was from desperation, or fear, or if it was an attempt to summon some last thread of strength, but it was there. And I was still shrieking as I stepped forward and swung the hammer as hard as I could into the side of his head.

Part Four

Forty-Seven

For Miriam Field, it's the waste ground.

It's a real place, and it's one she is forced to see every day, so to some extent she has become inured to it over the years. Miriam is a practical woman, after all – some say hard, even cold, as though she has no reason – and she knows deep down that it's only a patch of ground. It is *where* the thing happened to Jemima, not *what* happened. On their daily walks, Miriam manages to close her mind to the latter – and of course, nothing lingers here. There are no ghosts. Perhaps that's even sad in a way, because ghosts would imply an afterlife of a kind, and at least then there might be something for them both to look forward to.

She does dream about the place, though.

They are on their way back from the shops now, and it lies ahead of them. But first they must make their way through the small copse of trees where the attack occurred. The Edith Copse, they used to call it, although some of the locals remember and call it something else amongst themselves. For some reason, this part of the journey bothers Miriam less than the waste ground, maybe because the latter is the place where Jemima might have been stopped and saved.

Even so, she grips Jemima's hand a little tighter.

'Come on, love. Don't hang around.'

Miriam speaks to her daughter in an abrupt, authoritative tone, and anyone overhearing it would think her harsh. But over the years, she has learned that it's what Jemima responds to best. Cajoling rarely works. Her daughter needs firm direction in the same the way a three-year-old does, and she harbours any resentment at the abruptness for about as long.

Jemima is staring at the copse of trees, not with fear but curiosity, as though it is a harmless puzzle she can't understand. At her mother's words, though, she turns away from it, then keeps an awkward but eager pace along the footpath. It is heartbreaking for Miriam – it always is – but she doesn't show it. Emotion is a luxury she can't afford. This is just one more small sadness, and she stores it away out of sight with all the others.

Hard, even cold, they say. *Harsh*. But, really, how could she not be? For the best part of two decades, her days have been regimented blocks of bathing, clothing, feeding. She washes Jemima's hair and stubbornly applies make-up. There is this daily trip to the shop, and then the daytime television shows. The spooned food. The evening's careful outing. Miriam still loves her daughter, but it is an existence they have now, not a life, and time is something to be survived, for no real reason other than to reach more time. When the two of them first moved here, all those years back, it was a blow, but it felt like there was still time ahead of them – that the separation and downsizing had just been the temporary dimming of a bulb that could be made to blaze again. It was astonishing to discover how much harder life could make it for you, with just one sudden, awful snap of its fingers.

As they reach the top of the embankment, the waste ground opening up ahead of them, Jemima is dragging back again.

'*Come on.*'

Miriam gives her a harder pull, and then immediately feels bad. As much as she loves her daughter, it is sometimes difficult not to think of her as an object that won't stay put – one that topples over however hard you try to balance it. But she remembers sitting with Jemima in the hospital, begging her to survive those terrible injuries, to come back to her no matter what, and it's hardly fair to blame her now for having listened.

'Come on.'

She says it more softly this time, and even turns and gives her daughter a smile. *I love you. I love you still. More every day, in my own way.* But there is no sign on Jemima's face that she has registered the impatience, or the repentance. She registers so little. More heartbreak, then – and again, Miriam stores it away with the rest. The place it all goes to must be infinite in size. It contains the enormous thing that happened to Jemima behind them, and then a thousand tiny moments from every day since. Every time someone has done a double-take at her daughter's beautiful, ruined face, or made fun of her. The pebbles they sometimes throw at the windows late on. The wrestling and the hardship. The fact that after all this time, they are *still here* ...

Enough.

With the bag of shopping in one hand and Jemima's hand grasped firmly in the other, Miriam begins walking across the waste ground.

'Come on, love.'

In reality, it's only a place, of course. Just dust and rubble. Bleak and dirty, yes, but given time and opportunity, even the most bereft of spots can acquire a kind of beauty. Some evenings, Miriam has watched the setting sun split its colours through the copse of trees behind her, and now she sees it rising in front of them, making it easy to imagine that the estate ahead is ablaze in the morning light. If only.

They're about halfway across when it happens.

Jemima stops suddenly, the jolt from it hurting Miriam's arm. She turns to look at her daughter, who is staring vacantly at the estate ahead of them.

Oh God.

Because this has happened before.

'Jemima?' she says, but as always in these circumstances, her daughter doesn't respond. The concentration on her face is fierce but utterly still. It is like looking at a photograph.

Then, without warning, Jemima starts moving again, much faster than before, and quicker than Miriam is used to. Her daughter overtakes her, and then Jemima is the one urging *her* on for a change.

'Hold on, love. You know I can't go that fast.'

Miriam struggles to keep up. More heartbreak. The first time this happened, she thought a memory must have surfaced, and that Jemima was fleeing the trees behind them. But when they reached the estate, she saw that the smile on her daughter's face contained a trace of joy, albeit one that faded quickly, and she understood. A memory had surfaced, but not an unpleasant one. Jemima's body wouldn't obey her properly any more, but a part of her had remembered what it used to be capable of, and her daughter had been trying to run.

Hold on, love.

She doesn't say it, though. It's heartbreaking, yes, but the smile always lasts at least a few seconds. It's sad when it goes, not when it's there. Let her run.

As they stutter awkwardly across, Miriam looks towards the estate and sees that someone is standing there, silhouetted against the orange glow behind. They draw nearer, Jemima still leading her, and Miriam sees that the figure is a woman, dressed in jeans and a short black leather jacket. She is in her early thirties, with long brown hair tied back in a ponytail, and her face is disfigured. Certainly not as badly as Jemima's, but obviously more recently. One of her eyes is bruised, and her nose has tape over the bridge. As they reach her, Miriam notices more bruising around one corner of her mouth. Whoever the woman is, she has been in a serious fight.

And she is clearly waiting for them.

They come to a halt close to her, and the woman stares at Jemima's face with an expression Miriam finds hard to read. For a moment she feels indignant and protective, because even though her daughter is unaware of her appearance, strangers can be rude and mean, and she does pick up on that. But this woman's own face doesn't contain a trace of pity or disgust.

Jemima, for her part, is looking off into the middle distance, oblivious to everything. The faint smile fades slowly from her face.

Miriam lets go of her daughter's hand and takes a step forward.

'Can I help you?'

'No.' The woman, who is still staring, shakes her head, then turns to look at Miriam instead. 'I'm sorry. I tried your house first, but obviously you were out. So I came here on the off chance.'

'You tried our house?'

'Yes. Sorry.' She takes out her wallet and shows Miriam a badge of some kind. 'Detective Inspector Zoe Dolan.'

The name means nothing to her, but the title generates a thrill of panic, and she starts to run through a short mental list of relatives, friends, acquaintances...

'What's happened?'

The woman – Zoe – puts her identification away.

'Nothing. I didn't mean to alarm you.'

'Then ...?'

'I went to school with your daughter.' She turns back to Jemima and smiles at her. 'Hello, Jem. Do you remember me? It's Zoe.'

Jemima doesn't say anything, but it's strange, because she also doesn't react the way she often does towards strangers. When she's approached like this, she will usually turn to Miriam and almost press herself against her, the way a shy child might. Now, she doesn't respond at all, which is the way she acts around people she's more comfortable with. The silence pans out.

'Jemima doesn't talk much,' Miriam says.

'No.'

She says it plainly: a statement of fact. Clearly, she knows what happened to Jemima, and the way she is looking at her makes more sense now. She is a policewoman, so she wouldn't be fazed by the sight of such extensive injuries, but she also went to school with her, before the attack, so she is searching

315

for traces of the girl she once knew, and perhaps wondering how much of that girl is left.

Miriam is about to say something, but she's distracted by a sudden burst of laughter a short distance away, and she turns to see three young boys on bicycles. They're a familiar enough sight, and her heart sinks a little. Every few days she sees them, untethered and roaming the estate, and it's always the same. If it's not these ones that throw stones at their house, it's others like them. Right now, two of them are laughing while the third is clawing at his face, pulling the bottoms of his eyes right down and making grunting noises.

Miriam stares blankly back at them, putting this moment away with all the others. There is nothing she can do about it. She wishes she could make them both invisible, that they could get from place to place without being noticed, but that isn't—

And then she realises that Zoe is walking slowly and steadily towards the children. They fall silent as she approaches, but of course they don't ride away. When she reaches them, she crouches down beside the nearest and begins talking quietly to him. They are far enough away that Miriam can't hear what is being said, but she sees Zoe gesturing behind her, and then angrily to her own injured face. A moment later, she leans in a little closer, pulling the bicycle at an angle, and whispers something to the boy with such ferocity that for a moment Miriam actually feels scared for him.

Zoe nods and stands back up again, then looks down at the children, who don't look back at her. A few seconds later, the three of them cycle away, and Zoe stares after them until they are gone. Then she walks back over.

'Just children,' Miriam says sadly.

'It happens a lot?'

She nods, although there doesn't seem any real point in answering. It happens a lot. But there are a large number of painful things that happen a lot.

'Yes. We used to call the police, but they said there's nothing they can do. Just children.'

316

Zoe looks at her for a moment, and then at the estate itself. Finally she turns back to Jemima. If her daughter has noticed the exchanges, she doesn't show it. She is just standing there. Waiting.

'Is that right?' Zoe says. Although she's still looking at Jemima, it sounds more like she's talking to herself. 'Well, we'll see about that.'

Forty-Eight

For Karen Cooper, it was a small black book.

I had it in my coat pocket when I arrived at her house, and could feel the weight of it there, disproportionate to its actual size. That should have been strange, perhaps – but then again, it contained far more than it appeared to. It was heavy with things that weren't actually there.

We would come to that, but in the meantime I wanted to talk to her about her husband: to help complete the picture of Derek Cooper we had been assembling over the past few days.

I rang the doorbell and waited on the step. The visit had been arranged in advance, so at least she would have had a chance to compose herself to meet the woman who had put her husband into the coma from which he was unlikely to emerge. And there was the sight of my face, as well, of course. The blatant evidence of what he had done to me. The visible legacy of his violence, which in some ways we shared.

Karen opened the door, and for a few seconds we didn't speak. I smiled politely – professionally – as her gaze moved over my face, taking in the damage.

'He did that to you?' she said eventually.

'Yes.'

'I'm so sorry.'

I nodded once. 'I'm sorry too.'

'Please.' She held the door wider. 'Come in.'

'Thank you. Are the children ...?'

'They're still with my parents.'

She led me through the kitchen to the front room. It was the first time I'd visited the scene of Derek Cooper's explosion, and I glanced around as I followed her. It was easy to imagine the flurry of violence in the air as he attacked the officers, but the house also *felt* like him, somehow, as though a hint of aftershave lingered in the air, or as if he might be lurking in another room. It wasn't quite enough to give me flashbacks to the fight in Sharon's bedroom, but I still felt my chest tighten a little.

A dangerous animal is nearby. A monster.

Not any more, I thought.

The front room was minimally furnished and spotlessly clean. Everything looked expensive and *just so*, like a show home. He would have insisted on it, no doubt: demanded that she play the good little wife. Appearance would have been everything.

'How is she?' Karen asked, after we'd sat down. 'His last victim?'

That was me, technically, but I knew who she meant.

'Sharon Hendricks is in hospital,' I said. 'She's doing okay, actually, all things considered. And Kieran Yates's condition has stabilised. Right now, it looks like he's going to make it.'

'I'm glad.' She glanced towards the kitchen. 'I haven't seen her since. The lady next door, I mean.'

'Margaret Smith? She's barely left his side.'

Karen took a deep breath. 'I keep thinking about the way Derek used to look at her. At Sharon, I mean.'

'When he came to the shop to pick you up?'

'Yes. I suppose I noticed it at the time and just never really took it in. He looked at a lot of women. She was his type, of course, but it felt stupid to be bothered by it. She was a smart girl. Pretty. Could probably have had anyone. So she wouldn't have had anything to do with an older man, a married man. I was never worried. It was just Derek being Derek.'

'I notice you don't say that you trusted *him*.'

That got me a hollow laugh. 'Because I didn't. Why would I? He made it quite clear how *disgusting* I am.'

'Disgusting?'

'Yes. He never said it outright, but it was obvious. He used to look at me the way he looked at Sharon, but not any more. And I couldn't really blame him, could I?'

I shook my head. Karen was an attractive woman, albeit obviously still clinging – with the make-up and the clothes – to an ideal of her younger self she could no longer really attain. I wanted to understand.

'So he preferred younger women?' I said.

'Yes. And I'd trapped him, hadn't I? I know that was how he saw it, deep down. The kids, the house, me. He never really wanted the kids, and then he didn't want me any more either. He wanted something better.'

'Like what?'

'Like anything. That was Derek. He always wanted something better. And he always thought that whatever he wanted should be his by right. That he deserved it. Nobody crossed him.'

And nobody will need to again. But I didn't say it. Instead, I thought about what Karen had just told me, and remembered my impressions of the victims. They were all young, attractive and successful: women you could see on the arm of an alpha male, being shown off like a trophy or a badge.

It was easy to tell that Karen Cooper had been very beautiful once, but it was equally apparent that hers was the type of beauty that comes from maintenance: an act that becomes increasingly difficult to perform as time passes. The make-up she wore failed to mask her age, especially around the eyes, and whereas once she might have been vivacious and vibrant – full of hope for the future – now she seemed empty. Vacant, even.

Once upon a time, she would surely have been Derek's type, and I tried to imagine how it might have felt to him, anchored as the years passed to what must have seemed an increasingly rusty trophy, one that polished itself with ever-diminishing returns. Coming to hate her, not because of who or what she was, but what she wasn't. *Trapped. He always wanted something better.*

And eventually taking that hatred out on her, and on the girls he felt entitled to but couldn't have.

A lot of people felt like that, of course: constrained as the years passed; dissatisfied with the undeserved smallness of their lives. It could hardly be the whole picture. But Derek Cooper had been an angry, arrogant man, confined in a box he felt too tight for him, not good enough for him. I could at least begin to see it.

'Did he ever mention Adam Johnson?'

Karen shook her head. 'No. I had no idea. He was the other one?'

I nodded. 'Your husband used to go and talk to him about what he'd done.'

'Why?'

That remained a question, and I still wasn't sure I had a definitive answer. Johnson had assumed the man was trying to groom him – or at least involve and implicate him – but given Cooper's meltdown after Johnson's suicide, I wondered if there had been something more to it all along. Just as Johnson had phoned the helpline, I wondered if, for all his rage at the world, Derek Cooper had needed someone to confess to as well. If some of that *hate* might have been directed inwards.

'We don't know,' I said. 'But let's talk about your husband for now. He was out a lot, wasn't he?'

'Yes. But I just presumed he was with someone else. And actually, I didn't mind that. Not really.'

The first time I'd interviewed her, I'd thought that, despite the make-up, Karen Cooper was no actress. And I thought the same thing again now.

'He was out the night Amanda Jarman was murdered?'

'Yes.' She nodded. 'Not all night. But it was late, and he smelled of drink when he got in.' She seemed suddenly brighter at that. 'That was the reason I left the shop early that day. You asked me what we'd been arguing about? It was that. We didn't have the money for him to be going out drinking, but he didn't like me telling him what to do. You can't imagine what Derek could be like.'

I nodded sympathetically.

'So how come you didn't call her?'

Karen Cooper was nodding back. Slowly, she stopped.

'I'm sorry?'

'Amanda Jarman,' I said. 'Because the thing is, we've looked through her phone records. She was due at work that morning, wasn't she? Of course, she didn't make it in. But you never called to find out why.'

'I'm sure I did.'

'Really? What did she say?'

'I can't remember.' Karen shook her head. 'Well, obviously she couldn't have answered.'

'No.'

'Perhaps I'm mixing her up with someone else. I must be.'

I stared back at her, allowing any trace of friendliness to drain from my expression. To make it clear that she wasn't going to be able to bluff her way past this, and that *appearances* didn't count for much with me.

'Let's be honest here, Karen. Bit of a mistake, that, wasn't it?'

'I don't know what you mean.'

But the temperature in the front room seemed to have dropped a few degrees, and there was a hardness to her voice now. While I still didn't believe her, it was for a different reason. Rather than being a terrible actress, Karen Cooper was actually a pretty good one. It was just that now she was finding it hard to ad-lib.

I reached into my pocket and took out a small black book with a weathered metal clasp.

'This is your diary.' I undid the clasp, wondering if she'd had a chance to search for it yet and discover it was missing. 'We found it when we were searching the house. You'll forgive the intrusion, of course.'

I didn't look at her as I flicked through the pages. Karen

said nothing, but I could feel her gaze moving from me to the book and back.

'It's mostly trivia,' I said. 'Appointments here and there. Little notes about things too dull for us to bother deciphering. No offence. But then we saw this.'

I held it up and turned it around so that she could see the spread for this week.

'On the day Amanda Jarman was murdered, you've drawn an asterisk in a circle.'

I could tell from her face that she wasn't going to reply. I turned the diary around again, then leafed back.

'And look – here's Sally Vickers. Exact same thing. And then, hang on a second, here's Julie Kennedy, with another little asterisk. And so on. All the victims. And the strange thing is that these symbols *only ever appear on those dates.*' I looked up at her. 'It's almost like you were marking them for a reason, isn't it, Karen? Like you knew something important had happened.'

Again, she just stared at me. On the surface, her expression was utterly blank, but I thought I could detect panic gathering below.

'Why did you mark those dates?'

I let the silence pan out, giving her a chance, then smiled.

'Do you know, I thought you *might* say it was because those were the dates when Derek stayed out all night. But you don't think on your feet that quickly, do you, Karen? And of course, that would be ridiculous anyway. You read the papers. You must have put two and two together, assuming you didn't already know.'

'I don't know what you're talking about.'

'Don't get me wrong,' I said. 'It must have been difficult for you, working with all those beautiful young women every day, knowing it was them your husband wanted, not you. That he was disgusted by you. That he was a monster. I imagine you felt *trapped* too, in your own way.'

I leaned forward.

'I wasn't sure at first if it was just that some miserable little part of you was glad it was *them* he was hurting, not *you*. That would be horrible enough, wouldn't it? But now I wonder if maybe, deep down where you won't even admit it to yourself, you hated them as much as he did.'

And even though she just continued to stare at me, I could tell that I'd shaken her: that my words had hit home. She had known, all right – to some degree, at least. Of course, whether she was prepared to acknowledge it, even to herself, was another matter entirely.

'That's ridiculous,' she said quietly. 'And you can't prove it.'

I looked at the diary for a few moments, then snapped it shut, placed it back in my pocket and stood up.

'Not yet,' I said. 'But believe me, it'll all come out eventually. It always does.'

As I walked back to the kitchen, I focused my attention on the air behind me, making sure she wasn't going to attack me. It was almost disappointing that all I felt was her eyes following me to the door. I turned back to see her still staring at me. She was visibly trembling. Not because I'd caught her out, I didn't think – she was right that we'd probably never be able to prove anything – but because she knew. Well, whatever the exact truth about her involvement, she was going to have to live with it. However much she tried to pretend otherwise, she would always know.

'Sleep well, Karen.'

Back outside, Chris was waiting for me in the car. I slid into the passenger seat and tapped the dashboard.

'Let's go.'

'She didn't cop to it?'

'Not out loud.'

He started the engine and sighed.

'You've got to do everything yourself, haven't you?'

'No,' I said as we set off. 'Not everything.'

Forty-Nine

For Miriam, it was the waste ground. For Karen, it was a small black book.

So what was it for me?

I didn't know any more.

When I arrived at the care home the following day, I was met by the same nurse who had shown me to John's room the first time I visited. She must have noticed the damage to my face, but she didn't mention it. Perhaps she recognised my name from the news, and knew what had happened to me, or maybe it was just that the quiet gravity of the situation made my appearance irrelevant.

'Come quickly,' she said.

I followed her, moving as fast as I could. Sweat was beading in my hairline, tickling down my back. *We think you should come in as soon as you can.* Following the phone call, I'd driven fast across the city, but I was sweating as though I'd run the distance instead, and it wasn't the exertion that was causing my heart to pound.

'He's very comfortable,' the nurse told me. 'He's not in any kind of pain. He's really very peaceful.'

'Will he be able to hear me?'

'I don't know. I would have thought so.'

As we approached his room, I thought of all the things I needed to tell him. Not about Derek and Karen Cooper, because there was no need to weigh him down with another investigation now. About Jemima, perhaps. But mostly about him and about me.

I followed the nurse into the room.

For a moment, I couldn't see him, my view of the bed occluded by the doctor and another nurse, both standing beside it. The nurse who'd led me up here cleared her throat.

'Zoe's here.'

They turned around. It was the same doctor I'd seen before, and he nodded at me by way of greeting and moved aside. No doubt it was practical as much as anything, but I thought there was something nice about that consistency of care. The same face, always there.

I stepped across to the bed, unhooking my bag from over my shoulder, and sat down on the chair next to it.

Looking at John, I was sure he was already gone. He was propped up at a forty-five-degree angle, with his hands above the covers on either side of his body. It didn't seem possible, but he was even more emaciated than he'd been on my previous visit. His skin was entirely yellow. There was an odd sheen to it, as though he had been cast from wax, and he was painfully still, his eyes closed and his head tilted back. His mouth was open, with the lips sucked in and half covering his teeth.

'John?'

I watched him for a moment, certain – *he's gone* – but then realised that his chest was fluttering ever so slightly. I listened carefully, and heard thin breath, as distant as the weakest of breezes, the faintest of voices heard over a telephone line.

He was dying right now in front of me. I knew it, but it was impossible to make the thought land, though there would be time for that later on, along with the grief. Just then, all I felt was a tremendous and indescribable love for him. Many things can escalate, boil up, and culminate in one final explosion. It doesn't always have to be hate.

I reached out and took his hand, wanting him to know I was

here with him. His fingers flickered very gently against mine. I can never be sure, but I think he knew.

'We'll give you a couple of minutes,' the doctor said, and then the three of them retreated from the room, closing the door behind them.

Keeping hold of his hand, I leaned closer to the bed.

'John, there's something I need to talk to you about. Something I should have said before now.'

I told him that what he'd said about the time after your life being the same as before wasn't true at all. That it wouldn't be the same after he was gone, because in the time he'd been alive, he had touched the world and changed it, and the impact of that would live on.

I told him that he had helped so many people, and that all of them were indebted to him for the way he'd shaped their lives, whether they had been able to acknowledge it before now or not. I told him he had been wrong – that I couldn't have done it without him – and I thanked him for that. Then I told him that I loved him, and that I'd never really needed to wish that he'd been my father, because deep down where I wouldn't admit it, that was how I'd always seen him.

Finally, I told him about Jemima. Not the details, but that I was going to do what I could to help her and her mother. It was too late in so many ways, but perhaps it would be something. I told him that he had been a good man, and that I was going to try to be more like him.

By the time I'd finished, his fingers had stopped fluttering and his chest was still. I leaned even closer and listened for the sound of his breathing, but it was no longer there. He was completely motionless. The difference now, even from just a few minutes earlier, was obvious. He'd gone.

I kissed him on his warm forehead, then went outside to join the medical staff in the corridor.

I have no idea if John heard me that day. I don't know whether my words got through, and if he had at least a few seconds to hold them before they evaporated. And I suppose

I never will. But that's the thing, isn't it? We can tell ourselves anything we like. Sometimes it matters when we pretend, or even when we lie to ourselves just to make our lives easier. But not always.

And so I'll choose to believe that he did.